FIVE ELEMENTS. ON

FROM
BREATH
AND
RUIN

NEW YORK TIMES BESTSELLING AUTHOR

CARRIE ANN
RYAN

From Breath and Ruin: An Elements of Five Novel
© 2019 Carrie Ann Ryan
All rights reserved.

ISBN: 978-1-947007-72-7
Cover design by Charity Hendry
Book design by Inkstain Design Studio

PRAISE FOR
CARRIE ANN RYAN

"Carrie Ann Ryan knows how to pull your heartstrings and make your pulse pound! Her wonderful Redwood Pack series will draw you in and keep you reading long into the night. I can't wait to see what comes next with the new generation, the Talons. Keep them coming, Carrie Ann!"

—LARA ADRIAN

New York Times bestselling author of Crave The Night

"Carrie Ann Ryan never fails to draw readers in with passion, raw sensuality, and characters that pop off the page. Any book by Carrie Ann is an absolute treat."

—J. KENNER

New York Times bestselling author

"With snarky humor, sizzling love scenes, and brilliant, imaginative world-building, The Dante's Circle series reads as if Carrie Ann Ryan peeked at my personal wish list!"

—LARISSA IONE

New York Times bestselling author

"Carrie Ann Ryan writes sexy shifters in a world full of passionate happily-ever-afters."

—VIVIAN AREND
New York Times **bestselling author**

Carrie Ann Ryan's books are wickedly funny and deliciously hot, with plenty of twists to keep you guessing. They'll keep you up all night!"

—CARI QUINN
USA Today **Bestselling Author**

"Once again, Carrie Ann Ryan knocks the Dante's Circle series out of the park. The queen of hot, sexy, enthralling paranormal romance, Carrie Ann is an author not to miss!"

—MARIE HARTE
New York Times **bestselling Author**

To the first author I picked up.
The first book I read.
The book that started it all.
Thank you for sparking my creativity.
Thank you for giving me a chance.

FROM
BREATH
AND
RUIN

CHAPTER 1

The dreams didn't come often, but when they did, it usually took me far too long to realize I could find my way out of them. At least, *most* of the time, I could make my way out. Other times, no matter how hard I tried to shake myself awake or tear at the seams of what the dream could be, I was forced to live within them, in the nightmares that felt far too real.

My heartbeat thudded in my ears as I tried to get my bearings once again. The dreams were never the same in what happened or even where I was when they occurred, but there was a thread that seemed familiar, as if it were calling to me in a way I could never understand.

Sometimes, I was on the fringe, watching the court of royals dance and hide their daggers of both wit and steel. Then they'd bow and turn to smoke, the ashes of their lies and hidden admissions blowing away like dust in the wind.

Other times, I was in the middle of the action, hurtling from side to sid as towers fell, and water rushed by. Air blew through my hair, whipping it into my face, the earth below me trembling as fire rained down on all of us.

Tonight, however, the visions weren't either of those. Yes, I was in the present, the dream happening to me rather than me being a witness to an absolution I would never understand.

But I stood in a clearing, winter on my back, summer facing me down with wicked heat. Spring danced along my right side with a cool warmth that didn't make sense, while fall brushed my left, its warming coolness confusing me even further.

There were two shadows in front of me, their arms outstretched, each calling my name in whispers. I could only hear their breaths, not their voices, so I had no idea who they were or what they represented in this dream that I knew would linger long after I woke.

"Lyric," they called in unison.

"Lyric."

And though that was my name, it still didn't sound as if they were truly calling to me. Instead, it was if they called to the person they needed me to be. I wasn't that person, though. Wasn't what they needed, and I knew I may not ever be.

And while I still had the same body shape as I did when I was awake—my slightly larger-than-average curves filling out my dress, and my height just below average so the bottom of my hem slid along the mud—I wasn't truly *me* in the dream.

My blond hair blew in the wind, catching the light and making it look white at times, gold at others. The shade was always changing depending on how much sun I took in during the season, but in this dream, it changed with the direction I turned.

It isn't truly me, I told myself again. This wasn't my dress, this wasn't my life.

Those shadows couldn't actually call to me because I *wasn't me*.

"Lyric," the shadows called again.

"Wake up," the one nearest the spring side demanded.

"It's time," the one closest to fall whispered.

And though they were both whispers, they sounded like screams in my ear.

I jolted awake, my sweat-slick skin clammy as I tried to catch my breath. My tank was soaked, sticking to my body, and my shorts had ridden up as if I'd thrashed in my sleep. Considering my comforter was on the floor, and my sheet was currently a knot at the end of my bed, I would say that was probably exactly what had happened.

I swallowed hard, narrowing my eyes at the clock, trying to see what time it was. The sun was already up, even though it wasn't quite seven in the morning, but it was summer in Denver, Colorado, and that meant blue skies, bright sun, and the occasional rain that came out of nowhere.

I had my white curtains drawn, but they didn't really block out the light, so I'd learned to sleep through the rays on my face long ago. I had to if I ever wanted to sleep in. And since I was also a teenager, sleeping in was part of life—especially during the summer.

I might be eighteen, out of high school and ready to start college in the fall, but I still felt like the teenager who wanted to sleep in and not have to wake up early for classes. It didn't help that my walls were still a light lilac from when I'd been in my purple phase, and there was still lace on my curtains and the skirt of my bed.

My family made a decent income, but we were firmly in the middle of middle class, and these days, that meant there wasn't money to update my bedroom to something a little less tween girl and a little more college-bound woman. I didn't care too much, however. I wasn't staying here long. Soon, I'd be in a dorm at the local university, an offshoot of the University of Colorado since there was no way I could afford Boulder's campus. Plus, this way, I could still be close to home.

Because as much as I might think I was ready to start my new life and be an adult, the nightmares that had plagued me for as long as I could remember told me that I wasn't as grown-up as I thought.

Honestly, what kind of teenager still needed a nightlight because she was scared of the shadows?

Me, apparently. Lyric Camaron, the walking embodiment of indecision and someone not quite ready for anything.

I ran a hand over my face, holding back a gag at how sweaty I was, and let out a sigh. The dreams hadn't happened so often before, but now they came almost every other night, and I had no idea what they meant. I'd always had a vivid imagination, but my dreams took that to a whole new level.

I wasn't a little girl anymore, and yet I still dreamed of princes and princesses, of magic and might. I dreamed of courts and pretty dresses, and flowers and rain. Still, I thought that was probably all just a front for what the dreams actually carried. A veil across the hate and lies and mystery of everything that came with them.

I'd always secretly wanted to write them down, to make them into a book or just a few stories, but for some reason, I'd held myself back. There was no use documenting what never made sense. The dreams scared me even when they shouldn't, and writing them down would only make them more real.

And it wasn't like writing would help me in my real life outside of the dreams. I needed to grow up, stop thinking about fairy tales that weren't bright and shiny, and figure out what I wanted to be when I grew up. Because I wasn't a little kid anymore and, sadly, the time to make those choices had already started to pass me by, and I was struggling to keep up.

"Shut up, Lyric," I mumbled to myself. It was far too early, and I still wasn't awake enough for my mind to be going down that path. I'd likely be getting a very similar lecture from my parents over breakfast—and perhaps lunch and dinner—as it was.

They loved me, and I loved them.

And that meant I needed to be a better daughter.

The first step to doing that was getting out of bed and washing off the sweat that coated my skin. Then, I'd wash my sheets, air out my comforter, and maybe even go for a run so I could get the cobwebs out of my mind. I wasn't a coffee fan since I tended to need far too much sugar to even like it, so I couldn't have a cup of that to help. So, that meant chores and fresh air so I could get out of my funk, let the dreams lie where they needed to be—far from my reality—and get on with my day.

I could do that. Totally. If only I could get the images from the dream out of my mind.

Those two shadows had been in more than one of my nightmares, and I couldn't help but think that they meant something. Who or what did they represent? Why were they important? I didn't know if they were male or female or if they were truly people at all. If they were supposed to be love interests, then having them be either a man or a woman would only mean that my dream-self represented my real-self since I was attracted to both and had dated both in real life. But I still didn't know what the dreams or the shadows in them really meant.

In a few, the apparitions had moved, and I could almost imagine them wanting to be even closer. They always held out their hands, as if I had to make a decision between them, to go to one or the other.

The seasons coming at me all at once seemed like another symbol for choice and change, as well. The same with the instances where I was covered in earth or water, air or flame. All of it indicated choice.

So maybe the dreams didn't mean anything beyond what I already knew.

It was time for me to make a choice.

A choice regarding who I could be—who Lyric Camaron would be as an adult.

That choice seemed the hardest of all, and yet I knew it was important. All teenagers went through this, they all had to make decisions, no matter what course outside forces wanted them to take.

I knew there was a path laid out before me, one that would lead to a life not unlike the one I held now, one made of decisions that made practical sense. That was the one I knew I should take, the one that would be easier and yet far more thought-out.

And yet part of me wanted something different. I wanted to be a Lyric who wasn't so middle-of-the-road as I currently was as a bisexual teenager living in Denver, Colorado.

There were choices I had to make. Clear-cut ones that had nothing to do with royals and elements, nothing to do with seasons and change.

I would make the right choice.

I had to.

And I would ignore the dreams and the idea that there could be something more for me. There hadn't been before, and I wasn't going to lie in wait for answers that scared me, translations of dreams that challenged me.

I would make my own way, make my own choices.

And they would be the right ones because they would be *mine*.

The dreams would go away eventually.

They would fade just like the young girl I used to be. In its place would be the future I needed, the one I craved.

I told myself I wouldn't dream again. I couldn't.

Because I didn't want to know what those shadows meant. I didn't want to know why they knew my name.

I didn't want to know why it all felt so real. And, above all else, I didn't want to know why I saw those same shadows when I was awake. Because those were the ones that scared me. The ones that were far too real.

I was Lyric, the girl with everything to look forward to. I wasn't the girl who saw shadows, who had dreams.

I couldn't be.

CHAPTER 2

After I'd put my sheets into the washer, I set the load, took a quick shower to rinse off, and headed out for my jog. I'd decided to go with long, black leggings, a hot pink sports bra under two black tanks, and a black jacket that had air holes all through it and thumb holes in the sleeves. It was my favorite jacket of all time, and I was seriously disappointed when I went to buy another one and found out that they were no longer making them. There were already frayed edges on the cuffs and, sometimes, the metal on my purse got caught in the mesh of the body, making me wince.

The fact that I had such an emotional attachment to my running gear told me I needed to get out of the house more—and not just for jogging around the neighborhood. I huffed a breath as I slowly ran up the steep hill at one of the entrances to the sub-division, cursing the fact that I lived in a mountainous city. Sure, once you got outside city lines to the east, it was all flat planes and easy walking, but within the city limits and west toward the Rockies? Hills galore that did nothing but make my side ache as I ran.

I'd always been a runner, but never in an organized way when it came to school. I hadn't played sports or joined the cross-country team. While I played soccer and T-ball as a kid, I hadn't been particularly good at it, not enough to focus so much of my time on it. I'd even tried gymnastics and ballet as a little girl like most kids did, but it wasn't my thing. And while I enjoyed running—still do—doing it to compete took the fun out of it for me. I was always a little jealous of people who could put in that effort and still have fun, but for me, sports wasn't where it was at. I did well in school, knowing I'd need any academic scholarship I could get so I could go to college, but I'd had to work at anything not English-related. Writing I could do. Writing, I *loved* to do.

Differentials? Not so much.

I held back a shiver at that thought and pushed myself into my second mile. I wasn't going to do any more than that today since I wanted breakfast, and I figured that most of the strain from my dreams was now gone. But I thought I might go out again later in the day after the hottest part of the afternoon for another run. Increments worked best for me and my attention span.

I thought I caught a shadow out of the corner of my eye, but as I whipped my head to look at it, nearly tripping over my own feet as I did, I figured it was just my hair and a trick of the light. I wasn't seeing shadows outside of dreams. I *wasn't*.

I just needed to get those weird thoughts and remnants out of my head and start my day off better.

My parents hadn't been awake when I left for my jog, but thanks to the note I placed by the coffee machine, they'd know I was out of the house. I might be an adult, but I was still their child and living under their roof. There were rules to be followed, a curfew to be kept, and manners to be upheld. I didn't know how I was going to handle living outside of their rules when I went to the dorms, but I also didn't think I'd be the type to go crazy like so many of the stories I'd heard growing up. I didn't want to flunk out of college when I hadn't even chosen my major yet. And I sure as heck didn't want to end up drinking the whole time and wind up with a minor in possession misdemeanor or something that would forever stain my record.

No, thank you, evil temptation and all.

By the time I got home, my parents were off to work, but I knew I'd see them for dinner. My best friend Braelynn, and my ex-girlfriend/friend Emory were coming over to eat with us, and I knew my parents were excited to see what the other two ladies planned for college. In Mom's and Dad's way of thinking, if I knew what others were doing, it would push me to make a decision. The problem was, the more they pressured me, the more I wanted to hide in my shell like a turtle and not make a choice at all.

The dream came back to me, and I tried not to frown as I poured myself some juice and put two slices of bread into the toaster. Just because I was once again having weird dreams that I tried to make sense of, didn't mean they actually *meant* anything.

I had more to do today than think about nightmares that didn't mean anything more than I needed to watch what I ate before bed. Sure, it was summer, and I was between jobs since the coffee shop I had been working at shut down unexpectedly, but I had other things in my life. Like that whole deciding what I wanted to do with my life thing.

But first, I would focus on my friends and the certain impending doom from the conversation that would surely happen over mashed potatoes and roasted chicken tonight.

Oddly enough, I wasn't lulled into a sense of security once my parents came home and didn't once mention school or my future. I knew the talk was coming, but they were giving me time to drop my defenses so they could pounce.

I didn't know why I kept floundering whenever it came to making a decision about majors and life choices, but the enormity of it just seemed overwhelming. I was eighteen, an adult who could fight and die in wars, but I couldn't drink. I could buy cigarettes and vote, but I was still technically a teenager.

Having to make a huge life choice when all I really wanted to do was explore and learn and find out what suited me felt so far out of my depth, it wasn't funny. I knew thousands upon thousands of people did it every year, and many of them even went in not knowing exactly what they wanted to do—but they still had an idea.

Me? I knew what I loved, but I also knew that love wouldn't pay the bills. At least that's what I'd been told. And, frankly, I sort of believed it.

My mind had always been full of dreams and layers upon layers of vivid imagery my imagination would tumble over and over. I loved putting those visions into work, at least in my mind. Picking a major that worked with that, wasn't something my parents were going to go for. The idea of doing it all on my own, or choosing a major and finding out that I wasn't really good at it or didn't like it anymore was just too much.

It was all too much.

I saw another shadow out of the corner of my eye, and I turned, trying to catch it, only to see my father staring at me instead. His eyes were wide since I'd moved so fast, clearly startled.

"Whoa there, Lyric. Didn't mean to scare you." I looked like a perfect mix of my parents, something that I'd never truly noticed until I got older. I had my mom's blond hair and height, but my dad's light brown eyes. Everything else was a complete mix of the two, and I'd always loved that I knew where I came from, despite not knowing where I was going.

Dad continued. "I was just wondering when Braelynn and Emory would be here." Dad didn't particularly like Emory. Not because she was gay, and I was bisexual—that part he was totally on board with, and I knew I had the best parents for that part of my life—no, he didn't like her because she was my ex. He didn't get how we could still be friends after she'd dumped me. Frankly, I didn't understand it either. Sometimes, I felt like our friendship was fraying on the edges, but I didn't think that had to do with our breakup. We were just finding out we were two different people, and everyone was moving on to college anyway. It sucked, and I didn't know how I felt about it. I never did, really, when it came to Emory.

That explanation hadn't been good enough for Dad. I still didn't know how my mother felt about it since she was so good at hiding it, but she at least put on a better face.

"They'll be here soon." The doorbell rang, and I grinned. "And there they are."

Dad nodded and moved out of the way so I could make it to the door before Mom did. My parents were great, but they were parents and liked to know exactly what my friends were doing at all times, even if it wasn't their business. I was pretty sure all parents were wired that way, and I'd learned to deal with it.

Braelynn smiled widely at me, her shoulder-length black hair up in a ponytail so I could see the honey highlights she'd put in on the lower layers. Her moms hated it, and Emory called her a skunk, but I loved them.

"Yay for dinner. I brought rolls." Braelynn held up a basket, and I moved back to let her in, knowing that Emory was right behind my friend.

"Yay rolls! I know Mom will be happy since you and your moms make like the best bread ever."

"Totally true. I do have the best moms." Braelynn winked and handed over the basket as Emory sauntered in. Why she had to saunter, I didn't know, but whatever worked for her.

"I'm starving," Emory said in way of greeting before leaning down to buss a kiss on my cheek. She'd done that before we began dating and hadn't stopped. Since I didn't care either way, I didn't push her off. Once I started to care and put up those boundaries, she'd stop. That was who she was.

"I'm hungry, too," I said. "Hi, Emory."

Emory studied my face and frowned. "You didn't sleep."

I tried to school my features, but I knew I wasn't good at it. "I'm fine. Let's go finish setting the table."

"Hmm." That was all she said as she made her way into the dining room, saying hello to my parents as if she hadn't broken part of my heart and left me wondering what I'd done.

And...I had no idea where that thought had come from. Maybe I really needed more sleep and fewer dreams about random shadows, seasons, and elements messing with my head.

By the time we were all seated at the table, Braelynn's rolls like manna to us all, I was on edge since Emory kept studying me. I didn't know why, and it bugged me because I knew this dinner would only get worse when my parents brought up the dreaded subject of majors.

They always did, and I knew there was nothing I could do about it other than choose a freaking major. But I didn't want to make the wrong choice.

I couldn't make the wrong choice.

"So, Emory, what did you decide to study again?" Mom asked, not even trying to be subtle.

Here we go.

Emory shrugged. "Photography with a minor in history. I want to work for the AP or something, going around the world, taking photos of the people left behind in war and strife."

My parents nodded as if they totally understood and not just because they were happy Emory had chosen a direction for her life. It didn't matter that it was dangerous and could end up being a career that didn't keep her financially set, Emory wasn't *their* daughter.

"And, Braelynn?"

My best friend smiled sweetly. She was always so sweet, so gentle. I loved her to the end of the world and back and knew I'd chosen well on that first day of preschool when we shared our blocks.

"Vet school, eventually. I know it's going to be hard, but it's my passion."

I winced at that word. *Passion.*

I didn't have that, not that I could tell anyway. How was I supposed to know what to do when I still had so much to learn? I tried not to let any of those thoughts cross my face, however, because my parents turned to me, expectant looks on their faces.

They loved me. They truly did.

But they didn't understand me.

And the thing was, I wasn't so sure I understood myself.

CHAPTER 3

"So, that was awkward," Emory said as she kicked a rock down the street.

"Tell me about it. At least it wasn't *your* parents." I sighed. Braelynn shifted over on the sidewalk so she walked between Emory and me. I wasn't even sure Braelynn was conscious of the act since she was so good at mediating situations and tension with just her mere presence. At least that's what I'd overheard Mom say to Dad once. When I thought about it, I totally agreed.

"Your mom and dad mean well—" Braelynn began, but Emory cut her off.

"Oh, stop it. They aren't even here. You don't have to defend them. Your nose is already brown enough."

"Shut up, Emory," I snapped. "She's just trying to help."

"Then she should stop lying for them. Jesus." Emory folded her arms over her chest, and I held back a sigh. This was why it was hard to be friends with Emory. Her temper got the better of her, and she said things she late claimed she didn't mean. Though I was never truly sure I believed her when she apologized for it.

And those apologies were few and far between.

I ignored the weird feeling in my gut that told me that, no matter what choices I made when it came to my future, Emory might not be in it. Then I wrapped my arm around Braelynn's shoulders and pulled her in.

"I know Mom and Dad mean well, but that doesn't make it okay. Or, maybe it does, and I need to grow up and figure out what I want to do with the rest of my life."

"The fact you're going to college at all is a step. You've always been good at so many things and *liked* doing them. You aren't like me, who decided when I was seven and playing with my dolls and the neighbor's puppy that I wanted to be a vet. That's a little kid dream that I never grew out of."

"And you're going to rock as a vet. Me, on the other hand? I'm going to end up living with my parents until the ripe old age of forty when they finally kick me out."

"I'll let you have my basement before that happens," Braelynn said with a laugh.

Emory rolled her eyes, and I glared over at her. She didn't like Braelynn, and I was pretty sure the feeling was mutual. Fortunately—or fortunately for *them*, I guess—they wouldn't be together much longer. It sucked, but Emory was going to an out-of-state university, and Braelynn would be up in Boulder, while I was stuck at home, going to the other University of Colorado campus. I'd figure out my plans, I always did, I just hated the sense of uncertainty I felt, as if I were waiting for something to come, something I didn't quite understand.

We walked another block, the sun setting and the evening chill setting in. It was so dry in Colorado that any humidity that might have made its way through to the city was long gone with the sun as the temperature dropped. It wasn't crazy cold like the other seasons, but it still made me wish I'd brought my jacket.

The three of us had decided to walk after dinner rather than drive anywhere since it was a nice night and we had nothing better to do. I didn't have a car of my own anyway since I was saving for college and knew the bus system like the back of my hand. Braelynn had a car but didn't like driving with Emory because my ex was possibly the worst backseat driver there ever was.

Emory had a fancy SUV for winter, and an even fancier convertible for the summer thanks to her over-indulgent parents who had no idea what to do with their daughter's sexuality and their inability to deal with it. But nobody had objected to the walk, so here we were, walking with no direction like we were in middle school rather than being recent high school graduates.

We talked about nothing important, glossing over anything that could cause an issue since it felt as if all three of us were on edge for some reason, and turned a corner. I almost tripped over my feet at the sight of three people standing in front of a house I knew, the trio glaring at one another before seeming to realize that they weren't alone.

I knew them, of course, it was hard *not* to know the teenagers in my neighborhood since most of us went to the same high school—or rather, *had*. Those who hadn't gone there, opting for homeschool or private schools, still ended up in many of the same social clubs that a lot of us were forced into over the years.

Okay, so maybe *forced* wasn't the best word for me since I'd tried a bunch of things as a kid, attempting to figure out what fit me best. The fact that nothing had stuck wasn't something I wanted to dwell on at the moment, however.

Why?

Namely, the two girls in front of us, and the guy standing with them. The very tall, very built guy that was a couple of years older than us but who I thought always looked like the most perfect human specimen. Ever.

Rhodes Luce.

If I allowed myself to use words like *dreamy* for a guy, he was *beyond* dreamy. His light brown skin always looked silken and almost shiny as if he'd just finished a run and was glistening under the sunlight. His brown hair wasn't just a normal hue, it had what looked to be honey highlights woven in and was longer on the top than on the sides, giving him a disheveled look that made me want to reach out and mess with it myself.

Not that I would ever do that.

Ever.

Not even in dreams.

I swore I saw a shadow again out of the corner of my eye when I thought the word *dreams*, but I ignored it and pinned my gaze back on Rhodes as I stopped in place, my friends beside me.

Anytime I was near him, I couldn't stop staring. It wasn't just his strong cheekbones. Wasn't just his beauty.

No, it was his eyes.

They were so light, I swore they were silver. But people didn't really have silver eyes.

Rhodes, though? He totally could.

He wasn't alone, so I did my best to pry my eyes from him as I awkwardly waved at the bunch. To his left, Rhodes' younger sister, Rosamond, smiled brightly, her tunic dress blowing in the wind. I was pretty sure Rosamond had been a hippy in a past life and just hadn't wanted to stop fitting into the era. It worked for her with her flowing curls and almost luminescent brown skin. She looked like a New Age fairy or something, and the way she spoke and acted fit the description.

She'd graduated with the rest of us a few weeks ago, but I hadn't seen her since.

On Rhodes' other side stood another former classmate of mine. Alura.

And if I thought Rosamond was strange, Alura was even more out there. Her long, white-blond hair blew in the breeze that I swore sometimes only affected her—not that that was a thing, though it sure seemed like it. She had the most vivid blue eyes I'd ever seen, like something out of a movie with special contacts, and she rarely spoke.

Honestly, I hadn't even known that Alura was friends with Rhodes and Rosamond, but the three definitely seemed to know each other.

"Oh, hi!" Rosamond said, skipping toward us. "I was just talking to Rhodes and Alura about a hike tomorrow and was going to come by and see if you wanted to go, Lyric."

I blinked. I hadn't really hung out with any of them outside of school, and *never* with Rhodes. Sure, I had an awkward crush on the guy, but it wasn't as if I'd truly spoken to him beyond a few short words since he and Rosamond moved to the neighborhood a couple of years ago. He'd already graduated by that point, so we hadn't gone to school together, and I rarely saw him in the neighborhood since his parents worked a lot and I *never* saw them.

"A hike? Really?" Emory scoffed.

Rosamond glanced over at Emory, seeming to dismiss her with a single look. "Since we're going to the same campus, Lyric, I figured it would be nice to hang out a bit. You know? Oh, you guys should come, too," she said to Braelynn and Emory. "It's going to be a great day, and this way, I'm not hiking alone with Rhodes, who gets all growly when I'm slow."

"I don't growl."

And yet…he totally just growled.

Was I a puddle of goo just then? Because I felt like I was a puddle of goo. Emory glanced at me, and I had a feeling I wasn't hiding my inner thoughts well.

Holding back a curse, I smiled at Rosamond. "I think a hike would be fun. It's supposed to be good weather. What did you guys have in mind?"

Rhodes shrugged, and I did my best not to stare at his forearms as he stuffed his hands into his pockets. "A place we like to go to. It's about an hour outside of the city, but not too far. And the hike isn't that bad since Rosamond here can do it."

"I can hear you," she sing-songed.

"I know. I can see you." He gave me a wink, and I almost looked behind me to make sure it was me he was looking at.

From Braelynn's subtle nudge and Emory's almost inaudible growl, I figured it *was* me he'd been looking at.

Oh, my.

"What about you, Alura?" Braelynn asked, always the peacekeeper—and an amazing friend.

The other girl shook her head. "Not this time. It's not for me." She met my gaze with those piercing blue eyes and didn't blink. "But soon, I believe. Soon."

And with that, she turned and walked away without another word. The Luce siblings didn't look worried about what had just happened, but Emory rolled her eyes.

"No wonder they call her a witch."

"Be nice," I whispered. "Stop being so mean."

"Whatever. I have a thing with my parents tomorrow, so count me out." Emory looked over at me as if I should say no, as well.

I truly didn't understand the girl who had once been my closest friend and my first girlfriend. She wasn't who she once was. But the thing was, I wasn't either. Maybe that's why it was good that things were changing as quickly as they were.

"I'm in," I said quickly.

"Me, too," Braelynn added.

"What time and where should we meet you?" I ignored Emory standing at my side, trying to push back the little twinge inside me that indicated that this was just one more symbol of the end of an era.

Rosamond clapped her hands. "Oh, yay! I can't wait."

Rhodes looked at me, his eyes flashing that silver I thought had to be contacts. "I can't wait either."

I bit my lip as they told me the details, and I did my best not to look too excited. Because this wasn't a date. It wasn't something that was a new beginning. Not really. It was just a hike, a day out in the mountains, something all Coloradoans did as much as possible—at least the ones who loved nature.

And yet, even as I told myself that, I wondered if it was the truth.

Because this felt different. It felt important.

And for some reason, I didn't think it was only about the boy with the silver eyes in front of me.

CHAPTER 4

I wasn't a good hiker, but I was at least good at trying. Or so I told myself as I searched in my closet for my hiking boots. I had other shoes that would work for the day, but I knew somewhere in the back of my closet buried under my discarded shirts and pants, I had an old pair that I'd used a couple of years ago that were well-worn enough that I wouldn't end up with blisters.

The last thing I needed was to end up limping around a mountain looking like a dork in front of Rhodes.

Not that today would be about time with Rhodes. He was just going to be there with his sister, the one who had invited Braelynn and me. I hardly knew him. He might be the star of a few of my less drama-filled dreams, but that didn't mean I actually knew anything about the guy other than the color of his eyes, and the way his voice made me feel.

Really, I only had an inkling of who he was. Like how he was a couple of years older than Rosamond. But I didn't know where he went to school now, or even *if* he went to college or a trade school. I knew he must work out a lot since no one had that kind of body if they didn't at least try to take care of it, but I'd only seen him running in the neighborhood a few times over the past couple of years. I didn't know his hobbies, what his favorite foods were, or anything else about him outside of how he made me feel when I was near him.

Considering that I hadn't had that tingly feeling around anyone else, it had to mean something. Or it just meant that I had a giant crush and needed to get over it before I ended up making a total fool of myself and ruined any chance I had with Rhodes. Not that I really thought I *had* a chance, but I wanted to know more about him and, I had to face the idea that I really liked the tingly feeling he gave me.

Even if all today gave me was a few hours with said tingly feelings before I ended up in college, and he ended up…wherever and we never saw each other again, then it would be worth it.

I grinned in triumph as I pulled out my old hiking boots from beneath a scarf I'd forgotten I owned, and quickly put them on. I wasn't disorganized, but the back corner of my closet was forever the place that things went to hide—and perhaps never be found again. A shelf had fallen down a year or so ago, and I'd never fixed it. Because of that, it wasn't the cleanest, but I could close my closet door and pretend it wasn't there. I'd cleaned the rest of my room earlier today, and since I still lived under my parents' roof and therefore abided by their rules, I made my bed every day no matter what.

I didn't know exactly who I'd be or how I'd react to my own room when I lived in a dorm, but I figured I'd still end up making my bed every day. I enjoyed sliding into straightened sheets, and I liked the way my room looked when I didn't have my comforter in a ball on the floor. Since my dreams tended to make me roll all over the place and I kept sweating through my sheets, it only made sense.

I still didn't know what I was going to do about the whole roommate situation. The school hadn't given me a name yet since, apparently, something was still pending. I knew I had a room, I just didn't know who I shared it with. That meant I didn't have time to plan how I was going to ease the new person into my endless nightmares and dreams. I could barely handle them myself, and I'd lived with them my whole life.

How was I supposed to let someone else in on that part of myself?

Too bad I hadn't known Rosamond was going to the same school. If I had, maybe I could have asked to be her roommate. It still would have been awkward, but at least I'd seen her around school and talked to her many times before. She wasn't a stranger.

This whole growing-up thing and having to make your own choices that could change your destiny wasn't easy.

With a sigh, I pushed those thoughts out of my head because I needed to get a move on if I was going to meet everyone at the Luces' to catch a ride to the trail. I didn't need to think about what-ifs and what-could-bes when all I really needed to think about was trying to have fun before everything changed.

I had an interview at a local café in a couple of days so I could actually get a job with enough hours that I could save some money for school. But, until then, I was going to try and have a summer vacation. I'd just *be*.

And think about dreamy Rhodes, who I was trying really hard not to think about.

The doorbell rang, and I quickly tightened my ponytail and scurried to the front door. I hadn't bothered with makeup or anything special with my hair and had lathered on sunscreen, but now I was afraid that I hadn't tried hard enough with the whole looking-presentable thing.

Braelynn was at the door when I opened it, and she smiled brightly at me, her crossbody bag an older one I knew she'd taken on hikes before.

"Hey! I'm so glad you didn't go all makeup and glitter for Rhodes."

I rolled my eyes and let her in. "Am I that obvious?"

"Only because I've known you forever. You had those heart eyes. Or maybe unicorn eyes that are all glitter and like, boy-crazy. Rhodes is cute for sure, and that deep voice is something else. I think that's one reason Emory's not going, by the way. Not the only reason, because she's Emory and I'll *never* understand her, but she probably saw it, too."

I winced as I stuffed two water bottles into my backpack. We weren't going out for long, but the sun was bright, and I needed to stay hydrated, or I'd trip over my own two feet. I knew myself.

"Yeah, I can't help that. She's already dated two other girls since we broke up, so it's not like she's pining for me."

"Maybe not, but she also likes to keep you close. She already hates sharing you with me, and in the fall when we all go our separate ways, she's going to hate it even more. You know Em, she has certain boxes for everyone, and we need to stay there, or she stresses out. I know she's mean to me sometimes, but I kind of get it. Her parents throw money at her so they don't have to be there themselves, and in the end, she clings to you because she knows you won't fight hard to get away."

I frowned as we walked out of the house and I locked the door behind us. "I don't know if I like that assessment of who I am to her. I mean, you're right about her parents and the whole boxes thing. I was the friend, then the girl she liked. Now, I'm permanently in the girl-she-used-to-have box. I'm the ex, yet she needs to be my friend. And I know we won't be friends forever. I've seen the writing on the wall for a while now on that front, and it hurts to think about, but I get it. I don't know if I like the idea that I don't fight now, though."

We turned the corner and headed down the street toward the Luce house. We'd planned to walk there instead of leaving Braelynn's car at their place. It just didn't make sense.

"I said that wrong," Braelynn said. "I don't think *she* thinks you'll fight back because she doesn't have you in that box. I didn't mean you won't." She paused, and I frowned at her. "She underestimates you."

"Most people do, yet sometimes, I feel like I earn that." I shook my head when she gave me a questioning look. We were at the Luces', and I didn't have the time or the inclination to explain my weird thoughts about myself. I was in a time of self-discovery or whatever I read on that pamphlet Mom had given me. I just needed to start it. But today on a hike with a boy I liked and the girl I thought I could be friends with during college, as well as my *best* friend, maybe I could actually start the journey.

Rhodes was outside leaning against his SUV when we walked up to the house. I ignored those tingly feelings inside me once again. Or I tried. He was just a guy. A hot guy with wicked amazing eyes…but a guy.

I'd get over my crush and learn not to be a dork, but today, I could at least imagine what it might be like to get to know him better.

Just today, I promised myself.

Tomorrow, I would do the other things I had on my list when it came to the new Lyric—no matter how many times I had to rub my temples and grit my teeth to do so.

"Hey there," Rhodes said, his mouth quirking into a smile at the sight of us.

I once again ignored my body's reaction. This wasn't the first hot guy I'd seen, and hopefully wouldn't be the last. Today was about hiking and new friends, not wherever the hell my mind went when it came to Rhodes Luce.

"Hey," I said, hopefully sounding casual.

"Oh, good, you're here!" Rosamond skipped out of the house and locked the door, her backpack dangling from her arm. "We're all packed up, and have sandwiches and other snacks in the cooler in the back. We figured we'd either stuff them into our packs or come back for them after a shorter hike. It'll depend on how we feel when we get there, I guess. The start to the trail is only about thirty minutes away since we live so close to the foothills. I'm really excited!"

Rosamond's smile and enthusiasm about the day was contagious, and soon, we were climbing into Rhodes' SUV. Rosamond slid into the back seat, claiming car sickness, though I always thought sitting in the back made it worse, and Braelynn soon followed her. I found myself sitting in the passenger seat next to Rhodes. He had sunglasses over his eyes, and I missed seeing the color, though I didn't say that aloud. In fact, I didn't say much of anything as Rosamond and Braelynn took up most of the conversation. Every once in a while, one of them would say something, and Rhodes would look over at me, smiling as if I were in on the secret, and I'd smile back.

I continued ignoring the warm feelings in my gut. This was nice, though. And crushes were meant to be fun as long as you were careful.

After Emory, I was going to be *really* careful.

When we got to the place, I found out that the trailhead wasn't a marked one for the public, but one that only guides and advanced hikers knew about.

"Are you sure it's okay we park here and take this way?" I asked.

Rhodes nodded as Rosamond and Braelynn talked about what food to bring and what to keep in the SUV.

"We're fine here. We know the owners of the property since it technically begins on ranch land and goes into public land. They let us hike here as long as we keep it like we see it, and we do. We don't really bring anyone up with us, you know? So, it stays special."

He smiled at me, and I swallowed hard. I really needed to get my head out of the clouds when it came to this guy if I wanted to keep from tripping over a rock or something. I should be focused on other things. Having a thing for Rhodes wasn't going to help me make life choices or stay on track. Or even *find* a track I wanted. But, I could smile today. Tomorrow, I needed to get my butt in gear.

"Sounds like fun. We aren't taking an advanced hike, though, right? Because I'm a good runner, but I'm not so good with the whole direction thing."

"The mountains are always to the west," Braelynn called out, and I laughed.

"That helps in Denver when we're driving, not when we're actually *in* the mountains."

Rhodes chuckled. "These are the foothills, actually." He pointed to a large peak in the distance that seemed a whole lot bigger than I remembered when seeing it from farther away. "That's a mountain. We're not actually going there today. Maybe one day if you're in the mood, but that one we have to start way earlier, and I need to bring camping gear in case the weather shifts. Not today, though, so get that look off your face." He winked behind his glasses—I could barely see it through the lenses—and I held back a swoon.

Seriously, what was with this guy?

The four of us started off on the trail, Rosamond being our nature guide as she explained where we were going and what trees we saw and all that stuff. I knew most of it already, but she seemed excited to talk about it, so I didn't interrupt. She led while Braelynn walked behind her. I was behind Braelynn, while Rhodes brought up the rear. Every once in a while, when there was room for two-by-two, Braelynn and Rosamond paired up, and that left me with Rhodes. I wasn't sure if that was on purpose or not, but I didn't mind…much.

Only when I tripped over a root, and he had to reach out to catch me.

"Sorry," I said after the fourth time. "I'm not usually this clumsy."

"No worries. You're looking all around you rather than at your feet."

"There's so much to see," I countered. "I don't want to miss it."

"I know what you mean." He still held onto my hand, and I looked down at my feet so I didn't fall again. The heat of him was distracting. "It's beautiful for sure."

I ignored the fact that he was looking at me when he said it. Yes, it was a line, and yes, I totally liked it, but still.

About two hours into our hike, we were just about getting to the point where the Luce siblings said we should stop for lunch. I was thrilled because my stomach was *not* happy at the moment, and I knew I looked a mess with dirt on my face from rubbing my hands over it through my sweat. I'd put on two more layers of sunscreen during our hike, even though we spent most of the time under the shade of the trees. I couldn't help but be cautious when it came to my skin and the number of freckles I got.

I stood on the edge of a rock face, the incline far steeper than I remembered from when we'd walked up it. Suddenly, my vision blurred. I blinked, wondering if I'd gotten too much sun, and I heard Rhodes shout for me.

My foot slipped down the embankment, and I reached out to try and stop my fall.

But I knew it would be too late.

I looked down at the ever-growing abyss and swore I saw a shadow wrapped around my foot, pulling me down farther.

It couldn't be, though, because shadows with spindly hands did not exist.

But girls falling down the mountain because of a loose rock did.

I screamed, but it did nothing.

My head slammed into a rock as I fell, and only Rhodes' voice reached me, my name a shout on the air as darkness threatened and I succumbed.

I knew this was the end.

My end.

Before I'd even had my beginning.

CHAPTER 5

Screams.

Not my screams. Not anything that could come from my mouth.
I couldn't speak, I couldn't breathe, I couldn't *be*.

Strong hands wrapped around me, pulling me, tugging me.

There were scrapes, someone calling my name, someone else patting at
me, touching my head, my arms, my sides.

I could feel it all, and yet, at the same time, I couldn't feel anything.

I was awake, but I wasn't. Something tugged at me, but I couldn't tell
what it was, or what or who it could be.

The darkness came again, and I fell once more.

When I was finally able to open my eyes, I groaned, slamming them shut
again at the bright light hitting my eyeballs. Bile filled my throat and coated
my tongue, and I tried not to throw up.

I couldn't tell what was happening, but I remembered starting to fall down the incline, and I knew that once I opened my eyes again, it could be bad. Really, *really* bad.

I could feel someone next to me, their hands hovering over my body as warmth spread through me. I didn't understand what was going on, and I figured the odd heat flaring through certain parts of me where the hands touched had to be part of some weird dream I would likely forget once I woke up completely.

If I woke up.

No, no…I couldn't think like that. I would wake up. I had to.

I opened my eyes, and this time, the sun didn't blind me. Instead, a dark head of hair, the softest brown skin, and silver eyes filled my vision.

Rhodes.

Either I'd died and this was my heaven, or I was waking up, and he was there for me.

I didn't think I'd hurt this bad if it were heaven, though, so I had to hope that he was here to help after my fall.

"Lyric? Keep your eyes open for me, baby. That's it."

Baby? How hard did I hit my head? Surely I was imagining Rhodes' deep croon of a voice calling me baby.

I tried to swallow, wincing at the sour taste on my tongue and the papery feel of my mouth. "What…what happened?"

I focused on Rhodes' face, trying to get my bearings as the world slowly stopped spinning around me so I could see better.

"You're going to be okay," Rhodes said softly, his eyes narrowed.

That didn't exactly reassure me. I remembered falling. I remembered standing on the edge of the cliff, but not too close where I'd trip and stumble down. I remembered the wind in my hair and the smell of dirt and grass and trees all around me. I remembered the sight of a small lake off in the distance beside the large mountain Rhodes had told me would be too far for us to travel to.

I remembered all of it.

I also remembered the shadows pulling at me, tugging me down the cliffside as I screamed and fought against their hold before blacking out.

So, maybe I didn't remember the truth, after all, only my nightmares.

"You fell a little bit," Rosamond said from my side. "Bumped your head, but there's no blood, and everything looks good to me. Can you wiggle your fingers?"

I did, relieved to know that I could actually do so.

But how could I move my fingers? How was there no blood? And how was I okay if I had fallen from as high as I did? It didn't make any sense. None of it made any sense. Then again, neither did the idea that shadows with spindly fingers could pull me down.

Maybe I hadn't hit my head as hard as I thought I had. Still, clearly, I needed to get home and get some sleep or something.

"Good, good," Rosamond muttered under her breath. "You're all good, Lyric. No lasting damage. Just a little tumble, and Rhodes here got you right back up."

Rhodes grunted, and I blinked up at him. There was something in his eyes that I couldn't decipher. He was either really angry or worried, but I couldn't tell which.

"Let's get you sitting up. Then we'll head back home. No use keeping going when I'm going to worry about you the whole time."

I knew he hadn't meant it rudely. In fact, I thought he might have intended it a little sweetly, but I still blushed at his words. I didn't want to be a burden, and I wasn't that much of a klutz, but apparently, I'd ruined the day. Darn it.

"I'm okay," I said and pushed myself up to a seated position. Rhodes put his hands under my armpits to help me, and I bit into my bottom lip, embarrassed that he had to help me at all.

"Yeah, you are." Rhodes brushed the dirt off my back, and I slid my hands up my face and over my head. I couldn't even feel a bump or cut, so maybe the dream and the pain had all been my imagination.

"Do I have a concussion? I mean, I blacked out, right?" I was so confused, and I felt like I was missing something.

Rosamond met Rhodes' gaze, and they shared a look that worried me. "You didn't pass out. More like lost your breath because you fell like you did. It had to be a little scary. Seriously, Lyric. You're okay. Why don't you stand up?"

Before I did though, another thought came to me. "Where's Braelynn?" Had she fallen, too? Or maybe I hadn't fallen as far as I thought I had. Seriously, why did I feel like I was missing something big, or worse, that Rhodes and Rosamond were keeping something from me?

"I'm over here," Braelynn said from a rock nearby. "I got a little overheated." Her cheeks were red, and she had a faraway look in her eyes that worried me. I wondered what else had happened during my so-called not passing out.

"Let's get you home, then," I said quickly and tried to stand up. Rhodes helped me and didn't let his hand drop from me, going so far as to put one palm under my elbow as I took my first step to walk. I didn't have any trouble walking a straight line, and I felt fine, just confused.

I knew there had to be something more to what'd happened, but maybe I was just overreacting because I was embarrassed that Rhodes had seen me pass out like I had.

"Let's get you both home," Rhodes said under his breath and shared another look with his sister.

If I didn't want to go home and make sure Braelynn made it safely to hers, I might have questioned more. Heck, I probably would have stomped my foot and demanded answers. But I didn't think I would get them just then. Maybe not ever.

Perhaps my dreams were starting to take over my waking times. If I wasn't careful, I might fall for real.

The journey back to the car wasn't like it had been on the way there. I hardly noticed the trees or the path we were on. Rosamond led with Braelynn by her side, and Rhodes held my hand as we walked. I didn't read anything into it, I didn't even get that flutter and tingle that I usually did with his touch. Instead, I just wanted to get home so he didn't feel the need to take care of me anymore.

I hated being taken care of.

The drive back home was silent, no one even bothering to eat any of the food we'd brought. I sat in the back with Braelynn, wanting to make sure she was okay. But all she did was look out the window and drink her water. I did the same when I wasn't studying the rest of them. Rhodes parked in front of my house, which surprised me since I hadn't known he knew where I lived. Then again, I really didn't know much about him, did I?

Rosamond offered to drive Braelynn home just in case, and I was grateful. They piled into Braelynn's car and were out of sight soon after I'd said my goodbyes, promising Braelynn that I would call her soon.

That left Rhodes and me alone in front of my house since my parents were still at work. We hadn't been gone all that long, and it seemed as if I had ruined the day by tripping or whatever happened. My parents were leaving the next day for a trip to visit my grandparents, and I'd said I'd stay home since they were also going on a second honeymoon afterwards. I didn't want to go, and I knew they wanted me to stay home and think about my future anyway. As if it weren't something I'd been doing for years.

Rhodes walked me to my door, and I frowned up at him when he looked around the area as if checking for something—like those shadows I always saw out of the corner of my eye. But that wasn't what he was searching for, it couldn't be. They didn't exist.

"Stay inside tonight, Lyric," Rhodes warned.

I blinked up at him. "I thought you said I was okay?"

He frowned, his jaw tightening. "You are. And you will be tonight as long as you stay inside." Then he leaned forward and kissed my forehead, startling me into silence.

Had he just…kissed me?

Sure, he'd done it in an almost brotherly way, but now I knew what his lips on my skin felt like, and no matter what else had happened today, I would always remember that feeling.

But he was still being weird and cryptic, and I didn't like it.

"Whatever you say. I was going to stay at home anyway." I was so not a party animal, but whatever. Rhodes didn't need to know my plans, even if they were nonexistent.

"Good. Keep it that way." He looked down at me and cleared his throat. "I'm sorry today ended up like it did, but I'm glad you came out. I'm sure I'll see you around soon."

Then he just stood there on my porch, and I knew I had to get inside, or he'd wait all night for me to be secure. Apparently, Rhodes Luce was a little overprotective.

I walked into the house and locked the door behind myself. Only then did I hear Rhodes walk away and start his SUV, presumably driving back to his home.

Today…today had been weird. Something had happened near that mountain, something I couldn't explain. And while I wanted to believe that everything was okay, there was something inside me, something nagging at me, saying that waking up with Rhodes looking down at me was the end. Or...it was *an* end. And a beginning. It was important. So important that I kept thinking about it even as the thought tried to flitter from my mind.

A shadow passed by out of the corner of my eye, and I turned to catch it, only to find my own reflection.

My eyes were wide, my skin pale, my hair a complete mess.

I had fallen today, and they had said that nothing was wrong. If that were true, then why did I ache? Why did I feel as if I had fallen farther than they said?

Another shadow passed, and I closed my eyes. It was nothing. I wasn't seeing things.

I couldn't be seeing things.

Not again.

CHAPTER 6

Shadows clawed at my skin, tugging, digging, shredding, ripping.

I stood in the center of an abyss that wasn't an abyss, wind whipping through my hair as I twisted and turned in the tunnel of shadows. They screamed my name, whispered the same near my ears, their hot breath dancing along my skin with silky heat.

I tried to fight against them as sweat slicked my skin, and water sprayed on my face from a nearby rocky edge where the ocean met the land. The ground beneath my feet rumbled, and I dug my bare toes into the small, jagged rocks, ignoring the way they made my soles bleed as I tried to keep my balance.

The heat of a nearby volcano blistered my skin, its smoke and ash burning my eyes even as I squeezed my lids shut.

So many sensations, so many nightmares wrapped within a dream.

Only they weren't mere shadows like before. Instead of dark shapes out of the corner of my eyes that faded to mist once I focused, they now had fangs and eyes and sharp claws.

They were my nightmares.

They were my future.

Why I knew that, I didn't know, but it was the truth.

They clawed at me again, my blood mixing with the mist of death that surrounded me.

When one creature lifted its head, its sharp teeth in front of my face dripping shadow and darkness…I screamed. My throat burned as the sound ripped from my lungs.

And found myself sitting up, alone in my bed, my head aching, and my clothes sticking to my skin with sweat.

Again.

This wasn't the first dream I'd had, nor did I think it would be the last, but it had been one of the most vivid. I dreamed in color, with sound, and using almost all of my senses. When I dreamed, I swore I was either living inside them or close enough at least to watch them. It didn't matter if I was the observer or the protagonist, I always knew they were dreams, even if they felt far more real than reality.

And maybe that was my problem.

Yet, tonight? This dream was different. The shadows had faces this time. They had claws and fangs and desire in their eyes that spoke of damage and a craving for flesh. I didn't know why I knew that, but then again, it was a dream, and I tended to know more about the hows than the whys when I was deep inside them.

I was so tired. So tired of shadows. Tired of seeing them. So tired of dreaming.

I thought of the shadow I thought I'd seen when I fell and shivered. How I could be cold in a hot room covered in sweat, I didn't know, but I was freezing now. Rhodes and Rosamond had told me I slipped but hadn't hurt myself—not really. Yet I could remember the searing pain initially upon waking. Could remember the fall, the moment when I hadn't been able to feel anything below me for an instant, other than the spindly fingers of the shadow wrapped around my ankle.

It hadn't been real, though.

It couldn't have been, as I didn't have a single bruise on me, and the monsters from my dreams weren't real.

They weren't real.

And if I told myself that over and over again, maybe I wouldn't jump at every dimming of the light, or when I caught something out of the corner of my eye. Everyone saw things, they just didn't freak out like I did. Sometimes, it was a speck of dust that filled your vision but looked far worse. Other times, it was just a case of simple deja vu.

None of it was scary, and I needed to stop thinking it was.

With a sigh, I rolled out of bed and went about the now far-too-normal routine of washing my sweaty sheets and clothes. My parents hadn't questioned my late-night and early morning laundry habits, and I guessed it was because they assumed I just liked things clean. I suppose that made sense, only it didn't make me feel any better that I couldn't get over the dreams.

"I'm not going insane," I whispered to myself. Seeing things out of the corner of my eyes and having horrible dreams that pulled me in until I couldn't breathe didn't make me crazy. It just meant that I had an overactive imagination that wouldn't quit.

I showered quickly and, since the sun was already up, I decided to go on another early morning run. Maybe I'd stop by the local stand that served the best breakfast burritos I'd ever had on the way. Not the greatest way to reward myself for running—a greasy burrito—but after yet another nightmare, I figured I deserved it. I'd just run home faster once my stomach settled. My parents were already gone, having had an early flight, so I was alone now and would be for almost a month.

I put on my pink sports bra with the black lace-up front and sides and a tank over the top, along with my favorite mesh jacket since it was still a little chilly this morning, no matter that it would be way too hot later. I slid on my black leggings and shoes and put on the crossbody bag I used while jogging sometimes. It had a buckle that I could tighten easily and wouldn't jiggle too much as I ran. Not that I ran very quickly without caffeine, but since the dreams had put me in such a mood where I couldn't quite get my footing, running toward food and anywhere other than my bedroom would have to do.

My feet hit the pavement just as the sun peeked over the horizon. I should have stretched beforehand, but I'd known I needed to get away and give myself distance from my room and memories of the dreams. I let the strain of running up hills as my lungs struggled to adjust to the exertion fill me so I wouldn't think about what I'd slept through or the thoughts that were cycling through my mind a million miles a minute.

I wasn't going insane.

I wasn't having dreams that meant anything.

I didn't fall and hurt myself on the hike.

I didn't miraculously heal while others lied to me about it.

And I didn't see anything in the shadows.

It was just a figment of my imagination. I needed to get more sun yet stay out of the heat. I also needed more water and less junk food—the burritos I was on my way to consume notwithstanding.

I would eventually go through a night at some point without a dream that seemed to rip at my soul and steal my breath. I was going to make a decision about my future and stick with it. And, I would eat my burrito in peace and then run it off later because I wasn't going to feel guilty about it.

And I would do all this without losing my mind.

Because I *wasn't* losing my mind.

I took two more turns, passing Rhodes' and Rose's street along the way, and found myself in front of the burrito place, my stomach growling and my thighs and lungs burning. I'd purposely took the route that passed their street without me actually running on it. I don't know why I did that exactly, but it had been as if I were drawn to the Luces, yet knew I didn't want to be near them.

Plus, I didn't want it to look like I was stalking Rhodes or acting weirdly around him since I couldn't get the feel of his hand on mine out of my head— or the sensation of his lips on my skin.

I had so many questions, so many worries, and I was still fretting over a boy.

That told me I needed more burritos in my stomach and less stress about romantic entanglements. I'd be smarter to deal with the grease from the burrito than anything that had to do with the boy I didn't need to think about.

Thankfully, the little stand was open. I ordered a chicken and bean burrito, as well as a potato and bean one. I wasn't a fan of eggs inside a tortilla, but this place made different versions for breakfast. I didn't drench them in hot sauce like I might have if it were later in the day, and I counted that as a breakfast win.

I took a seat on one of the outside covered benches and dug into the potato and bean burrito, saving the chicken for last. That one was usually hotter, and I didn't mind cold chicken as much as I did cold potatoes. I was picky when it came to sneaking away for breakfast burritos, but at least I had a system.

I let the sunrise slide over me as I finished the first burrito, annoyed with myself for forgetting to order a bottle of water, as well. I'd get one after I finished the second half of my breakfast so I could let my stomach settle a bit before jogging back home. Not the smartest move on my part this morning, but it wasn't like I was thinking clearly.

I swallowed the last bite of potato and froze when I caught something out of the corner of my eye.

"It's just a shadow," I whispered to myself. "A normal shadow. It's not real."

But as I turned, able to look away, I didn't know if I was telling myself the truth.

Because it sure as heck *looked* real.

The creature stood on all fours, its head coming up to just about my shoulder height as it clawed at the trashcan nearest the street. If it didn't look like something that crawled out of my darkest nightmares, I would have thought it a stray dog or very large cat, looking for scraps. Maybe even a bear from the mountains that wandered too far into the urban areas.

But strays weren't that big, and bears didn't have massive iron-and-silver-tipped claws that shone in the sunlight.

I knew this…whatever it was. I had seen it before.

Only, I hadn't been awake at the time.

It had long, pointed ears, and longer teeth that jutted from its open mouth as it drooled a pool near its front feet. If it had been standing on its hind legs, it would have easily towered over me. It had large muscles but a slender body as if it were ready to run toward its prey and spring at any opportunity.

And, for some reason, I knew if the…*thing* looked at me, I would be its prey.

I held my breath, wondering when I had truly gone off the edge and started seeing things. Because this monster was created of shadow but made of flesh and bone. I could see that now. This was what I had seen out of the corner of my eye for far too long. Now, I could see it in truth.

I was sure I would ask myself why later, but for now, I just froze, my other burrito left untouched and cooling on the table as I watched the shadow-monster dig into the trash without making a sound. It didn't even rustle a single piece of paper or water bottle, and I had no idea how it did that.

Because it isn't real.

I ignored the words in my head that I knew were the truth and did my best not to breathe too loudly or cry out at the sight.

When the burrito stand lady walked past the trashcan to talk with another person walking near, I blinked, and the shadow was gone as if it had never existed.

Yet I *knew* it had.

Because I couldn't be losing my mind, I *couldn't*. That meant something else was going on.

I needed to talk to the one person I trusted more than anything to make sense of it all.

I threw the last of my breakfast away, my stomach roiling at what I'd just seen—or perhaps *hadn't* seen—and jogged to Braelynn's house. I texted her on the way when I stopped at a corner, waiting for a car to pass, and hoped she was awake.

Me: *Are you up? I need to talk.*

Braelynn: *Just up now. I'll meet you at the back door.*

I quickly put my phone into the pocket of my jacket, letting out a deep breath. I knew I could count on Braelynn, and the fact that she hadn't even asked *why* I needed to talk to her so urgently and in person meant everything.

I was just about to turn onto Braelynn's street when I heard someone call my name.

"Why are you running this early?" Emory asked as she ran toward me, her keys in hand. All of us lived near each other since we were in the same school district and neighborhood, but with everything on my mind, I'd forgotten that Emory lived on the way to Braelynn's place. "Now you have me running."

I stared at the girl I'd once thought I loved before I realized that it was only an infatuation of young hearts, and knew that Emory should probably be part of this conversation, as well. She might not be my best friend, and I knew that our lives would be going their separate ways, but I also knew she would be the voice of reason while Braelynn would help me settle my nerves. I needed them both, and yet I was afraid of what they might say.

"I'm headed to Braelynn's to talk about...well, I need to tell her something. Can you come, too?"

There must have been something in my voice because Emory gave me a weird look. "Everything okay, Lyric?"

I started to nod before shaking my head. "I don't know. Can you come?"

She stared at me long enough that I was afraid she was going to say no, but then she stuck her keys into her pocket and shrugged. "Okay. You're being weird, you know?"

"I know, but...but thank you." I turned and walked the rest of the way to Braelynn's, Emory right behind me. My friend sat on her back porch, a cup of tea in her hand, and a small frown on her face. I knew the mug held tea since Braelynn wasn't a huge fan of coffee, and it was too early for hot chocolate for her.

"What's wrong, Lyric?" Braelynn stood up and set down her mug.

"Can we talk inside? Or somewhere private?" I didn't want to air all my dirty laundry and insanity to the world. It was bad enough that I was about to do it in front of Braelynn and Emory.

"My parents are out of town, so, of course. I only said go through to the back because I was already sitting out here enjoying the morning." Braelynn took a step toward me and hugged me close. I held her back, my nerves soothing ever so slightly just by being in her presence.

"Let's get on with it then." Emory said. "I was on my way to get a latte, and now I'm caffeine-less and hungry."

I pulled away from my best friend and turned so the three of us could walk into Braelynn's house and into the living room. Once we were seated, however—me beside Braelynn on the couch, and Emory sitting on the chair in front of us—I had no idea where to start.

How could I tell the two people who knew me better than most that I was seeing things? And that I thought that, somehow…something was connected to my fall up in the mountains. An accident that the others said wasn't as bad as I thought it had been.

"Spit it out," Emory said. "You're starting to freak me out with all your lip biting and hand wringing. It's not like you."

"Emory…" Braelynn began, but I held up my shaking hands.

"No, I'll start. I know I might sound like I'm losing it, but I want you to hear me out. Okay?"

Braelynn took my hand in hers and gave it a squeeze. I settled immediately. She was always so good at that. "Of course."

Emory didn't say anything, yet I hadn't expected her to.

I didn't know where to begin, so I just started…hoping I was doing the right thing.

"Sometimes, I think there's something in the shadows. Something more than a trick of the eye."

The others didn't say anything, and for that, I was grateful. So, I continued.

"You know how you think you see something move and yet when you look, nothing's there? I've had that in my life. I've always looked, as quickly as possible, but I could never catch it. When I was little, my mother used to say that it was fairies and magic, and only the 'special' could see. But then I got older, and I stopped telling her I still saw the shadows."

I took a deep breath, and Braelynn squeezed my hand again. Emory looked bored, and I had no idea what to do with that reaction.

"But the shadows are growing. At least, in my mind. I think something happened to me on that mountain. I don't know what, but...I don't know. I've been having dreams. Or, I guess nightmares. I don't know. But I can't sleep, and I swore I saw a monster today while getting breakfast, the same ones I've been seeing out of the corner of my eye, and similar to the ones in my dreams."

"You're kidding me," Emory drawled. "How much sleep did you get last night?"

I looked down at my hands, knowing I deserved any reaction she gave me. "Not enough. That's for sure. But that's the problem. I've been having dreams for as long as I can remember. Vivid ones."

"We all have dreams. Not everyone is special or magic. No one is." Emory rolled her eyes, and she was lucky I didn't smack her. I knew I was probably making no sense, but I was also baring myself to her, and she was being a brat about it.

"That might be true, but I still think something happened up there. I remember falling, Braelynn. I remember the pain and thinking it was going to hurt and yet I woke up and you looked confused and Rosamond and Rhodes said I was fine."

"You fell?" Emory sat up straighter. "Why didn't you tell me?"

"Because it all happened so fast and, honestly, they said I wasn't hurt.

But I *remember*."

"I told you going on that hike was a bad idea."

I pinched the bridge of my nose with my free hand, Braelynn still holding my other and staying quiet. "I know, but that doesn't help now."

"And, for hell's sake, Lyric, you aren't making any sense. You're talking about dreams and monsters and shadows, and yet going on about falling? I don't get it."

"I don't either," I snapped. "That's why I'm here. I'm trying to get my thoughts in order. I saw a *monster*, you guys. It had claws and big teeth, and I didn't move so it wouldn't look right at me. I don't know if that was the right thing to do, but I *saw* it. I've always seen shadows, always felt them in my dreams, but nothing like this. And the only thing that's changed is the hike. It has to connect. Or, maybe I'm really just seeing things and need to be committed. I don't know, but *something* is wrong, and I can't keep it to myself anymore. Not if I want to keep my mind intact."

We were quiet for a long while, my mind whirling, and Emory glaring until Braelynn's voice punctured the silence.

"I think we should talk to Rhodes and Rosamond."

I turned to her. "Why? Do you believe me?" I hoped she did because I didn't want to be alone. I had known deep down that Emory wouldn't believe me, but Braelynn... Braelynn understood me.

She had to.

Braelynn met my gaze with sad eyes before nodding. "I don't see shadows or monsters, but I know something happened on that cliffside. My brain is trying to tell me what that is, yet it's all fuzzy. I don't remember you falling, but I don't remember how you ended up on your back with the others hovering around you either. I think we need to talk to the Luces because I know something happened, yet I have...nothing. It's like there's a gap when I try to remember, and that scares me."

My heart thudded in my ears, and I swallowed, my mouth suddenly dry. "I...I don't know what to ask them, but I think we need to go."

Emory let out a sigh. "I think you've both been watching too many scary movies. But if you think the twin freaks are hiding something from you, don't let me stand in your way. In fact, I'll be right by your side because I don't like the idea that they'd hurt you. Or lie. Or whatever."

It was as good as I would get from Emory, so I took it. The three of us looked at one another, and I knew as we made our way to Rhodes and Rosamond's that something important was happening, something that could change everything.

I had seen a monster today—not just a shadow.

I had changed—not just my circumstances.

Somehow, I knew as soon as we met with them, everything would be different. I should be running the other way. I should be thinking about my future and not things that could and should not be. Yet I couldn't stop my path, couldn't shift my direction away from their home.

Something was coming.

Or rather, I feared, something was already here.

And I was in the middle of it.

CHAPTER 7

I stood on the doorstep of a home I'd never been in before, but I knew who lived there. It was a decent-sized ranch home and only one story, but I knew the back faced the mountains, so there had to be a few good views that way. Not all homes here were two stories, and many were split-level thanks to all the hills, but this one was pretty simple. Only, it didn't really feel simple just then. Nothing did.

Rhodes and Rosamond were private people, and I'd only ever been in their SUV, and that was just yesterday—the same day I had miraculously survived a fall that had to be far worse than they said it was.

I had no idea why my mind kept coming back to that fact, but I knew it had to be true. There was no way I could have imagined everything that had been happening to me recently, and while I didn't know if it was all connected, I *did* know that there were two other people who had been there

Or, perhaps they'd call me crazy and help have me committed because I felt like I was one nightmare and shadow away from that already.

But I'd seen the fangs.

I remembered my dreams.

I could still feel the air on my face and the feeling of that *thing* tugging on my ankle as it pulled me down.

I remembered the fear.

No, I wasn't going crazy.

But I didn't feel sane either...

"It's early, but whatever. I still can't believe you didn't tell me you fell. Like, what the hell, Lyric?" Emory narrowed her eyes at me before ringing the bell.

I winced at the sound, realizing it was, in fact, really early. In actuality, there probably wasn't a reason for us to be here, ready to...what? Ask them point-blank if they lied about my fall and how I magically healed before seeing monsters?

Ugh. I was so stupid. Like, how on earth did any of this make sense? I needed to go home, pop an aspirin, and forget everything I thought I saw. Forget the fact that Braelynn felt like something was off, as well. For all I knew, she was only feeling the way she did because I was, and somehow I'd convinced her that something was wrong.

"We need to go." I blurted the words and took a step back, nearly falling off the stoop as I did.

Emory took my forearm in a punishing grip, frowning at me. "We're not kids. We don't ring and dash, dude."

I didn't have time to respond to her, not that I knew what I'd say anyway, because the door opened, and Rosamond stood there, her brows drawn together.

"What's wrong, Lyric?"

Emory stepped in front of me, and Braelynn had to hold my hip for a moment to keep me from falling. That step and I were not getting along today apparently as I'd tripped more than once today.

"I'll tell you what's wrong. You let Lyric get hurt and, apparently, you're lying about it. I knew you two were freaks, but I didn't realize it was this bad. What the hell did you do to her? Don't make me hurt you."

"Emory." The steel in my voice must have reached her because she turned her head, her mouth parted, and her hair swishing over her shoulders.

"What?"

"Stop it. Don't be a bitch because you're annoyed I don't tell you everything." I let out a breath, trying to gather my thoughts. "Can we come in, Rosamond? I know it's early and we're here out of the blue, but I have something to ask you."

"*We* do," Braelynn added beside me. "If it's okay. Please. Thank you." Braelynn was rambling at this point and I let out a breath, wondering what we were doing here and why we'd come as a group as we had.

Rosamond looked between the three of us, a curious look on her face that I couldn't read. She was about to step aside when the hairs on the back of my neck rose, and something skittered just out of my line of sight.

A shadow.

I turned, my heart beating fast as I tried to catch what I thought I could see out of the corner of my eye. But before I could fully turn, Rosamond shoved her way through the three of us, moving Braelynn and Emory to the sides and me backwards enough that I almost fell. Again.

"What the hell?" Emory asked, turning, a glare on her face. She shoved her dark hair back behind her ears and moved toward Rosamond.

Braelynn put out a hand, stopping her, and Emory glared at her instead. "Stop. Something's wrong."

"I'll tell you what's wrong. We shouldn't be here."

"No," Rosamond said softly, her hands outstretched, and her long, dark hair blowing in the wind. "*They* shouldn't be here." And with those oddly terrifying words echoing in my ears, I finally looked at what Rosamond saw.

"Oh, God." I hadn't even realized that I'd said the words aloud until Braelynn and Emory both looked at me, confusion on their faces. Maybe they couldn't see what I could, what Rosamond obviously could, but that wasn't any different than before. Perhaps I was truly losing my mind.

The monster I had seen at the burrito place had found friends, and they were prowling toward the house. The shadows each had long fangs, dark eyes that glowed red, and even longer claws that dug into the ground, tilling the soil and browning the grass.

Rosamond stood in front of us as five monsters crawled our way. I had no idea what she was doing. She was so small, like a tiny dancer, and yet she looked as fierce as a warrior right then, ready to battle against these...*things*.

Rosamond looked over her shoulder at me, and I swore I could see something in her eyes that spoke of someone far older, something that spoke of memories and an age that didn't make sense.

Then she turned away and held out her arms. She whispered something under her breath, and a bright light shot out from her hands, making me take a step back into Braelynn. A film slid down from the sky, almost like when you break an egg over a glass bowl, and the sides become harder to see through. Now, I could only see the lawn, my friends, and those monsters. It felt as if the rest of the world wouldn't be able to see what was going on within the bubble, and yet we couldn't truly see outside of it either.

Or, maybe I had hit my head, and none of this was real.

Then, a monster jumped.

Rosamond ducked out of the way, and I ran toward her, knowing I wasn't strong enough to help. But I couldn't just leave her alone out there.

"Get inside!" I yelled to my friends. "Go!"

Emory turned on her heel, but as soon as she did, one of the shadows grabbed her ankle, tossing her off the steps. She fell hard and didn't get up. I screamed, but before I could help her, another shadow picked up Braelynn and threw her into a car. It didn't seem like it was too hard, but Braelynn let out a soft sound and then passed out, lying near the tire as the shadow turned away and stared at me.

Directly at me.

"Crap."

This was real. All of this was real. And I had no idea how to fight these things. I wasn't a fighter, I wasn't even good at watching action movies because I got bored. I looked over to my right, and Rosamond was fighting four of the monsters, moving her hands in weird patterns I didn't understand. Somehow, without even touching them, the shadows flew away, hitting the ground hard and making deep grooves in the yard where they landed, only to scramble back and try to get at Rosamond again. She seemed to be holding her own, even if I didn't know how she was doing it.

That left the fifth monster to me, it's dark, ash-covered skin reminding me of a picture of a Hell Hound I'd seen when I was younger. Maybe it was from the pits of hell, and this was my apocalypse.

The thing lurched toward me and met my gaze. I couldn't look away, but I couldn't run either. I knew it would chase me, and I couldn't leave my friends lying unconscious, possibly hurt—or worse.

I swallowed down the bile that threatened to rise at that thought, then ducked quickly when the shadow jumped at me. Somehow, I remembered my meager self-defense training from my single class and rolled over my shoulder to land on my feet. I didn't do it particularly well and almost fell on my face, but the shadow's claws at least missed me.

I whirled around, then fell on my side when the shadow jumped again. That time, I hadn't been fast enough. It raised a clawed hand at me, and I shielded my face, knowing that I wouldn't be quick enough to get away, but hoping it would miss me somehow.

Or maybe I just knew that I wasn't strong enough to fight.

If I got out of this alive, I'd find a way to learn. I never wanted to feel this helpless again. But before I could lament even more, the shadow screamed, a terrifying, high-pitched sound that made me shut my eyes…but only for a moment.

I needed to know what had made the shadow shriek.

Because if something could hurt it, it could hurt my friends and me, too.

But as the shadow was tossed off of me, I saw that it wasn't another monster.

No, it was the boy with the dark skin and the silver eyes.

The one I had come to talk to.

Rhodes growled, and the earth shook beneath me as if it were just as angry as he was. Or maybe I was the one shaking. I didn't know, but I knew I couldn't stay where I was for long. I crawled away, my legs too weak for me to stand yet. I tried to get to Braelynn since she was closer, but I kept looking over my shoulder to see what Rhodes and Rosamond were doing, not quite believing my eyes at what I saw.

They both moved their hands in motions too fast for me to truly see, seeming to blow the monsters away from them and into the ground with such force, I could feel it through my hands and knees as I crawled. The shadows bled red from where the rocks cut into them and from where Rhodes stabbed at them, and I knew I'd never get the image of the battle out of my mind until the day I died. I just hoped that day was a long time from now.

I finally turned away from the fighting that was so out of my depth and stood up on shaky legs, trying to run toward my friends. Maybe if I could get to them and pull them into the house, I could call for help. I didn't know who I could call in to fight demon shadows, but perhaps I could do *something*. Though as soon as I got to Braelynn, I remembered that I shouldn't move someone that could have a back injury. The same with Emory. Tears threatened.

I was weak.

Darn it, I was so freaking weak, and I hated myself for it.

So, I forced back the tears and went to Braelynn's side, cupping her face. "Braelynn, be okay. Please, wake up."

Her eyes fluttered open and, this time, I let the tears fall. She looked confused but didn't move, and I knew the fear wasn't over, not by a long shot, but she'd opened her eyes, and that had to count for something.

Before I could say anything, though, something tugged at my shoulder and dragged me a few feet away from her. I kicked and screamed, then lost my breath as I looked up into the red eyes of a shadow.

Only, it wasn't a shadow. I knew that now. It wasn't just something from my dreams or a trick of the eyes.

It was real.

And it hovered over me.

Waiting.

And since I hadn't been able to fight back in my dreams, I kicked out and punched, trying to do *something* instead of just lying there, waiting for the thing to end my life. The impact of the kick rocked my body, and I teetered on my other foot, but I didn't fall.

The monster growled at me, so I kicked again, my foot aching from the second impact.

It lowered its head, so I punched it in the mouth, the shock from the blow sending a hot wave of pain down my arm.

It didn't do anything.

Just hovered.

Then it screamed when Rosamond jumped on its back like she was riding a bull in a rodeo. I'd never seen anything like it. Of course, as of ten minutes ago, I'd never seen anything like this at all.

No, that wasn't right, I'd seen one at the burrito stand, but I hadn't fought it, I hadn't seen someone ride one while fighting and using strength that seemed to come out of nowhere.

I crawled out from under the shadow, caught sight of Rhodes fighting off the other four by himself, and got to my feet again. Out of the corner of my eye, I saw a branch near the edge of the house, so I ran toward it, hoping I would be fast enough. *You are a runner*, I reminded myself. I was good at something. Though it wasn't like I could do much with that skill. I dragged the branch over to where Rosamond fought the other shadow monster and slammed it into the creature's side. It cried out, looked at me, then screamed again when Rosamond did something with her hands. It was as if she were dancing her hands in the air, her fingers moving in an intricate pattern, pushing and pulling in a way I didn't understand.

Suddenly, the red light in its eyes faded, and it fell to the ground.

I blinked, then looked over to the side, only to see Rhodes doing the same to two more of the shadow monsters, leaving three large bodies on the ground as the other two fell back, circling us. I swayed on my feet, dizzy and confused, but I kept myself up. Rhodes stepped toward me, then widened his eyes.

I looked over my shoulder and, this time, it was me who screamed, not the monsters.

The other two shadows had circled us, and in doing so, something dark that looked like a portal from a movie I had once seen opened up near where

Braelynn lay, still so still it scared me. The monsters jumped over her, though, and came straight for me.

I fell to my knees as one slammed into my side, the pain ricocheting through me. Nothing was broken, but I knew I was bruised. And, it wasn't over.

The shadow loomed over me, and then everything changed. It all happened so quickly, I felt as if I were missing pieces. Rhodes was suddenly by my side, pulling me away as he shoved something into the shadow, but then he yelled for his sister, horror in his eyes.

I looked over only to see that the other monster pulled at an unconscious Rosamond. It tugged her toward the dark circle that held no light, only something that spoke of distance. When it stepped through it, Rhodes tugged me closer, away from the dead body of one of the monsters that had tried to kill me, and then he screamed.

Rhodes screamed.

Because the portal or whatever it was closed, and Rosamond and the monster were just…gone.

His sister was gone.

Gone.

Just…not there anymore.

But I was still here.

And so was Rhodes.

If he hadn't been trying to save me, he might have been able to help her. Save her.

"Damn it," Rhodes growled. "The Negs aren't supposed to have that magic. Rosamond!" He screamed her name again as if she could hear him where she'd been pulled to.

Silence. That was all I could hear then. Silence.

I smelled dirt and fire and didn't understand. It was like my dream, but it was real.

I hurt, and the horrors were real.

And the dread in Rhodes' eyes was all too real.

"What just happened?" I asked, my voice raw from screaming. "Where's Rosamond? Where did they take her?

Rhodes didn't answer me. Instead, he looked over his shoulder, his jaw tightening as the thin veil that had somehow surrounded us seemed to shimmer before disappearing completely.

"We need to get inside."

Emory stood up behind us. I hadn't realized she'd woken up. "No, what just happened?"

Rhodes took my arm and pulled me up. "The Negs are here, and your world, your *everything* is just beginning."

I had no idea what he meant by "Negs" or his weird proclamation that made no sense, and yet I knew he wasn't lying.

I hadn't been hallucinating. I wasn't losing my mind. But now that I'd seen a glimpse of whatever the heck was going on around us, I wasn't sure I wanted that confirmation, because it meant it was real.

I wanted to wake up from this dream that wasn't a dream, only I didn't think I'd have that option.

I didn't think *any* of my choices would ever be the same again.

CHAPTER 8

"I'm not going inside with you," Emory spat, holding her head. "I'm going home and forgetting this ever happened. I don't know what the heck is going on with you and your weird sister, but I want no part of it."

Rhodes didn't spare her a glance. Instead, his attention was on me, his silver eyes pools of fury.

"Lyric."

I blinked, my head aching, and my body throbbing from the fall. "I…what?"

He reached out as if to cup my cheek before freezing and lowering his hand. "We need to get inside. I'll explain…well, I'll explain as much as I can. But we're not safe out in the open here."

"And we'll be safe in your house? I don't think so. Come on, Lyric."

Emory folded her arms over her chest, but I looked back at Rhodes, knowing that I couldn't go home. Not yet. Not until I knew what was going on.

"You'll tell me everything?" I asked, needing to know the answer even if I was afraid of what he might say.

Once again, he reached out, but this time, he took my hand. I ignored the pull I felt at the contact. It didn't make sense. It couldn't. "Everything I can."

It wasn't the answer I wanted to hear, but it seemed it was as good as I would get.

"Okay, then."

Relief covered his face for a brief moment before something in his eyes changed, and his features tightened. I didn't know what it meant. But Rosamond was gone, something had attacked us—something I couldn't explain but, apparently, he could—and so many other things had happened that it was no wonder I couldn't read his face.

Though I never had been able to before either, even in the brief interactions I'd had with the boy I dreamed pretty dreams about.

There was nothing pretty about what had just happened, however, so those thoughts were long gone from my mind as Rhodes pulled me toward the house, reaching out to guide Braelynn in, as well. Emory stood to the side, glaring at all of us before muttering something under her breath that I couldn't hear and following us into Rhodes' house.

I tried to take in what I saw, what I *had* seen outside, but it wasn't easy, not when I still shook, and my knees ached, while my hands were covered in dirt and scrapes. My friends stood on either side of me, Braelynn standing stock-still, her eyes wide even as she no doubt took everything in, as well. Emory stood off to the side, her eyes narrowing further as she glared at Rhodes, who stood in front of us.

"Take a seat." Rhodes cleared his throat, his voice a growl. "Please."

"I don't think so."

I closed my eyes at Emory's biting words. I was tired, confused, and honestly…scared. "Emory. Stop it. Just stop it."

"I can't believe you're going to kowtow to this guy. What the hell happened out there, freak? And why do you think we want to hear any of what you have to say?"

Rhodes folded his arms over his chest and gave Emory a bored look. "That's a contradiction in questions. Either you want answers, or you're not going to believe anything I say. Which is it?"

"Stop." My voice was low, but Rhodes heard it because he turned to me, something soft in his eyes for just a moment before his expression turned hard again.

"There are things you need to know, Lyric. Things you should have been told before now."

That made my back go up. "Then, tell me."

"Lyric—"

"Shut up, Emory! Just let him tell me what the hell is going on. Something just came out of the *shadows* and attacked us. It *took* Rosamond, and we're just supposed to pretend that it didn't happen?"

Emory glared. "I didn't see any of what you say, Lyric. I didn't see anything except you and Rosamond running and then falling from what looked like thin air."

"I didn't see the monster either," Braelynn added quietly. "But I know something was there. I saw the shadows, just not…not anything tangible. So why did you see it, Lyric? Why now and not before?"

We all turned to Rhodes, who finally sighed, a defeated look crossing his face. "You can see what lurks beneath the shadows, Lyric, because of who you are and because of what happened in the forest. As for Braelynn, I don't know why she can see at least part of the shadows. There's a reason, but I don't know what it is. Emory sees nothing because that's what all humans see.

Just figments of their imagination. Maybe a glimpse when they're not paying attention, but never in full."

"The fall?" I sank down onto the couch, my knees weak, not from information but from everything that had happened a few moments ago. I was a runner, not a fighter. And I had no idea what might come at us next.

Rhodes ran a hand over his face, and I noticed the blood on his knuckles. Any other time, I would have reached for him, to help him clean them, to help *any* of my friends, but I wasn't sure what I could do. I didn't feel like I could do much of anything at the moment except try to listen and hope I could either make sense of it or wake up from yet another nightmare.

Emory paced beside the couch, her arms folded angrily over her chest. Braelynn went to the chair closest to the sofa, almost curling into herself. My friend was far too sweet for this, far too innocent. I wasn't the nicest person, wasn't the one who made good life choices all the time, but Braelynn was. And now, something was changing, and I was afraid it was all my fault.

Rhodes sat down on the table in front of me, reaching out carefully to cup my face with one hand. Emory growled beside us, but I didn't think it was from jealousy. No, Emory was pissed off that she couldn't see what we could, or rather, what *I* could, and she hated being out of the loop.

"You fell," Rhodes said softly, bringing me back to the conversation.

"Something grabbed my ankle. I didn't really fall, did I? Not like…not like what I'm trying not to remember."

Rhodes pulled away, and I immediately missed his touch. At the same time, I was annoyed with myself for thinking of something as trivial as a crush and an innocent touch at a time when I thought I might be losing my mind. Not to mention, Rosamond was out there somewhere, and I had no idea where or how we were going to get her back.

"I think something grabbed you. A Neg."

I frowned. "A Neg?"

"It's…a shadow. The negative space of all that is light and magic, as well as everything that is dark and magic. It rests in the unrest of the in-between."

"Magic." I blinked. "You're saying magic is real."

"Let's get out of here, Lyric. He's spouting nonsense, and I'm not here for that."

"It's not nonsense. I *saw* things, Emory. If you're going to keep interrupting, just go. Okay? Just go."

"I'm not leaving you alone with him."

"She's not alone," Braelynn said, her voice louder.

"Like you count."

I closed my eyes, taking a moment to myself as I tried to get the two people who'd meant the most to me for so long to stop fighting. No, that wasn't right, I needed Emory to back off and not react out of fear. She wasn't hateful exactly, but when she got scared, she lashed out, and people got hurt. Braelynn understood that, but it didn't make it right.

"Enough," Rhodes growled. "This doesn't concern you, but as Lyric's friend, you can stay. Just remember, this is my house. You'll respect Lyric and Braelynn, or you'll leave. I don't care if you feel you have the right to be here. You don't."

Since I'd tried to get Emory to stop before, I didn't say anything for a moment. I hated that she didn't listen, but I also didn't like being walked on. If and when I figured out what was coming or even what was happening, I didn't think Emory would be a part of my life for long afterwards.

"Go, Emory. I'm tired of fighting with you, and this is important." I looked at her and tried to see the girl I had once cared for instead of the angry woman in front of me who pushed at me daily. "Can't you see that this is important?" I pressed my hand to my chest, my heart racing.

"I'll stay. For you."

I didn't know what that meant, but I was too tired to think about it more. "Then let Rhodes explain. Let *me* try to understand and see if he's lying. Let me make my own choices." I'd said that before in another context, and she must have remembered because her eyes flared before she gave me a tight nod. I turned back to Rhodes, and he gave me an approving look. As I wasn't in the mood for looks or whatever approval he thought I needed, I just blinked slowly.

He cleared his throat. "I should start at the beginning."

"Please."

"The world is far bigger than you know, Lyric. Than any of you know. While the human realm is part of it, it's not the only part. The Maison realm, the one I'm from, lies on the human realm as if they overlap but don't take up the same space in time."

He'd mentioned magic before, and I hadn't really understood. He was talking realms and monsters and magic and so much more. Parallel dimensions? Was that even right? I didn't understand any of it, and it confused me more than I wanted to admit.

Was I still dreaming?

Or was I losing my mind?

Or maybe…just maybe, Rhodes was telling me something that would explain much, even though I didn't know why it would.

"You're going to have to slow down. Maison?"

"It means home," Braelynn whispered. "Right? It means home."

Rhodes smiled. "Yes, in English, Maison means home. It's the name of our people, as well as the full realm. But the realm isn't whole, not anymore. That's why I'm here." He let out a curse that made me widen my eyes. "Sorry. I'm going about this the wrong way. Rosamond should have been the one to explain all of this. She's the one who's good with words. I was just here to protect her. And, well, to find you."

"Me? Why would you need to find me?"

"See? I'm not doing this right." He stood up quickly, running his hands through his hair. "I need Rosamond to tell you this, but since she's not here, that's not helping. And I need to go *find* her, but to do that, I have to leave you alone, and that's not something I can do either."

"Do you know where she was taken?" I asked, worried about the girl I'd thought could be my friend.

Rhodes nodded and then shook his head, confusing me even further. "I don't know which territory she was taken to, but I know the Negs took her away from the human realm."

"You say 'human' as if…as if you're not human. But you look it." I let out a breath. "I think I'm having a panic attack." I took a deep breath, and he shook his head.

"You're not panicking. You're confused, and you want answers. I'm trying to give you them, though I don't know how or where to start. Even your friends look a little more panicked than you do. Why is that?"

"Shock?" I asked, looking down at the scrapes on my hands.

"Maybe. Or maybe it's because you know that you're supposed to be here, that you're here for a reason. That everything you're seeing is slowly making sense. You know that something's a little different."

"I *don't* know."

"Then let me tell you about the Maisons. One thousand years ago, there was one realm of magic, the Maison realm. It's still there, but not like it was. The realm before held five kingdoms with five kings and/or queens who worked together to keep the Maison people safe and maintain the balance of magic."

"Five kingdoms," I whispered.

The memory of how my dreams always separated into five parts—sometimes only four—came back to me, but I didn't understand.

"Yes, that of Fire, Earth, Water, Air, and Spirit."

I'd instinctively known that before he spoke it, but I still didn't understand.

"Sounds like a children's game," Emory whispered.

"There's nothing game-like with what happened. Over five hundred years of peace and small skirmishes passed, and many of those in the kingdoms intermated, the magics soon becoming tied to one another in pairs—save for the Spirit Wielders." He cleared his throat. "Earth Wielders and Fire Wielders became close, while the Water and Air Wielders did the same. The Spirit ones were always separate, but they were few and far between. Always."

"You're saying you're a…Wielder? Is that what you're calling it?"

Rhodes nodded, then held out his hand. His silver eyes brightened, and a small tunnel of wind formed on his palm. I sucked in a breath as Emory backed up quickly, and Braelynn leaned forward, awe on her face.

"Wind," I whispered. "You Wield wind?" Magic. I was looking magic directly in the face, and I wasn't running away screaming.

It was true.

It was all true.

And I knew I wasn't dreaming.

"Not only." He leaned forward and picked up the glass of water I hadn't noticed was there. The wind tunnel faded, and as he poured the water into his cupped hands, not a single drop fell. Instead, it swirled over his hands and through the gaps in his fingers, glimmering in the light. When he set down the glass and held up his other hand, the wind tunnel appeared once more. Then he pushed his hands toward each other, the wind and water colliding, creating a vortex of air and water that left me stunned.

Magic was real.

"That wasn't a parlor trick," Emory said quietly, her voice wooden.

"No," Rhodes said softly, then snapped his fingers and the wind went away, the water going back to the glass in front of him. "It's not."

"It's real," I said at once. "But I still don't understand. Why did those... Negs, you called them? Why did they come after Rosamond?" Why had I been seeing them for so long?

"I don't know if they were after her or you, but before you ask why, let me continue. Where was I?"

"I think the kingdoms were about to fall," Braelynn answered. "At least that's where the story seemed like it was headed."

Rhodes tilted his head as he studied her. "How did you know that?"

"Aren't all great civilizations doomed to fall? At least without change?"

I stared at my friend and was once again in awe of her brilliance, an intelligence she hid because, sometimes, she didn't want others to know. Rhodes saw, though, and for that, I was grateful.

"You're right, Braelynn. There was a war. The Fall. The first High King of Obscurité wanted to ensure that no Fire or Earth Wielder touched the Water or Air Wielders. The Obscurité kingdom was created after Earth and Fire came together for so many years. The Lumière came from Water and Air."

"Light and darkness," I put in. I don't know why I interrupted, or why I felt the need to say the words, but I knew their meaning, at least from my French lessons in school.

"You know your languages," Rhodes put in.

"Only some. Did your kingdoms name themselves from our languages, or was it the other way around?"

Rhodes gave me a look and then continued. "I don't know why the High King of Obscurité started the war, or why the King of Lumière fought back as he did. During the skirmish, the final Spirit Priestess, the one who ruled the Spirit territory, was killed trying to lead the innocent out of the Maison realm and into the human one. Upon her death, the Maison realm fractured into two distinct kingdoms, splitting the magic of five into two sets with the Spirits forced to hide amongst the humans. There are Spirit territories now, but they are empty wastelands to the north and south of what used to be the realm's center."

"You're saying there are Spirit magic users…Wielders in the human realm?" I paused. "In *this* realm?" I was trying my best to keep up, but I felt as though I were walking through quicksand, five steps behind wherever Rhodes thought I should be.

Rhodes nodded. "They hide so well that no one can find them. And for good reason. There are magics I don't even know about that could be used with them. Both dark and light. I'm glad they're hidden away sometimes, because I don't trust everyone in any territory. They'll be safer here. You know?"

I didn't, but I nodded anyway.

"The two high kings who started the war, died in the split, leaving their son and daughter to take the mantles. Each blames the other for the deaths and the fracture and have been at a stalemate for five hundred years."

My eyes widened. "You said *blames*. As in…as in they're still alive?"

I didn't ask if they were real or not, not anymore. I'd seen the shadows, had seen how Rosamond tried to protect us, had seen Rhodes' magic. Yes, he'd lied about my fall in the woods with the shadow, the Neg—something I would ask about soon—but he was being forthcoming…maybe a little too communicative.

"Yes." He let out a breath. "There's a lot more. So much more, that I don't know if I can even explain it all or if you'll understand it all in one sitting. But there's more. Believe me. The current high king and queen of the two kingdoms of the former Maison realm are still at it. We're still at war, just at a stalemate… until we find the one who can bring us together. The new Spirit Priestess."

Numbness settled over me, and I looked at Rhodes, confused. What was he talking about? And why did I feel a little spark in my chest like his words should mean something? It didn't make any sense.

"Spirit Priestess."

"There's a reason you're here, Lyric. A reason the Negs can find you so easily. A reason they were after you in the first place. A reason you can see them beyond the fact that the magic we used to heal you jumpstarted everything you were blocking. And a reason you know I'm telling you the truth."

I shook my head, standing up quickly. "No. I believed you before this. I saw your proof. But I don't believe you otherwise."

"You're the Spirit Priestess, Lyric. Or at least you will be. You're the one." Rhodes met my gaze, the intensity shocking enough to pull me out of any sense of connection I might have felt just then.

I blinked at him, then turned on my heel to leave the house. I'd thought I had answers up until that point, but now I knew it had been a lie.

I wasn't important.

I wasn't a prophecy.

I wasn't who he was looking for.

I was just me.

And that *had* been enough.

CHAPTER 9

"Lyric."

At the sound of Rhodes' voice, I didn't stop, though part of me wanted to. I went to the door, put my hand on the handle, then remembered what had been outside these walls just a few short minutes ago.

Were the bodies still out there? Had anyone seen what had happened?

I didn't understand the complexities of it all or get how the world around us hadn't seemed to realize that there was a battle for life and death going on around them. No one had noticed that Rosamond was gone. That she'd disappeared into a black hole of…something magical that I had no name for. Everything that had just happened seemed ripped out of books and movies, and I had no idea what to do with it all.

How to process any of it.

"Where did Rosamond go? Are the Negs gone out there? What if someone sees them or what happened to your yard? What was that thing that took Rosamond? Not the Neg, the other thing. The thing the Neg pulled her through. Why can I see these things, Rhodes? And don't call me what you did…I'm not that. But, truly, why can I see them?" I took a deep breath, the silence in the room thick and heavy. "Why could I always see something?"

I hadn't realized that he was behind me until he put his hand on my shoulder, his warm breath near my ear, sending shivers down my spine.

"I don't know where Rosamond is exactly. The magic from the Negs felt of Fire and Earth, so I'd say they came from the borderlands between the two territories in the Obscurité Kingdom. That doesn't mean she'll end up there when this is all said and done. But that's where the Negs came from. Therefore, that's where they'll go back to in order to travel. As to *why* they took my sister… I don't know. But she's strong, Lyric. Even stronger than I am in most cases. She's had over four hundred years—four hundred and ten in fact—to learn her powers."

I turned in his arms, aware that Braelynn and Emory were standing behind him now, their eyes probably as wide as mine had to be.

"Rosamond is *four hundred and ten years old?*"

Rhodes quirked a smile, but it didn't reach his eyes. "The Maisons live long lives. We're not immortal—the wars we fought for countless ages have proven that—but we don't age past our twenties."

I looked at his face, trying to figure out how old he could be. There were no wrinkles on the brown of his skin, no signs of age at all. He was just Rhodes, the most beautiful boy—*man*—I'd ever met.

I'd thought he'd just graduated high school a few years before me. I'd thought Rosamond had graduated *with* me.

What else had been a lie?

"And how old are you? Not twenty or whatever I thought you were."

He frowned, his brows drawing together. "I'm two hundred and eight.

Not that much older than you in terms of Maison years. Rosamond is quite a bit older than me."

My mouth went suddenly dry. Rhodes was almost two full centuries older than I was. That was insane. But, then again, much about this day and week had been nuts.

"You don't look a day over one hundred," Emory said dryly. "But I still don't believe a word out of your mouth. It seems to me, all of this, the rock-climbing incident, everything that just happened outside, the fact I was just thrown to the ground by something I couldn't see, all revolves around *you*. Not Lyric. So, we're leaving."

Emory tugged on her shirt, the tear at the bottom widening. I hadn't noticed that she'd torn it during the fight, but then again, I'd been so focused on not dying, I hadn't been aware of a lot of things.

"I need to stay, Emory. I need to find out more. And I need to know if Rosamond is okay."

I looked over at Braelynn, trying to see if she was hurt. She'd been so quiet, but everything had happened so fast, I didn't blame her. I was only speaking at all because I needed answers. I'd spent so many nights fighting my dreams, I couldn't stand back anymore. At least, I didn't think so.

"Are you okay, Braelynn? You hit your head pretty hard."

She tucked a piece of her dark hair behind her ear and nodded. "I'm fine. I didn't hit my head, actually. I just got the wind knocked out of me, and it took me a minute to figure out what was going on. But I'm with Lyric, Emory. I don't want to leave either. I need to know what happened and understand why I can't see the shadows clearly but I can almost see them. Something's going on, something bigger than us and our fighting. So, I'm going to stay and see what Rhodes has to say."

Once again, Emory folded her arms over her chest. "I'll stay too, then.

I'm not leaving you both to get murdered by this guy who can bury you in dirt or something."

I closed my eyes and willed myself to find patience. Emory was freaking out and being annoying and rude about it, but other than physically forcing her out of the house, there wasn't much I could do. She didn't listen to me. Not anymore. Though, in retrospect, I wasn't sure if she ever had.

"I'm glad you're staying, but I don't have much time to tell you more before I need to go." Rhodes looked at me, studying my face as if he were searching for answers I didn't even know the questions to. "Or maybe *we* need to go."

He'd said something similar before, and I still didn't understand.

"Before you ask anything else, let me answer your other questions," Rhodes cut in. "The Negs are gone. Their bodies turn to literal shadow in the human realm once they're dead. Humans don't see them unless they are truly looking, and humans rarely want to look. The reason no one saw the fight was because Rosamond put up a shield. I had to break through it to get to you because I could see through it since it was made of Air magic. But because I had to break through it in order to help in the fight, the Negs were able to open a portal. Only they have the ability to do that because they aren't of life but rather the absence of life."

"Death?" Emory asked.

Rhodes shook his head. "It's not that simple, and I don't have time to explain the intricacies of the magics of the realm. At least not right now. The Negs that have Rosamond have a lead, and it's going to take days as it is for me to get through the southern Spirit territory entrance and then through the Earth territory before I can even get to where the Negs came from." He let out a deep breath. "As for why you can see the Negs, why you can so readily believe magic even as it's shown to you? You know the answer to that,

Lyric. Deep inside, you know. But if you don't want to deal with that right now, I understand. It's a lot. But know that there are many in the human realm with blood of the Maisons. Over the centuries, my people have left the two realms and their wars, deciding to live among the humans instead. And when they do, they age, they marry, they have children, and then they die. They aren't like the Spirit Wielders, who have shielded themselves from others, walking amongst the humans for an eternity. Instead, they forsake their magic, but their blood is still the same. Their children, their children's children, and their children's children's children, will still have traces of magic, even if it's dormant."

He looked over his shoulder at Braelynn. "That could explain what you're seeing, but I don't know. Rosamond would know more, but I'm not her. I need to find her, though. I need to go to my family and tell them what happened."

"You can't just call?" Emory asked, but I didn't know if she was being sarcastic or not. "Plus, you made it sound like you're going on a long trek or something through your realm. You can't just drive or fly there?"

Rhodes shook his head. "No. Our kingdoms, the Obscurité and the Lumière, are so rich in magic, that the technology you use here doesn't work. No phones, no cars, no computers. It's very...medieval. They even dress differently in each territory, nothing like we do here." He pinched the bridge of his nose. "That reminds me. I need to change."

"We're coming with you," I blurted.

"You'll be in the way," he said quickly, then cursed under his breath. "I didn't mean it like that. Okay, I did because you don't know the area, and bringing humans into the kingdoms is forbidden, but I need to move fast, Lyric. I don't want you to get hurt."

There was a warm undercurrent to his last words, but I didn't have time to focus on it, not when I *knew* I needed to go. Magic was real, and it was right in front of me.

"You said I was a Spirit…whatever. You said I was *something* more than human. Braelynn, as well. I don't know if I believe that, but if it's true, then shouldn't I be there? Shouldn't I see why all of this is happening?"

"You mentioned that the children of the war came to the human realm to find the Spirit Priestess," Braelynn put in, and we all turned to her. "That she's the one that can unite the kingdoms. And if you say that's Lyric, shouldn't she be with you?" She paused and met my eyes, something in her gaze that worried me. "Shouldn't you protect her?"

"Braelynn…" I began but didn't know what else to say.

Once again, Rhodes cursed. "You're right. I know that. But Rosamond was supposed to *be here*. She's the one with words. With answers. I'm the one with the muscle." A blush stained his cheeks when he met my gaze, and I tried not to notice how attractive it was. He let out a breath. "I can't just leave you here in case another Neg comes, or if the Obscurité scouts find you first."

There was something in that statement that worried me, but Rhodes continued so fast, I didn't have time to comment on it. I'd ask later, along with the thousand other questions I had for him.

"Okay, I think I have something that will fit you all. At least Rosamond does. But if you come with me, you need to do what I say. We're not going to the mall or even to downtown Denver late at night. We're going to a warring kingdom, one where I'm the enemy because I'm not Obscurité. My magics alone could get me killed. The fact the three of you look human could get you killed. The fact that you carry the sense of the Spirit Priestess could get you killed. Or worse." He paused, and I didn't know if it was for effect, or if he was just now realizing what he was saying. "Are you sure you want to come?"

I wasn't sure. Not by a long shot, but I knew I had to go.

"I'm coming," I said quickly. "I can't let Rosamond get hurt any worse than she already might be. She saved my life."

And I needed to know more about what was happening to me, but I didn't voice that. But from the look in Rhodes' eyes, I didn't need to.

"I'm coming, too," Braelynn said. "Lyric doesn't go anywhere without me." She said it with a smile, but I reached around Rhodes and took her hand, giving it a squeeze.

"That *is* true," I said, trying to grin, but I knew it didn't really reach my eyes.

"I guess that means I'm going too because there's no way I'm letting Lyric—or Braelynn for that matter—get hurt because of *you*." Emory raised her chin as she said the words, but I saw the fear in her eyes. She hadn't seen the monsters, but if we went into the territories…the kingdoms or realms, or whatever he'd called them, I was afraid there might not be any hiding from them.

Rhodes gave a tight nod. "Then we leave soon. You can text your parents, give them a story about a road trip, I don't care. Make sure they don't come looking for you, don't realize that you're not where you say you are. You're all adults now, and if you're careful, it won't seem like you've been gone for long or doing anything you shouldn't. You won't need anything from this realm anyway. I have packs, food, and Rosamond should have leathers for you."

My and Braelynn's parents were out of town anyway, and Emory's didn't care what she did. But it still seemed insane. Though all of this was insane.

Rhodes turned away then, heading to the back room. I met Emory's gaze.

"Did he just say leathers?" I asked, a little startled.

"Apparently, we're trying all new things today," she said with a snort, but I wasn't sure if I could find anything funny just then, not when my world had been turned upside down.

Everything had changed, and I didn't know where I was going next, but I knew wherever it was, it was meant to be. I knew I was going to the right place.

I just prayed I knew what to do when I got there.

CHAPTER 10

We stood on the mountainside, the one past where I had fallen thanks to the Negs—a name I now knew to use rather than *the darkness* or just *the shadows*—and I knew this was where it all changed.

We hadn't hiked this far the first time I'd gone with Rhodes into the woods, but we had seen this peak. This had been the mountain far off in the distance that Rhodes had commented on. Only, it wasn't as far as I thought it was, not when Rhodes knew the shortcuts to get us to the place we apparently needed to be.

The last time I had been in these woods, I had been thinking about my dreams, had been remembering the shadows, but had also thought of the peace sliding through my body and the fact that I was free of stress just for a small moment. I had thought about Rhodes being near—the boy I had a

As it turned out, I didn't know him at all.

He wasn't just a boy, wasn't even a man close to me in age.

Wasn't a man at all.

A human.

He was…he was a Wielder. A Maison.

And though I still didn't quite comprehend what any of that meant, somewhere deep in my heart, I knew the words he had told me were true. Magic was real, the world was far different than I thought it could ever be, and my stress about what my major would be in college seemed so far off in the distance, I could barely reconcile the fact that it was truly my problem.

Rhodes had called me the Spirit Priestess, yet I didn't know what that meant.

I was just me. Just Lyric.

I wasn't their savior.

I wasn't the one who would put their world back together, sew up the kingdoms to create one full realm, and prevent a war or whatever the heck he thought I could do.

I wasn't going to do that because I was just me.

How could I be the person Rhodes said his people needed when I didn't even know what the kingdoms or the realm that used to be were? I'd never seen them, never even knew they existed until just now. None of this made any sense to me, and part of me questioned why I was standing here next to the boy who'd changed everything.

I had to stop calling Rhodes a boy.

There had been nothing *boy* about him even when I first caught sight of him and had fallen in love with those eyes of his. I'd only called him that because I was still in high school and calling him a man seemed…wrong.

But I wasn't in high school any longer.

I wasn't just a girl.

And he wasn't just a boy.

And if I kept thinking about Rhodes and what I should call him, it would mean I didn't have to think about exactly where I was standing and why we were here in the first place.

While on our first trip, this place was where he'd said the hike would be worse. That it would burn, ache.

And he'd been right.

My thighs felt like they were on fire, and my lungs burned just as much. I swore my body shook from exertion, and no amount of water Rhodes forced down my throat helped. I had thought I was in shape, curves and all. Apparently, I had been wrong.

Braelynn and Emory were behind me, each leaning on rocks as they fought to catch their breaths. I still couldn't believe both of them had come with me to help find Rosamond, but Braelynn had wanted to be here because of what the other woman had done for us, and for other reasons I had no idea about I was sure. I loved my best friend, but sometimes she was far more secretive than even I had been with my dreams and shadows.

The idea that Emory was also here confused me because I wasn't sure she even *liked* me anymore. Our constant arguing and fighting for what felt like dominance—at least on her part, for me it was so I could be seen and could be a person in her eyes—had taken up so much time recently, I didn't know *why* she was here.

Maybe it was to watch out for me.

Perhaps it was to make sure Rhodes didn't get me killed.

And maybe it was for reasons of her own that she didn't want to share.

That meant it all came back to me, though. Why *I* was there. There was something deep down inside me that wouldn't be silent. It was as if my dreams were no longer during sleep but waking ones where I had to venture through them and figure out exactly what they meant.

I didn't understand it, and it all felt like it was far more significant than anything I could ever be or want to be. But I had to be here. I had to go with Rhodes, even if I slowed him down, and I had to find a way to make sure Rosamond was okay.

Rhodes' sister had sacrificed herself to save my friends and me, and I couldn't—I wouldn't—forget that. I couldn't forget the way the Negs had growled and clawed their way toward me, nor could I forget the look on Rosamond's face when she was pulled into that portal to wherever. Had it been the place between the Earth and Fire territories? If that were the case, and Rhodes was from the Water and Air territories, I knew this wouldn't be easy for him. But he didn't want me out of his sight, and I knew, I *knew*, I had to be here.

I had to finish climbing this mountain, no matter how hard my lungs worked at the moment, and I had to see what was on the other side of whatever the heck this all was.

"Are you ready?" Rhodes asked, his eyes narrowed as he studied my face. Out of the corner of my eye, I could see Emory and Braelynn stand a little straighter. I let out a breath, thankful that it didn't burn as much this time.

"Ready for what?" I didn't want to lie, but I also didn't want him to leave me behind. I wasn't strong, I wasn't a fighter, but I was a runner. That had to count for something—even in a world I didn't understand.

Rhodes frowned, then turned slightly so he could point at a dark slash in the nearest mountain. Whenever I was in the Rockies, they almost didn't seem real. It always felt like they were paintings of what mountains should be, large slopes and sweeps from a paintbrush to depict dimension with grays, blues, greens, and browns. And little Bob Ross trees like my mother used to call them that looked like tiny, feathered dots rather than towering shadows.

But now, I was in the middle of them, and the dark slash looked to be an entrance to a cave I hadn't noticed before.

"What are you pointing at?" Emory asked. "All I see is more mountain. If this is where you're going to kill us and stash the bodies, just know I'm not going down easy."

Rhodes let out a breath. "There's nothing easy about you, Emory."

I held back a snort since I agreed with him, but this wasn't the place for that. "I see a cave entrance. Is that what you mean?"

As soon as I said the words, pinpricks of sensation danced along my skin. I gasped, my fingers tingling and the hairs on the back of my neck rising. I felt like I had to sneeze, my nose itching and my eyes watering.

Rhodes moved a fraction, blocking the cave entrance from view.

"You can feel it, can't you?" he asked, his voice soft. "The magic from the other kingdoms? I would hazard a guess that the closer we get to the crack in the Spirit territory, the more you're going to be able to feel it."

I swallowed hard, able to breathe a little easier since Rhodes was now blocking my view somewhat. "Magic? You're saying I'm feeling *magic*?" At some point, I was going to wake up from this dream, and everything would make sense again.

Or, I wouldn't, and I'd drown in the shadows.

I ignored that odd thought and stared at Rhodes.

"Is it like someone is just brushing your skin, making you edgy, almost like you have to sneeze or scratch an itch?" Again, his voice was low, and I could feel Emory and Braelynn walking closer.

I nodded, not sure if I wanted to voice the truth.

Something flashed in his eyes, and one side of his mouth quirked into a smile before his features cooled.

"I don't see anything," Emory grumbled. "Are you sure you're not here to kill us?"

Rhodes gave my ex a look that I couldn't read, but I had a feeling he didn't want to answer her. Not because he was actually going to kill us, but because, like usual these days, Emory was annoying him like she did me, to the point the idea of me murdering *her* wasn't all that far-fetched.

"If I concentrate, I can see the entrance, but it gives me a headache if I try for too long," Braelynn put in. "I have no idea what that means, and I'd say I need to sit down, but I don't know if I want to sit here for long." She looked over her shoulder as if she could feel something threatening, and I did the same, only I was so edgy from whatever magic Rhodes was talking about, I didn't know if something was coming for real or not.

"I still think you have some Maison blood in your veins, but I can't tell what territory you'd be from," Rhodes said quickly. "The fact that you can see the entrance at all means once we get over there, you might start feeling things differently over time. My magic isn't as strong in the human realm as it is over there. Just be prepared for anything, okay?" He looked down at me. "As for you, well, your magic shouldn't show up right away. I don't think, anyway. It's not supposed to."

I blinked. "My…magic?"

He winced. "This is why I need Rosamond." He cursed under his breath. "I need my sister for more than this, but yeah, she would be able to explain better." He squared his shoulders. "I know you don't want to hear it, but you're the Spirit Priestess, the one we've been looking for. That means, you have magic. Or you will. We don't have to talk about it now, we can wait until we get my sister, but just stay by my side. Okay? All of you. No matter what happens, no matter what you see, I'm strong enough to protect you all. We just need to get to my friends on the other side, and then we can make a plan to get to Rosamond."

I didn't want to believe him, but then again, the tiny pinpricks of so-called magic on my arms weren't going away. If anything, the sensation was intensifying. The wind slid through my hair, the breeze almost calling to me as it did in my dreams. I didn't understand, but then again, I didn't understand much of what was going on.

I hated the unknown. There was a reason I didn't know what to do next with my life because I needed answers. And, because of that, I felt like everything was slipping through my fingers, making me feel like I was two steps behind whatever was happening in front of me.

"We should go," I said quickly. "We can't let Rosamond wait any longer." I ignored the flare in my chest as whatever was going on in front of me pulsated as if it had *heard* me. Or maybe I was just trying to rationalize everything I was feeling and making things up. At this point, I couldn't tell.

Rhodes gave me a look as if studying me to make sure I wasn't going to run away. I couldn't run away, not then. Not when my dreams were starting to become reality, and I'd seen the monsters from my nightmares come to life and *steal* one of the people I thought could be a friend if I'd had more time.

Maybe I was still dreaming. But it wasn't as if I could turn my back and walk away now. If this was real, if this were all truly happening, then I needed to see it through. I'd never thought of myself as particularly brave before, but something was pulling me toward that cave entrance. If I were in the middle of a horror movie, the viewers would probably be screaming at me to not go into the scary, dark cave and instead run away, but I couldn't. Not when I knew there was something more going on. There had to be.

"Stay behind me. Whatever you see, just keep moving. We're heading into the Spirit territory because it's the only way to go from the human realm to where we need to go. It should be empty, but that doesn't mean anything.

There could be Obscurité soldiers guarding the entrance or even traveling through. Negs can make their way through the area, but I can take care of them. You just need to stay out of the way, or you'll get hurt."

He looked at me as he said it, but then looked over his shoulder to peer at Emory and Braelynn, who each nodded in turn. Then he faced me once more.

"Lyric?"

I met his silver gaze and nodded. "I'm ready."

The lie fell easily off my tongue, but as I said it, I knew I'd never be truly ready, even if I tried to be.

Rhodes reached out and squeezed my shoulder, the familiar warm sensation sliding through me so quickly that I almost tripped as I leaned into him. I quickly righted myself, my face heating, but he didn't comment on it—and, thankfully, neither did my friends.

Rhodes turned from me then, rolling his shoulders back so he looked even larger than before, and started toward the cave entrance.

"I still can't see where we're going," Emory said quickly from my side. She and Braelynn had each moved to stand on either side of me, though soon we'd have to go single-file to fit through the tight entrance. "It's disconcerting to say the least."

"I can see it a little more clearly with each step we take," Braelynn whispered, her voice a bit shaky before she cleared her throat. "We're going the right way, though. I think we're *supposed* to go this way. Do you get it, Lyric? Is it the same for you?"

I looked over at my best friend and nodded at the comprehension in her gaze. "It's the same."

"I'm only going because I don't want you to be killed or hurt following this crazy man into danger. I also want to know what threw me onto that lawn. I might not have been able to see it, but I *felt* it. And let me tell you, that's not a sensation I ever want to feel again." Emory grumbled as we climbed over a fallen tree right at the entrance to the cave. Rhodes turned back to me, holding out a hand, but I had already moved over the obstruction, not needing his help but grateful he was there.

I didn't know what I was supposed to feel toward him now, or what I was going to do with my crush now that I knew it was so much more complicated than it had been before. But thinking about small things like the fact that I was still attracted to him and got butterflies at his touch made it easier for me to think about the larger issues that meant my world had changed dramatically. I could think of both, as long as I didn't do anything stupid and end up hurt because of it.

"Hold onto the back of my shirt." Rhodes' voice pulled me out of my thoughts and into the present. Where I was about to walk into a set of territories that I knew nothing about and was, apparently, a key player in.

No, I wasn't going to think about that.

Not now. Maybe not ever.

"Why?" Emory asked, her voice acidic. I knew she was scared though, because heck, so was I.

"Because we're about to slide through the crack in the magic, and I want to make sure you don't get lost. Lyric, hold onto my shirt, Braelynn, hold onto Lyric's, and Emory, hold onto Braelynn's." His voice was low, authoritative, and I quickly reached out to grab his shirt, ignoring the fact that my fingers brushed the strong muscles of his back even through the fabric.

"What if we get lost?" Emory asked.

"You don't want to know." After Rhodes' cryptic comment, he gave me one last look, then turned away, taking a step toward where the thickening air tugged at my skin, the ground beneath my feet rumbled, and whatever was inside me, reaching out for whatever was on the other side, shook.

I took a step, keeping Rhodes' shirt firmly in my grasp, and then all hell broke loose.

Magic, at least I *thought* it was magic, slammed into me, pulling at my hair, my skin, my *soul*. It felt as if claws were digging into my body, ripping apart my flesh, breaking my bones, and trying to rearrange me into something I could never be. I screamed, or I tried to, but no sound came out because no air could get in.

I could smell the scent of ash and flame, feel the dirt beneath my feet and on my skin, could taste the salt of an ocean on my tongue, and yet I knew none of it was real.

It couldn't be.

But as I opened my eyes that I didn't know I had closed, I knew I wasn't in the cave anymore. I was...*here*.

I wasn't home.

But I was *here*.

Wherever here was.

Then someone screamed, and the shadows came again. This time, I knew it wasn't a dream. This time, I wouldn't be able to wake myself up.

This time, they were real.

Again.

CHAPTER 11

"Lyric, get down!" Rhodes shouted at me as two Negs slammed into him. He hit the ground, rolling over on his side as he slid from underneath the monsters from my dreams that were far too real now. He was on his feet in the next instant, his hands moving in front of him in a complicated set of movements I couldn't follow.

But even as I looked at him, his words came back to me, and I went to my knees just in time to watch a Neg fly over me, his claws snapping at air right where my head had been only a moment ago. I rolled to the side, far less gracefully than Rhodes had before, my backpack digging into me, and scrambled to my feet so I could see where Braelynn and Emory were.

Braelynn ducked under another Neg, but the shadow monster wasn't really going after her. No, it seemed to have its sights set on Rhodes and... me. So, when Braelynn moved out of the way, the Neg didn't attack her. I'd never been so grateful for anything, because while I might not know how to fight, Braelynn was even less learned. She was the brilliant one, while I was the decent runner. Though those labels didn't really mean anything since, apparently, we weren't in Kansas anymore.

Or even in the *human realm* anymore.

Emory stood motionless as she watched what was going on around us. I had a feeling whatever had blocked her from seeing the Negs before was no longer a problem while in the Spirit territory.

I swallowed hard, trying to get my bearings as another Neg came at me. I couldn't duck away in time, but I could run to the side as fast as possible. My legs burned as I made my way to where Rhodes stood over the last of the fallen Negs. He must have used his magic to drown the Negs when I was looking over at Braelynn and Emory because both of the shadows were covered in water, unmoving.

"Rhodes! Behind me!"

I hated the fact that I was bringing more danger to his side, but I had no idea what to do, and he could take care of it. All I could do was run. I didn't have any magic, no matter what Rhodes might think, and I knew I was so far out of my depth, I wasn't sure I'd ever see the surface again.

Rhodes looked up at me, his eyes wide with panic as he ran toward me, his arms outstretched, magic pouring off of him in waves as he muttered something under his breath that I couldn't decipher. That's when I noticed another Neg out of the corner of my eye—barreling right toward me.

I didn't think I would be fast enough this time.

Dread crawled over me as I tried to run faster, but it was no use, there was nowhere I could go and be safe.

Then there was a shout, a deep voice I didn't recognize, but one that Rhodes must have because his eyes narrowed, and a grin covered his face. This wasn't the time for smiling, so I had no idea what it meant. Then, I saw him.

A man with wide shoulders and long, blond hair tied back in a leather strap. He wore the same leathers that Rhodes did, ones that clung to his body—I still couldn't get the image of Rhodes in his new clothes out of my mind. And the other man held a sword.

An actual metal sword that sliced through the neck of the Neg that had been coming at me from the side.

Before I could process what I had just seen, Rhodes was by my side, shouting something at the Neg behind me, the shadow so close I could feel the darkness of it, the heat of its void along my skin. Water from a nearby stream I hadn't noticed slammed into the Neg, and soon, the shadow monster was on the ground, screaming in agony.

The other man came up to us then, slicing out with his sword, ending the Neg before it could scream again and maybe alert any others that were there.

I held back a shudder. I *really* didn't want to see any more Negs just then. I hadn't even gotten a good look at where we were, and I knew we still had a long way to go. Yet the fight had come out of nowhere. As if the creatures were waiting.

And perhaps they had been. Rhodes had mentioned that anything could be waiting on the other side of the entrance, and he'd been right.

"Where's your sword?" the other man asked Rhodes, putting his weapon away as he glared at the man by my side. "Coming in with just your magic and three Danes? What the hell were you thinking?"

I didn't know what Danes were, but I had a feeling the term had to do with not being a Wielder.

"Luken," Rhodes rasped as Emory and Braelynn came to my side, each so close to me that I could feel their bodies shaking. We had no idea what was going on, and I didn't know if the fight was over or just beginning. "Thanks for the assist." Then the two clasped forearms and hugged each other as if they hadn't just killed monsters and almost been killed.

As the two stood next to each other, I couldn't help but compare them. The guys seemed to be friends, or at least knew each other enough to fight alongside one another and embrace as if they hadn't seen each other in years. Was this Luken of the Lumière Kingdom, as well? Rhodes had said the Lumière was involved in a constant war with the Obscurité, and that he'd have to hide who he was once we made it to their lands to find Rosamond. With that said, Luken had to be of the Lumière.

I didn't think he was a Spirit Wielder. In my head, those looked like monks or priestesses with long, flowing robes, all quiet and unassuming. I didn't know why exactly that was what my brain conjured up, and I could be totally wrong, but from the way Rhodes had talked about them, they seemed even more otherworldly than the actual *other world* I was currently standing in with dirt on my face.

The two men were about the same height, with Luken maybe an inch taller. And while I had thought Rhodes was wide with muscle, Luken was even more so. Luken's skin was a pale bronze, as if he spent time out in the sun. In contrast, Rhodes' was a soft brown that shone in the harsh light that hovered overhead.

Luken's hair was far longer, his eyes a little more wicked, the same with his mouth, and he looked like he was the kind of guy who could laugh with you even as he cut off the head of a Neg. And since that was what he was doing with Rhodes at the moment, I assumed I was on the right track when it came to him.

If Luken were in this realm, broken as it was, and had called us "Danes," then that meant he had to be a Wielder, right? If he was from Lumière, then it meant he was either Air or Water, or like Rhodes, a mix of both.

I didn't know if it was proper to ask those kinds of questions. Like how you didn't go up to someone and ask their sexuality, you probably didn't go up to someone and ask about their magic.

I honestly had no idea what was going on.

Nor did I think I was going to figure it out anytime soon.

"Who's blondie?" Emory asked, her eyes narrowing.

Rhodes turned at her words and once again studied my face. I didn't get why he did that so often. It was as if he wanted to make sure he knew what I was thinking before he did whatever he planned to do next. Or maybe I was just seeing things. I didn't know exactly, but there was something…*there*. I didn't know what it was, but it was something.

I'd quite possibly hit my head when I rolled away from that Neg.

"Lyric, Emory, Braelynn, this is my best friend and fellow soldier, Luken." Rhodes pointed at each of us during the introduction, and I didn't miss the fact that he paused at my name.

Luken gave everyone a nod before staring at me. Just like Rhodes. Okay, his staring didn't feel exactly like Rhodes' did, but I was getting a little tired of all the gawking.

"Thanks for the assist," Emory said, repeating Rhodes' words and folding her arms over her chest.

Luken raised a brow at her. "From what I saw, you were standing and staring at the Negs while Rhodes and I did all the fighting. But sure, you're welcome."

"And you're an—"

Rhodes took a step forward, holding out his hand. "Enough, you two. We don't have time for whatever barbs you're both about to toss at each other. We might have made it into the Spirit territory, but we still have a long way to go until we reach Earth lands, and I don't really feel comfortable with all of us out in the open like this just shooting the breeze."

I agreed with him on that since now that my adrenaline from the fight and the initial magic was wearing off, I felt like there were a thousand eyes on us even though, if that had been true, Rhodes would have noticed and said something. At least, I hoped he would.

"Let's get going," I said quickly, not wanting Emory to start yelling. And, frankly, I wasn't comfortable standing around waiting for something to happen. The Negs had been waiting for us, either by design or randomness, and I didn't want any more of their friends to show up. Not to mention the fact that *anyone* from any of the territories could show up at any moment and, since my friends and I were *Danes* as Luken had put it, I didn't want Rhodes getting into trouble or ending up with a similar fate myself. I wasn't going to think about the fact that Rhodes thought I had some power, or the idea that Braelynn might have Maison blood in her veins. It was all a little too much right then, and I was in so deep, I knew I'd probably made a mistake somewhere along the way. But I couldn't go back now, so moving forward was the only way to go, even if I was heading straight into danger.

"Sounds good to me," Luken said, staring at me again. "And while we're headed to a place I think we can stay for the night while we figure out what's next, my buddy Rhodes here can explain to me why there are Danes with him."

Rhodes whispered something into his friend's ear, and from the way Luken's eyes widened when he looked at me, I didn't think it had anything to do with Rosamond's kidnapping and everything to do with what Rhodes thought I was…or what he thought I could be.

Wonderful.

Rhodes searched my face before speaking. I didn't know what that meant, but my heart still raced from before, and I felt like I was in quicksand.

"We're headed to the Earth territory, which is east of us. The Fire territory is north and east of us." He pointed in the direction we were headed, then frowned. "And to the west is the Air territory, with the Water one north of that. We aren't going there, though. Not when we need to find Rosamond."

"Let's head out," Rhodes began. "Luken, you lead. Braelynn and Emory, follow him. Lyric, you're with me, covering their backs."

"And you get to spend more time with Lyric, *covering our backs.*" Emory snorted but didn't otherwise complain as Luken started off toward the dark mountains that I was just now seeing in the distance. If we had come from the south and were now in the southern Spirit territory, that meant we were heading east, to the Earth territory.

There was still so much I needed to know, and when we got to wherever we were staying for the night, I was going to sit Rhodes down and have him explain more to me. The little bit we'd gotten from him before had been a lot of information at first, but now I knew it had only scraped the surface. I had run headfirst into this new world because I felt guilty about Rosamond's kidnapping, and something inside me told me to go with Rhodes. Not to mention that he hadn't wanted me to stay behind where he couldn't keep an eye on me. But, in the end, I knew I was out of my depth and a liability. Maybe I wasn't able to fight for myself, not truly, but if I gained as much knowledge as I could, at least I wouldn't run face-first into danger by accident.

The others started off ahead of us, and I fell in step with Rhodes, keeping my mouth shut. I didn't know why I was still attracted to him like I was when this was in no way the time or place for that, but I also needed to get my feelings and thoughts in order. Rhodes needed to keep an eye out or whatever he'd been clearly trained for, and I didn't want to distract him.

And now that I could focus on something other than shadow monsters with large teeth coming at me, I finally took in my surroundings. If I were going to be any help on this journey, I should probably start doing that sooner, but I never said I was a fighter or someone that would be helpful in finding Rosamond. I only knew I *had* to be here, and Rhodes had agreed.

When Rhodes had called the Spirit territory a barren wasteland, he hadn't been overexaggerating.

The world looked as if it had a light sepia haze over it, not bright, but not quite in shadow either. I didn't know if this was what it would be like in all of the territories, or if it was just in the Spirit area. And if the latter was the case, was it because of what had happened when all of the Spirit Wielders left the broken Maison realm to hide in the human one? Or had it always been like this?

"You look confused," Rhodes whispered as he walked over the desert-like area, stepping over stray rocks and petrified branches and trunks. It looked as though there might have been a forest here at some point, but it was long gone, with only sunlight and pale dirt and sand for as far as the eye could see until you looked far west or east—toward the other territories.

I looked up at him for a brief moment before looking back down at my feet and the area around me so I didn't end up tripping and causing a scene.

"Of course, I'm confused. I'm still not sure how I ended up here."

Emory and Braelynn were up ahead of us, not talking to each other or even Luken, who was a couple of feet ahead of them, his destination apparently on his mind because he only looked back every once in a while to help Brae over a fallen log. Emory wouldn't take any help, and I wasn't surprised. That was Emory, always fighting against anything that made her feel weak.

Since I didn't want to fall on my face, I let Rhodes help me over a log that wasn't easy to walk around especially since it would take much more time and effort to do so. There weren't too many downed trees around us, but most were large enough that climbing over them was easier than straying from our path.

"You're here because you need to be. Because you're braver than you think you are, Lyric. You wanted to help Rosamond, and I'm betting you want to find out more about who you are, too."

"I'm not brave," I said quickly, letting go of his hand as soon as I was over the petrified log. I missed the warmth immediately, and berated myself for liking it in the first place.

"You are to me. Bravery doesn't mean wielding a sword. Or even an element. The fact you're here is answer enough for that. But back to what I was saying before. You look confused, but not only for the whys of how we're here."

I looked up at his face, squinting in the harsh light above him. "You're far too perceptive it seems."

Rhodes shrugged, looking around for what I guessed were possible dangers. I was glad he was the one doing it because I honestly had no idea what to look for.

"I have to be. It's my duty in more ways than one. Now, why don't you tell me what put that look on your face originally."

I was the one who shrugged this time. "I don't know, really. I was just thinking about how barren this place looks. And I wanted to know if all the territories look like this, or if this is how it looked before the war."

Rhodes tilted his head as we walked, studying me once again. "Each territory looks different and tends to model the element it's made of. It's hard to explain unless you're there and looking at it. As for this territory, it didn't look like this before, no, though I don't know what it looked like when people lived here. I'm younger than the war, remember?"

I winced. "Let's not talk about the age thing. It makes me feel like I'm a baby compared to you." And I did *not* like that feeling one bit.

He shook his head and reached out to brush a piece of hair from my face. It was all I could do not to gasp and end up tripping.

"I told you before, you're about the same age as me if you count in

Maison years. Time moves the same way here as it does in the human realm, if that's what you're wondering. We're not going to return to your house with a hundred years passing or anything."

I hadn't known that was a worry until just now, and I was a little glad I didn't because my stomach was already turning.

Rhodes continued, "I'm still young compared to many, so while I might have more years under my belt than you, in how the others see me, I'm a... young adult. Just like you."

The fact that his words soothed me worried me. I liked how he looked at me, how he was finally speaking to me. But I didn't know what it all meant.

I didn't seem to know what any of it meant anymore.

But when he reached out again and gave my hand a squeeze, I put some of my worries out of my head and tried to live in the moment. Because if I worried about everything I didn't understand and what else we might face as we searched for Rosamond, I wasn't sure I'd be able to function.

And as it was, I knew I'd need everything I had to make it through.

I didn't need to be a Wielder to understand that.

CHAPTER 12

We walked for over two hours, my water from my pack drained, and my legs aching and burning by the time Luken stopped us for the night near a copse of trees I'd been staring at for ages. I hoped this would be where we stopped to rest.

I hadn't been able to see much other than the trees the entire time we walked, as all I'd wanted to do was sit down and find a way to be safe. I wasn't a warrior, that much was clear since all I'd been able to do during either fight was roll and run away. Rhodes and Luken had done all the actual fighting, the saving. It wasn't even a balm to my injured pride that Emory and Braelynn hadn't been much help either. They were just as lost as I was, and yet Rhodes thought I was something special. Something to help their realm? I wasn't even close.

My friends and I wouldn't be anything but dead weight when it came to this new place, and now I had a feeling I'd set us up for failure by even trying to demand that I come. The fact that Rhodes had wanted me by his side to keep an eye on me didn't warm me as much as it should.

"Here should be good for the night," Luken said once the five of us were situated between two large trees that still had their leaves.

Once we'd reached this grouping of foliage, I realized that we were no longer in the deadlands of the southern Spirit territory anymore. Or, at least it looked that way. Luken and Rhodes hadn't mentioned that we'd made it to the Earth territory yet, so I didn't know if we were in a new place or if this was just a different part of the southern Spirit territory.

As I was already out of the loop and behind on so many things, I figured it was time for me to at least try to speak up.

"Where are we?" I asked Rhodes. I didn't know Luken, and though he seemed to be a nice guy, he didn't know me either. The fact that I didn't know Rhodes as well as I thought I had—which hadn't been much to begin with— wasn't lost on me.

Luken pulled off his pack and set it down to lean against the nearest tree, his gaze darting between Braelynn and me and back again. He didn't look at Emory, but then again, since she refused to look at anyone, instead choosing to glare at her surroundings with folded arms, I didn't blame him. I didn't know why Emory had come. She didn't seem to really want to be in my presence other than to yell at me recently, but now she was here. And, as evidenced by the Negs' attacks, we were going to have to work together to find Rosamond and get out of this alive.

"We're still in the Spirit territory," Rhodes answered, pulling my attention away from Emory and back to him. Out of the corner of my eye, I saw Emory huff out a breath, and I did my best to ignore her. I really didn't know why she'd come with us, and I didn't know what she was going to do now that we couldn't return without help. Rhodes and Luken weren't going to just stop and take one of us back if we were scared. We should have thought about that before we took Rhodes' extra packs and supplies and came along on this journey I wasn't sure we should even be on in the first place.

"It looks so much more…" I didn't know what word to use that could describe the beauty of the place. Yes, the other part of the Spirit territory had been beautiful in its own way, but the starkness of it just reminded me that it had once been different. Not that I knew what it had looked like before exactly. Even Rhodes didn't know for sure, but the deadness coming from it was clear. This part, however, had green trees and dark soil as if it were much more fertile and not afraid of the death and bareness that lay beyond it.

"Alive," Braelynn finished for me, standing by my side and looking at Rhodes, as well.

Rhodes and Luken met gazes, and I wondered what their evident silent communication was about. Though, right then, I pondered a lot of things. Rhodes turned back to Braelynn and me and tilted his head as if looking for words.

"We're on the border between the Spirit and Earth territories. We're close enough now that sentries might find us if we aren't careful, but we're in a good position that most of them won't venture this far out. On each border between the territories, the land represents the melding of the two. Earth clearly has more sway here, but my teachers told me that it used to be different, more a blend of Earth and Fire, as well as Water and Air."

"Not that our teachers ever told us what it really looked like," Luken said, rolling his eyes and his shoulders after he did so. "No one likes to talk about what it looked like *before*, so they don't talk about it much at all. Those that remember, either hide it because it hurts, or because it gives power to those below them. There are those who don't want others to remember. So they make *sure* others don't remember it."

Rhodes frowned at his friend. "That's not always the case."

"What? You're saying that all of our territories are perfect little happy, warring people?" This time, Luken snorted. "They like us ignorant and beneath their notice."

I didn't know who *they* were, but from the way Luken and Rhodes glared at each other, I had a feeling this wasn't the first time the two had had this argument.

Rhodes finally cleared his throat and pointed to the set of trees behind me. "We'll set up the tents over there. It'll be dark soon since the sun is just setting, and I'd rather get our camp set up before we have to do it in the dark."

"I'll take guard duty first," Luken said, pushing off from the tree he'd leaned against. He patted the hilt of his sword. "You help set the girls up and get some sleep. I know you've been wired over in the human realm. Use the time to get used to being back." Then he moved forward and hugged Rhodes tightly. "Welcome home, brother."

Rhodes' lips quirked into a small smile as he pounded Luken on the back. "Be safe. You know we can't be caught here."

"Of course." Then, Luken was off, blending into the trees as if he'd never been there in the first place. I so wanted to learn how to do that, but at this point, I would settle for walking along a straight path without tripping over my own two feet or a root from a tree that seemingly came out of nowhere.

"So, we're camping in tents? How long is this going to take? Not the tents, but the whole finding your sister thing. Because you weren't really clear on that."

Rhodes glanced at Emory as she spoke, but it was me who answered, tired and sore, and not in the mood to deal with Emory's tone.

"It'll take however long it takes," I snapped. "Rosamond was *taken* by those Negs. She saved our lives, and I'm not going to let that be in vain. So, if it takes days...*weeks*...then I'll be right here, figuring out what to do next, even as I'm doing it. If you have a problem with that, Emory, then you shouldn't have come. But griping and snipping at every little thing will just make this trip that much harder. I honestly don't know why you're here, but now that you are? Don't mess this up because you're pissed off at the world."

"I'm not pissed off at the world, I'm mostly just pissed off at you right now. Why are we here, Lyric? We're not fighters, we're not even aliens or whatever these guys are."

"Maisons," Braelynn cut in. "They are Maisons. Wielders. You know that. Stop acting like you're above them because you're scared."

"Shut up, Braelynn. I didn't ask you."

"That's enough," Rhodes said quietly, but his voice stopped us all. "If you yell any louder, we might as well let the Earth Wielders know we're here, waiting to encroach on their land so we can get to their other border. Go set up your tents. They're in your packs and are larger than they seem thanks to an Air spell. I'll help you take them down in the morning and put them back into your packs. Go now, but do it quietly. I'll make a fire so we can actually eat tonight."

Then he turned on his heel, and I knew my cheeks were red. Fighting with my friends in front of the person who was protecting me and the one I had a weird crush on? Not the smartest move. But it wasn't like the latter mattered at all. No matter what Rhodes said, he was still older than me, and I had far more important things to worry about outside of the fact that I liked his eyes.

Emory sneered, then went to her pack. Braelynn gave me a sad look, then did the same, so I opened my own bag and pulled out the small bundle of cloth that looked to be the only thing inside that resembled a tent.

Warmth spread over my fingers. I knew that feeling.

Magic.

I didn't know why I could sense it now—maybe because I was in the other realm. And perhaps Rhodes was right, and there was something different about me. I wasn't the Spirit Priestess like he said, I couldn't be, but there had to be a reason I had been drawn here and could feel and see the things I could. Maybe I was what they thought Braelynn was, someone of the blood.

Putting up the tent was relatively easy since it wasn't a bunch of poles and stakes. By the time the three of us had put ours up, Rhodes was back with firewood and had a small fire going in front of him. He had his hands above the flames, looking as if he were warming himself, but from the way he whispered, I had a feeling he was doing something far different.

"I'm using my Air Wielding to keep the sound and sight of the fire from prying eyes. You can only see it because you're close to it. If any of the sentries get close enough to see it, they've made it past Luken, and we're already in trouble."

I nodded, trying to soak everything in. My head hurt, and I knew I'd already taken in too much information in such a short period of time, but I couldn't tell Rhodes to stop teaching me new things—not when I craved to know more.

"Do you need me to set up your tent?" I asked.

He gave me a strange look. "If you'd like. I'd appreciate it. I need to cook us some dinner so we can get to sleep early. I know you're tired since you're not used to hiking like we did, and frankly, we need to get up before the sun rises so we can get through the border undetected."

I nodded then went to his pack, doing the same with his tent as I had with mine. Since Braelynn had put herself between Emory and me, I set up Rhodes' tent on the other side of mine, making a semi-circle. It was ridiculous that the action sent a little thrill through me since it was just a tent and it wasn't as if they were touching, but thinking about silly things like that was easier than thinking about the harder ones like a new life and this new sense of being that threatened to overwhelm me.

Emory and Braelynn were silent, Braelynn looking thoughtful while Emory sulked, as we met Rhodes by the fire. He'd cooked what looked to be stew in a pot, looking very human-gone-camping rather than the warrior he'd looked like before, in a world that I didn't understand. A world I wasn't sure I fit in.

Rhodes must have caught my look because he said, "We're eating some of the supplies that might not do well once we hit the other territories. The magic around here is relatively dull since no one lives in this territory." He paused. "Well, not *no one*. But the people who might live here won't reveal themselves."

"What?"

Rhodes winced, his cheeks darkening, and I was pretty sure he was blushing. "Rumors and myths surround both of the Spirit territories. About what it used to look like, and the people who used to live here. Since the Spirit Wielders were always so reclusive when they lived within the Maison realm, most of us have never seen them do magic, or even know what their power entails. It's all such a mystery that some say a few Wielders remained here. Others say that those who camp—longer than we are tonight, those who aren't just passing through—are fugitives or refugees from other territories that don't want to be found."

Rhodes dished out our dinner as he spoke, leaving some in the pot for Luken I assumed. I kept my attention on him, soaking up every piece of information I could. Everything was new to me, yet at the same time, it was as if I had always known that I needed to *know* this. It didn't make any sense, but then again, nothing about the past few days did.

"So, there could be other Wielders around other than the Earth sentries you're worried about?" I asked, taking a bite of the stew and not really tasting it.

He nodded. "Luken is keeping an eye out, and so am I for that matter."

"And we're eating the stew now because...what? Magic will make it bad?" Emory asked, clearly not believing a word Rhodes was saying. That didn't surprise me since she didn't want to believe anything he said, no matter what she saw with her own eyes.

"Yes." Rhodes shrugged, finishing his stew. "The magic in these territories is so strong that it affects all things that come from the human realm. So, any food, canisters, clothes, or anything that was made there will disintegrate, catch on fire, or make you sick after a while. So, we're going to use up the food that I brought since it's hard to find good hunting areas in this realm. But, from now on, Luken and I will find what we need."

"I can help," Braelynn put in. "My dad taught me how to make traps and things when I was little."

Rhodes smiled softly and nodded.

"I can't help with that, but I can learn," I put in, hating the feeling of being the useless one.

"You will." He met my gaze. "You're going to help because you're going to unlock your powers and figure out who you are and what it means to be a Spirit Priestess."

"Seriously? Stop with that garbage," Emory snapped, but I held up my hand.

"I don't think I'm who you think I am," I said softly. "But let's for a moment pretend that I am."

He gave me a look that said he wanted me to believe and, thankfully, Emory shut up. "Okay." He was so close to me on the fallen log just then that I could feel the heat of him against my thigh. I tried to ignore it. There were more important things going on than what he did to me.

"You're saying the Spirit Priestess can Wield the five elements. But how do you go about unlocking them? You say that I'm here, that I have all of these…*powers* inside of me and I'm supposed to know how to use them."

"You *won't* know how to use them, you'll need to be trained, but they *are* there, Lyric."

"How can you tell? How do you know I'm her?" My heart rate sped up, and my fingers grew tingly. I felt like I was having trouble breathing, and I knew if I weren't careful, I'd have a full-blown panic attack.

"Because I've been searching for you for what seems like all my life. I know you, Lyric."

He leaned closer, and I did the same, drawn to those eyes of his. When Emory coughed, I blinked and pulled away, the moment broken since I'd forgotten that my friends were still there, watching Rhodes and me talk.

"I know you," Rhodes whispered again so the others couldn't hear, but I didn't say anything back. I wasn't sure I could. Because even though I didn't want what he said to be true, there was something inside me telling me to listen.

And that part scared me more than the Negs.

Because if it was all true, then my part in this was just the beginning, and there would be more to come than a camping trip and searching for a friend.

Much more.

CHAPTER 13

I woke up to the sound of someone outside, rummaging around as if they were looking for something in the near-dark. Blinking the sleep away from my eyes, I tried to adjust to my surroundings, taking a moment longer than I should have to realize that I was in a tent, but this wasn't a camping trip with Braelynn.

No, I'd walked into another realm with Rhodes, Braelynn, and Emory, meeting up with a Wielder named Luken. And after dinner around a fire, Rhodes had helped the three of us get settled in our tents before leaving to trade positions with Luken so the other man could eat. But not before giving me a lingering look that I knew Emory hadn't missed.

The sound came again, and I hoped it was Luken or Rhodes moving around, or even one of my friends. Because if it weren't, it wasn't like I could do much but kick out and hope I connected. And maybe run away. But to where?

Luken for some help. Because there was no way I was going to continue on this journey without knowing at least some ways to protect myself. The self-defense class I had taken had been helpful, but it hadn't been enough for things like Negs and fighting against beings who had magic.

I didn't want to be the weakest link.

And I'm not, I reminded myself. I'd fought back, at least a little, while Braelynn and Emory had either been frozen in place or knocked out. That had to count for something.

A scratch on the outside of my tent, like fingernails sliding along the cloth, had me freezing, my heart once again racing.

"Lyric, I know you're up."

Rhodes.

That was Rhodes' voice.

My whole body relaxed, and I sat up then rolled out from under my blanket, already in the leathers and top I'd borrowed from Rosamond's closet. Not only had I not brought anything to sleep in since there hadn't been space to pack, I'd also wanted to be ready to run at a moment's notice. I'd even kept on the boots.

I crawled out of the tent, aware that I hadn't brushed my teeth or even my hair, but I was half-awake and wanted to see what Rhodes wanted.

He looked up at me from where he knelt on all fours. He crouched beside the opening of the tent and put his finger to his mouth so I wouldn't speak. His eyes were dancing, and I had a feeling I looked a little ridiculous.

Not like I could change that.

Thankfully, he moved out of the way and stood up, holding out a hand to help me up when I finished crawling out of my tent. I swallowed hard at the contact of his skin to mine, wondering once again what it was about him that drew me in.

He kept his hand on mine, pulling me around the tent area to the small stream I had heard when we first got to the campsite. I had yet to see it since we'd crashed after dinner rather than washing up before bed.

"Luken slept for a bit but is out on patrol again. I'm going to let your friends sleep for a little while longer, but then we need to get moving. But I figured you could use some time alone while you clean up for the day." He paused. "Not that you have a lot to clean up, but you know what I mean."

I raised a brow. "Thanks. I think."

He rubbed the back of his neck, for once looking like he was actually my age instead of this older entity he'd suddenly become when he first showed us his magic.

"I know this is a lot for you, Lyric, and I wish Rosamond was here so she could explain things better."

"If she were here, I wouldn't be in this realm," I reminded him as I bent down to the stream to let my hands touch the water. The fact that it was ice-cold cooled any blushing I might have done.

"I don't know about that." He crouched down next to me, his hands sliding through the water near mine. "You're here for a reason. If you weren't who you are, do you really think I'd have let you come into the realm with me to find my sister? You've never been here before, and this is going to be dangerous, Lyric. It's been a walk in the park so far."

We'd been attacked by Negs and had hiked until my legs felt like they were going to fall off, but if that was what he called a walk in the park, I wasn't going to be scared off. Not yet.

"I might be a liability, but it's too late now."

"I didn't say you were a liability."

I glared at him. "You might as well have said it." I might be a burden, but I was the only one allowed to think that.

"What I was saying," he continued, "is that you would have come here anyway. The realm needs you. The people need who you can be."

"Not who I am." I hadn't meant to say the words, but they were out, so I continued. "You and Rosamond came to me and wanted me to go hiking. You wanted to be my friend because you thought I was this *person* you needed for your realm. You don't need *me*. You need me for what you think I can do, not what I can do right now. Don't forget that, Rhodes. But don't forget that I'm not that person either. I don't know if I can *ever* be."

Rhodes dried his hands on his shirt, then reached out to cup my cheek. I froze, and my mouth parted as he moved closer.

"I saw you before I knew who you were. I didn't seek you out because I thought you could help me." He paused. "I can't make connections, Lyric. I couldn't. Not when I knew I'd have to pack up and move to another place to search, or come back here and help my family before I moved back to the human realm to look for the Spirit Priestess. For you. But I saw you before I knew," he repeated. "I want you to know that."

"What are you saying?"

He shook his head, sliding his thumb along my cheekbone. "Nothing we can do anything about right now. This is all too much for you as it is. My ramblings won't help."

His *ramblings*, as he'd called them, were the only things making sense in a nonsensical sort of way. But I didn't say that. It would only make things harder for me as he lowered his hand and stood up.

"Rhodes…"

"You're here. And you're worth more than you think you are. Not just because of the blood in your veins, but because of your soul. Remember that as things change, and other things get harder."

I opened my mouth to say something, when Rhodes stiffened, his hands shooting out, and the water around us foaming into waves at his feet.

"What is it?" I whispered.

"We're not alone."

CHAPTER 14

I stood up slowly, my eyes wide as I tried not to make a sound. Rhodes tilted his head as if listening for something, his fingers twitching. I guessed he was ready to use his magic, like Luken would have likely had his hand on the hilt of his sword.

Rhodes put his finger up to his lips as if telling me not to say anything. I gave him a look that I hoped spoke volumes because I wasn't going to talk right then, not when I had no idea what was going on, and the only way to defend myself was to use the small amount of skill I'd learned in a class with *humans*. Or, I could run.

But I had no idea where I could run to.

Learning how to defend myself was now going to the top of the list of priorities.

Once again, all hell broke loose.

Rhodes leapt forward, pushing me down to the ground as he raised his hands into the air and swished them back down again in a rapid movement that was almost too fast for my eyes to follow. I hit the dirt next to the stream, hard, my shoulder stinging as I rolled to my hands and knees, desperate to get up again.

I turned to see a man in dark brown leathers and a green tunic standing in front of Rhodes, his scarred hands out and moving in rhythmic motions similar to Rhodes' as he growled something low.

Rhodes shouted, and I turned toward the other side of the stream as the ground beneath me quaked, rolling in waves just like the water that Rhodes had started to use against the man in green.

Earth Wielder.

This had to be an Earth Wielder, probably one of the sentries Rhodes and Luken had talked about the night before. And if there was one of them, there might be more. I didn't have any powers or even a weapon, but I didn't want to leave Rhodes alone. Since I didn't know if the Wielder in front of me could control just dirt like he was currently doing now or the rocks themselves, it wasn't like I could throw a rock and try to distract him. For all I knew, he could control it somehow and use it against me. But I also couldn't stand by and do nothing.

That wasn't who I was, even if I hadn't known that particular fact about myself until this whole series of events started.

Rhodes moved his hands in front of him again as if pushing them against a wall with all of his strength. A massive wave of water from the stream shot past him toward the Earth Wielder.

The Earth Wielder threw up his hands, a wall of rock and dirt appearing in front of him suddenly, blocking the wave of water and stopping it from potentially drowning him.

I'd never seen anything so magnificently horrifying in my life.

Nothing seemed real, yet I knew this was my new reality no matter what I might be afraid of.

Before I could quite comprehend everything that I was seeing, two more men dressed in similar clothing came out of the trees, their arms outstretched, and their eyes narrowed.

Now it was three against one—I wasn't counting myself in this battle—and Luken and my friends were nowhere to be seen. I hoped with everything I had that the girls just didn't hear what was going on, and Luken was too far away to help. I didn't want to think about anything else that could explain their absence.

I flinched at the sound of something to the side of us and turned. "Rhodes!" I called out. "Look out!"

He didn't look back at me. Instead, he turned to face the other two sentries who had joined the fight. Now, there were five of them against Rhodes, and Rhodes not only had to keep himself alive and uninjured, but he had to somehow keep his attention on me, as well. I was a liability, and the idea that he could get hurt because of me made my pulse race and my fingers tingle.

"What are you doing here, *Prince?*" One of the newer Earth Wielders asked Rhodes, his voice a low growl.

Prince?

Rhodes was a *prince?*

So not the thing to be focusing on just then, but…a prince? The man had said "prince," and Rhodes hadn't corrected him. That was something else to file away under things that constantly surprised and worried me.

I was only two feet away from Rhodes, standing behind him with my hands at my sides, trying not to make any sudden movements and gain the sentries' attention.

"Just passing through," Rhodes said casually...*too* casually. He was up to something, and I wished I knew what it was. Because I had a feeling things were about to move quickly, and I needed to be prepared. Did mind-reading come with this powers thing Rhodes had talked about? Because that would be useful just then. "We're still in the southern Spirit territory, so there shouldn't be any cause for attack."

The first sentry who'd come upon us narrowed his eyes. "You're near our land. You know the laws. You're a Lumière. You're too close to the Earth territory, and you know it."

Another added, "You know the boundaries, can feel the magic as you get close. We don't take kindly to strangers on our land." Then, the man looked over at me, and I stiffened even more. "Nor do we want Danes here."

"Yeah, Rhodes, what are you doing with a human by your side? They aren't supposed to be in our realm."

"And I thought you were on the hunt for the fabled Spirit Priestess?" the first sentry asked, his eyes on me. I didn't blink, didn't breathe. Instead, I stood there and hoped he didn't want to get any closer. "In fact, I heard you and your sister were planning to stay there until you found her. Now, look what I see...a human by your side. One without powers. Yet the Priestess would need to unlock hers according to legend. Am I right?" The sentry tilted his head, his eyes gleaming, and his hands twitching as if he were ready to use magic again.

I stayed still, not knowing what to do. If this man thought I was the Spirit Priestess, would he try to take me? Or worse? Rhodes had said that whoever the Priestess was, she could unite the realm. But he hadn't said how that would happen, or even if everyone *wanted* that to happen at all.

From the glint in the sentry's eyes, I didn't think he was on Rhodes' side in that thought. It didn't matter if I *was* her or not, because if this man and his team thought I was, then that's all that mattered. And considering that I didn't have anything to defend myself with, this wouldn't be a battle I could win. Not on my own, and looking at the numbers, maybe not even with Rhodes.

"She's with me," Rhodes said with a warning in his voice. "We're not on your land."

"You attacked me with your Water Wielding."

"Because you attacked first," Rhodes said simply. He held out his hand, not looking over his shoulder, but I knew he was talking to me when he said, "Come here."

I did, keeping my eyes on the first sentry who had seemed to take a liking to me. I slid my hand into Rhodes', the warmth of his skin settling my nerves. I didn't know what would happen next, but I wasn't alone, and that counted for far more than I knew.

"I think we should take her with us," the first sentry said smoothly, his gaze never leaving mine. "If she's who I think she is, she'll be worth something."

"For the queen?" another asked.

Rhodes' hand tightened on mine at the word *queen*, and for some reason, my entire body cooled as if someone were walking over my grave.

"She's not going anywhere," Rhodes bit out.

"Oh, I think she is, Prince. After all, we outnumber you, and your little human can't fight for herself."

"So be it," Rhodes mumbled, then leaned over to me and whispered in my ear, "Hold onto my waist and, no matter what happens, don't let go."

"What?"

"Now."

I moved, letting go of his hand to wrap my arms around his waist. The hairs on my forearms and the back of my neck rose as I did, and I didn't know if it was because I was this close to the heat of him, my body pressed to his, or the fact that he had his arms out, magic swirling all around us.

The water from the stream stayed where it was, so I knew he wasn't using his Water Wielding. Instead, he must be using his Air Wielding. The others scrambled around us, shouting at each other as the ground beneath my feet started to rumble.

Rhodes chanted under his breath, an almost haunting melody, in a language I couldn't understand with meanings I knew could break me in two if I fully comprehended their intent.

The world split open, the sky falling. I was sure this was the end, only... it wasn't.

Rhodes had summoned a tornado.

An actual *tornado*.

"You won't take her," Rhodes shouted over the screaming air, the sound like a train coming close, the world truly ending.

The others screamed, the ground no longer shaking from the Earth Wielders but from Rhodes and this power.

And he had power.

He was power itself.

My arms tightened on his waist as the eye of the tornado settled upon us, and I looked up, my heart beating so hard I could practically feel it in my jaw, my cheeks, on my tongue. I couldn't see where the others had gone, but I knew they weren't there anymore. They'd disappeared along with a few trees and part of the stream itself as Rhodes continued chanting. Somehow, he was the epicenter of this magic. It didn't harm him, and because I was touching him, I was safe, too.

Safe with Rhodes. Something I'd always felt yet tried not to dwell on.

As Rhodes slowed his chant, something changed. My hands slipped, and I gasped, only I didn't fall away from him. The magic coming from his hands, from his body, slammed into me, and something inside me snapped.

I let go completely, unable to hold on any longer, my body flying away but not up. No, I moved out from Rhodes, the toes of my boots skimming the ground as I opened my mouth in a soundless scream.

Rhodes turned on his heel then, his hands falling as the magic cut out like someone had turned off a switch, the absence of power like a painful burn.

"Lyric!"

He sounded as if he were in a vacuum as he reached out to me, his eyes wide in panic. I didn't move, didn't breathe. Instead, I focused on what that snap had been inside of me. My hair flowed all around me as if wind had come out of nowhere, sliding around me with gentle yet unfamiliar caresses.

My heart beat hard once, twice, then something unlocked as if it had been there all along. As if I had been waiting for this moment.

I threw back my head and screamed. This time, the sound ripped from my lips as if it had always been there, waiting for this time, this moment. Air slammed out of me, knocking Rhodes back and making the trees that reached toward the sky in prayer sway.

I fell to my knees, my body shaking, my hands once again tingling as I tried to understand what had just happened. I looked up, shoving my hair out of my face as I searched for Rhodes, but he was already there in front of me, kneeling and cupping my cheeks.

"Lyric? Lyric, are you okay? You're...you have Air, Lyric. That was Air." His voice sounded like a whisper and a shout all at once, the awe in it frightening even as his presence gave me the strength I didn't know I needed.

Air.

What I felt and what he said came together, and I tried to form the words I needed.

I had Air magic. I was an Air Wielder.

And that meant… that meant what he'd said could be true.

I could be the lost Spirit Priestess.

The one to save them all.

The one to bind.

And I had no idea what I was going to do about it.

CHAPTER 15

"Lyric."

I blinked, catching my breath as the world restarted. Rhodes knelt in front of me. I didn't remember going down to my knees at all. He had his hand out, tentatively brushing the tips of his fingers along my cheekbone. I didn't lean into his touch, but a part of me wanted to.

"What just happened?" I asked, my voice wobbly but clearly not as shaky as my hands. I balled them into fists, digging into the ground between our feet.

"You just unlocked your Air Wielding. It was…it was beautiful, Lyric. The power. I can't describe it. It's raw, elemental magic at its finest, but it's *yours*."

I pushed that to the side for a moment, knowing it was important. But I wasn't ready to face it. "What happened to the sentries? The Earth Wielders? Where did they go?" I had a feeling I knew the answer, but I needed to hear it from Rhodes. I needed to know that there was no going back from this.

A shadow passed over Rhodes' face before he answered. "They were going to take you and possibly tell the others who you are. I couldn't let that happen."

"Because I'm your property?" I asked, harsher than I intended.

He blanched, shaking his head. "No. Never. You're always going to be your own person, no matter the power you Wield. And I'm going to do everything in *my* power to make sure it stays that way."

There was something in his eyes that told me he was telling the truth, even if I had a feeling that neither of us truly understood what was coming—me even more so.

"Then what happened to the sentries, Rhodes?"

His throat worked as he swallowed hard and, once again, he looked younger than his actual years. "I killed them. I didn't want to. I wanted to get out of this without killing a single person, but this is war, Lyric. They were going to kill me and take you, doing whatever they wanted in order to attain their goals. I didn't know if that meant using your powers for themselves, selling you to the highest bidder, or delivering you to my enemy, the queen. I couldn't let that happen. Any of it. And I'd do it again, Lyric. That's the kind of man I am. I'd do it again to protect you. To protect my people."

I leaned forward, so close we were only a breath away. Rhodes froze. I didn't know what I was doing, but I wasn't going to kiss him, not yet.

"It's okay." It wasn't. I wasn't sure if it would ever be okay. This wasn't my world, no matter how much Rhodes wanted it to be. And killing was wrong. It had to be wrong. But I also couldn't judge him. He'd saved my life and his own. I would find a way to make peace with it the longer I stayed here, but it was something I had to do myself.

His shoulders relaxed, and he pulled back slightly so he could look me in the eyes. "We need to find the others and get out of here. We made a lot of noise and did enough damage that it won't be long until we're found again. I don't want to head into the Earth territory until we're a little less conspicuous. Okay? Lyric, tell me you're okay."

I didn't think I'd ever be okay again, what with the actual *magic* slamming into my system and unlocking a piece of myself I'd tried my hardest to ignore, even when it had been part of my dreams for as long as I could remember.

"I'm fine."

A lie.

"I think you will be. I think you're stronger than you know, Lyric."

"You don't know me, Rhodes." I didn't know myself anymore.

"I might not know all of you, but I know parts of you. And if you give me a chance, I'd like to know more."

I didn't know what he meant by that, and I wasn't sure I wanted to follow that train of thought, not when so much else was going on.

"What am I?" I hadn't meant to say that, not even in the whisper it came out as.

"You're Lyric. The Spirit Priestess."

I shook my head. "I can't be. I can't have this magic."

"Yes, you can. You have to. Because you're who you need to be. Who you've always been, Lyric. You've always been who you need to be." He paused. "Who I need you to be." He cleared his throat. "And when we find Rose, we'll figure it all out. Together. But first, we need to find Luken and the others."

Rhodes stood up quickly and held out his hand. I placed my palm in his, coming to my feet and dusting off my pants. Rhodes kept my hand in his for a moment before giving it a squeeze and letting go. I would have felt lost if I hadn't realized that he needed both of his hands to use his magic and protect us.

Magic I apparently had, as well. Power I had no idea what to do with.

"I can't lie to myself and say I don't have Air in me," I said quickly. "Not when everything just happened, and I can feel it bubbling up inside me, wanting out. But what am I going to do with it, Rhodes? You're a century older than I am, and I assume you've had training."

He looked over his shoulder and nodded. "Almost since birth."

"So, I have no hope."

He shook his head, then looked forward with me following behind. "There's always hope, Lyric. Without hope, what's the point of all of this?"

I didn't have an answer for that, so I asked another question. "So, what am I going to do?"

"I'll train you. Luken will too for that matter. Rosamond would be the best, though. So, we're going to find her."

I moved forward and put my hand on his back as we walked. "We will. I know we will."

He didn't say anything, but then again, he didn't need to. The reason I'd come into this realm was for Rosamond, and maybe for what I was feeling now, but mostly for Rosamond.

We didn't have to walk toward the camp for long before Luken burst out of the trees, sword in hand and blood on his face and trailing down his arm.

"Rhodes. The tornado you?"

Rhodes nodded, moving forward. "You okay?"

Luken looked over at me, his eyes widening a fraction, and nodded. "Had to deal with five sentries, but then again, it seems you had your own party to deal with."

It wasn't phrased as a question, but Rhodes answered anyway. "They're dealt with."

"Braelynn and Emory?" I asked, walking past the two men to look toward the camp. "Are my friends okay?"

Luken nodded. "They're hidden. I kept them safe, don't worry, Priestess."

I whirled on him, glaring. "My name is Lyric."

He held up one hand in surrender, the other still holding his sword.

"Sorry. I just noticed someone has a new power that wasn't there last night, but don't mind me. I'm just going to do another check before we head out of this place to somewhere safer. As for your friends, they're around the bend. I told them to keep quiet, and Braelynn will do it. Emory? I'd hurry, or she's likely to yell down the whole canyon."

I started running toward where Luken had pointed, Rhodes right behind me. I needed to make sure my friends were okay. If I thought about them, then I wouldn't have to think or worry about anything else.

Emory was the first one I saw, her arms folded over her chest as she glared at me. "Where were you?"

"Are you okay?" I asked, ignoring her question. "Braelynn?"

My friend walked out from behind a boulder and nodded. "I'm fine. Luken took care of us. Are you okay, though? You look shaken and really pale."

Braelynn came forward and wrapped her arms around me. I hugged her back, my soul settling. I didn't know why, it just did. Braelynn was my rock, my touchstone. I didn't know what I'd do without her. That I had been worried about what would happen when we separated for college seemed so long ago, and now we were in a different realm, a power untamed and raw and pulsating inside me scratching to get out.

Luken and Rhodes were near us now, Luken packing things up as Rhodes came closer.

"We should go," he said. "Now that we're all together, we need to find another camp before more sentries come looking for their lost teams."

"How did they find us anyway?" Emory asked. "I thought you said we'd be safe."

I turned to her, tired and not in the mood to deal with her. I hadn't been in the mood to deal with her for a while, and I hated myself just a little bit for it.

"You're breathing, aren't you?" Luken asked, shrugging when Rhodes gave him a look.

"You know what?" Emory asked, and I had a feeling none of us were going to like what she had to say. "I'm done. We're leaving, Lyric. We're going home. This isn't our world. Isn't our problem. I knew we shouldn't have come to begin with, but I wasn't about to let you get kidnapped by this idiot."

"I'm not leaving," I cut in before Rhodes or Luken could say a word. Braelynn stood by my side, giving me strength. "We're here to find Rosamond. We're here for her, and for me. At least I'm here for myself. Because something happened, Emory. There's something inside me that wasn't there before. And I can't leave now, especially when I know something is different about me."

"They're brainwashing you."

"Do you think so little of me that I'd let them do that?"

"I think you want to be important and you'll do anything to make that be true, even if you lie to yourself and everyone else."

I took a step back as if I'd been slapped. I'd never heard such hatred in Emory's words before, not directed at me—or anyone else for that matter. What had happened to her that she hated everyone so much? Including me.

"There's no call for that," Rhodes added. "If you have a problem, talk it out. Don't lash out because you're scared."

"I'm not scared." Emory lifted her chin. "I'm just not going to be led around by delusional liars."

I put my hand over my heart, my eyes narrowing at the girl I'd thought I could one day love. "I feel it in *here*. The difference. Something's going on, and I have to see this to the end."

Emory sneered. "Then it will be our ends, too. I'm leaving."

I took a step forward. "You can't leave. We can't waste time going back with you, and the only two people who know the way back need to go and find Rosamond."

"I can follow our trail. I'm not an idiot. I'm not staying here, and you can't make me. I'll scream and fight and make sure everyone around us hears. Because you're all seeing thing that aren't there. There's no way this is happening. It's a bad dream, and once I get out of here, it'll all be over, and we can go back to normal."

Emory was the only delusional one here, but I had no idea what I could say to change her mind. She shoved past me, and I tried to grab her to stop her before she did something stupid, but she whirled on me, slapping me hard across the face.

"Don't touch me, you freak."

I blinked, holding my hand up to my stinging cheek. "You hit me."

"And I'll do it again if you force me to stay."

"What is wrong with you?" Braelynn asked.

"I'm not a little weakling who needs to stay by perfect Lyric and her perfect boys and their perfect little made-up world like you, Braelynn. Stay if you want, but I'm done."

"If you go, you'll probably end up dead," Luken put in, not sounding like he cared in the least.

Rhodes' jaw tightened as he moved forward but, thankfully, Emory didn't try to hit him. "Never hit Lyric again. Do you hear me?"

"And what are you going to do about it?" Emory asked, her voice dark.

"Lyric will take care of you herself, I would imagine. But if she doesn't want to, I'll take care of it." He handed her a pack—shoved it at her actually. "Stay on the path we made. It'll be visible for another day before the winds take care of it. Move fast, drink water, and keep the sun to your right. You'll see the break in the realms on this side of the magic line, but you won't once you move through it since you're human. Go quickly, and don't look back.

If you do, I don't know what could find you. The Negs might be out there, Emory. I can't help you. I need to find my sister, but if you don't want to be here, I won't force you to stay. Go. I hope you make it, mainly because it would hurt Lyric if you don't."

I moved forward and reached out, but Emory took a step back. Once again, I felt a slap that wasn't physical.

"Emory. Don't do this. You're going to get hurt."

"I'll take my chances with the Negs over you."

Then she turned on her heel and left me behind—left everyone behind. I couldn't stop her, and I didn't want to go after her, not when I knew I needed to stay.

Part of my life had just walked out on me, leaving me in the dust. Yet I didn't go after her.

I stayed in the present. Stayed with those who understood what was going on inside me, way more than I did.

And I didn't break.

I didn't cry.

Because there was nothing left to cry about.

Not anymore.

CHAPTER 16

We moved to the new camp soon after, walking in silence as the depth of what had just happened sank into me. Not only with Emory leaving, but with…everything.

The magic.

The fighting.

The loss of life.

Everything.

Trying to be strong when I honestly didn't feel like it and when all I wanted to do was find a log to sit on and cry out all of my tension, frustration, and fear was exhausting. I had to keep going. I had to pretend that I was stronger than I was. And I had to figure out what to do when Rhodes came to me and asked me how I was feeling about having one of my powers unlocked.

One of my powers.

As if I had more.

But if part of what he'd said was true, why couldn't all of it be?

And by thinking that statement, I felt as if I'd just sentenced myself to a future that could wipe out who I was while burying the old Lyric and everything she might have cared about. Emory was already gone.

I couldn't explain the difference I felt inside of myself from only a few hours ago, the changes from a few days ago, but I knew I needed to—at least to myself.

Luken was off, once again doing patrol. For some reason, though I didn't know him well or his facial tics, I had a feeling he hadn't liked the fact that he hadn't been there for his friend when everything happened. Yes, Luken had been fighting his own set of sentries at the time, but I could tell that he wanted to be everywhere at once, trying to help his *prince*, in any way he could.

Oh, yeah, that was another thing that tilted my axis off-kilter.

Rhodes was a prince. That meant that Rosamond was a princess. Maybe? I didn't know the line of succession or royalty rules when it came to the Maisons, nor did I know what it meant for the two separate kingdoms in this realm and their war.

For all I knew, people who could Wield two elements were called princes. I had so many questions for Rhodes, so many things that needed to be answered, and yet I was afraid to start asking the questions.

And I hated being afraid.

"She'll be okay," Braelynn said as she came forward, a bladder of water in her hand. "Emory is strong and knows what she's doing. Most of the time. She's just stubborn and in her own head, thinking that she's always right no matter what the actual answer is. She'll follow the path, and she'll be home in no time. I know Luken and Rhodes would go with her if they could, but she was being unreasonable. We need to find Rosamond, and Luken isn't going anywhere without Rhodes. They're best friends, and he's Rhodes' right-hand man."

I raised a brow as I looked at her, taking the water from her and storing it in her bag. We were in charge of dinner that night, using up the last of the human-realm supplies as the guys put themselves on security. I didn't care that others might think it was women's work and that we'd been segregated. Braelynn and I had no idea how to fight, and though I apparently now had a new Air power I didn't know how to use it.

"You sound like you've been talking to Luken more than I thought."

Braelynn's cheeks pinked, and she shrugged before opening the final can of stew. "Emory was off muttering to herself about being stranded in a bad dream, and I was keeping Luken company, watching what he was doing so I didn't feel too useless."

I winced. "You're not the only one feeling useless right now." I picked at a stain on my shirt, wondering when I'd gotten it. Probably from one of the many times I'd hit the ground recently, or just from our hike. Looking clean and like I belonged here wasn't something that would happen anytime soon, I feared.

"But you're apparently this super-magic person who has a new *power*," Braelynn said with a wink and sat down next to me on the rock. "Are you okay? I mean…how does it feel?"

I pressed my lips together, trying to figure out how to answer that. "I have no idea." I looked down at my hands, spreading my fingers, palms up. "I feel like I have this…*something* inside of me. Something that if I just reached down and touched it, I could use. But what can I use it for? What if I hurt someone or myself because I'm so inept at it that I end up screwing everything up before I even really learn it?"

"Lyric. You do well at anything you put your mind to."

"That's so not true. I'm average." That had been drilled into my head long ago.

Braelynn pushed at my shoulder. "You're not average. Shush, before I kick you."

I couldn't help but smile. "You wouldn't kick me."

"I might. I might do a lot of things people don't expect me to. I'm here with you, aren't I?"

I turned to face my best friend, reaching out to grip her hand. "I never thought you'd back away. Because that's what you do. You do anything to help your friends. This might not be something we'd ever thought we'd do…" I paused, and she snorted. "But you never back down. I mean, you threw yourself in front of Emory more than once."

"Yes, because standing up to a bully equates to hunkering down from the tornado your boyfriend makes."

"Rhodes isn't my boyfriend." *Yes, because that's the important part of what she said.* "Plus, he's a prince. Did you hear that part? A prince."

Braelynn rolled her eyes, and I could almost believe that we were back in school, talking about our days rather than in a new realm on the verge of something far greater than ourselves with magic and Wielders and powers.

"He's pretty enough to be a prince."

I rolled my eyes and leaned on my friend's shoulder. "I think we need food. Or sleep. Or something that's not going to make us loopy."

"I'll start working on dinner. Why don't you go talk to Rhodes, who is walking towards us, his eyes only on you to the point where I don't think he even notices I'm here."

I was the one to blush this time. "Shush. Go think about Luken or something."

"Maybe I will. And, Lyric? Don't think of yourself as average. Anything you put yourself into, *really* put yourself into, you excel at. You might stumble at first, but once you make a decision, you're the best person for the job. Don't forget that. Okay?"

Then she was off, moving toward the fire Rhodes had made, stew in hand, and Rhodes was suddenly in front of me, a curious look on his face.

"What is it? Do you need me for something?"

He murmured something under his breath that I couldn't hear, and I stood up, wondering what was going on.

"Luken is on patrol. If it's okay with Braelynn, I'd like to pull you away from dinner duty to see what we can do about starting your training." He frowned. "I can help you with Air and Water, but when we get to Earth and Fire?" His frowned deepened. "We'll need to find someone we can trust to help you train in those. And that's going to be a problem. And don't even get me started on the Spirit Wielding…though Rosamond might be able to get us a contact for that. Once we find her."

"I'm fine with making dinner," Braelynn called out. "Go learn all the things, Lyric."

I felt like something else was going on beneath the surface. But it wasn't like I could ask him all of his deepest darkest secrets. I didn't have the right to those.

"You're saying the fact that I'll unlock the rest of the magics is a done deal? That I'm not somehow just an Air Wielder who didn't know I was?"

Rhodes shook his head, reaching out and gently brushing his finger along my chin. "I *know*. I just know. And that doesn't help you at all, does it?"

I let out a soft laugh. "Not so much."

"Come with me, just over to the clearing so I can show you a little bit of Air Wielding. Nothing too dangerous or powerful, but it's using the smaller abilities, the idea that you can hold air in your hand and pull it from the oxygen around you, that paves the way for true control and ability."

"You mean like a mini tornado in my hand?" I asked, following Rhodes to the clearing. I waved at Braelynn, who went back to cooking, and knew that Luken was around, watching over her as much as he was his best friend and me. I didn't know why I trusted Luken as much as I did so soon, but there was just something about him that told me he'd do anything in his power for the three of us.

Emory, on the other hand…

I pushed her and those thoughts from my mind. The control I would need for what Rhodes wanted to teach me wouldn't happen if I were thinking about Emory.

When we made it to the clearing, Rhodes turned to face me, and I had to stop from moving forward and brushing his hair from his face. In addition to the pull I felt to this realm, there was a connection between us. And based on the way he looked like he also wanted to move forward, I wasn't the only one feeling it.

Now probably wasn't the best time to think about that, however.

He cleared his throat. "Not a tornado. That's something you'll learn at the highest level. Not that you will necessarily *need* to learn it. I mean, if Rosamond's wishes come true, then you'll only have to learn the basics for a while, and everyone will come together because of your existence and not because they're forced into it by war."

I blinked. "That's a possibility? I'm still getting used to the idea that I *have* an elemental power. What do you mean *war?*"

"We're already at war, Lyric. We've been at war with each other for centuries. And unless something radical changes, we're going to be at war for a few more centuries at least."

That didn't sound disconcerting at all. "And the Spirit Priestess—what I supposedly am—she's supposed to stop that? How?"

"If I knew, I wouldn't feel like I was out of my depth here. There's a reason I want to wait for Rosamond to tell you things. There are some things I literally don't know. No matter how close I am to the crown and the history of it all."

That gave me the opening I'd been waiting for. "The crown? So, you're really a prince like the sentry said?"

Rhodes gave me a tight nod. "The King of Lumière is my uncle. My father and mother are the lord and lady, but I get the prince title until my cousin, next in line to the throne, has children. It's complicated, and I don't pay much attention to it. I'll never be the king. That's not my fate, and I'm fine with that. I've trained to be a warrior, just like Luken. We've fought and trained alongside each other for most of our lives, even though our bloodlines couldn't be more different."

"What do you mean?"

Rhodes pinched the bridge of his nose. "The Maisons tend to be more titled and cast-like than most of the human realm. Luken's parents weren't married when he was born, and his father hasn't claimed him, so they call him a bastard. But since I'll fight anyone who uses that title near him, they don't tend to call him that more than once."

"People can be cruel. I'm sorry."

Rhodes shrugged. "Luken is the best man I know, and the one person I'd want at my side no matter what. For now, he's keeping an eye on the perimeter and Braelynn, while you and I train. So, let's get to it." Rhodes widened his stance, brushing off our conversation. I was fine with that. We'd gone down a lane I hadn't expected, and it seemed to hurt him so I wouldn't press.

It wasn't my business anyway.

"Do what I'm doing," he started. "Keep your feet slightly apart. There you go. And hold your hands out like you're cupping water from the stream."

"Okay." I did as he asked, feeling silly.

"Now, I want you to close your eyes and think about the power inside you. It's light, it's hollow, but it has a force that flows within that vastness.

Imagine that you're grabbing that energy as if it's a string that can be wrapped around your hand. Does that make sense?"

It did, and I wasn't going to think too hard about *why* it did, or I'd lose my concentration and ruin it all.

"Okay."

"Good. Now, tug. Just a little, nothing too crazy. Just like a brush of knuckles along skin."

I did as he asked, then fell back on my butt, a force of wind pummeling me so hard, I fought to catch my breath. I opened my eyes to see Rhodes in front of me, cursing as he threw his hands to the sides, dissipating the wind and sending it through the large trees surrounding us.

"Okay, so that was a little too much all at once."

I winced and let him help me to my feet. "I'm not going to be really good at this."

"No, I don't think that's the problem. When children learn this, they actually take multiple tries just to find that thread, and even more attempts to pull it. Nothing usually happens, Lyric. Your problem, I think, is that you have *too much* power within you." He let out a breath, and I tried to understand his words. "So, we're going to take it slow. Because I have a feeling once you get the basics, a tornado is going to be the least of our worries."

"That doesn't sound ominous or anything."

He grinned, and I couldn't help but smile back. "Okay. Let's do it again. But go about one-thousandth that strength. Okay?"

I nodded. "Okay. Maybe you should take a step back or something."

He raised a brow, giving me a far too cocky look. "I think I can take anything you give me, Lyric."

Okay, then. "Whatever you say. Just don't blame me if you end up flying into another realm I don't know about."

He snorted and nodded toward my newly cupped hands. "Close your eyes and try again. Just a little bit."

I did as he asked and focused on the power. I wasn't afraid of it, not really. To be truly afraid of it, I'd have to understand what it was, and I wasn't ready for that. But I focused on the tunnel of air, then the thread that I tried to visualize. And this time when I thought about tugging, I didn't, I just brushed it with my mental hand. A simple caress, not even a full touch.

"Lyric," Rhodes whispered. "Open your eyes."

I did, meeting the silver of his gaze.

"Look down."

When I did, I gasped. I held a small wind tunnel, pieces of dirt and a tiny flake of a leaf swirling clockwise so I could see it.

As soon as I focused on the tunnel in my hands, however, it dissipated with an audible *poof*, leaving me cupping nothing but true air. My heart beat a fast staccato.

I looked up at Rhodes, the smile on his face as wide as mine must have been just then. "I did it!"

"Yeah, you did. I knew you could."

Then I jumped into his arms, wrapping mine around his neck. "I did it! I didn't knock down a tree or myself or anything."

He wrapped his arms around my body, holding me close, my feet off the ground. Suddenly, I realized exactly what I'd done and where I was.

"You did it. And on the second try, too. I knew you were special, Lyric. From the start."

And before I could think about what was happening or what I was doing, Rhodes lowered his head and pressed his mouth to mine. I closed my eyes, getting to know the feel of his soft lips against mine.

It was only a bare instant of contact, a brush of lips that felt as if the air between us were charged, and yet nothing had changed beyond the fractional moment of sensation.

He pulled back, and I opened my eyes, meeting his gaze again. We didn't say anything. But then, we didn't need to.

Things had changed.

Again.

Now, I just had to decide what that meant.

CHAPTER 17

The next morning, we were no longer waiting to see what would happen if the sentries found us. Instead, the four of us stood near a new line of trees that were apparently the border to the Earth territory.

Since Rhodes mentioned that the magic from the Negs smelled of dirt and flame, he'd said it meant that Rosamond must have been taken to the border between the Earth and Fire territories. Only we couldn't get there directly through the southern Spirit territory. We had to get through almost the entire Earth territory without being detected before we could even *start* on Rosamond's trail.

Along the way, Luken and Rhodes asked people discrete questions and listened in on conversations to see if there was any news about Rosamond. A kidnapped Lumière princess would be news, after all.

What it all meant, was that we were going to be on the road for far longer than a few days. I had known that going in, but now that I'd seen some of the magic and felt it, the scope of what we were doing seemed far greater than trying to find one person in a world that didn't make sense.

We hid behind a large tree and the bushes surrounding it. Luken was up front, scouting the area, while Rhodes stayed behind with Braelynn and me. The guys made hand movements, but this time, I knew they weren't using magic, but instead talking to each other in a way that I recognized from TV shows, the way soldiers did. I had no idea what they were saying, but I was soaking it all in and staying out of the way. My fingers once again itched and tingled like there was magic inside me waiting to get out.

Rhodes had said that the build-up could happen over time and that I'd get used to it as well as learn how to alleviate the pressure. However, standing outside of the small, hidden entrance that we were about to use to get into enemy territory wasn't the best place for me to ask him more. I fisted my hands at my sides. Braelynn gave me a weird look that I shrugged off as I tried to ignore the burn. Nothing happened outwardly, so I hoped I wouldn't blow our cover—literally, since I was afraid I'd end up with a small tornado or a blast of wind because I couldn't handle the power inside of me.

I pressed my lips together as I thought about the words I'd said to myself earlier.

The enemy.

We were heading into the Obscurité Kingdom, and I'd just thought of them as the enemy. Not because I thought of them as *my* enemy. But because they were Rhodes' and Luken's rivals.

The guys were of the Lumière Kingdom, and that meant anyone from the Obscurité Kingdom was their adversary. If either of them was caught in Fire or Earth territories, they could be tried and found guilty of trespassing—and probably a hundred other things.

I was walking into the middle of a war I had only the barest of details about and shouldn't be part of. But, I felt what I now knew to be Air running through my veins, and knew there was more to come. At least that's what Luken and Rhodes thought, and since they'd been right so far, I was having a hard time finding a reason to doubt them outside of sheer panic and fear.

Once we passed the trees in front of us, we'd be in a new kingdom. The only thing I knew about kings and queens came from history books, watching the press on the princes and their weddings, and random TV shows where everything seemed dramatic and over-the-top.

Now, I didn't know what to think anymore. Honestly, it didn't matter anyway. This wasn't fiction. This wouldn't go away because I wished it would. There was power in me that I couldn't deny anymore, and I was going to be smart about it. I had to learn how to use it. But we were here not only for what was going on inside me and what could be coming next, but also because a friend was in trouble, Rhodes' *sister* was in trouble, and we couldn't let her down.

We needed to find her.

No matter the cost.

"You look a little pale," Braelynn said from my side. We weren't whispering, but we also weren't talking at our normal volume. With the sentry attack the day before, and Emory leaving without looking back, we were more than cautious when it came to who could be listening and what might be coming at any moment.

"Just thinking about what we're about to do and the fact that we have to get to the place where Rhodes thinks Rosamond was originally brought. That doesn't mean we'll actually find her there, though."

"Then we'll follow the trail to discover where she was taken afterwards."

I looked over at my friend, who had braided her hair away from her face, making her look younger than usual. Or maybe I just felt older than I had even the day before.

"How do you know there will be a trail?"

"Because there's always a trail," Braelynn said simply.

"But in real life? I don't know about that."

"You have to at least try to believe in it. We're about to head into a place we've never been before. And it's going to be filled with magic we've never seen before. I mean, I'm not really used to the fact that Rhodes and Luken can use Air Wielding or that Rhodes can also Wield Water. Don't even get me started on you right now, though I totally believe in you and everything you can do and will do."

When Braelynn rambled like this, I knew she was nervous, but I let her go on, knowing we both probably needed it.

"We don't know what's coming, and the two people who might actually have a clue, have to hide who they are because of what they can do. I don't know if other Wielders can figure out what kind of power someone has, or if everyone in this realm actually has Wielding abilities, or if it's just a few that do. Either way, Rhodes and Luken will have to try and hide who they are. *You* will have to try and hide who you are." Braelynn looked down at her empty hands, a frown on her face. "And I have to somehow figure out why I'm here. Because it's for a reason. I wouldn't be here otherwise. I wouldn't be here as a hindrance without knowing that I was here because something pushed me. I can see the Negs for a reason. I could see the portal for a reason. Now, I just need to figure out what that is."

It was the most I'd heard my friend say in one sitting in ages, and I had a feeling it had everything to do with the fact that Emory wasn't with us. I'd been the one to bring Emory into our lives, and I hadn't truly noticed the effect it had on my best friend.

I wrapped my arm around Brae's shoulders and gave her a squeeze. "I'm sorry I wasn't around enough. I'm sorry I didn't stick up for you."

Braelynn gave me a weird look and then shook her head. "You know, for some reason, I just followed your train of thought to figure out why you'd say that right then. Emory wasn't the nicest to me, but I stood up for myself when I needed to. It's not always easy being her friend. Frankly, I don't know if I would have continued to be so if I didn't love you like a sister." She shrugged. "I don't hate people, and I don't hate her, but I'm glad she's not here." She winced. "Even if I'm scared to death for her at the same time. I hate conflicting feelings, but that's how I always feel when it comes to Emory."

"Tell me about it." I snorted, once again pushing thoughts of my ex out of my head. There wasn't anything I could do now about her leaving. And a small part of me was waiting for her to come back and find us so we could continue our journey together. That wasn't going to happen, though, and a small part of me hated myself for not going after her.

That was one regret I would always have, no matter what I needed to do now that the next step of our journey beckoned.

"Ready to go?" Rhodes asked as he came up behind us. I jumped, startled since I hadn't heard him approaching. I eyed Braelynn since she hadn't moved. Apparently, I was more on edge than I thought.

"Yes," I said, not exactly lying.

Luken moved up to stand on Braelynn's other side and winked. He smiled at all of us, and though it reached his eyes, I could tell that he was nervous, as well. Never a good sign when the guy who was the actual fighter of the group looked uneasy.

"What are we expecting to see when we get through those trees?" I asked, settling my pack more firmly on my back. We had no more human realm items on us. Everything we carried had been made here and taken to the human realm by Rhodes and Rosamond before. It felt strange that it *didn't* feel as weird as it should, but then again, at some point, I would wake up from this dream, and hopefully, I wouldn't feel like throwing up as everything started to change yet again.

"First, you're going to feel the wards. They're at each boundary and can also circle homes, the court areas, and anywhere a Wielder with a particular affinity is able to put one up to protect and warn. This is the weakest point of the wards Luken and I could find. We should be able to get through undetected because they're for barrier-use only, not for alerting. It takes immense power to keep those going. And with the crystals failing, that's not going to happen at all points of the borders anymore."

I froze. "Crystals?"

Luken cursed under his breath, and I looked at Rhodes, who shook his head. "Later."

"There's going to be a whole dissertation later at this point."

"And we'll get to it. But first, we need to get through the wards. It shouldn't hurt, not these ones, but it won't be comfortable. When we get to the other side, we're not only going to be in the Obscurité Kingdom but also on Earth territory. Luken and I can't sense Wielders near, but we'll have to be cautious in case the wards are dulling that. We know the path we need to take when we get there, but it's not going to be easy, and it's going to take time. We're going to have to go the long way to avoid a few areas that Wielders like us can't get through. And, Lyric? We'll train as we go. I promise you."

I looked at him for a moment before nodding. "Okay. Let's go."

And with that, Luken took the first step toward the gap in the trees, Braelynn right behind him. It didn't surprise me that my friend was so quick off the mark. She needed to find answers just like I did, but she was even more out of the loop than me it seemed. Or maybe I was the one falling behind. It didn't matter because, somehow, we'd find a way to get all the answers we needed.

There wasn't another choice.

Rhodes put his hand on my shoulder and gave it a squeeze. "I'll protect you, Lyric. You have my word."

But who will protect you? I didn't say it, but I knew the answer would be Luken or anyone more qualified than me. I felt like a flea at this point.

Instead, I said, "I need to learn how to protect myself."

He squeezed my shoulder a second time before letting his hand fall. "That we can do. Now, let's follow before Luken and Braelynn end up alone in the Earth territory without us."

I quickly looked away and moved toward the gap in the trees. As soon as I stood between two large trunks, I could feel the wards pulling at me. It was almost a warmth that spread through me, like when you got too close to a live outlet or electric pole that buzzed loudly enough to make your teeth ache.

Rhodes walked beside me as we crouched through the wards, his hands free to use his Wielding. I kept my palms out, as well, but I didn't know what I would do if I needed to use my Air. Maybe instinct would take over, and I wouldn't end up hurting those close to me.

The warmth intensified as we made our way through. It didn't push or tug at me. Instead, it wrapped around me like a warm blanket and clung to me, seeming to not want to let go as I took my first full step into the Earth territory.

When the wards let go, its fingers trailing down my back like a soft caress, I shook off the sensation and crouched down behind Braelynn, Rhodes doing the same at my side.

"We're good for the time being," Luken said softly. "Let's get to the other side of that hill since I don't sense anyone else around us. We can plan our next move there."

Rhodes nodded, and I followed Luken and Braelynn, Rhodes right behind me as the four of us made our way through the trees and over the slight hill covered in spongey grass and long, green reeds that blew in the wind.

We were in the *Earth* territory, and it was so unlike the Spirit territory that it was almost like blinking color into existence.

Everything was so...*green*. And brown. But mostly green. While the trees in the Spirit territory had sparse leaves and aging trunks that were pale in color, varying in size, the Earth territory had every shade of green and brown imaginable.

I hadn't even thought about the idea that there were shades of brown until that moment. I mean, I knew there were, but right then, it was all so vivid and real, that I hadn't known the truth behind the beauty of the color.

The whole area was surrounded by deep forests and small hills, with mountains with rounded peaks in the distance, rather than the jagged tops of the Rockies. A stream bubbled behind the vale, but the water was so clear you could almost ignore that it was there. Instead, your eyes were drawn to the lush foliage all around the area, and the multi-colored rocks and pebbles shining under the gleam of the water itself.

Everything screamed health and gardens and...yeah, *green*. There was no other word for it, it just was.

I had no idea what Earth Wielders could do with their magic besides shaking the ground like the sentries had, but I knew it had to be great since the concept of earth was more than moving rocks and looking at a tall tree and seeing how it connected to those around it.

There was so much here that it was breathtaking to behold, and that was saying something, considering I lived in one of the most beautiful places in the world.

And just when I was about to tell Rhodes that, I froze, the sound of a foot on soil so faint I didn't know why I had even heard it in the first place stopping me.

But I wasn't the only one to hear it, as both Luken and Rhodes stiffened, as well.

And that's when the earth moved beneath my feet.

Moved.

CHAPTER 18

Rhodes cursed under his breath and rolled to his feet as if walking on actual air rather than the rolling ground beneath us. Since I had no such talent, I dug my fingers into the dirt and grass, the soil sliding under my fingernails, and tiny rocks cutting into my skin. I just hoped to keep from falling down the hill itself and into whoever waited below.

Luken had his arm around Braelynn, holding her close to his side as he dug into the hill with his free hand, as well. That left his sword on his back with him unable to use it to protect any of us, but as he was keeping Braelynn safe, I didn't know what else he could do.

Rhodes was near me in the next instant, pulling me into him with one arm as he used the other to do his Air Wielding. He rolled me under him, and I once again dug my hands into the ground beneath me. He shouted something at Luken, but I couldn't hear it over the rumble of the hill beneath

And that's when the rocks started falling.

Braelynn screamed, and Luken pulled her closer, rolling down the hill a bit as rock after rock, and boulder after boulder pummeled the hillside.

Rhodes leaned down and shouted into my ear so I could hear. "We need to get to the other side of the hill near those trees. Earth Wielders can shift the ground beneath us if they have a strong enough Wielder."

He moved us both to the side as another boulder hit far too close for comfort. The rock smashed into the ground, leaving a crater-sized hole after it rolled down the hill again, but when it hit the hill, a chunk of it broke off and shattered into a thousand different pieces.

Instinctively, I threw up my arms, using whatever Air Wielding I could summon. I only ended up with slight pockets of air, pulsating toward the jagged shards coming at my face. The magic warmed my fingertips and pulled at my lungs, stretching them and making them ache, and I knew I was doing it wrong but I didn't know what else to do to make this work.

Thankfully, whatever I managed to do worked slightly, and most of the small rocks flew in the other direction towards the hill itself—and not into Luken or Braelynn. I was honestly surprised that it had worked at all and that I hadn't hit anyone with the other rocks.

However, I hadn't been able to stop all of the shards from coming, and one sliced into my upper arm, tearing through my tunic and leaving a gash behind. Another carved a gouge into my cheek, the sting making my eyes water. I held back a cry and put my hand up to my face, trying to see how bad the bleeding was, only to let out an audible hiss since the action scraped my tunic into my other wound.

Rhodes cursed above me and sent a shockingly powerful wave of Air Wielding toward the crater and yet another stone that came for us. Then he tugged on my arm, and we were crawling over the hill, trying to keep our heads down.

Though there weren't any sentries or Earth Wielders on this side of the hill, we weren't exactly on a mountain. That meant that no matter how far we went down on the other side or ducked, the Earth Wielders could still throw things over the top and hit us. For some reason, they weren't coming after us physically, and while I wondered about that, I could only focus on trying to follow Rhodes to the copse of trees.

The ground beneath us shuddered again, but not as violently as the first two times. Luken was right behind me, Braelynn right below me at my side. I heard Luken clearly when he shouted.

"Their Earth shaker is losing steam. Not as powerful as they seem to think they are."

Rhodes looked over his shoulder for a brief instant, his eyes narrowing as he took in my face and the cut there before looking forward again. "There're still too many of them." My hopes plummeted. If Rhodes were worried, I wasn't sure how we were going to get out of this.

Somehow, we made it to the line of trees that ran up the hill and were able to hide behind a few of them as the rocks and dirt continued coming. I had no idea what the Earth Wielders were trying to accomplish, but if they wanted to bury us in mud and rocks after crushing us with those stones, they were well on their way to succeeding.

"Those don't seem like normal sentries," Rhodes said, looking around a tree and trying to duck out of the way. I didn't know if the Earth Wielders knew our exact position, and I tried not to make any sudden movements to give us away.

Plus, I was scared out of my mind and frozen in place.

Regardless, I wasn't moving unless someone told me to run. To say I was once again out of my depth would be an understatement.

"I know what you mean," Luken added, his voice low.

"Why do you think that?" I asked, my voice a whisper.

"Right, they seem to be acting like the others that found us in that camp," Braelynn put in, and I nodded, not that I truly knew what had happened at the camp with Luken, Braelynn, and Emory. We hadn't had time to get into specifics, but I had seen what the sentries did to Rhodes and me, and what Rhodes had been forced to do when the others had become interested in me.

I didn't want that to happen again, but I wasn't sure if we would have a choice.

Rhodes frowned before he explained. "The ones that came at us at the camp were organized and in formation. They were on-duty guards, who wanted us away from the border and probably would have taken us in. Only one of them actually used deadly force, if you remember, and that one got a look from his no-doubt superior. I don't think those sentries would have killed us right away. These guys? They're playing games. They're throwing rocks where they know they won't hit us directly but where they can still weaken us. Their Earth shaker, the one that can move the ground beneath our feet and even use the soil like waves of water, is already burnt out. If he weren't, we'd still be rolling like before. It's like they're a team…but not really. They're just throwing everything they have at us, and it doesn't make sense. I don't know if they want us dead, or if they want to take us in. Either way, it just feels…different. The magic is a little rawer, a little edgier."

I nodded. "You're right. I mean, you know you're right, but I can feel the difference in the magic, too." I stretched out my hands, shaking them a bit. "It doesn't feel as…staticky as it did before. I know I'm new to this, but…"

Rhodes reached out and squeezed my hand before lowering it and going back to looking around the trees for who was coming for us. It was a little too quiet right then for any peace of mind. "You might be new, but Luken and I can feel your potential power. There's nothing slight about it, Lyric. You need to trust your instincts."

Since I didn't know if I had any instincts to trust, it was a moot point. Before I could say anything else, though, the trees around us shook, and I blew out a breath, my hands out. I didn't know if any Wielding I did would help or cause more harm than good, but I wasn't going to go down without a fight. Neither were Rhodes or Luken with his sword, for that matter. Only Braelynn had no Wielding to speak of, but she still stood with her chin high, and I knew she'd fight with her bare hands if she had to. We might be out of our depth, but we'd learn.

There wasn't another choice.

The four of us moved along the trees, falling to our knees as more rocks slammed down around us. The ones after us had to know where we were, but they weren't coming directly for us. Maybe it was a game to them, or perhaps they had other plans. Either way, I really hoped there was some way out of this.

I didn't want to see what might happen if we weren't strong enough to protect ourselves.

"Hell," Rhodes whispered. "I can't tell how many of them there are, but from the magic alone, there's got to be what, fifteen? Twenty?"

Any hope I had plummeted. Twenty Wielders against two trained ones, a weak one with no knowledge, and a human who might be somehow connected to the Maison realm... It didn't bode well in terms of numbers.

"That sounds about right. And you know what they're doing, don't you?" Luken sounded like he wanted to tear into something but held himself back.

"It's a damn trap."

We were being herded, and there was nothing any of us could do about it.

Rhodes cursed again and turned to me. "I can't use all of my force because there's a chance they can get to you or Braelynn before I can get to them. And if they find out who I am, who *you* are, it will be even worse. I'll fight, Lyric. You have my word, but if it comes down to something I can't do, even with Luken by my side, you and Braelynn need to run. Run back to where we were before, where we entered this kingdom and territory, and find the path to get home."

I shook my head, not believing what he was telling me to do. "I'm not leaving you."

"And I'm not going to let you get hurt because I can't protect you. I'm strong, Lyric. Probably stronger than all of them down there, but I don't know how good I'll be when it comes to fighting against all of them at once, or when I'm depleted after being out of the realm for so long."

"You need the realm to keep your magic?" Braelynn asked as if reading my mind since I had the same question.

Rhodes nodded. "Being close to our kingdom and the crystal within the court itself helps us. It's why those of immense power usually stay within the court walls. I'm fine, and will be fine. I'm not weak and can Wield two elements, but it's a little trickier if I don't want to leave a pile of bodies behind, *and* if I want to keep the two of you safe."

He reached out and brushed the blood off my cheek, his gaze going dark. "Though it doesn't seem like I've been doing too good a job with that."

"I'm fine," I said, ignoring not only the pain in my cheek but also the way his touch made me want to lean into him. This wasn't the time or place, and I knew that, but it was getting harder to ignore him, no matter that everything seemed to be literally crumbling around us.

"No, you aren't. And they're going to pay for spilling your blood." There was a promise in his voice that should have worried me, but it didn't. Instead, I blew out a breath, then pulled Rhodes to the ground as another rock slammed into the tree shielding us.

Then there was no more time to think, no more time to talk.

The fight was on.

Four men came out of the clearing, and Rhodes went at them. One of the Earth Wielders, dressed in dark brown leathers and a darker tunic along with a dark green scarf over his head, grinned at Rhodes like a wild man before bringing his hands out to either side of him, palms and fingers outstretched, before slamming his hands together directly in front of his chest.

When the earth moved in waves beneath my feet, I knew the man was the Earth shaker.

And since the other three surrounding him, dressed in a similar fashion but without the bandana, showing off their various shades of brown hair, were opening and closing their hands as they moved their arms, I had a feeling they used a different variation of Earth Wielding.

All of them looked like pirates, and I couldn't help but hold back a laugh at that thought. Earth-Wielding pirates, who pillaged the Earth itself with their power in order to…what? Kidnap or kill us? I wasn't sure who they were, but they weren't anything like the sentries from before.

Stones and rocks lifted from the ground all around us, heading straight towards Rhodes. Before I could blink, Rhodes had his arms out, and the wind around us swirled, shoving the rocks back to where they'd come from.

The Earth shaker didn't move, unfazed, but three of the rock throwers ducked out of the way. I assumed those were the weaker Wielders since the last one standing snapped his fingers, and the rocks crumbled to dust.

And though the Earth shaker seemed the cockiest, I had a feeling that one might have more power.

Other Wielders came at Luken, who had Braelynn to his back. There were more of them coming up on his side, and though he was strong and had his sword out, one of the rocks slammed into his head. I screamed, running to him, but Braelynn was already there, her hand covering the wound. That left her vulnerable, though. It left them both in the line of fire. When the

Wielders came at all of us again, I could only throw out my hands and pray that whatever power I had was enough to protect my friends.

It wasn't enough.

It wasn't even close.

I knocked two men off their feet, but the others came closer.

They didn't hit us again. Instead, they smiled and grabbed at Braelynn and Luken, coming for me, as well. I didn't run away, knowing I could never leave my friends, but when Rhodes put his back to me, I knew there was nowhere to go.

We were surrounded.

We were trapped.

We'd lost.

CHAPTER 19

It turned out that the Wielder who was the best with stone happened to be the leader of the Earth-Wielding pirates. I didn't know the actual name of their crew, but they would forever be called that in my head. It kept me sane, or at least as lucid and rational as I could be trapped in a new world after being captured by an enemy with no name.

I only knew the guy was the leader because the others looked to him for orders, even if it was an all too casual glance that maybe he thought none of us would see. The group had come at us quickly after Rhodes put down his hand, signaling a surrender. They'd forcibly taken Rhodes by the shoulders, pulling him away from me. He'd kept his gaze on mine, however, and I'd known that, somehow, we'd find a way out of this.

Some of the other pirates had picked up Luken, carrying him to the wagon where they forced Rhodes, Braelynn, and me to get in. They didn't touch me or Braelynn, and I didn't know if that was because they didn't want to hur women, or because they wondered who these two Danes were in their land.

Only, I wasn't a Dane…was I?

I was an Air Wielder, and perhaps more, though I couldn't tell yet. Rhodes and Luken thought I was, so maybe it was true, but I had a feeling I couldn't let these Earth Wielders know who I could possibly be.

Now the four of us were sitting in a cave, chained to one another and covered in dirt. The pirates hadn't thrown it at us, but between crawling inside the wagon and then being dragged through the cave, we couldn't help but be covered in grime. As the pirates walked by, they looked far cleaner than we did, and I figured that had to do with the fact they could just Wield the dirt off if they wanted.

Or maybe I was focusing on trivial little things like that because I had no idea if we were going to live through this or not.

The shackles around our wrists sent a buzzing sensation through my body, and I had a feeling that if I tried to find my Air and use it, I wouldn't be able to. Since the pirates didn't have many guards on us, Rhodes and Luken must have felt the same thing, or at least something similar, as neither of them was fighting back. The pirates hadn't even taken Luken's sword. It was still strapped to his back. His face was bloody from the attack, but he was awake and alert now, and looking angrier than I'd ever seen him in the short time we'd known each other.

Our backs were to the wall, Luken's sword digging into the dirt, and I knew our captors had put us here to wait. I didn't know what we were waiting for exactly, but I knew something was coming. This was one of those times I wished I could read minds so I could see what the plan was. I didn't want to die here. I didn't want to die at all. But I didn't know what would happen next.

My body ached, and my palms were damp. I could smell decay in the air, and the scent of wet soil that was almost cloying. Water burbled in a creek somewhere nearby, but I didn't know if it was from outside or if we were so deep in the cave that it was from water *inside* with us.

I looked over at Rhodes, hoping there was something I could do, but when he looked over my head, I knew that our time for planning was over. Sadly, there hadn't been any planning at all.

"You know, I wasn't expecting to find an Air and Water, an Air, a baby Air, and a Dane while walking through my territory. Sometimes, I'm just lucky I guess."

The stone Wielder, the leader, grinned at us when I turned my head to face him. I swallowed hard, hoping I wouldn't throw up. Somehow, this had become my life, and I wasn't going to back down. There wasn't any time for a freak-out, and acting like I was scared would only make things worse.

"I'm Slavik, leader of my group here. Some call me 'King,' but you know how calling yourself that can get you beheaded quickly around here. I mean, Queen Cameo doesn't care if it's said in jest. She'll call down an execution just because she broke a nail, let alone if someone's trying to usurp her throne. She's been High Queen of Obscurité for five hundred years, and it still doesn't seem like it's enough for her."

The man shrugged and went to sit on a large, flat rock that had been placed right in front of the four of us. Slavik looked like he liked an audience as he spoke, but I wasn't sure what he could possibly want from us. Though I now knew the high queen's name: Cameo. And since she was Slavik's queen, that meant she was queen of the Obscurité, the one who ruled the Earth and Fire territories and the borderlands in between.

Slavik crossed his ankle over his knee and leaned back against the dirt wall. "Now, when Zeke was alive, he held her back some. But it's been forever since he died, and most people don't remember the old king. But, really, he just married into the job, so who knows what he could have been without Cameo by his side. Now, since there are always eyes watching, always ears listening, let's be sure not to call me the pirate king. I go by Slavik." He winked. "But you can call me a pirate king when we're alone if you want."

It wasn't until Rhodes growled low in his throat that I realized that Slavik was talking to me. I held back a shudder and tried not to react, but from the way he looked at me, I hadn't held back the revulsion or fear. It didn't help that he'd called himself the pirate king like I'd thought in my head. If it wasn't obvious from how they all dressed, I'd have assumed he read my mind. Rhodes hadn't mentioned that talent with any of the elements, but for all I knew, it was something special only Slavik could do.

"Pirate king," Rhodes said with a snort. "Really? That's what you're going with?"

Slavik narrowed his eyes. "You look familiar, Lumière. Do I know you?"

"You act as if I should know *you*."

I stayed as still as possible, hoping that Rhodes had a plan other than annoying Slavik. I just didn't want the so-called pirate king's attention on me...though I really didn't want it on Rhodes either.

Slavik narrowed his eyes. "You're Lumière, you wouldn't know me. But the Obscurité? They know me. Some fear me. Some realize I'm doing what must be done."

"And what is it exactly that you're doing?" I hadn't realized I'd spoken until the words were out of my mouth, and Rhodes stiffened at my side. Braelynn leaned into my other side, and I could see out of the corner of my eye that Luken glanced at me for a moment before looking around the rest of the cave, probably trying to keep everyone in his sights.

"What should be done," Slavik snapped. "We take what we can from those who don't know any better. They aren't using it, and our world is dying. Our *people* are dying. If we don't take it, then who will? Who will use it? The power, the gold, the homes, the food. If it lies in waste, then there's no use for it."

"You're some kind of Robin Hood?" I asked, aware that I probably shouldn't be speaking, but I couldn't help it.

The pirate king narrowed his eyes. "Who?"

I bit my tongue. Just because Rhodes had come into the human realm and probably knew some of the shows and movies from my world, didn't mean everyone else did. And Rhodes had said that there were no human inventions in the Maison realm. No TV, no movies, nothing that magic and elemental Wielding could interfere with.

"Never mind."

"Hmm." He ran his hand through his hair and studied us. He had dark hair and darker brown eyes, with skin only slightly tanner than mine. I didn't think it was from the sun, but more natural. Most of the people I'd seen in this territory had skin in various shades of white and brown with their only similar characteristic being their hair color and the style of their clothing. I didn't know if all Earth Wielders had brown hair, but the pirates and sentries seemed to.

"You're stealing from people because you think it's your right, or that you can since they aren't using it properly or something. Well, we have nothing for you, so why are we here?"

I truly needed to shut up. Luken kept giving me weird looks when he wasn't keeping an eye on our surroundings. Braelynn looked at me like I was insane, but Rhodes looked at me as if he trusted me.

Me.

The one who had no idea what she was doing.

"You really do like to ask questions, don't you?" Slavik narrowed his eyes at me, but there was a grin threatening. It was as if he liked to watch us to see exactly what we would do, and so he could be as outrageous as he wanted to be.

I honestly didn't know if me asking questions would get us killed or not, but I knew I couldn't just lay down and let them do whatever they wanted to us. I wasn't going to let my friends—the people who had tried to help me— die because I wasn't brave or strong enough to prevent it.

"There's no hope left here. The Earth territory is dying. *Every* territory is dying. The crystals that we need to survive are fading away."

I looked over at Rhodes, who didn't look back at me. But I could see the tension in his jaw and knew that whatever this pirate king had to say, it was important. And it was something Rhodes apparently wasn't ready for me to hear. I didn't know what that meant, but I wasn't happy about it. Because Rhodes was supposed to tell me everything. Or at least that's what I thought.

After all, he kept saying that he was waiting for Rosamond to come back. For us to find her so she could explain everything to me. But he had only been giving me little nibbles of exactly what was going on in this new realm.

And to say I was scared was an understatement.

"I can see by your face that you didn't know about the crystals." The pirate king glared at me before shrugging. I was truly afraid he was going to figure out that we had come from the human realm, and either our cover would be blown, or he would find another way to figure out exactly why we were in his territory.

"The crystals fuel each kingdom. I hear, before the war, before the Fall, there used to be one big crystal. But for all I know, that's just a fable that was told to children so they knew exactly how everything used to be one, and how it all used to be perfect peace. That's crap if you ask me. Because our world needs war. It's what drives the kings and queens of our lands. Greed, war, strife. All of it has always been part of our history, and the fact that we just happen to be two kingdoms now? That just adds more blood to the battlefield."

"So, there are two crystals then?" I hadn't meant to ask that, and from the way Rhodes glared at me, I knew I shouldn't have. Because anyone in this realm should know that.

But the pirate king wasn't looking at us. Instead, he was buffing his nails like he had nowhere else to be. As if he hadn't shackled us in the middle of a seweresque cave.

"There are two. A dark and a light. You can guess where those are, I'm sure. Within each kingdom, in the main courts, the crystals lay in wait. The king and the queen each take their power from the crystals. Everyone should be taking their power from the crystals and, therefore, feeding their power back into them. Apparently, it's a symbiotic relationship or some jazz like that. But as the magic fades from our realm, so do the crystals. Our land and our people are dying, and so is our magic, day by day. We have more Danes than we ever had before, and that is saying something. Our realm is dying, *everything* is dying. And that means I and my men will do whatever we need to, to make sure we stay alive. Because no one cares about what we do. Not even a little."

"You sound like you believe that we're already dead. That we're just walking around as husks, waiting for the end to truly come."

I looked over at Rhodes after he'd spoken, wondering if he was baiting Slavik or truly wanted to know the answer. I didn't know if *I* wanted to know. Because I knew there was a reason Rhodes wanted me in this realm. The Spirit Priestess had to do something, had to *be* something. And if that something meant bringing the kingdoms together, and maybe stopping the magic from dying, perhaps that was something he should've told me to begin with. Waiting for Rosamond wasn't an option anymore, not when I already had one element unlocked and I was truly afraid of what might happen when the other four did. If they did.

"The Spirit Priestess is a lie." Slavik raised his chin and glared at all of us.

160

"It's a myth that comes from wanting hope, and it only leads to more death. The world around us is fading, just like those crystals. And there's nothing we can do about it. The kings and queens send their children out into the human realm to find the lost Priestess. But if she is so important, why would she be hidden away? If she knows how to help us all, why would she hide from us? You know why? Because she doesn't care. Or she doesn't exist. And so, I really don't care what all of you think. But you *do* have something I want."

I met Slavik's gaze. "And what is that?"

Slavik grinned, and fear slid down my spine. "You have power."

And then, more magic fizzled in the air, the earth beneath our feet shaking, and I knew the Earth shaker was back.

Then Braelynn screamed.

They moved us to a new Earth dwelling, something made of dirt and mud and slightly underground. People were lying dead around us or were dying. They were trapped, just like we were. If we didn't find a way out, we'd be dead just like the rest of them. It made me wonder if there were truly good Earth people around, or if everyone in this territory, in this kingdom for that matter, was lost.

They separated us, Braelynn going somewhere with Luken after she had screamed. Someone had come up from behind us, tugging on her hair and putting a blade to her throat. She had stopped screaming when she realized what exactly was touching her skin, but I'd almost screamed for her.

They had pulled my friends away, taking Rhodes in a different direction than me, and I just prayed that there was something we could do.

But I didn't think there was.

Not when I didn't have any power, and not when I had no idea where we were.

CHAPTER 20

"There's still hope."

I almost jumped at the cracking voice, then looked to my side. What I had thought was a bundle of blankets, was actually an older woman with lines on her face that spoke of time and knowledge.

I looked over at the woman sitting next to me, and all I wanted to do was hold her close and tell her that everything would be okay. Or maybe I wanted her to do that for me. Fear crawled up my spine and slithered down to my stomach.

I was honestly so scared, but I knew if I just kept breathing, if I just kept hoping, maybe there would be a way out of this.

But Rhodes and Luken hadn't looked as if there would be a way out of this when I'd seen them last.

So, maybe there really wasn't a way.

"I know who you are."

My eyes widened at the woman's words, but I didn't say anything back. What was there to say? I had never met her before in my life, therefore, I had no idea who she was, so she couldn't know who I was.

She wouldn't know my name. Wouldn't know my friends. And she wouldn't know that I was a fragile new Air Wielder, someone who really wasn't supposed to be here. I had a façade on, I was a fake. And Rhodes wanted to believe that I could be the savior? All I could do was say the wrong thing and get put into this Earth jail. A prison filled with people screaming, people dying, people giving up.

And the thing that hurt the worst? I didn't know if they were dying because of what the pirate king was doing, or because what he'd said was true and all the magic—and therefore the people's will to live—was finally gone. That there was no hope.

That they didn't believe in the Spirit Priestess.

"I know you don't know what I'm talking about. But I know who you are. I know what you're supposed to do. And you're not supposed to be here. Maybe it would be easier for the others if you lay here forever and no one found you. But I know that's not the case."

Shivers racked my body, and goosebumps pebbled my skin. I had no idea who this woman was, but her words were starting to freak me out.

"What are you talking about?" I whispered the words, afraid Slavik or someone would come in and hear me. I didn't want the pirate king to know who the others thought I was, and honestly, I didn't want him to be near me at all. Because I knew the next time I saw his face or that of any of his men, it might be the *last* thing I saw. And the fact that I could so clearly and calmly think that told me my life had truly changed since I'd woken up from my nightmare. Or had emerged into a new one.

Because this was far worse than any dream I'd had of the four elements, where I had stood between the four directions. This was different than the darkness coming at me, the shadows cloying. This was real. And this told me that maybe those nighttime visions that I'd had for so long were far more real than I wanted to believe.

"I know who you're destined to be. I can tell," the woman continued. "My sister wasn't who you are, but she held some power. She left this realm long ago, telling me she would come back for me. But she never came back. I always assumed someone found her and took her from this Earth. And not just the part that we lay in now. The one that holds us all."

I looked over at the woman and frowned. "Are you talking about the Spirit Wielders?"

I had whispered the words, hoping no one would hear. But no one was listening to us. No one was doing much of anything. After all, Slavik had been right. It seemed there truly was no hope when it came to this place.

"Yes. She had some Spirit power, but mostly Earth. There must have been someone in our line long ago that was a full Spirit Wielder. But those don't exist anymore, do they? They faded into the Danes and the humans over time. Extinction is such a dirty word, but it's something that comes close to what we face. And now look at what we've become. We're fading, falling, breaking into a thousand pieces of nothingness. But now, you're here. I always knew you would come. I always knew that, one day, I would meet you, and I would know what to do when I did. Because I always believed. The others told me I shouldn't, but I did."

I couldn't say anything. What was there to say? Rhodes had spoken to me about being a Spirit Priestess, and the way he had spoken seemed as if there was some hope. But I was only a vessel, a weapon. Then again, he hadn't told me enough for me to truly understand what he meant by Spirit Wielding or the elements or anything. I was so confused when it came to him in general, and it wasn't just because of my feelings for him, it was everything surrounding us.

"What is your name, darling?"

"Lyric."

I didn't think there was a reason for me to hide that from her, not when I had no idea if I'd ever see the sun again. If I'd ever see my friends again. If I'd ever see Rhodes again.

Why I was so morose just then I didn't know, but it was probably because I was stuck in an Earth cave dwelling thing somewhere below ground—or maybe I was above ground, I couldn't tell anymore since this hut or whatever it was, was both above and below. But I did know that someone wanted to hurt me, wanted to hurt my friends, and they had separated us. There was no more strength in numbers.

And no matter what I did, what I tried, I couldn't get these shackles off my hands. I couldn't use the Air magic that I had just found within me. And I had no idea how to unlock the other magics, the other elements that Rhodes said I possessed. For all I knew, I was just a baby Air Wielder with no real strength or power. For all I knew, this was just another dream that I would wake up from, screaming.

But I wasn't going to wake up.

Not this time.

"Lyric is a lovely name for the Spirit Priestess."

I didn't say anything. I wasn't sure what I *could* say to her. I couldn't give her hope, and I couldn't tell her I wasn't the Spirit Priestess. Because from the look in her eyes, the idea that I was that and could survive, could exist at all, was the only thing keeping her going.

Or maybe I was putting too much stock in two words that could possibly mean nothing. Perhaps I was making it important so I had hope.

Because this wasn't my life.

And yet, it was.

And if I were going to escape, I had to stop thinking that this wasn't my life, that this wasn't the way I would survive. I had to be stronger than that.

"I won't ask you what you're doing here. I won't ask why you're here at all. But know that the others will hear of you. They will whisper at first, and then the words will come in waves. People will follow you, people will fear you, but people will love you. And I know what I'm supposed to do now. And when the time comes, I want you to remember me."

"What's your name?" I asked, my voice soft. I didn't want to think too hard on the words that she'd said. There was so much pressure surrounding me, so much pressure within me. And because it all came at me at once, I just wanted to try and forget, at least for a moment. And if I could focus on others, focus on what was important beyond myself, maybe I could come back to what I needed to think about later. Apparently, I was better at digging my head into the sand than I thought.

"Magda."

The woman reached out and gripped my hand, and the strength inside her bones shook me, shocking me right to my core as if I were standing on an electrical grid.

I'd stood at this spot before in my dreams, facing one direction, the other directions pulling and tugging at me until I could no longer breathe, could no longer see, my life forever altered.

I did not know this woman, but she knew me.

In her eyes, I saw the darkness, the blood, the ritual. I saw the Fire, the Earth, the Water, the Air. I saw it all, and I saw my fate.

Only I couldn't understand what any of it meant.

"Your friend, the one you search for, she's far, but you will find her. I never found my sister, but you will find who you seek. She is like me, this girl, but of Air and Water."

I blinked, trying to catch up with everything the woman was saying, and everything going on inside my head. It was as if I were two steps behind and didn't understand what was going on.

"What?"

"The one you seek. She's a Seer. Like me. Though I believe she's far stronger. Find her, Lyric. Find her before the others do."

The ominous tone in her voice sent another shiver through me, but I tried not to let it show.

This woman was a Seer. An actual Seer. I was done telling myself that none of these things were real, not after everything that had been happening.

"A Seer? As in, you see the future?" Just because I had read a few books in the fantasy genres, didn't mean I actually knew what any of the titles in this world meant. This wasn't a dream, wasn't a book. This was a realm where I had to keep up because there was no going back. Not anymore. The fact that I was so far behind already was not lost on me, but I was trying to catch up. I was.

Only, I was afraid I wouldn't be able to.

Until it was too late.

Magda reached out and patted my hand again, her skin cool and leathery as if she'd worked with her hands all her life. Yet her bones held so much strength.

"Yes, something like that. It's different for each of us, but your friend, she's the strong one. I can only See when I know it's going to be important to me. Not that I can See everything important in my life. But I know when I need to do something for the greater good."

Then she stopped speaking and leaned against my shoulder. I squeezed her hand, my shackles clinking, and hoped that we could get out of there. I didn't know where this woman's home was or even if she had any family, but if we found a way out, I was going to ask Rhodes for help. Because even in these few moments of speaking with this woman, she had given me strength so I didn't freak out and start crying.

Because I knew if I started crying right then, the severity of the whole situation and everything that had happened over the past few days would hit me. And I knew it would be too much.

I sat there, listening to others speaking to one another in soft tones, some crying, and I let Magda sleep. Her soft breaths were interrupted every once in a while by a rasping cough, and I knew if we didn't get out of here soon, she wouldn't be long for this world.

But before I could figure out exactly how to get out of there, a door opened, and a sliver of light shone through. I pulled my hands away from Magda and tried to shield my eyes from the obtrusive light. I didn't know how long I had been down there. Honestly, I didn't know how long it had been since we came into this realm from the human one at all at this point.

When my eyes adjusted, it wasn't Slavik who walked towards me though, it was the Earth shaker. The one in the bandana who glared and held immense power. Magic he was loose with and didn't use to the best of his ability. He waved it about and didn't save it. So much so, that Rhodes and Luken had said he exhausted far too quickly. I knew that power was held in reserves and it took time and practice to learn how to use it sparingly as well as save some over time. This man, apparently, used his up too fast. If I got out of this, I didn't want to be that kind of Wielder.

I almost snorted—as if I was actually going to get out of this.

The Earth shaker put his finger to his lips and grinned.

And I knew I wasn't going to like what came next.

I wasn't going to like anything this man did.

With a snap of his fingers, the torches around us lit, and I blinked.

He wasn't just an Earth shaker, wasn't only an Earth Wielder. He was a Fire Wielder, as well. I had to wonder if the pirate king, Slavik, knew that. I didn't even know how one could tell if someone was a Wielder. And I didn't know how I could tell what kind of Wielder they were at all, other than the element they Wielded. Rhodes and Slavik seemed to know without seeing it, but not all of the sentries did, and neither could anyone else I had met.

Magda was different.

I just hoped that this Earth shaker, this Fire Wielder, didn't hurt Magda.

"Slavik doesn't know I'm here, but I wanted to get to know you. There's something different about you. Your name is Lyric?" I must've started at his question because he grinned again. "I heard the boy with the dark hair call you that. Or rather, that man. I know who he is, Lyric. I'm not going to tell Slavik that though because I enjoy watching my king act as if he knows what he's doing."

The way the Earth shaker said "king," I knew he didn't respect Slavik. He was following Slavik for some reason, but I wasn't going to ask what that reason was. I didn't want to know too much or delve into the depths of pirate politics—if that was even a thing.

I just wanted to get out of here and find Rhodes, and then Rosamond.

But I knew it wouldn't be easy, no matter what the Earth shaker said or did next.

The man tapped the top of his head and then pointed at me. "You see, I know you're an Air Wielder, but you sent us something different. I don't quite know what it is. But I bet you if I take this boulder to the side of me and crush your cute little arm with it, you'll tell me. Or maybe, I'll use the torch that I just lit and burn you. Just a little. Do you know what burnt flesh smells like? It doesn't smell like bacon or a roast, I'll tell you that."

He gave me a look that sent bile up my throat. I tried not to throw up.

"It smells…I don't know, like a long summer day when you've been outside too long, and you're just starting to feel the heat. Like when you're coming home from a long day, and you can smell the barbecue over a fire. That's the smell. Of course, not all smell what I do, and not all enjoy the scent of burnt flesh. Not all relish the sound of screams as I crush people to death with my Earth. Slavik lets me have what I need, though. He doesn't know it, but he does it because he doesn't look beneath the surface. And once he realizes what I can get out of you—because I know you'll give me something good—it'll all be worth it. I know there's something different about you. He'll understand why I needed to hurt you. Slavik always understands, even if it takes him a little while to get it."

Magda didn't move, but I had a feeling she was awake. All were alert in this prison, listening for what the man would say next. Waiting for what he would do.

"After all, he never comes down here to the chambers. He thinks that I've let all the prisoners go. He thinks that once we take what we want, what we *need*, the others go back to their little homes to live their sad little lives. But that's not the case. Though what Slavik doesn't know won't hurt him. And it surely doesn't hurt us."

I stared at this man, wondering how the hell I had gotten into this situation. Slavik really didn't know what this guy was doing?

Who was truly ruling here if they were all like this? Or maybe it was complete anarchy, sadists doing whatever they wanted with true horror enveloping us.

This time, I couldn't stop the tears from falling as I tried to move back from him. I knew that if he caught me, if he touched me, it would hurt.

He bent over me, his breath so close I could smell it. It smelled like rotten eggs, and like someone who hadn't brushed their teeth in far too long.

When Slavik had been close before, and even when the other Earth Wielders had gotten too close, they hadn't smelled like this.

This man, whatever his name was, was literally rotting from the inside out, and he knew it.

But I think he liked it.

The others in the chamber looked around at us, either cowering in fear or looking as if they wanted to help. But they were in shackles, too, and most of them looked far weaker than me. I couldn't tell if they were Earth Wielders or any other kind of Wielder, but I knew I was in this alone unless my friends could find me.

And as soon as the Earth shaker, the nameless man I knew could be the last face I ever saw, leaned even closer, Magda reached out and cupped my cheek. The movement was so quick, so startling, that the man moved back, his eyes wide.

"What do you think you're doing?" he asked, his eyes narrowing. He held out his hands, and I knew he was ready to use his Wielding. I just didn't know if he was going to try Earth or Fire. Either would hurt.

I kept my eyes on him, but it was Magda I listened to. "It's okay, darling. I know who you're going to be. And I know what is coming for all of us. Now, close your eyes, and know that they're coming for you. Don't fret, Lyric. You have far more precious things to do in life than worry about an old woman." I didn't know what she meant by that, but then she snapped her fingers and slammed her hands together. The pure power radiating off her shook me to my bones.

The entire chamber shook, as well, the walls shedding dust trails as they moved back and forth. The man in front of me, the one I knew I would one day need to learn the name of so I could scream it as I made him hurt for what he most likely did to all these people, took a staggering step back.

And then Magda slammed her hands again, this time into the ground between us. A hole in the wall to the right of us opened up, and light poured through. People screamed, rolling out of the way to avoid the falling debris. Another wave of dirt slammed up into the air, smacking the torturer down. It didn't kill him, but it knocked him out. I only knew he was alive because I could see the rise and fall of his chest.

Then Magda smashed her hands down onto my shackles, and the bonds fell away. I looked over at her and gasped. Her eyes were bright white, her hair blowing in a wind that wasn't there. "What's going on?"

She reached up and cupped my face again. She looked at me, but I knew her eyes weren't seeing, not the way I saw things. "Don't worry about me. I knew what I was holding within me. And I knew what I needed to use it for. I was just waiting for you. Go now, the others will be waiting for you. Dry your tears, Lyric. We're going to need your strength. Don't worry about those of us in here. The prisoners will get out, and they will find *their* strength. They will remember the girl that they met that stood up to the pirate king and his torturer, his Earth shaker. They will remember her. You."

And then Magda closed her eyes and slumped against me. I let the tears fall. She might've told me not to cry, but I knew I couldn't hold it back when it came to watching her die in my arms.

And I knew that no one could miss the fact that a huge wall had just been knocked down in the middle of the pirates' prison. So, I scrambled to my feet, laying Magda down so it looked as if she were sleeping. I was too weak to actually pick her up and carry her with me, and I didn't know what I was going to do as it was. So, I went to the others who were still sitting, looking to be in just as much shock as I was.

"Are you still shackled? Let me help get you out."

One of the men shook his head and bravely got to his feet as I helped him up. He met my eyes with the brown of his gaze. He looked at me as if he knew me, knew who I was.

"We've got this. We'll make sure Magda gets to her family. Go, find your friends. We know who you are, Priestess. We've always known. Find the strength. Find the will. And we will find a way to help you."

I had no idea who these people were, but as I heard Rhodes screaming my name through the hole in the wall, I knew I had to leave. I couldn't find my friends and figure out exactly what we needed to do next if I was still down here. There were a few stronger people who had been shackled, but somehow, Magda had broken through all of the shackles with that one slam against my bonds. These people would be able to help each other out. I needed to get out of there before the pirate king came down to investigate the noise.

"I…I'll try to help. I promise."

"You are. That is what I promise."

I gave the man a nod, even though I wasn't sure what he'd meant by that, helped more people up on my way out, and hoped they would be safe without me. I was just through the hole when Rhodes came out, his eyes wide, and his skin pale. He cupped my face and smashed a kiss to my lips that went straight to my toes, but not to my head because I could barely think of anything but Magda and the people behind me. When he pulled back, he helped me through the wall completely.

He'd kissed me.

Kissed me like he'd thought I was dead.

I knew there were more important things I should be thinking about. And, honestly, I couldn't even focus on Rhodes or what had just happened. I could barely feel my lips, let alone remember what his felt like. Rhodes had no words for me, neither did Luken or Braelynn who had joined us. I knew they would tell me what we needed to do and what had happened to them, but I couldn't listen to any of it now.

I could only think about the woman behind me. The one who had sacrificed herself with the last of her power to get my friends and me out.

She had given everything for the promise of a vision that I didn't know would come true. Something I didn't even know the meaning of because I hadn't seen it myself.

I just hoped that this wasn't the end. And I prayed that it wasn't just a bloody beginning.

Because even though I had known I was lost before, I knew I was even more so now.

Magda had died for me, and I had no idea what that meant.

Only that I'd never forget her.

Or forgive myself.

CHAPTER 21

"How did you get out?" I paused. "I mean, to get me."

Though the man had told me to go, we ended up going with them for the first part of our escape. We'd run out of the place alongside those who could run with us, pulling still more along until we were forced to split up. I could barely remember any of it. The shock of it all was far too much for me. We hadn't stopped to make sure everyone was okay or even to ensure that they had a place to go.

We'd trusted them to find their own way because we'd be targets, putting a bullseye on them. The prisoners had understood.

Though I was the one who had voiced the question, I wasn't sure my brain would be able to process what Rhodes was about to say in response. My head hurt, my feet hurt, my hands hurt.

But nothing hurt more than my heart. My soul.

Every time I closed my eyes, I saw Magda's face.

Every time I closed my eyes, I saw the face of the man I'd talked to and the others I had left behind.

It didn't matter that he had been the one who told me to run. That he'd run behind me with the others. That, somehow, he believed in me, or what I *could* be. Magda had died because she believed I was the Spirit Priestess. And I was so busy trying not to think about what that meant, that I hadn't been able to help her in the end.

What kind of person did that make me?

What kind of person was I that I could leave those people behind, even after I'd tried to help them out of their shackles, after I tried to help them stand? I had left them after running through the forest, but I hadn't stayed with them. I hadn't gone with them to make sure they actually found a place to hide. I had left them because I needed to run to safety.

That man had told me to go, said the others would be safe. But what if that wasn't the case? What if I had convinced myself to believe him because I wanted to fight for myself? And only myself.

"Lyric? What's wrong?" Rhodes cursed under his breath, and I looked over at him. There was a jagged cut along his cheekbone that I wanted to reach out and try to soothe. I didn't know when he'd gotten hurt because it hadn't been there before we were split up after we'd met Slavik. Maybe it had happened when the wall had fallen, or perhaps it had happened before that when we'd been apart. I just didn't know. But did it really matter?

"Lyric? Did he hurt you? Did any of them hurt you? I didn't see Slavik again, but that didn't mean there weren't more of his people there. If I could go back and kill them all for you, annihilate them for myself for that matter, I would. But we had to get out of there when we had the chance. We wouldn't have been able to fight against them all, but I swear I would have found a way if he hurt you."

I didn't reach out and touch him, but I did lean over just a bit so my shoulder brushed against his. The warmth of him seeped into my bones, but I still felt cold. I didn't think I'd ever be warm again after seeing Magda's eyes. She'd had so much power within her, and it was clear she had been saving it because of something she'd Seen in a vision. She'd needed it because I was the one who was supposed to get out of there. Not her. Because, apparently, that's what visions did. They took the power from one to give to another, even if only metaphorically.

If I had ever felt so insignificant and powerless before this, I couldn't remember, and I knew it would pale in comparison to how I felt right now.

How was I supposed to show my worth? How was I supposed to prove to myself and the rest of them that I was worth their sacrifices and heartache?

They wanted me to be this Spirit Priestess, but I didn't even know what that meant.

"Slavik wasn't there," I answered instead. I pushed those thoughts out of my head, knowing they wouldn't help anything right then. Rhodes didn't want to give me any answers, and frankly, I wasn't sure he had any to give. Once he found his sister, I'd find out the next step. As long as I had that goal, I could put one foot in front of the other. I just needed something to work towards.

"But someone else was there?"

"The Earth shaker. He was a Fire Wielder, as well. Did you know that? He said Slavik didn't."

Rhodes shook his head. "No, I'm usually pretty good at figuring out which elements someone can Wield, but not in every case. And if he was hiding it that well from Slavik, he was probably doing it for a reason."

I traced my fingers along my knee, my hand brushing against Rhodes' thigh as I did so. The contact made me suck in a breath, but I ignored it. I had to if I wanted to get through my thoughts about everything that had happened.

"I think he just wanted to make sure he had some power over the pirate king. He didn't hurt me, but he threatened to. I don't think he actually knew who I was, but he knew I was important to you. Because he knew who you were. I don't know what he was going to do with that information, and I think he's still alive, so he could still hurt you with it. But I knew he was going to use me to get at you. And then Magda saved me."

"That older woman? There were tears running down your cheeks, and you were calling for her as we ran from the building. Did we leave her behind with the others? I'm sorry I had to pull you away, but I told you I wouldn't have been able to fight all of them all at once, not when I didn't know if you were hurt or not."

"Magda died. She was an Earth Wielder and a Seer. She had all this power that she had saved up just for that moment. And she used it. Used so much of herself that she died right in my arms. But she broke the shackles, and she pushed that Earth shaker away. She brought down that wall to bring you into my room and then out of the building itself. She did all of that because she said she had Seen it in a vision, and yet there was nothing I could do to help her."

Rhodes wrapped his arm around my shoulders, and I leaned into him, needing his strength more than I cared to admit. This wasn't my world, wasn't my life, and yet the more I said that, the more I realized that wasn't really true anymore. Because here I was, living in the moment, trying to figure out exactly what I was going to do next. And if I needed to lean on someone just for a moment? I was going to do it.

"I'm so sorry. I wish there was something I could do, but there isn't. I've seen so many people die because of the crystals fading and the war that we're fighting that I don't think everyone realizes where it started to begin with.

But the realm is dying, I told you that, Lyric. And I know with you, there's hope. I didn't want to put all that pressure on you, and that's why I wanted to wait for Rosamond to tell you everything. But now I feel like I probably should have told you more than I did."

He sounded like he was truly sorry, and I understood why he hadn't given me an entire backstory and full details of a history that was far older than anything I could imagine. But it was still hard.

I shook my head, but I didn't pull away. "You can tell me in the morning. I don't think I can learn anything new right now. But Magda said something that I wanted to ask you about. That is after you explain to me exactly what happened down there because I'm still a little lost."

I looked up at him, and he frowned but continued answering my initial question. "They put Luken, me, and Braelynn in a different room. There were others with us, and they were shackled just like we were—like I assume you were. No one came in, no one left. It was actually quite...well, not as eventful as what you went through," he said with a wince. He pinched the bridge of his nose and let out a sigh.

"Forget I just said that. There's nothing uneventful about what happened down there. I just haven't had enough sleep, and I'm saying stupid crap that's going to end up making you hate me. I hate seeing people suffer. I hate when I'm unable to help them, and I hate even more when I have to leave them behind. But as soon as that wall came down and I saw you, I knew I had to get you out of there. I knew there were others likely coming, and we had to just get out of there. Luken and I tore a hole through the other side of the wall as soon as our shackles fell off. And we made sure that there was a way for people to escape. And though they were right behind us and we helped them out of that place, I knew we wouldn't be able to stay with them. I knew we'd have to split up. Even before I found you, I made sure that no one could get back into that room. Meaning Slavik and the others would have to go all the way around to get to those people. It gave them a chance, at least. And in the morning, we can go back. If that's what we need to do."

I shook my head. "There was an Earth Wielder there, an older man, not as old as Magda, but one with strength. I have no idea how I could tell that, but it's just something I knew."

"You're starting to be able to sense the strength of someone's elemental Wielding. It'll get a little sharper as time goes on."

I took in that information, looking down at my hands. So much had changed, and there was no going back. "That man told me to go. Said that he would make sure the others got to where they needed to be, as would the other able-bodied people. He looked into my eyes and promised me that and told me to run. I think he knew what I am. Or at least what everyone thinks I am. I tried to help everybody I could, but then you were there, and we had to go. At least I know they got out of the building before we were forced to split up."

"I think...we'll make a better decision next time." Rhodes let out a breath and removed his arm from my shoulders, before turning to face me. "All I could think about was getting you, Luken, and Braelynn out of there. We made a way for others to get free, and made sure as many as possible used it, but it wasn't enough. Not really. And I'm never going to make that mistake again, Lyric. But you have to know, your safety comes first."

I raised my chin and looked into those silver eyes of his. "Because I'm the Spirit Priestess?"

"Not just because of that. I hoped you would know that by now." There was a heat in his voice that hadn't been there before, and I didn't mistake what it was, but I didn't know what I could do about it just then.

I remembered that he'd kissed me. I recalled the taste of him, the feel of him. A kiss with a boy you liked, a man you admired, a crush that you never thought would happen, was supposed to be in the heat of the moment. Those were always the best ones. But the fact that it had happened with everything else crashing down around us? That was just a little bit too much for me. At least for now. Later, I would talk to him about it. Later, I might move in for more. But for now, I couldn't get Magda out of my head.

"Are Luken and Braelynn asleep?" I changed the subject, a little scared of what would happen next and not wanting to talk about it. I was getting really good at avoiding tough topics, and I wasn't proud of it.

"They are. I'm keeping my senses alert, and then I'm going to go on patrol. We don't have our bags from before, so our campsite is really just a bed made of leaves and whatever Luken could find. But we'll make do. We'll get what we need, then we'll trade with those we find, and we'll make sure we get to the border to find my sister. And then...we'll go home."

My eyes widened. That was the first time Rhodes had ever mentioned the second half of his plan—if there was even a plan at all. "Home? My home, or yours?"

Rhodes ran his hand through his dark hair. "My home in this realm. I think it's time you see the Lumière Kingdom, rather than the Obscurité."

I went to bed soon after that announcement, wondering what my life would have been like if I hadn't fallen from that cliff, hadn't been pulled down by the Negs. Then again, somewhere deep inside I knew I'd have found a way here anyway.

The dreams, the fact that I hadn't made a decision about my future, all of it had seemed to push me in this direction.

By the time the first call of the birds I hadn't paid attention to before filled the air, I had been awake for over an hour. I hadn't slept as much as I should have, but the fact that I'd gotten any sleep at all counted as a win for me, especially considering everything that had happened.

Together, the four of us gathered what supplies we could, Luken somehow finding us two leather satchels to carry gathered berries and water. I didn't ask where he'd gotten them, but when I gave him a look, he told me that he'd taken them from two sentries that wouldn't miss them. The sentries were still alive but were going the other way.

I probably should have worried more about the stealing, but at this point, I could only take one step at a time and keep going.

"Are you okay?" Braelynn asked as we hiked through the forest and down a hill. We'd all been pretty quiet the entire trip, but then again, we'd just escaped a kidnapping and a near-death experience, so being quiet sort of made sense.

I glanced over at my best friend and gave her a tight nod. "I'll be okay." Not a lie, but no, I wasn't okay.

"I'm sorry you lost your friend." She reached out and squeezed my hand, and I swallowed hard, thinking of Magda and then Emory.

"Thanks for being here. I don't know if I could have done this without a familiar face."

She squeezed my hand again before letting go, so we each had better balance. "Rhodes seems like a familiar face."

I blushed, I knew it, but when it came to Rhodes, my feelings were all over the place. "And you and Luken?"

Braelynn blushed as well, and I held back a laugh. Talking about boys and crushes, even if we didn't talk about it in detail, seemed so normal. I needed that.

Rhodes held up a hand, and Braelynn and I crouched behind a large bush. We'd learned to hide when he did that. Since someone walked toward us at that moment, I was happy we'd moved quickly.

The man looked to be older than Rhodes and Luken, but then again, I couldn't tell ages anymore, not with some being *centuries* old, and their kind not aging past their twenties. The guy who approached was an Earth Wielder, though I still couldn't explain how I knew that, only that his power felt warm—yet not hot—and soothing—yet not fluid.

"I know you," the man said, looking at Rhodes, and I tensed.

"I'm sure you're mistaken," Rhodes said casually. "We're just traveling through." He tilted his chin toward Luken, and I held my breath, knowing if I made a sound, I'd give my and Braelynn's position away. I had my hands spread, ready to use whatever Air I had in case this man moved too quickly, or if he wasn't alone.

"No, I know you." The man held up his hands, and the four of us tensed. "I'm not going to hurt you, and considering how much power the crystal has leached from me over the decades, I wouldn't be able to even if I tried. But I *am* honored to meet you, Prince."

Rhodes didn't say anything as the other man bowed his head, and it struck me again that the man who had been helping me through this was a *prince*. There was so much about him that I didn't know, and yet I wanted to know more.

Needed to know more.

But these days, it seemed I needed a lot of things I couldn't have.

"I know you don't believe me, but there are others who want peace, as well. I've tried to send word to those in your kingdom, but I'm not sure it went through."

"Word?" Rhodes asked, his voice low.

"My group and I were looking for food and saw your sister. The queen's men had her, though she scented of Negs, as well. She was going north toward the Fire territory, and I can only assume the court since they were the queen's men. We were too weak to help her, I'm afraid, and would have only put her in more danger if we tried, but they weren't hurting her. She was going with them, surrounded, but she looked unharmed."

I bit my lip so I wouldn't call out and ask questions. If what this man said was true, Rosamond was *alive*.

Rhodes asked a few more questions before Luken moved back toward the two of us.

"Can we give him any of our food or water?" I asked, my voice barely above a whisper. "I know we don't have much, but he looks hungry…and worn down."

Luken met my gaze and nodded. "We have little to spare, but we can spare just enough. I was coming here to check on you since there is no one else around. If there were, we'd have been able to sense them."

"We're fine," Braelynn answered for both of us.

I nodded, then opened up my pack to see what we could give the man who had given us hope. How could he have faith at all when the world seemed to be fading around us? I didn't know, but I admired him for it.

When the man left, Rhodes came back to us, sitting down on the ground behind the bush next to Braelynn and me.

"Do you believe him?" I asked, handing over the water bladder.

He nodded. "Thank you. And yes, I do. But I don't know why I do."

"Because your sister is a Seer, and you're a Truth Seeker," Luken said with a shrug.

I straightened. "A Truth Seeker?"

"You don't sound surprised that Rosamond is a Seer…" Rhodes met my gaze, and I nodded.

"Magda mentioned it."

"I see." I didn't know what he saw exactly, but then again, I couldn't read his mind.

"Is it true?"

"Yes, Rosamond's a Seer. My grandmother was a Truth Seeker. She could find the truth in someone's words and actions. Even in their intentions."

"Like a lie detector?"

"What's that?" Luken asked, and I remembered that the other man hadn't been to the human realm before.

"No, a Truth Seeker is even deeper than that. I'm not one, despite what Luken thinks."

"You know when someone is telling the truth. At least, most of the time."

"Maybe, but I don't know if I always believe that."

"So, you think the traveler's telling the truth then?" I put in. "About seeing Rosamond?"

"Yes. And that means the queen wanted Rosamond, not just a random Neg."

I froze. "Because Rosamond's a Seer." It wasn't a question, but Rhodes nodded anyway.

"And that means Queen Cameo needs something from my sister. We're going to go to the border like we planned because it's on the way, but I have a feeling we'll be going farther north than we intended."

I shivered, not wanting to enter the Fire territory or the Obscurité Court. There was something there that scared me yet pulled me at the same time, and I didn't know what it was. I only had one element of magic so far, and it was of the Lumière. I wasn't sure I wanted the other elements if it gave me this sense of foreboding.

But before I could ask anything else, Rhodes stood up and held out his hand. "We need to keep moving," he said, and I placed my hand in his, knowing he was right.

Braelynn took up beside Luken, and the four of us continued our journey, my feet aching, and my body beyond tired.

But I couldn't stop moving.

No matter what.

And because I was so tired, I almost missed the way Rhodes tensed.

I turned at the sound and froze.

We were surrounded.

Again.

And this time, it wasn't pirates.

This time, it was the Earth sentries.

And they weren't alone.

CHAPTER 22

There had to be forty of them.

Forty.

All wearing dark green and brown leathers and tunics, looking far cleaner than the pirates had, and more like they were wearing a uniform instead of just regular clothes.

I was so tired of losing, of not being strong enough, but when it came to numbers, we just didn't have them.

"Haldar. Long time, no see."

I figured it was probably never a good idea when the people surrounding us, their arms outstretched, ready to use whatever Wielding they had, knew who Rhodes was. Or rather, in this case, Rhodes knew who *they* were. Because each time we met someone who Rhodes knew the name of or vice versa, it either ended in bloodshed, screams, or us having to give up because

Rhodes had said that it would be hard for him to blend in because, apparently, he was known in this realm, no matter the kingdom he was in. With his dark looks, silver eyes, and elemental magics, I could understand that. I was just starting to realize the power he held, and it was intense. The fact that he was related to the King of Lumière, the sworn enemy of the queen of the territory we were currently in, probably wasn't good either.

But I didn't really know the politics behind that, or even the histories beyond the initial story where the two kingdoms became sworn enemies. What I did know, was that I didn't think we were getting out of this on our own. We would have to go wherever these sentries wanted us to go. Or worse, not go anywhere.

Luken had his sword in his hand, and Rhodes had his hands outstretched, ready to use his Wielding. So, I did the same, knowing I didn't have quite the power the others did, but I had enough running through my veins that maybe I could at least get Braelynn out.

She was the defenseless one in this, the one that was here as my touchstone, the one who wanted to find out more about this place that called to her. And the only way she could defend herself was with whatever she held in her hand.

Out of the corner of my eye, I saw that she held a small dagger, one that Luken or Rhodes had probably given her, Luken if I was thinking clearly enough. I didn't know if my friend knew how to use it, but my best friend might have even more hidden depth than I realized.

"Rhodes. We found the pirates, or what was left of them." Haldar was a big man, his voice bellowing throughout the trees as he spoke. He had his hands on his large stomach, looking like he was ready to throw his head back and laugh at any moment.

"What did you do to them?" Rhodes asked. "Because we weren't the ones who left the bodies behind. That was all Slavik and his men."

I didn't open my mouth and correct Rhodes because even though Slavik had been the one in charge, he hadn't been the one torturing those people. That had been the Earth shaker, the one with the hidden Fire Wielding power.

"Oh, we left the pieces of the pirates that were left behind by their ilk. Though we didn't find the leader. Those we did find though, were sure quick to tell us who they had found. A dark-haired man with silver eyes that happened to possess elemental Air and Water Wielding? Of course, it had to be you, *Prince.* And they said this Wielder was running around with a man with a sword. We knew that had to be the bastard, Luken. And as for the two women he was running with? That I didn't know, but I am pleased to meet you now."

He winked as he said it, and my skin crawled. This man didn't make me feel like the Earth shaker did, like I wanted to run and wash off any evidence of his existence. But he *did* make me feel like he laughed at us because he could. Because he thought he was better than us.

Haldar bowed as if he were meeting a king, or rather a prince, and I barely resisted an eye roll, even with how inappropriate my thoughts were. Apparently, living for centuries didn't change the showy and odd nature of some people when they wanted to treat others like they were nothing. I wasn't going to say a word or even move, considering he had thirty-nine or so other people around him—all ready to hurt us if needed. At least that's what I figured they were doing, since they surrounded us with their arms out, ready to Wield at any moment.

"What do you want from us?" Rhodes asked, a growl in his voice. "Because it's not like we can do anything for you. We're just passing through, you know why we're here."

That made me pause, but then again, if that Earth Wielder from before had known, maybe others did, too. If Rosamond were a princess of the Lumière, then her kidnapping might be out in the open at this point.

Haldar grinned. "Looking for your dear sister? Oh, the story's out on that, and your uncle isn't pleased. Didn't he want you to find the Spirit Priestess just like our own prince is trying to? And what did you do instead? You lose your sister to the queen. So, you don't really need to go through these lands anymore in secret, do you? Unless you want to be on the wrong end of a sentry's knife or their Wielding. Because the queen's guards are on the lookout for you. And my lord and lady will give you to them if you don't do what we want."

These were Earth Wielders, meaning they worked for Queen Cameo. But if this lord and lady Haldar spoke of weren't part of the queen's court, were they the Lord and Lady of Earth? But wouldn't they answer to the queen? I figured Haldar was just messing with us at this point. If we were taken to the Lord and Lady of Earth, then we'd be as good as in the queen's hands.

If the queen was Rhodes' enemy and had taken Rosamond?

Then I didn't want to be near her. Or her prince, who was apparently also looking for me.

"What do your lord and lady want?" Luken asked, his voice casual. Too casual.

Haldar sniffed in Luken's direction. "I don't listen to what a bastard asks me."

Rhodes was the one to lunge, but Luken held him back. "You don't need to defend me, Rhodes. I know who I am. And I'm not some lackey for a lord and lady who live in a pile of dirt."

The other Earth Wielders moved closer at that dig, and Braelynn stepped slightly to Luken's side. That left me closer to Rhodes, but we were still surrounded.

"Watch what you say." Rhodes raised his chin and brushed off Luken.

"If Luken asks you a question, then you better answer it. Because he's mine."

"Ah, so you're sleeping with the help now? Or are you just keeping your women with you for that?"

Haldar glared over at us, but I didn't meet his eyes. I didn't want him to look too deeply and sense that maybe I was what everyone was looking for. It's not that I wanted to feel like I was important, but if Rhodes thought I was, I didn't want to be a chess piece in a game I was very much unprepared for.

"I'm going to ask you then, what do your lord and lady want?" Rhodes glanced over at me quickly, but then kept his attention on the ones that could hurt us. I wished there was something I could do, but all I could do was keep quiet and stay under the radar.

"That is something my lord and lady will tell you themselves."

Rhodes threw up his hands into the air, and the other Earth Wielders tensed. That made me pause. We couldn't win against this many, but apparently, they were still afraid of Rhodes' power. Good to know.

"You've got to be kidding me. You want us to go all the way across the Earth territory just to meet your lord and lady?" Rhodes spat. "That's going to take days. Days that Rosamond doesn't have. I can't let my sister die because the Lord and Lady of Dirt want to speak to me."

"Watch your mouth, Prince. You're just the nephew of the king. You're nothing. You're not even a true heir. Your sister is the one with the power, you're just a minion like your little bastard friend here. You were looking so long for a Spirit Priestess, yet you couldn't even find her. All you found was some defective human and a weak little Air Wielder. So, why don't you just come with us...or *don't*. I'm sure the lord and lady can tell what they wanted to say to your dead bodies. You might have power, but you can't match all of us at once."

Rhodes' fists clenched at his sides, and I couldn't help it, I reached out and put my hand on his arm. I didn't want him getting hurt because he was angry. Upset that he couldn't fight back because we were outnumbered. Mad because nobody respected Luken. And incensed because we were so out of our depth it wasn't even funny.

"We'll find her," I promised, my voice a whisper.

But Haldar heard. "Listen to your whore. Now, let's go."

Rhodes didn't attack at that word, but I flinched. Instead, Rhodes glared, and then the four of us were off into the caravan. Not defeated, but outnumbered.

And I hated it.

CHAPTER 23

I knew that some part of me had wanted to see all of the Earth territory. I had wanted to see the mountains and the dark plains of soil. I had wanted to see the streams and the forests that were so rich with greens and browns, that it took my breath away. I had wanted to see all of that, but not practically chained by impotence.

They hadn't put shackles on us like the pirates had, but they kept us surrounded at all times, to the point we were always so outnumbered we couldn't actually fight. Maybe if there had only been twenty men, we would've been able to get out of it. I had enough power in me to take down one or two, Braelynn could run, and I was a runner, as well. Maybe if I were actually trained, I would've been able to help.

But there had been no time for that. Everything kept coming at us one thing after another, and I felt like I was drowning. My hands burned, and my too much.

So, as we walked, Rhodes took my hand every once in a while and showed me how to make little tornadoes, small brushes of air. The magic swirled within me, and it felt like I was breathing. I could feel my control returning with each passing moment. I was doing *something*, and it had to count.

But the Earth Wielders watched us, and they were paying us too much attention. I just had to hope that they thought I was really just there for Rhodes' pleasure, for his entertainment. And not because I was truly coming into my own, as whoever I was meant to be.

It took six days to get across the Earth territory.

Six days.

They had wagons for us for some parts, but we walked for most of it. My boots were worn, and I had blisters that bled. My body ached, and I felt as if my hip might pop out of place at any moment. I was only eighteen, yet I felt far older. But now we were at the Lord and Lady of Earth's estate, and the grand scale of it took my breath away.

The whole place was made of dark stone with vegetation everywhere. The building looked like a castle, with turrets aplenty, but it wasn't overly done. There were moors and mud pits as if the land needed to showcase all of Earth and not just the pretty parts.

People worked all around, keeping their eyes downcast as they kept to their business. Some looked beaten down, but not physically. It was as if they were losing the hope to believe in something. And if it was true that the crystal in this territory was fading, leaching the power out of its people, I could understand the looks on their faces, the sadness in their eyes when they glanced at me. Only, the peeks were rare, and most of the people didn't even look.

But the building itself where the Lord and Lady of Earth lived was glorious. It was exactly what I had pictured in my head, thinking of a castle where a lord and lady would reside.

Luken had explained to me along the way that there was a lord and lady of the element in each territory. Here, the Lord and Lady of Earth were Valor and Zia. Rhodes knew them personally. Considering that most people I'd met were hundreds of years old, having histories with those of the same hierarchy made sense. Valor and Zia also had a daughter, but Rhodes didn't tell me her name, only that he knew her, as well. It didn't sound like she was his friend, though.

He'd also explained to me that Zia was Cameo's younger sister. And when the former king of the Obscurité Kingdom died in the Fall, Cameo had become queen, and her sister had married the current Lord of Earth, Valor.

If Cameo had been the one to kidnap Rosamond, for whatever purpose, I didn't have a good feeling about going into this building, this castle. Because the Lady of Earth was the Queen of Obscurité's sister. And unless they didn't get along, then nothing good could come of this.

We moved through the castle without pause, and Haldar ended up putting us in a large room that had two bedrooms attached to it.

It was strange being in this place after spending so long under the open sky. I had bathed in lakes and streams. I had tried not to remember exactly what a hot shower felt like or even what my favorite hoodie looked like. Because that was long gone, out of my mind, maybe out of my memories forever. I knew that enough time had passed, that my parents were likely looking for me, or perhaps they were too focused on themselves. They may not even be home yet.

Either way, I tried not to think about all of that. Instead, I focused on what was in front of me, and the Wielding I still needed to learn.

I needed to change into the new clothes they provided for us. I might have felt odd about that, but the leathers I had borrowed from Rosamond were torn, bloody, and in need of repair—or even thrown away. Braelynn's hadn't fared much better. My tunic had holes in it, and it was also covered in spots of blood. I wasn't really happy about that because it just reminded me that we had fought. And lost.

They dressed us in fighting leathers again, but I didn't know exactly what that meant. Rhodes and Luken had moved over to one bedroom, while Braelynn and I went to the other. We took turns taking showers, though they weren't the same type I was used to. There was a mechanical system that pulled water like a rainfall down onto me as I bathed, but it wasn't the metallic system from before. I knew there had to be some type of metal in this world, but I didn't know exactly what had been invented yet—or what worked with the magics. It wasn't like the human realm was completely closed off from the Maison realm. And unlike the humans, the Wielders knew what the human realm was. So, for all I knew, while they might not be able to take all of the technology from the human world, they might be able to at least use some ideas. Or, maybe they'd closed themselves off completely, except those like Rhodes, who had been looking for me.

I ran my hand through my wet hair, annoyed with myself for even thinking about that.

I didn't want to think about being the Spirit Priestess. Because I had no idea what it meant. But the hope in others' eyes when they said that title, when they told me they knew who I was? That scared me more than anything. I didn't want that hope. I didn't want that pressure. I just wanted to find out who I was, but I had a feeling I wasn't going to like the answers along the way. Even if I made all the right decisions, I knew that not everything would be in my hands.

Namely, what we were doing right now. I quickly braided my long hair, keeping the front parts that were shorter a little bit in my face. It wasn't like there was a blow-dryer to help me get ready for the day. I wondered when I'd actually see my blow-dryer and then wondered if I'd *ever* see it again. Not that it actually mattered. I didn't *miss* my blow-dryer, but I did wonder what my old life was like. Because if Rhodes were right, and we were going to his kingdom after we found his sister, then maybe my time here would be far longer than the few days I'd thought we would spend here.

After all, we had already been here way longer than I had planned.

I shook my head and then tried to keep my thoughts on the goal at hand.

Braelynn was dressed in leathers similar to mine, though her tunic was slightly darker than the pale cream of mine. We'd each used the scarf that was given to us to sort of make a belt to keep the shirts from billowing around us. It was still an odd form of clothing, and for some reason, I had imagined them giving us dresses to wear. But this wasn't some Regency novel, and I wasn't some fair maiden.

Yet, sometimes, I kind of wished I didn't have to learn to fight.

At other times, I wished I had learned way before this. Or at all.

Brae and I met up with Luken and Rhodes in the connecting room. They each had showered, looking far cleaner than I had ever seen them—at least since we'd started our journey. Luken wore a shirt similar in color to Braelynn's over his leathers, while Rhodes wore one similar to mine.

Luken's sharp cheekbones glinted under the light as he stared at Braelynn, and I had to wonder what was going on between them. I was hiding from my feelings about Rhodes, and he kept dropping hints of what he felt for me. It seemed that Luken and Braelynn were far closer than they had been even just a day before. Luken stepped in front of Brae and brushed a lock of hair behind her ear before giving her a small grin. I hadn't really seen Luken smile that often, but the way he looked at my friend told me that he should be smiling more.

I looked up at Rhodes and met those silver eyes, but I didn't smile. I did hold back a slight sigh. He was honestly so handsome, it was hard for me not to stare. But I was better than that, and we had things to do.

A lord and lady to meet.

"You look good," Rhodes said quietly.

I glanced up at him again. "I guess we look a little cleaner, at least."

"Not much you can say. They let Luken keep a sword since it's an heirloom that nobody wants to take from him, but they took away the rest of my weapons. All our weapons. But because we're in a situation where we don't know what's coming next, I did sneak out and get us a couple of knives."

He handed over what looked like a steak knife but with a gilt blade and gems along the handle. My hand shook as I reached out to grip it, not knowing exactly what to do with it.

"This is the pointy end. We'll teach you the rest later. I wish there had been more time, and there should have been so much more. And I'm sorry that you've just been thrust into this situation. But I'm going to train you. You're already so much better with your Air Wielding than even I was when I was learning. You're going to be able to defend yourself, and remember, use the pointy end."

"Where did you find these?"

"In one of the spare bedrooms next door. It was probably a gift from the lady to one of the guards. It's not a big deal, and I don't think they'll even be missed. They weren't in a nice box or anything, just thrown in a trunk. We need weapons, and I don't want to just rely on my Wielding just in case there's some magic I don't know about here, trying to hamper us like those shackles."

"Makes sense. Thank you."

He leaned forward and cupped my face, and I let myself lean into his touch, even for the barest of moments.

"You're welcome, Lyric."

Someone had left food at the front, and I just now saw it. My stomach growled, and I looked over at Rhodes, who gave me a nod. "I can do a little Air Wielding trick to see if there's poison, but it's not fool-proof. I don't think the Lord and Lady of Dirt will want to poison us, though. They want answers, and they want to look good."

"Why do you call them the Lord and Lady of Dirt?" I asked as we all went to the table and started making our plates. There were juices and fruits and some cold meats. It was a decent spread, and far more than I'd expected. Part of me wanted to fold it into a napkin and hide it for when we were on the road again, but I didn't think that would be quite useful. Plus, I had nowhere to put it in my tunic—I'd barely been able to stash my knife. They had taken our packs, as well.

"I call them that because I don't like them. They've always had an air of superiority about them, and they've always hated me for some reason. I have never known them to be cruel, though, so I guess that counts for something."

"It wasn't Slavik, by the way, who did all of that back with the pirates. It was the Earth shaker. I should have told you that before."

"I figured, that didn't seem like Slavik's way. But thanks for telling me." Rhodes went to help me make my plate, but I stepped in, wanting to do it myself. I hated the fact that I couldn't do so many things on my own, but when Rhodes gave me a look, I just shrugged and leaned into him. I could care and touch and get close, but I also needed to do things myself.

In a world where I felt like I had no power, I knew I was being irrational about the little things, but I couldn't help it.

We all ate, listening to and telling more stories that we had overheard, and things we'd learned over the course of our six-day journey. I wanted to ask more poignant questions about the kingdoms, but I didn't think this was the right time. Anyone could be listening, and if I were the one who lived at this estate, I would have probably been eavesdropping.

By the time we finished eating and cleaned up, Haldar was at the door again. He seemed to be waiting for us, and since he'd arrived at just the right moment, I knew they had been watching us.

"Haldar, what is it you want from us?" Rhodes asked.

Haldar just grunted and turned on his heel. I guessed that meant we were supposed to follow him. So, the four of us did. Luken covered Braelynn so Rhodes was near me. I had a feeling that if a fight were to break out, I would be by Rhodes' side, and Braelynn would be by Luken's. We'd coupled off and hadn't meant to, but I'd been learning my Wielding slowly and surely. I'd be able to defend myself, and Rhodes believed in me. That had to count for something. I thought about the blade secured at my side and wondered if Haldar knew about it. If he did, he didn't seem to care. If he didn't, that meant he hadn't been listening quite as closely as I thought.

We walked into what could only be called the throne room, and I almost swallowed my tongue.

Large, long bronze and brown and gold draperies hung from the ceiling like in the Tudor times in England. Three massive chairs were set up front on a dais. One, the tallest, where the lady would likely sit, and the second and third ones slightly lower—the last maybe for their princess. Everything was gold and gilded and bronzed. It reminded me of metals and rare soil. There were gems all around, and that brought to mind the fact that gemstones were found in the earth like diamonds were made from thousands of pounds of pressure.

All within the earth itself.

This was the Lord and Lady of Earth, not *dirt* like Rhodes joked. This was Valor and Zia. Zia being the sister of Cameo, the Queen of Obscurité.

Haldar gestured for us to stand in front of the thrones and then looked at the two people sitting there. The princess's throne was empty, and I knew she had to be gone. Because with the grand show they were giving us now, she would have more than likely been there in all her glory to show off if she were there. Zia sat in her throne, her dress large and billowy. The fabric was gold and brown, but not just a dull brown, one that glinted under the light and was rich like dark chocolate. It was absolutely gorgeous. The lady's dark hair was in an elaborate braid that went all around her head, crowning the waves that cascaded down her back. She had pale skin, so light that she looked almost pure white compared to the darkness of the room. But she was stunning and so stoic, I didn't know if she was even breathing.

Valor was just as pale, his hair just as stark and rich. He didn't smile. He didn't even look at me. Instead, he only glared at Rhodes. He had a sharp nose and sharper cheekbones. His jaw was defined and looked like it could have been cut from granite. He might have been handsome if he didn't look so scary.

He wore fighting leathers and a tunic, as well, but his looked to be of a far better quality than ours, and his shoes shone in the light.

For some reason, to me, he looked like he might have fought at one point in his life. It looked like he was most comfortable in these clothes, but it was clear he hadn't been on a battlefield in enough years that he didn't quite know the proper dress. It was like he was playing a part, but he wasn't sure what he was doing.

Valor spoke first, pulling me out of my thoughts.

"Why are you in our territory?"

"We're looking for Rosamond. But you know that, don't you?" Rhodes asked, his voice calm. So calm, that I had no idea how he was feeling, but I knew that whatever he felt had to be intense enough that he was forcibly holding himself back. We stood shoulder-to-shoulder in front of the lord and lady of the estate, of an element, in a realm that wasn't my own but seemed to be mine in the end. It was so jaw-dropping that I felt like I was just following blindly, not taking action.

"If you're looking for your sister, then why are you doing it on my land? Do you think I have something to do with your Lumière kin? If she's here, she shouldn't have been. You know the laws. You stay away from my kingdom. I stay away from yours."

"Your kingdom? Don't you mean your territory?" Rhodes asked, his voice a low growl.

I stiffened. It seemed that the Lord of Dirt wanted the queen's throne. He might have misspoken, it could have been a misstep, but from the glare on his face, and the glint in his eyes, Rhodes had been right in assuming what Valor's motivation was.

He wanted to be the King of Obscurité. He'd even married the daughter of the former king. But it wasn't good enough.

Now, he had power over the four of them.

"I want to know why you're here. And why you brought this one."

He looked directly at me then, and I raised my chin, almost shaking. I couldn't show weakness, no matter what.

"Because she is mine. You don't have to question that. I'm just looking for my sister, and I have my team to do it."

"Odd team you've made here." When Valor looked at me again, I *knew* he knew who I was. What I was. But he wasn't going to say anything, not yet. Valor seemed like a calculating man, and he wasn't going to use the Spirit Priestess chess piece until the right moment.

This wasn't a man I could trust, but then again, I wasn't sure who I *could* trust.

Valor was silent for so long, that I was sure he was going to sentence us to death, Rhodes being a prince of the Lumière or not. But then he spoke, surprising me to my core.

"You can leave, but you owe me a favor. Remember that. You'll owe me, Rhodes. All four of you will owe me. And I will call upon it one day."

Rhodes didn't say anything, but I looked over to see that he had his jaw clenched. He didn't like this any more than I did. It was a bad idea, but I didn't know any way out of this. We needed to get out of here, and we needed to go to the border between Earth and Fire…and perhaps into the court of the Obscurité itself.

I didn't know if any of that would be any better, nor did I know if we would even find Rosamond in the end.

But as we made the pact with the Lord of Earth, I knew this would come back to haunt us. I just knew it.

No matter when it came.

CHAPTER 24

It took another eight days to reach the Fire and Earth border. Along the way, the four of us trained. Braelynn and I both trained in fighting techniques, Luken being the best help with that, and I trained longer hours with Rhodes, learning different Air Wielding techniques.

We didn't know when my other elements would unlock, but once they did, I knew I'd have to find new trainers. Not for Water since Rhodes could handle that, but we'd have to find someone Rhodes trusted to teach me Earth and Fire Wielding.

Considering that the only Earth Wielders I liked that I had met so far had been in chains and were now in hiding, I wasn't sure what we'd do when the time came for that. And I didn't know what would happen to unlock my other Wielding elements—if I even had them. When I unlocked Air, I had almost died. I'd been so angry about what had happened with Rhodes and those sentries that it had nearly been too much. I wasn't sure I wanted to face similar situations.

But I couldn't just walk away from it. Not anymore.

As we walked through the Earth territory, word must have spread throughout the land that we were allowed there. I wasn't exactly sure how that worked since the queen's guard was apparently still on the lookout for us, but the Lord of Earth had sent word that we were allowed to cross.

Maybe there was some weird territorial dispute I didn't understand, but I just thanked whatever was happening that we didn't have to fight the entire way back through the Earth territory to get to the Fire-Earth border.

We went a different way than we had before when the sentries took us. This time, we saw beautiful waterfalls and gorgeous lakes. The water wasn't as crystalline blue as it sometimes was in the Rockies or even the Cascades in the human realm, but the lush vegetation around the bodies of water just made them seem healthy and whole.

But, for some reason, that was one of the only things that seemed that way. Everybody just seemed tired here, and no matter where we went, it only seemed to get worse.

"Rhodes? Why does everyone look so tired?" It was a legitimate question, but I knew I'd surprised him by asking it out of the blue.

"What do you mean?" Rhodes handed me a piece of jerky, and I ate it, not liking the taste but not complaining. The Lord of Earth, for some reason, had given us a few supplies for the trip and some money. I didn't know why, and I didn't even want to take it at first, but Rhodes had told Valor that he would pay him back and that whatever money the lord gave, it had nothing to do with the pact they'd made.

Valor seemed to agree. I didn't know how Rhodes would pay him back but considering that he was a prince, maybe he had more money than I knew. Not that I actually knew anything about what kind of money they used here since the coins all had different symbols on them that I couldn't read. I'd ask to learn what those meant later. Apparently, there was a universal coin in all of the territories that traversed both kingdoms as if it weren't a big deal that there was a centuries-old war going on.

Every time Rhodes used the coins, Braelynn and I had been on another mission, whether it was washing our clothes or just getting clean in general. The men hadn't asked us to handle money yet, and I figured it was because they knew we didn't know how to count it with all the different denominations. If I were going to stay in this realm longer, I'd need to learn.

"I mean, everybody looks sad and drawn. Is it because of the crystals?"

We were less than a day's walk from the border and were taking the night to try and recharge before we went through. It would be a new setting, a different group of sentries. The borderlands was a territory handled by the queen's guards mostly, but also by both the Fire and the Earth territories. It made for a lot of fighting between them all, and that meant that most people chose not to live there at all since they'd have to deal with three governing bodies and territorial skirmishes. Plus, apparently, the Negs tended to stay in the borderlands, enjoying the chaos and the lack of anything substantive. I had no idea what to expect because it would be the mixing of two elements, but I was still glad we were getting close.

"Yes, it's because of the crystals," Rhodes explained. "Long ago, way before I was born, and even before Rosamond was born, there was one crystal. It was made of all the light and darkness and all the stars. It fed the Maisons, and we, in turn, fed it. It was a symbiotic crystal that allowed our Wielding to evolve over time into what we needed it to be, and to branch off into the numerous kinds of Wielding there are within each element."

He paused, frowning at me as if he were trying to remember the story. "The crystal was large, but it fit perfectly in the center of the main court.

Eventually, as the kings and queens of each elemental kingdom slowly melded into just the two and the Spirit territory that never had a king or queen but a Priestess, the crystal started to change."

I nodded, gesturing for him to go on. These were stories he'd been taught as a child, that much I knew, but I was so behind, I was soaking up every bit of information I could.

"The crystal, instead of being made up of all of the colors, almost like a rainbow, became light or dark on any given day. It was like it was…sick, trying to decide what it should be. And when the Fall happened, and the two kings died, causing the kingdoms themselves to split and practically destroying what the Maison realm had once been, the crystal itself broke in two."

My eyes widened, and I leaned closer. "So, it wasn't just a fight over land, it actually had to do with the Wielding and magic. Like everything?"

Rhodes reached out and tangled my fingers with his. He gave them a squeeze but didn't let them go. I looked down at our entwined hands just as he did, but neither of us moved away."

"It *was* everything. The people split into different factions, and the new king and queen rose up from the darkness. Or rather *in* the darkness—and the light. The crystal, in its two new forms, was taken to each of the separate courts. But because of the way the land is allocated and split, the courts are actually quite close together. Only a small border separates them, and even then, I swear sometimes you can look right into the Obscurité Court from the Lumière Court. They used to be one, but now there's meant to be two."

"Do you live there, then? In the Lumière Court?" There were so many things about Rhodes I didn't know. I knew what was in his heart, and the strengths he had. I knew how he fought, and who he fought for. I thought I knew the man, but I needed to know more about him. More about his likes and his dislikes beyond what we'd seen in the Earth territory or even in the Spirit one. It was hard to find times like these when we were constantly on the run, but with Luken and Braelynn off near a stream spending time together, this gave Rhodes and me time to ourselves.

"I don't live in the same castle as the rest of my family. I live in the court, though. Or at least I have rooms there. I've been living in and out of the human realm for so long that I haven't been back in a while. But I did grow up there, in the court. With my cousin, Eitri."

I knew my brows rose as I asked, "Eitri? If he's your cousin, then he's a prince of the Lumière?"

Rhodes snorted, and I had to figure there was a wealth of history there as he spoke of his family. "Yes, just like me. Although I tend not to think of myself as a prince. Not anymore. I used to be the only prince, and then a few decades after I was born, my uncle and aunt had Eitri. So, technically, my new title is Lord, but people call me 'Prince' as an insult here. And it just sticks. I tend to answer to Prince, Lord, warrior, or simply Rhodes."

There was nothing *just* about Rhodes, but I didn't say that. "So that means Rosamond is a princess and a lady?"

"Yes. Brokk, my uncle, the King of Lumière, is my father's older brother. Durin and Áine are my parents. Brokk married Delphine, and now it's all one big, happy family. It all ends up a bit incestuous, or it would if we didn't live for so long and didn't stay in our positions for centuries. Because my mother's parents are the Lord and Lady of Air, while my parents are actually the Lord and Lady of Water."

I almost choked on my food. "Seriously? How did I not know that you were next in line for the Lord of Water? And related to the Lord and Lady of Air? Not to mention the king, or that you're entirely Lumière, even more so than Eitri, considering both of your parents."

Rhodes shrugged. "Who would rule what was all decided long ago, and they were all from the same main families. Lands changing hands at the estates and the ruling doesn't really happen in our world. Unless there's a battle and someone dies. Or someone is poisoned. There have been a few poisonings in the lower courts."

"There are lower courts?"

"Yes, but those aren't lords and ladies. It's more the people who run each of the small cities and towns. We've gone through a few of them as we made our way here. Think of them like...mayors, or governors. But they all answer to the main lord and lady of that element."

"And you seem to be related to almost all of them, at least within the Lumière."

Rhodes grinned at me, and I couldn't help but smile back. He had that effect on me. "Pretty much."

He stopped smiling and continued. "Our light crystal is fading just as much as the dark crystal. The people of the Earth territory do have a worn look about them, and I don't know if it's like that in the Air or Water territories, or even the Fire. We'll see what the Fire people look like soon, but it's been so long since I was home—at least what Lumière is home-wise—that I just don't know. And the thing is, if those not in the court are hearing about the crystal, and it's not just rumor, that means it has to be pretty bad, and will likely get worse the closer we get to the court itself."

"So, what are we going to do?"

Rhodes played with my fingers as he frowned. "Well, we're going to find my sister. We're going to go into the Fire territory, and I hope to hell we don't have to go into the actual court, but if we do, we'll figure it out."

I was the one to sigh this time. "And then I need to figure out what my job is."

"I don't know what that entails, Lyric. I wasn't just pulling you along this whole trip, waiting to tell you as much as I could. I seriously don't know what you're supposed to do. Rosamond is a Seer. She's the one who's supposed to know these things. I was just supposed to find you. Protect you."

I understood that now, though I hated that we were both so in the dark about so many things. "How did you find me? I mean, how did you know? Is there something about me?"

Rhodes met my gaze, and it looked like he almost lowered his head before he thought better of it. I wish he wouldn't have thought better of it. We'd only shared a few kisses since our first, but I wanted more, even though it might not be the best time. But, sometimes, you just had to take a leap, and that was what this whole thing was for me.

"I knew who you were because I was pulled to you. But maybe that pull wasn't just because you were the Spirit Priestess." His voice had gone husky at that, and I had to wonder exactly what he was thinking at that moment.

A pull? That was almost romantic, but I knew he had to be speaking of something else right then.

"And there was Alura."

I paused. "Alura?"

"You know her, from school. Actually, you saw her talking to me and Rosamond near our house."

I tried to think back to all those days ago, even though they seemed like years. Decades. And then I nodded. I could remember seeing Alura with her white-blond hair, long and straight and almost flowing without actual wind as she spoke to the siblings. Alura had always seemed not quite part of this time, and if she were the one to tell Rhodes that I was a Spirit Priestess? What else was I missing?

"Is she a Wielder, as well?"

"Yes, but I don't know what kind." Rhodes squeezed my hand then leaned forward and brushed his lips against mine. I pulled back, but only because I was startled. When he didn't pull away quickly enough, I pressed my lips back to his.

"Sorry, I've been wanting to do that for a while," Rhodes whispered after a few moments of just *us*.

"I don't mind. But, Alura?" I couldn't get distracted when it came to Rhodes. Although it was really hard to stay focused with him sometimes.

"I don't know what kind of Wielder she is, but she's strong. And old. I don't know why she felt the need to tell us, but Rosamond trusted her, and Rosamond doesn't trust easily. So, I trusted her, as well."

I thought on that. "It's all a bit daunting, isn't it?"

Rhodes moved so we were both sitting next to each other on the log and then shifted me so I was leaning my back against his chest. I felt protected, and I didn't feel protected often. Not anymore.

"It's always going to be daunting, Lyric. I don't think it's *not* going to be daunting anymore. I wish I could say I'm sorry that I brought you here, but I can't. I'm not. Not when you're already so good at Air Wielding, and I just know you'll be good at whatever else you need to pick up. My people need you, even if you don't hold the title yet. And I know you're not ready for it, but my people need you."

"And who are my people, then?" I hadn't meant to say the words, hadn't known I was truly feeling them. Was I that lost? Had I forgotten who I was altogether?

Did it matter at all?

Rhodes moved so we were facing each other but still cuddled into each other. "I don't know. But I can be your people if you want. And Braelynn is your people. And I bet Luken would be your people."

For some reason, Emory's face filled my mind for just a moment. I hoped she had found her way home. If someone had caught her, we would have heard by now, especially with the way news tended to travel here when it came to outsiders. At least, I hope we would have.

I only had to hope that no news was good news. I still couldn't believe she had just up and left like that. It was so irresponsible. I knew I should have fought harder, but then again, I had to be here. There was a reason I was here, and I couldn't leave yet.

I tried to push those thoughts out of my mind and worked to listen to the man in front of me, the one holding me. Rhodes told me more about his childhood, and his annoying cousin, and it felt like I was almost at home again. It seemed that everybody had family issues, only Rhodes' problems happened to have Wielding and elements and a king and a queen involved.

Everything was changing, once again. Soon, we would be inside the Fire and Earth border and then in the Fire territory itself.

And I was ready. As ready as I would ever be.

But was I ready to be what the others thought they needed me to be? That was the question.

CHAPTER 25

I had been to the Red Rocks of Colorado numerous times and had spent far too many hours of my life taking photos and generally breathing in all I could of the Garden of the Gods near Colorado Springs.

But all of that breathtaking beauty paled in comparison to that of the Fire and Earth border.

It was as if the rocks had been molded by the gods and goddesses, from the heavens above.

Everything was red and brown, a mixture of all the colors of that spectrum. I almost couldn't believe what I was seeing. Great stacks reached up to the sky, others were rounded but still tall. If I looked hard enough, I could see different shapes within the stones themselves. I remembered at Garden of the Gods, it looked like two camels kissing, and I swore I could see something just like that here. Nature, or maybe it was Wielding, had created these. And just looking at it all took my breath away. I struggled to take it all in, its beauty overwhelming and invigorating all at the same time. It was beautiful, a perfect blend of Earth and Fire.

Rhodes gripped my hand, and I looked up at him, smiling for the first time in what felt like forever.

"It's beautiful."

He gave my hand a squeeze and followed my gaze. "I agree. It's been years since I've been here. It looks much the same, although the people are a little different.

"Sadder?" I winced. "That wasn't nice."

"But not wrong."

Those at the border looked much the same as those in the Earth territory regarding mood and attitude. People milled about in the different shops of the market right at the border crossing. You could buy food and different things that you might need for a long journey. Some people were selling trinkets, and I knew that they were handmade and possibly well-loved from some of the hands that I saw moving with gentle care as they offered their wares. The shop owners were a mix of Earth and Fire Wielders, and I only knew that they were Fire Wielders because Rhodes pointed them out. They looked just like the Earth Wielders, a mix of everybody—skin tones, hair, eyes, all different people with different backgrounds—and yet they all had power.

Their power, though, was almost sootier, warmer, hotter. It took me a while to realize it.

If I stood near one of them for too long, I swore I could smell smoke.

Or maybe that was just my imagination running wild.

There weren't that many trees here, and what was left was a little bit ragged, a little more barren. They weren't as white and stark as they had been in the Spirit territory, and I guessed that once we reached the Fire territory, things would look even more different.

It seemed after thousands of years, that once the people who resided in the territories lived there long enough, their land changed with them. Or maybe it was more like the people adapted to the land.

Part of me wanted to know the answer to that. The rest of me knew that I had so much more to learn. That maybe it would be a little too much all at once.

"I'm going to go get some more food for the travel," Luken said, pulling Braelynn with him. "You guys want to go make sure we have enough water and bedding?"

Braelynn blushed as Luken said the word *bedding*, and my brows rose. Okay, apparently, those two were further along in their relationship than I figured. Or perhaps I was seeing too much into my friend's reaction. Either way, Braelynn winked at me before turning and walking away with Luken.

I looked up at Rhodes and squeezed his hand. "Are you ready?"

Rhodes smiled down at me and kissed me. Kissed me right in the open, and I couldn't help but part my lips and let his tongue brush along mine. Shivers ran down my spine, and I smiled as he pulled away. It was strange, finding someone that you cared about when everything else seemed to be changing and falling apart around you. Or maybe that was when you saw what was truly there and clung to what was important. I didn't know the truth behind it all, but I wasn't going to run away because I was scared. I hadn't left yet, and I wasn't going to leave Rhodes.

The hairs on the back of my neck stood on end, and I frowned. I turned to look behind me but only saw people milling about, nobody really looking at us. I looked up at Rhodes again, who was looking in the same direction I was, his jaw tight.

"What is it?"

"Nothing." He shook his head. "I'm just seeing things."

Rhodes didn't just see things. Now, I was worried. But he tugged on my hand, and we went to go see some of the sellers. We picked up another couple of bladders to fill with water, and a sturdier backpack for me. The Lord of Earth had given us a couple, but it was always nice to be prepared, and I didn't know exactly where we were going. Because, apparently, as soon as we reached the middle of the borderlands, that's where most of the Negs would be. And that was where Rosamond had been taken initially. Or so we assumed.

That weaker Earth Wielder had told us that he had seen her but hadn't told us where exactly. Had she been moved through the Earth territory? Or had she been pulled towards the court itself to meet the queen? I didn't know, and I didn't think Rhodes did either. But we were on alert.

"Do you think we'll find Rosamond soon?" I asked, my voice soft.

Rhodes brushed his knuckle along my cheek before sighing. "It would make things easier if we did. But things haven't been easy yet, have they?"

"You aren't lying there. So, I guess we have to look for some bedding?" I cleared my throat, and Rhodes gave a hearty laugh.

"Yes, because right now, we only have two rolls, and they're pretty thin. Though I don't think Luken meant exactly what you and your friend thought. I saw the way you two blushed at each other."

I couldn't help it, I blushed harder. "Anyway, where do we find that?"

Rhodes gestured off towards a few stalls at the other end of the row. "Over there, I think. There should be some blankets, too because once you hit the other side of the border, the temperature drops."

"I don't know why, but I kind of assumed that once we reached the Fire territory, things would get hotter."

"That can be true in some places, but in other places, it's like the heat has been completely ripped out of the area to feed another. It's like that in the Earth territory, too. Did you notice? That some parts are much greener than the others, while others are far more brown? The climate in the Fire territory should be warmer, but that comes from the Wielding itself. It won't always be that way, and the border itself is where everything mixes. That tends to get a bit chilly." Rhodes winked down at me, much like Braelynn had done to me. "But don't worry, I'll keep you warm."

I rolled my eyes. "Smooth. Did you learn that in the human realm? Or do all the Wielders learn lines like that?"

Rhodes laughed, his head thrown back. I had never seen him look more handsome. Maybe it had to do with the fact that he just seemed happy right then. At least it looked like he didn't have the weight of thousands of answers and questions on his shoulders. He had so much responsibility, and even though he was far older than I was in years, we were similar in age if you thought about experience of the Maison realm versus the human one.

Together, we picked up a couple of blankets and a couple more rolls. We attached them easily to the packs, and it was still light enough that I didn't feel the strain of it. I might be a runner, but I wasn't in as decent shape as I needed to be apparently. But over the past couple of weeks, my muscles had grown leaner, and I had gotten a bit stronger. My endurance was up as well, even though I fell asleep hard every night.

But I hadn't had the dreams.

I hadn't had a single nightmare since I came to this realm. I hadn't seen a single shadow, hadn't had the feeling of someone watching me.

Maybe that was because I was here? Perhaps it was because something was waiting for me on the other side of this journey.

I didn't know, but I hadn't slept this well in years. Maybe it was because of exhaustion. It didn't matter, though. I would just have to find a way to make this new part of myself work.

We made our way back to the edge of the market where all the stalls were and met up with Braelynn and Luken. We made sure all of our packs were together before we moved farther into the borderlands as one. For some reason, I had thought it would be more momentous, much like when we had gone from the Spirit territory to the Earth one. But instead of wards or anything, it was just a simple barrier, practically drawn in the sand. I could feel the magic against my skin as we walked across the new part of the border, so I knew there was something there, but it was different. It was as if these two were part of the same kingdom, therefore their securities would be different because there were two territories involved.

Or maybe I was just exhausted and not thinking clearly. Knowing me, it was probably the latter.

We walked for a good two hours, talking about nothing in particular, when we came across a cactus flower. I hadn't seen any vegetation yet, so seeing a cactus at all surprised me. Then again, it was almost as if we were in the desert, so I guess that made sense. I looked down, my eyes wide as I looked at the bright red flower on the green plant. The red was deep, like blood, but with bright pinks along the edges. Rhodes touched my shoulder, and I looked up at him.

"It's beautiful. I don't think I've ever seen anything that color before."

"Keep looking," Rhodes whispered. He gestured with his hand, and I looked at the flower again.

The bloom opened up, and I sucked in a breath. It wasn't just a flower anymore, it was fire. Actual fire as the bloom opened fully and spun. It was like little bursts of flame dancing along the edges of the flower, and then the bloom became the fire.

I had never seen anything like it. It was beautiful.

I had always liked fire as a kid. I'd loved campfires and playing with matches. I always did it safely, even though I knew that what I was doing was wrong.

But I've always loved fire.

Watching the flames dance along that flower, each petal becoming a new flame, I knew I would never see anything this beautiful again. But I didn't tell Rhodes that, not when his two elements were the exact opposite of what I saw now.

One day, I might be able to Wield what I saw now. I didn't think that day would come soon, though. I didn't know what would happen when I unlocked that part of myself, but when that day did come, I just hoped Rhodes understood that I would hold two elements that were of his enemy.

I didn't like that train of thought, so I pushed it away. After all, the Spirit Priestess was supposed to bring everybody together. Right?

I was putting too much into these flowers. I just shook my head.

"It's beautiful," I repeated. "Should we keep going?" I didn't think anyone heard that last part though since they were all looking at the cactus flowers.

Braelynn moved to my side. "You're right, Lyric. It is beautiful. Although I don't really know what you would do with that?" She studied the flowers in front of us, and I smiled at my friend. She was asking the questions that I couldn't because I was too afraid of what Rhodes would think. That was annoying, and I had to stop it.

Luken answered, "Fire Wielders use them sometimes. Because, sometimes, they aren't able to make Fire from nothing. Others can only play with fire or make it dance. They can't create it."

Rhodes nodded. "And those who can't create it, use things like this. It's how some Air Wielders can only use the air around them if it's a windy day. And some Water Wielders can only use water if they have a pouch on them or if they're near a body of water. It all depends on what type of Wielder you are." Rhodes' explanation made sense, and I nodded before we continued on.

That's when the Negs came.

The hairs on the back of my neck stood on end, and bile rose up my throat as I looked around. The shadows out of the corners of my eyes formed, and then they weren't just shadows anymore. They were the monsters from my nightmares.

Long fangs, dark red eyes, and they looked like they had come from the bowels of hell.

There was more than one, more than three, more than the five I'd seen before.

I counted them as they circled us, coming out of the mist. There were seventeen of them in total.

Seventeen of them, and only four of us.

Braelynn held out her dagger, and Luken his sword. I held out my hands, much better with my Air Wielding now than I was with the blade. Rhodes did the same with his hands and put himself in front of me. That angered me a bit, but I understood. He was protecting me. He thought that was his role.

I would have to learn how to protect him, as well.

Then, the Negs attacked. They came at Braelynn and Luken first, their mouths open, drool dripping down their chins, but when the drool hit the ground, it sizzled like acid, and my eyes widened. That was way different than it had been in the human realm. I had to wonder how much more dangerous they were here than when they were in a world of muted magic.

Two Negs came at Rhodes, and he ducked out of the way, pushing me down. I hit the ground, my hands stinging from the soil and dirt digging into my palms. I wanted to yell at him for that, but I couldn't. He was just doing his job, after all.

I rolled away, this time standing up and pushing out my hands at the same time. I tugged on the Air Wielding within me and pushed.

Air flew through me, spreading along my fingers and out through my fingertips. The Neg in front of me flew back twenty feet at least, rolling and then slamming into the ground. The Neg next to him jumped, and I threw my left hand out, tossing that Neg into another.

Training with Rhodes and Luken had helped, and learning to focus on what was inside of me helped even more.

More Negs came, and I knew we were going to lose if we didn't find a way to stop them. Luken stabbed one and then another. Somehow, he was able to toss one over so Braelynn could finish the final stabbing. I didn't know where they had trained to do that as one, but I was grateful that Braelynn wasn't alone, that she wasn't defenseless. I put my back to Rhodes and hoped that we could somehow work as a team, but it wasn't working.

More Negs than ever came at us, more than I dared to think about.

They just kept coming, their claws digging into the soil. Rhodes took out one, then another, then two more. I took out one, tossing it to the ground so hard it didn't get up.

But I was lagging, my reserves not as strong as they should be. I had to focus harder than Rhodes did, and I didn't like it. I knew I was better than I had been the first time we fought, but I wasn't good enough yet. But I damn well would be soon.

Then, a blur of dark shadow and fire came out of nowhere, surprising me. I looked over at Rhodes, who glared but didn't attack the latest shadow.

Only it wasn't a shadow.

It was a man. A man with dark hair, light brown skin, and dark, *dark* eyes.

It was when he met my gaze that his eyes widened for a fraction of a second, and I lost my breath. I had never seen this man before, but I felt like I knew him. Why was that? It didn't matter, I didn't have time for this.

I turned away from the man, hoping he wasn't the enemy and instead someone who could help us. After all, we were fighting Negs.

Weren't all Wielders against the Negs?

The stranger held out his hands, and flames danced along his fingertips.

221

I sucked in a breath.

A Fire Wielder.

The first I had seen in action.

I used my Air again, throwing a Neg out of the way. Rhodes was working with three more, but they kept circling him.

Then the stranger slammed up his hand, and a wall of dirt pummeled one of the Negs attacking Rhodes.

A Fire Wielder *and* an Earth Wielder.

It seemed this man had many talents. And, since he was helping Rhodes, he appeared to be on our side. At least, for now.

The stranger reached out and plucked the bloom from the cactus. Instinctively, for some reason, I held out my hands and blew my Air towards his Fire. The man met my gaze again and nodded, and then both of us pulled our hands back ever so slightly before pushing with all our might. The Fire erupted, egged on by my Air, and it hit a group of a dozen Negs all at once.

The screams hurt my ears, making it hard for me to even see because it hurt so much. But then there were no more Negs. There was only breathing, and the feeling that something had changed.

We were all silent for moment before Luken went to Rhodes' side, and Rhodes got into the stranger's face, practically growling. The other man didn't look fazed, however. If anything, he looked bored.

"What the hell are you doing out here?" the man asked Rhodes.

Rhodes lifted a brow. "Easton, thanks for showing up. We don't need you." I had never heard anger like that in Rhodes' voice before. Yes, he had acted haughty towards the Lord and Lady of Earth, but this was different.

Who was this Easton?

"Go home, Easton. Go talk to your mother. Ask her why she has my sister."

Easton snorted, and I froze, not sure I heard correctly. "My dear old mother doesn't have your sister. She wouldn't do that. She knows the rules. She's the one who made them with your favorite uncle."

I stood there transfixed. Easton was Cameo's son. This was the Prince of Obscurité. A prince of Fire and Earth. His mother was the one who had supposedly taken Rosamond. The one who had her guards looking for us. The one who had people looking for me. I took a step back, and Rhodes put his hand over mine, pulling me behind him.

This time, I didn't mind that he was protecting me. Because I wanted a good look at this stranger, this Easton.

Easton's gaze went to the place where Rhodes touched me, and he narrowed his eyes before blanking his face. I had no idea what that was about, but I didn't focus on it. This man was the son of our enemy, the one who threatened everything Rhodes and I wanted.

Rhodes lifted his chin. "Your mother has my sister, and you know it. I wouldn't be here otherwise."

"You don't know what you're talking about," Easton sneered before turning to me. "You better go home, little girl. This isn't your fight. You're just going to get hurt."

I blinked since he was talking to me, not sure why he was doing so at all. "I'm not a little girl. And I don't need to go anywhere."

Easton met my gaze for a moment before turning his head away. "Suit yourself. But the longer you stay here with him? The more likely it is you'll get hurt. This isn't for you. Go home."

Then, he turned on his heel and left, and I had to wonder how he had gotten here. How had he been at the right place at the right time? Yes, he had saved us from the Negs, but who had sent them in the first place? Maybe it was just a coincidence that the Negs happened to be here. After all, this is where they lived.

Or, maybe Easton had been the one to send them.

His mother *had* sent the originals.

And he was the Prince of Obscurité.

CHAPTER 26

We slept that night on our new rolls an hour from where we'd fought the Negs. We'd known we would have to sleep in the borderlands themselves before we entered the Fire territory, but it was hard to fall asleep so soon after the battle, so soon after the confrontation with Easton.

Rhodes didn't want to talk about the other prince, and I didn't want to push, not when we were so close to our original goal. There might not be any sign of Rosamond, but we were getting closer. I could feel it.

By the time we ate and cleaned up, the sun had set, and the temperature had indeed dropped dramatically. I was glad that Luken had told us to purchase blankets. I lay in my roll next to Braelynn, the two men on patrol since they both said they wouldn't be able to sleep anyway. It stung that they could go longer without sleep, but Luken had explained that it was because they were Wielders. Since they aged slower, they also burned less energy. I didn't understand it, but they hadn't needed the amount of sleep Braelynn and I did over the course of the trip.

Tonight was no different.

Braelynn had fallen asleep after Luken told her a story, soothing her in their own private moment. But it had taken me longer to succumb.

The dreams hadn't made it any easier.

The dreams that hadn't haunted me since the human realm.

The dreams that were back.

I didn't want to believe the nightmares were coming for me, were there to keep me up at night and pull me in, forcing me to let go. But then again, they'd been gone for so long, maybe it was time for them to return. I'd had my reprieve.

I might be living in a new world, one where I could physically see the difference between the paths that I took, but it didn't seem to matter anymore.

Because the dreams would tell me exactly what I needed to see. Maybe it was time for me to actually look at them. I supposed it was time for me to truly understand what they were trying to tell me.

Or maybe I was losing my mind, one element at a time.

The dream began like it always did, dark, shadows, a pause where I had to figure out exactly where it would begin—or maybe where it could end.

Once again, I stood at the convergence of four elements, four directions. Earth rumbled under my feet, the Air slid through my hair. Water sprayed along my face. And the heat of Fire singed my skin.

I hadn't known all of this was true before. I hadn't known that the elements that haunted my dreams were the ones from the Maison realm. I hadn't known that, one day, I would be able to feel one of those elements deep within my soul, that I might be able to feel the others once they were unlocked.

So, as the elements brushed against me again, I tried to take a look into my surroundings. This time, unlike so many other times when I was a passive participant, I knew where we were.

This time, I knew where we had been all along.

We were in the southern Spirit territory. Or maybe not, if the northern Spirit territory looked the same, but I had been in a place that looked just like this, and from the feel of it, I knew we were there.

Maybe I was at the point where all the elements met, or maybe I was just in a symbol of what the Maisons needed to believe in. I wasn't sure, but I knew that outside of the elements that hurt my skin, that made it hard to breathe, that made me feel like I was fighting a war that never ended, there were landmarks that told me I was near the Spirit Wielders. The white trees, the bleached sand, the never-ending sun that never seemed to brighten anything it touched.

This was the Spirit territory, and I wasn't alone.

I looked around, and the shadows came at me. I almost screamed. I tensed, trying not to show my panic. These were the same shadows as before. Could they get into my dreams? Had they been haunting me this entire time?

I didn't know exactly what they could do, but since we were here, I didn't think I would be able to fight back like I could in the human realm.

Or could I?

Maybe I could use Air more here than I could in the real world because this was merely a dream.

But before I could form a plan for exactly how to save myself in a world that didn't make any sense, the shadows shifted. Suddenly, they were no longer what I feared could be the horror. Instead, I was surrounded by twelve people in long, cream robes.

It was as if each person stood at the hour mark of a clock, their heads down, the hoods of their robes covering their faces. I could see the long, flowing hair of some of them, one blond, two brown-haired, one red, but from the builds under the robes, some could have been men. I just didn't know.

But these people, whoever they were, circled me. They were closing in, taking one step at a time, each to a tone that I couldn't quite hear but could feel in my bones. I tried to catch my breath, but I wasn't sure I would be able to. Then again, when was the last time I'd been able to fully catch my breath at all since everything started?

I knew this was important, I knew this wasn't just a dream.

None of the dreams I'd had before were truly dreams either.

The one at twelve o'clock slid her hood from her head and looked at me, her wide eyes staring as if she were seeing into my soul. The figures to my right and left slid their hoods back, as well, and I assumed the one behind me did the same, if the rustling was any indication. The one before me was beautiful, stunning. She took me in as if she were trying to see every inch of me, every ounce of the person that I thought I could hide, of the person that I didn't even know I was. But there was beauty there I couldn't quite comprehend.

Her long, strawberry-blond hair tumbled around her shoulders, blowing in the wind I could feel yet knew wasn't coming from the same direction as the wind hitting my face.

In fact, if I looked at each person, we seemed to have our own wind, our own elements.

It didn't make any sense. Then again, I was in a dream, after all.

"Stay with the light. And the darkness."

I blinked as the woman spoke. I didn't understand.

"What? What do you mean?"

The one at my three o'clock spoke, her voice deep. I looked over at the woman with dark skin and darker eyes. "You must choose the path."

The one at nine o'clock spoke, and I turned to a man with light brown skin and hazel eyes. "You must choose the path," he repeated.

The one at six o'clock spoke, and I turned yet again. This woman had long, straight, black hair, her cheekbones severe. She looked stunning. Gorgeous. And I was scared of her. "We are the Spirit Wielders. The ones who must hide with the humans because of what's become of our realm. Do not fear us, do not forget us. But know that one day we will come back."

"Then why aren't you here now? If you can get into my dreams, if you're truly who you say you are, why aren't you *here* with the rest of us, trying to figure out what's going wrong? Doesn't the realm need you? It's dying. I've seen the people. They say it's because the crystals are fading. Don't they need you?"

"Of course, they do. The Maisons need all five elements to truly thrive. But we can't survive right now in that realm. You will know more when the time is right. But know that you must choose your path."

I turned away from the woman with the dark hair and back to the original woman at twelve o'clock. The figures stationed between the cardinal directions hadn't removed their hoods, and I knew they were likely just there so their powers could be used. They wouldn't speak.

The other woman spoke. "Stay with the light and the darkness. Don't fold. Don't run. Learn the gray."

"And know that others watch you. It is not who you think it is."

I turned to the man that had spoken and screamed as fire erupted all around us. It didn't make any sense. Heat blasted, and the others shrieked. The hairs on my arms singed, and I shook myself, trying to catch my breath as smoke billowed around us. I ducked, my mouth open in a scream, but I didn't have enough air to actually make a sound.

Everything burned.

Everything hurt.

And I didn't understand why.

"Learn the gray. Stay with the light. Stay with the darkness."

All of them spoke at once, and then *they* screamed, the fire erupting. I covered my face, trying to stop what was happening and wake up. But I couldn't. Instead, I opened my eyes and looked around.

Someone had attacked the Spirit Wielders as they had come to me in my dreams. Someone was coming after them. Someone was coming after me.

But who? Who would want to do this?

I looked through the fire, through the smoke that tasted of ash, and I gasped.

It was the crystal.

The dark crystal.

The one from the Obscurité Court.

The one that was dying, yet somehow fed the magic in the Earth territory as the people in turn strengthened it.

Queen Cameo was the one in charge of it, the one who ruled using it, and yet I could see it through the darkness. Whoever was near the crystal at that point had to be the one attacking me. But I didn't know what to do.

And then a dark shadow stepped in front of the crystal, and their arms went out, their magic pouring through them.

Their Wielding far stronger than mine.

Was it the queen?

Was it Easton?

Was it someone I didn't know?

I didn't know what I could do next. I threw up my hands, using my Air, but I knew it wouldn't be enough. I wasn't strong enough for this. I didn't know what I would be able to do, but I was going to need more than one element, more than a few weeks of learning how to prepare myself if I were going to save myself, my friends, and maybe even a kingdom or two.

The figure in front of me raised their hands once more, and fire burned around me.

I screamed. Alone.

The Spirit Wielders had left. Whatever had let them come into my dreams to try and speak to me, to warn me, to confuse me, hadn't been enough against this Fire.

It hadn't been enough against the crystal that might've been fading but had more than enough power to come out to us all.

And as the fire came at me again, the earth rumbling under my feet as if I would fall at any moment, I woke up. My eyes went wide. But I wasn't how I was when I had fallen asleep.

Flames covered my body now, dancing along my skin in an arcing burn. I could feel the heat, sense the singeing of the hairs on my legs and arms, the filaments burning into dust and ash.

I shook my hands, then my legs. A scream almost escaped my mouth, but I blew it away, afraid that I would catch the tent fully on fire or end up burned. But then Rhodes, who I had forgotten had slept next to me, sat up quickly. His arm blazed with fire on his tunic, and he shook it out, not uttering a word as he focused on me.

I sat up, my heart racing, and used the rest of my Air to get the fire off my body, out of the tent, and off the man that I thought I could love.

After his patrol, he had slept next to me, our bodies brushing but not fully touching. He'd wanted to make sure I was safe, and I had been able to truly fall asleep when he was near me. It hadn't meant anything that the dreams came to me when he was there.

It only meant that I had finally been able to sleep deeply because he was close. Because I had felt safe.

And then I had hurt him.

I had burned him because of my dreams.

The fire hadn't completely gone out, and the tent above us still burned. Rhodes used his Water Wielding to put it out completely, but the skin beneath his tunic on his right arm was singed, blisters already forming.

My dreams had hurt him. *Something* had attacked him. *Was* it my dreams? Or was it whoever had tried to attack me through them? It didn't matter. It was dangerous for him to be around me.

"I'm so sorry," I said, finally able to catch my breath. "I didn't mean to hurt you."

He shook his head and reached out to cup my face. "You didn't."

I pulled back, afraid that I'd burn him again with just my touch. I tried to ignore the disappointment in his eyes, but it wasn't easy. "You're bleeding. Your arm is a blister right now. I burned you. Fire Wielding burned you."

He swallowed hard, and I watched his throat work. "It was the dream. Have you unlocked your Fire Wielding? If so, then it might happen. Air has such force, such tenacity, but it's harder to initially hurt someone with it. That's why Fire is such a dangerous element to have. And why so many go crazy when they can't master it. They become insane because of the flames within them, the heat singeing their souls and their minds. Those that harness the Fire have to be so strong, have to almost be cold in the end. It's almost as if they aren't the same person they were when they started. I'm not going to let that happen to you." He cupped my face, and I closed my eyes, leaning into him. I felt like I could breathe with him, even if I was shaking. "I care about you, Lyric. You're a part of me, and I don't know why, and I know it's too soon, and I know we need to worry about the rest of the world before we can worry about us, but I care about you. I'm not going to let the Fire Wielding take you. Okay?"

My heart practically skipped a beat, my body shaking at his words. I knew this was important. Then again, everything was important lately.

I nodded, unable to actually form the words. Did I care about Rhodes? Yes, I had let him sleep next to me, knowing I would be safe in his arms even if he didn't hold me the whole night. I knew that there was something important where he was concerned. I had felt a connection to him from the first time I saw him, and as the days progressed, as the weeks passed, I knew that he was someone important to me. I knew that I wanted him in my life, I just didn't know exactly what that meant. There was so much going on around us that I needed to focus on. I knew that.

But it was hard not to want to focus on him, as well.

He used his Water Wielding to somehow soothe the wound on his arm, and I wanted to cry. My eyes stung, but the tears didn't come. Honestly, I was probably too shocked to cry.

Someone had tried to attack me through my nightmares, and it had hurt Rhodes.

When I explained the dream to him and then explained the rest of my dreams, he had nodded but hadn't come up with an explanation. I hadn't expected him to. Not really. The dreams weren't for him.

They were mine.

But I knew that someone had tried to attack me through them, just as the Spirit Wielders had tried to warn me.

I wasn't going to refute who I was anymore, wasn't going to deny what other people wanted me to be.

They wanted me to be the Spirit Priestess.

I didn't know if that would ever come to pass. I didn't know if I had that type of power. But I was going to help find Rosamond. And I was going to make sure Rhodes was safe. And maybe I could even help find Emory again.

Because right then, I almost felt like it was time for me to go home.

Everything had changed, and everything was going so fast. It was hard to keep up when all I wanted to do was take a break and try to catch my breath—and maybe just go home.

But when I went back to the human realm, would I be the same?

Would home be the same?

Would Emory be the same? Would she even be there? I wasn't sure what to think. A small part of me wanted to run back to find her, to make sure she was safe, but that would never happen. I'd never be able to go back the way she had. And I didn't want to. Not really. The idea of finding her was a small, misguided wish that would likely hurt more than it helped.

I couldn't do that to myself. Couldn't do that to the others. I couldn't do that to Braelynn. I couldn't leave her, not when she was forming something with Luken…and when she was connecting so clearly with the land around us.

Braelynn was fighting. Fighting for herself and smiling and laughing. And truly acting as if she belonged here. Braelynn didn't have a single Wielding aspect to her. She didn't have a connection to a single element, yet sometimes it felt like she was far more connected to this territory, to this kingdom, to this realm than I was.

And maybe that was because Braelynn knew who she was, or at least had an idea of who she could be.

And I was only just beginning to discover those things about myself.

Was I making the wrong choice? Should I leave and let Rhodes use his powers and strength to find his sister? Was I just in the way?

Those had been the questions plaguing me since I first stepped foot in the Maison realm, and yet with the dreams from the Spirit Wielders, and the person that attacked me full-on with Fire, and even the earth rumbling beneath my feet, I knew I couldn't go home.

I might've wanted to turn tail and run, but it wasn't my time.

I had to face whatever was coming head-on.

I had to face the fact that even in my dreams, I could hurt Rhodes.

I had to find the strength and the talent. I had to find the will.

I couldn't run away. I could run far, I could run fast, but I had to run towards the problem, not away from it.

No matter the cost.

CHAPTER 27

The Fire territory was nothing like I'd imagined.

I'd had a lot of time to think about what each of the territories would look like, especially after seeing the lush landscape of the Earth territory. Yes, there had been times when there weren't trees or water within the Earth territory, but most of the land had been the dark browns and tans of dirt, and the dark and light greens of grass and moss. The foliage had been lush, plentiful. Because even as the people were dying, the land seemed to be thriving.

Or maybe that was just the parts I had seen. The realm here was so vast, I knew it would take me months, years, perhaps even a decade to see everything I could see. I had only been on two paths—one to the Earth territory estate, and one back from it to the border. For all I knew, the Earth territory looked completely different on the other side. But from what I had in what the people could do.

So, when I first stepped into the new territory, away from the border where the red rocks loomed stark against the blue sky, and the fire cactuses bloomed, I couldn't quite believe my eyes.

There was everything here: trees, mountains, even a burbling brook.

It wasn't a barren landscape of fire and doom.

This wasn't hell, or what I had thought hell might look like. Because that's what I had imagined the Fire territory would resemble. Lava, pools of fire, ash raining down from the sky. I had no idea why that was what had come to mind, but I couldn't help it. The Earth lands and people had made sense in a way given its name and what I had seen firsthand.

Fire, it seemed, had more complexities.

Yes, the mud and the dirt did have a reddish hue, but then again, so did many lands in the human realm. There were trees, but they weren't as green and thick as the ones in the Earth territory. These seemed to be ones with spindly branches, but they still produced leaves. The shoots weren't as green, but they weren't on fire either.

Even as I thought that, I saw another cactus flower in the far distance, its bloom aflame. I had to wonder if maybe there was a Fire Wielder around, using that blossom for their magic.

Maybe there were trees like the cacti. For some reason, I wanted to see those blooms if they existed.

Looking around, I saw there were plants that had almost pom-poms on them. I remembered seeing trees such as that in a child's book when I was little, and then again for real at a country club I had gone to with a friend. The trees were perfectly pruned, at the club at least. Here, there seemed to be some angles to them, but most of them were round. A pom-pom.

They were the same colors as in the children's book. Dark purples, reds, and browns. The colors of autumn.

And then it hit me. That is what the Fire territory looked like to me. Autumn.

My favorite season. I loved the idea of leather coats and knee boots. I loved hot coffee after a whole season of just iced ones. I loved scarves and gloves. I loved the scent of the changing season that only seemed to happen when autumn came.

The Fire territory didn't smell like autumn, not the way I was used to, but it did seem to scent of something fresh and new, almost rebirth.

That sort of made sense. Because a phoenix could rise out of the ashes, after all.

Rhodes squeezed my hand, and I gave him a look, nodding as we continued on. We were attempting to keep silent, trying not to let anyone really focus on us. Rhodes had used his Water Wielding to somehow dull our powers.

I wasn't sure how he had done it, and he'd said it drained him, but he had wanted to make sure that any others we saw couldn't tell that we were Air or Water Wielders. So now, we all looked like Danes to them, almost like Braelynn.

But he made us look like the Danes who came from the siphoned magic, not like humans born without power.

Luken had explained that Danes were those who were either born without magic or lost the Wielding ability over time. As the crystals faded, so did the Wielding power of those who were weak to begin with. Even some far stronger suddenly lost their magics.

Those were the Danes that others whispered about in quiet and hushed tones when no one else could hear.

I didn't know why, and I wasn't going to ask. Not when even Luken himself seemed a little worried about it.

So, thanks to Rhodes' Water Wielding, we now looked like Danes—even Braelynn who had the same Water Wielding spread over her, so it didn't look like she was human.

After we had slept the night before in our tents, mine now slightly singed, we quickly packed up and let Rhodes use his Wielding. Sweat had beaded on his brow as he worked, and I had wiped it away, wishing I could help. It would have been so much easier for all of us if I had Water Wielding. But instead, I only had my Air Wielding. And while it was helpful and it was gaining strength, and I was acquiring skill, I was still missing four of my other elements.

Rhodes had promised me they would come. But maybe they wouldn't emerge until we found Rosamond and she could help us.

We made our way through a tiny forest and found ourselves near a village. What I saw there almost changed my mind about what Fire Wielders could be. From how the war had sounded in the stories I heard, and the way we had been attacked in the Earth territory as a result of people scared of us—or scared of what was coming—I had assumed that the Fire territory would be just like that.

The Earth territory had people who looked downtrodden, who appeared like they were in pain. As if they had been losing their power day by day—which they had.

Here, children laughed in the street.

Kids with dark red hair, and strawberry blond. Children with black hair, and light chestnut. Youth of every skin tone, and race. All of them living in the Fire territory…and laughing.

They were chasing each other and playing games. All the while, the adults watched the children move, keeping a close eye on them as they worked in their market stalls, or spoke to each other over a meal at a cafe.

There were actual areas where people bought food and ate it. It wasn't like in the human realm with little tables and chairs and servers. But it was a place that people could go to sit down and just relax.

For some reason, I hadn't known that this could exist. This carefree atmosphere. Not here. Not when we had been on the line and fighting just to survive this whole time so far. We had been on this journey, trying to figure out exactly who we were. Or maybe that was just me. Regardless, the people here, they seemed happy. Maybe some of them looked a little tired as if their powers were being leached, or maybe I was just seeing things.

I wanted to ask Rhodes about it, wanted to ask if this is what he had expected. Wanted to inquire if he had seen it before. But there was such animosity between him and the Fire Wielders, I wasn't sure I *could* ask him.

I remembered that boy, that man, Easton, and the way he had glared. The way he had told me to run away. The way that he had called me a little girl.

There'd been something between Rhodes and Easton. Bitterness I knew had a deep history that Rhodes would likely not tell me about. I had tried to ask once, and he had waved me away, saying that Easton was a prince of the Obscurité, and therefore, Rhodes' enemy.

Apparently, it didn't matter that my goal here was to bring these kingdoms together.

Because if the princes were enemies, that meant the war was still going on. And I didn't know what it would mean or take to bring everyone together. I could barely figure out how to make sure I didn't take misstep after misstep. I hadn't been able to keep Emory with us, how was I supposed to hold a whole realm together?

I shook that thought away as Rhodes took my hand, and we kept going. There would be time for dwelling on all that later. I couldn't get ahead of myself.

People nodded at us, some smiling. We did the same back to them as if we were just four Danes walking together from one point of a village to another. I didn't know what others saw when they looked at us, but they didn't run away. They didn't whisper in hushed tones about the strangers that shouldn't be there.

I leaned over to Rhodes and asked him a question. "Are there travelers here often?"

Rhodes looked around and then leaned over to whisper back to me, a smile on his face. I didn't know if it was real or not, considering we were undercover. "Travelers come here often. They trade, they stay overnight. We'll walk through this town and one more before the night. And, if we're lucky, there will be an inn that will take our coin."

I almost sighed at the thought. An inn. A place with a roof. And maybe, if I *was* lucky, a tub.

I hadn't taken a real shower since the Earth territory. And that had been at the estate when I was just trying to figure out how to use their equipment.

Yes, I had taken baths in rivers and lakes and streams, but it wasn't the same. Rhodes had bought me soap made of lavender and other ingredients, so I knew I smelled good, but there was a difference between smelling good and feeling good.

From the way Rhodes winked at me, I had a feeling he knew where my thoughts had gone.

"I hope I didn't moan out loud."

He just shook his head and laughed, and then took my hand again.

I leaned into him, trying to think of this as just a casual walk on a lazy day, not a journey through enemy territory as we tried to find Rhodes' kidnapped sister. If I thought about that, it all seemed too much.

I just wanted to breathe and maybe imagine myself on a date—perhaps a double date with Braelynn and Luken. I knew that wasn't the case, however, and I knew that wasn't how things would end up.

But as we walked out of the little town towards the desert area, I had a feeling that this was just the beginning of the Fire territory. There was even more to come. More that could surprise even Rhodes.

As we walked through the desert, it wasn't like any barren land I knew. It didn't feel like it was too hot or that we were out of water or anything. There was just flat land all around us with no mountains, though I had seen some far in the distance when we first entered the territory.

"This part will be a few miles, but not more than we've done in a day before. We have water, and there's a couple streams up ahead. But there're also the lava pits, so we'll have to be careful."

I tripped over my foot at Rhodes' words, and he caught me. "Lava pits?"

"You didn't really think we'd enter the Fire territory without lava, did you?" His sarcastic tone made me raise a brow.

I continued to walk but gave him a look. "You don't have to make fun of me for not knowing this stuff. I think I'm doing pretty well for being completely new."

Rhodes looked down at me and squeezed my hand before leaning down to brush his lips over mine. I ignored the flutter in my stomach. "I'm sorry. I didn't mean to make light of your question."

"No, I'm just a little touchy. When I was first thinking of the Fire territory, I thought of lava. And then I saw a town with smiling and laughing children and I got a little confused."

Rhodes looked a little confused himself for a moment before giving me a nod, his eyes dark. "There're a lot of different areas in every territory. The town we just passed through is near the border, so they deal with a lot of new people. It also seems strangely untouched by war. At least on the surface. But we're still in the Fire territory, so we need to be careful. I don't know how long the Water Wielding spell I used will last. Probably not much longer. Maybe not even past the morning. So, we're going to have to be on the lookout."

There was an underlying tone of tension beneath his words, and I knew it probably had to do with the fact that we were in enemy territory.

A place that I could one day hold the element of. If I didn't already.

I wondered once again if he'd understand and accept that. If he could deal with the fact that I would eventually hold two elements that weren't his—three if you included Spirit. But I wasn't sure I could, since I had no idea what kind of Wielding that entailed.

The elemental Wieldings in my head at least made sense. I hadn't seen them all in action yet, at least not every aspect of them, but I had seen enough of each to understand the basis of them. I had only seen the Spirit Wielders in my dreams, and even then, they hadn't done more than speak words that made no sense.

According to them, I had to find the gray. Both the light and the dark.

Did that mean I needed to make sure I found all of the elements? Or did that mean I had to ensure that I didn't just stay in one territory at a time?

Or maybe I was just reading too much into words that didn't make any sense at all.

We were just walking across a bridge when Rhodes stopped and pulled me behind him. I frowned but looked under his shoulder, my eyes wide once I saw what he did.

Tiny little flames danced along the desert. If I looked closer, I could see an actual form in them.

These weren't just mini-fires that came out of nowhere.

"Firedrakes," Luken said under his breath. "I didn't think those were still out here." There was awe in his tone, so I looked over at the man. My brows rose.

"Firedrakes?"

Rhodes was the one who answered. "They're like mini dragons that can either make their whole body fire or use the flame like the dragons in your old stories. I didn't think they came down here too much. The queen likes them, and they usually stay near her. These seem to be young, though. They aren't really afraid of people."

I understood what Rhodes meant as two little firedrakes came over to us. I didn't feel the heat as they slid over the bridge and danced around between us like two little squirrels, or maybe tiny dogs trying to yip at us. I wanted to reach down and pet one. Or maybe let it fall asleep in my hands and curl up into a ball. That's how adorable they were. But as I looked up at Rhodes, a smile on my face and a giggle ready to escape my lips, I knew that there was something really different about me.

He had an affinity for Air and Water. He was of Air and Water.

But I wasn't.

The fact that I had always liked fire wasn't something I had told him. But from the way he looked at me, I knew he could see it.

The firedrakes danced between us some more and then kept moving on until they disappeared behind a set of trees. I hoped they would be okay. I was actually a little worried about them. But Rhodes assured me that they would be fine. That this was their natural habitat, and they were safe.

I looked over my shoulder one more time, wondering what the firedrakes would see on their journey, even as I worried about my own, and then I followed Rhodes and the others down the path.

We did indeed stop at an inn in the next town. The shower I took felt like nothing before. There was a fire in the hearth, and embers of flame—also known as Will-o'-the-wisps—lit up the town where they danced in lanterns. It was amazing, all of the ways the people of the Fire territory used flame around them.

Some Fire Wielders used it to cook, others to warm themselves. Still more used it to build and cut things.

It was as if the Fire was part of them, and it wasn't dangerous. I knew I only saw part of it, just like I had only seen part of the Earth territory.

But it all had to mean something.

We had gotten two rooms at the inn, and though I was anxious at first, I ended up sharing with Braelynn and not Rhodes. Rhodes and Luken would share the other, though I knew one of them would likely be in the hallway for most of the night. They would take turns keeping guard like always.

Braelynn and I needed more rest than they did, and we weren't as trained as they were. We were getting better, but sleep would definitely help. We settled into our beds, and I tried to take in everything that had happened so far. Today had been a relatively uneventful day, and yet I had seen so much. And so much still confused me.

"Are you okay?" Braelynn asked.

I blinked at the sound of her voice and turned on my side so I faced her fully. "I am. I think I'm just tired."

"You're right. I'm tired, too. But, Lyric? I feel like we should have been here long before this. It feels like home. Does that make sense?"

I nodded that I did get it, though I wasn't really sure that was a hundred percent true.

"And, Luken? I like him, Lyric. I like him a lot." I'd never heard Braelynn sound so sure of anything. I loved it.

I smiled at my best friend and snuggled into the pillow. "I assumed so. And I like the way he is around you, and the way he's helping you figure out exactly how to fit in here. You're such a strong fighter, Braelynn. It's pretty amazing to watch."

And it was. Braelynn was a far better fighter than I was, though I relied on my Air Wielding more than I did on my fists. For now, at least.

"Lyric?"

"Yes?"

"Maybe the human realm didn't work out for us the way it was supposed to. We both know that we didn't fit in, not the way others did. But maybe... this realm? Maybe this realm could."

Braelynn didn't say anything else, and I didn't say anything in return. What was there to add?

Because I totally agreed with her.

This is where I was meant to be. This is why I couldn't make a decision when it came to anything in the human realm.

But now that I was here, I knew there were more steps I needed to take.

Figuring out what those were, would be the hard part. The part that could take everything I had.

And maybe more.

CHAPTER 28

The next morning, things had changed. Not in a way where the world around me had changed, or even that *I* had changed. But I had a sense that something was different. We were still walking through the Fire territory—hopefully on our way to see Rosamond.

For some reason, I knew we were on the right path. It wasn't as if I'd ever been here before. Or that I knew where I was going. But Rhodes did. And he was so sure of his convictions, I had to believe in him.

Because if I didn't believe in him, I was afraid I wasn't going to believe in much else.

Along the way, the Water Wielding glamour that had washed over us earlier to hide our powers dissipated. Rhodes didn't offer to redo the magic, and I knew it was because he was conserving his strength. We were headed into the unknown, and were already walking through it with our heads held

But that meant that Braelynn looked human, not even like a Dane, and I looked like the Air Wielder I was.

It was odd that I could think of myself as an Air Wielder so soon after not knowing any of this existed. But it wasn't like I could deny it. I could feel the power running through my veins. I could feel the Air dancing on my fingertips as I let the power eke out of my system in that little game Rhodes had taught me.

When Rhodes used his Air Wielding, it was more a sharp caress. He could go slow with it, or he could force the Air and make it into a weapon. He was strategic. Precise.

The fact that he had made that tornado to take care of those sentries back when we first entered the Earth territory told me that he had been angry.

He had been scared.

He had been protecting me.

Luken, on the other hand, was brute force. A weapon. And I really liked how he fought. I didn't think I'd ever be able to fight like him, would never be able to use my Air Wielding like he did. But he was a force to be reckoned with.

He had trained me along the way through the Earth territory on our way to the border. He fought with such strength and determination. It was a little scary to think that he held so much raw power within him.

While Rhodes could add his Water Wielding to his Air or even use his Water Wielding separately, Luken only had his Air Wielding, just like I did. But Luken had years, no…decades of practice. He had trained himself to be the force and weapon he was.

I would never be able to Wield like that, and that was just fine with me. I could fight alongside Luken, and maybe figure out how to pull these broken territories back together.

Rhodes told me that Rosamond would explain everything and tell me exactly what I needed to know. I hoped that was true, because I had no idea what was going on. All I knew was that these people needed help, and if there was a way for me to do that, I would.

We were following a path that Rhodes had found after he talked to a few people who hadn't minded that Rhodes was a prince of the Lumière. In fact, they had seemed to like it.

I didn't understand the politics here, but I knew it was far deeper than one side of a territory or another. The other Wielders, the Fire Wielders, had said they'd seen Rosamond pulled through here. Rhodes was talking to more now, and I moved forward a little just so I could hear. One of the Wielders was tall, wide, and had a scar down his face. The other was smaller, even wider than the first, and had a burn on his chin.

"You saw her here?" Rhodes handed over a coin, and I knew he was paying them for their knowledge. We didn't have many coins, but Rhodes had enough through trade and whatever other means he'd come about it, that we could at least pay for information.

"Yeah, with the guard," the smaller Fire Wielder said, a frown on his face. "But they didn't look like the queen's guard. I don't know who told you they were the queen's guard, but they didn't look like them. They had the leather chest plates. You know, the one with the huge wolf on it. That wolf isn't of the queen. Those are the knight's."

Luken stiffened beside me, and Braelynn leaned into him as if soothing him. I frowned and looked at Luken and then at Rhodes.

Rhodes hadn't reacted to the Fire Wielder's words, at least not physically. But I could tell that whenever those words meant, they weren't good.

Rhodes spoke with the Fire Wielders a bit longer, paid them a bit more, and then we parted ways. I moved closer to Rhodes, not taking his hand but close enough that I could feel the heat of him. We kept going, walking in silence for a few moments before I finally had to speak up.

"What do the wolf symbols mean? Who is the knight?" I kept my voice low in case anyone could overhear us. But we were in a forested area with large trees that burst into flame every once in a while, before going back to looking uncharred. Like a phoenix. There were few buildings and even fewer people. We weren't in the red rock area of the border anymore, nor were we in a true desert like when we had seen the firedrakes. We were going into more diversified land. There were pools of cold liquid that sometimes boiled out of nowhere. There were volcanoes that spewed where I could actually see the lava and feel the heat of it from far away.

Everything was red or black, and yet when the two met, they became beautiful, bright colors that didn't make any sense.

The Fire territory was truly gorgeous, maybe not as lush as the Earth territory, nor was it as barren as the Spirit one, but there was a beauty here that was a sight to behold, a beauty that spoke to me.

A beauty that I didn't want Rhodes to know I recognized.

Maybe that was wrong of me. Maybe I needed him to understand that the Fire called to me just like the Air did. But now wasn't the time. "The wolf means they are guards of the knight. Not the queen." Rhodes' voice brought me out of my thoughts, and I turned to him even as we continued walking.

"And who is the knight? And why do you sound like you're worried?" I reached out and squeezed his hand before letting it go. We were still on guard, and I didn't want us to get distracted. "Weren't we worried before that it was the queen?"

"The queen has one right-hand man. The knight. He is her advisor. Her warrior. Her crude object. Her blunt force. Lore is a bastard. I've always hated him. In fact, some people think he is the reason the queen's husband died. And it wasn't like the stories say."

I almost tripped over my feet at that. "They think the knight killed the queen's husband, the king?"

Rhodes let out a breath. "I don't know. I don't know what the truth is. All I know is that the king's dead. Easton is the prince. And Cameo is the queen here. Her knight is her only advisor, and it said that he spewed poison into her ear. Of course, that could just be what the Lumière say. I don't spend much time in the Obscurité Court. I spend a little more time with the Lumière. Not much these days, though."

I shook my head, utterly confused, and stepped over a rotting log. Rhodes reached out to steady me, but I held my own, my legs stronger, and my balance better than it had been before we started this journey. "But if Lore killed Cameo's husband, why would she keep him at her side?"

"That's a question I'm not sure I can ask. And I sure can't answer. All I know is that if the knight is the one who went after my sister, there's more at play here than them just needing a Seer. And I don't know if these Fire Wielders are right, or if the Earth Wielders were right about the queen. Maybe the queen's guard gave Rosamond over to the knight's guard. I don't know, but I'm not happy either way."

"Why? Beyond the obvious," I added quickly.

"Because Queen Cameo might be the most powerful Wielder in this kingdom, but the knight, Lore, fights dirty. He uses all sorts of magics that no one else will touch. He truly is the evil that others say he is. I'm not saying that he's the poison to Cameo's ear, but he's more dangerous than most people think."

"Then what are we going to do?

"We're going to find my sister."

We kept walking, taking breaks to eat, and only sleeping for an hour or so at a time. There wasn't much time to find Rosamond. We were still so far behind, between everything that had happened in the Earth territory and the fact that I was so much slower than the rest of them—even Braelynn—it was just taking an exorbitant amount of time.

"Do you think it's true?" Luken asked as we sat around the campfire. "Do you think it's true that the knight is actually the queen's soulmate? That it wasn't her husband, the king?"

I blinked. "Soulmate?"

Luken and Rhodes met each other's gazes and looked decidedly uncomfortable. Now, I really needed to know what Luken was talking about, and why he refused to meet my gaze. And why Rhodes now refused to look at me.

"I don't know about the knight and the king and the queen. You know rumors. Everyone seems to spread them, and none more so than at the court itself." Rhodes poked at the fire, using his Water Wielding so no one could see the light from a distance.

"Is there something magical about the soulmates of Wielders?" I asked. "Or are you just saying that the knight and the queen love each other?"

"I don't know if Lore could ever love." Rhodes' voice sounded bitter, and I had no idea why. "But, no. Soulmates are a little different when it comes to Wielders."

"And what are soulmates?" Braelynn asked, speaking up for the first time. She had been sleeping against Luken's side, exhausted after our day. I was tired, too, but it was hard for me to sleep when I had so many different thoughts going through my mind.

"It is said that, with Wielders," Rhodes began, clearly uncomfortable, "and soulmates, there is only one matching soul within all of the lands for each Wielder. Just like in those human and mortal stories of princes and fairy tales and magic. But, like I mentioned, it's a little different when it comes to Wielders."

"How?" My voice was a soft breath. This time, Rhodes finally looked at me. I knew Luken and Braelynn were still staring at us, listening and waiting for what Rhodes had to say. But right then, it was just the two of us. It was a culmination of everything that I'd been thinking about since I first saw him. Since I had first heard about what a Wielder was. Since I had first heard about the magic running through my veins.

"Soulmates create a bond. It's different for each person. For each Wielder. There's only one for each of us within the lands, and most of the time, it's within their own element. But, as we know, the elements tend to meld over time, and that's how we ended up with the territories, how we ended up with the kingdoms themselves. But soulmates are each Wielder's true halves. There's no one else for them. No one stronger, no one they could love and cherish more 'til the end of time."

"You know love doesn't always have to do with soulmates," Luken said, anger in his voice.

I didn't ask what he meant by that because I had a feeling whatever Luken would say about love not entering into the equation with soulmates might hurt him more than any of us. Maybe I would ask Rhodes about it later, but I wouldn't ask Luken. There was pain underneath Luken's anger, and it wasn't my right to know.

"You're right about that," Rhodes said. "But for most, and most of the time, it's someone they truly love. And it's destined. Sometimes, there's a connection right away. Sometimes, the bond takes time. Sometimes, they don't know until it's almost too late. Bonds can create anything between two Wielders. Some can hear each other's thoughts, some know where their other half is across the world. Others can share mortal wounds."

Rhodes finally looked me straight in the eyes, and I saw the hardness there, the heat. "Mortal wounds?"

I didn't know why, out of all the things he'd said, that was what I asked about first.

"It is said the connection is as strong as titanium. As strong as the five elements in one. So, if one of the Wielders is almost slain and they suffer a mortal blow, the wound will appear on the other. I don't know if it actually happens because it's been centuries since anyone's ever documented it. It might just be a myth. But if the connection is there, it could happen."

There was a rustling sound. Out of the corner of my eye, I saw that Luken and Braelynn were walking off together, whispering to one another. But I kept my gaze on Rhodes.

"Why are you looking at me like that?" Once again, my voice was soft, barely a whisper.

"Because ever since I looked at you, I knew there was a connection. A feeling. I know it's important, that you're important not only to this realm but also to me. I hope I'm important to you, as well." He paused. "I just wanted you to know."

And then he didn't let me think. He pressed his lips against mine, and I knew that this was vital.

But before I could ask him more, before I could figure out exactly what had happened, I heard a scream, and both of us were on our feet. I ran behind Rhodes, finally reaching where Luken and Braelynn were headed.

In front of us, the ground had caved in. I looked down into a crevice, tears suddenly streaming down my face as I screamed.

Luken held on to a ledge of the crevice, holding Braelynn to him, and I knew that my friend was hurt, bleeding. But I had no idea how we were going to get out of this.

"Hold on!" Rhodes screamed. "Just hold on," he screamed again at Luken.

I went down to my knees and tried to pull, using all of my strength to try and save Luken and Braelynn. But it wasn't enough. They were being yanked down, much like I had with the Negs while in the mountains. Rhodes might have been strong enough to pull them up, but we couldn't exactly reach them at the best angle either.

Then the ground fell away beneath us, and suddenly, we weren't in the desert anymore. We were at the bottom of a crevice, a swamp under our feet. It smelled of putrid disease and decay. Fire burst out of geysers with irregularity so I couldn't figure out exactly where and when it would come. Luken held Braelynn, her arm close to her chest. It didn't look broken, but they were both bruised. My body hurt from the impact after the fall, but the swamp floor wasn't as hard as the desert would have been.

Rhodes cupped my face, checking for injuries, and then we looked around, trying to figure out exactly how to get out of there. The fire burned, scorching us, licking at our skin. Smoke filled our lungs, and I knew there was no way out. No matter what Air I could use, along with Rhodes and Luken, it wasn't enough.

Somehow, we were in a fire swamp at the bottom of a ravine. It didn't make any sense. Whatever Water Wielding Rhodes used wasn't enough. The walls of the gorge around us started to close in, and I knew that this wasn't natural.

"It's the knight!" Rhodes screamed over the din. "This is his magic. I can taste it. He's the only one with the power to do something like this. We're not going to be able to fight this with anything from Lumière." Then Rhodes looked at me, and I sucked in a breath.

We weren't going to get out of this with anything from Lumière. That meant Air and Water couldn't fight against the knight's magic.

"Why?" I knew he wasn't going to have the answer that I needed. There was nothing I could do. I didn't have any of my Obscurité Kingdom powers. I didn't have Fire and Earth.

I wouldn't be enough.

"The knight uses magic that forces sacrifice. They say he was the one that used the Spirit Wielders. He was the one who took their magic," Rhodes began. "He breaks the greatest taboos and uses Wielding in ways that it isn't meant for. This is him. I know it down to my bones. And we're going to try and climb out of here because I don't know any other way to stop this Fire."

Rhodes kissed me then, putting everything into it, but I pulled back, my arms, my legs, my whole body shaking.

We weren't going to get out of this alive without some form of Fire or Earth Wielding.

And I didn't think the boy we saw before, the Prince of Obscurité, was going to save us this time.

We were going to have to save ourselves.

Or die trying.

Fire burst out of the ground again, and Braelynn screamed, once again holding her arm against herself, a wicked burn across her skin. Luken tried to use his sword to direct his Air Wielding at the flames, but it only made things worse. Rhodes threw himself in front of me, the fire coming at us both. And I just knew that he was going to die.

Sacrifice himself to save me.

I knew that if I didn't do something, my best friend, the boy that I thought I could maybe be connected to—the one that could be my soulmate—and the man that I thought might love my best friend could die.

We could *all* die if I didn't find a way out of this.

My body warmed, my head aching and feeling full.

That's when the earth trembled beneath my feet. This time, it rumbled into my bones and into my heart.

I closed my eyes and thought of the ground around me, the dirt and the soil and the trees.

We were in the Fire territory, but there was earth all around me.

And then I screamed, something unlocking inside of me with such force that I fell back into the rock wall, my teeth clacking, and my jaw tense. I hit my skull hard, and I thought I could see stars behind my eyelids. I knew my head was going to hurt later, that every single bone in my body would feel like it was broken.

But I was going to save my friends.

Because there was no other way out of this.

My body shook once more, the energy and power within me brutally bursting from my skin with such force, I wasn't sure I was even in the same place anymore. That I was myself.

And then I had Earth.

Another power that I didn't understand.

The power that was ours.

A power that was part of everyone.

Yet it was mine.

Mine.

And then the Fire around us was smothered under the soil. I pulled at the rocks and the dirt and everything around us I could use and stamped out that heat. Somehow, I was able to direct it so it didn't hit my friends. Rhodes looked at me, his eyes wide, and I didn't see fear there. But there was *something* I didn't quite understand.

Truth.

Power.

Awe.

My friends came at me, coming close so I didn't have so many areas to protect.

And then we were saved.

All the Fire was gone.

And we were okay.

Rhodes opened his mouth to say something to me, and I tried to figure out exactly what I was thinking. I attempted to stop my hands from shaking, and I wiped blood away from my nose, knowing I had used too much Wielding all at once.

But I had unlocked my second power.

My second element.

I had Earth. I had Air.

And I could be the Spirit Priestess.

And then there was Fire again. A wall of flame that covered us.

And I screamed.

CHAPTER 29

I woke up in a room that had nothing to do with the fire swamp or forest I had been in when the wall of Fire came at us. There were stone walls all around me, charred with soot, the stone itself dark. There were long windows up high, far higher than I could climb or hope to reach. The windows had chains on them that dangled in the wind.

I knew it was daytime because of the light shining through the windows, but I didn't stand in the light.

Instead, I lay in the shadows.

My body hurt as if I had been pushed through a grate, as if I had been pulled through a tunnel. Somehow, the wall of flame had brought us here. And I didn't think it had anything to do with people on long journeys, not like when we had been in the Earth territory.

This was magic I didn't know. This was Wielding I didn't understand.

his eyes closed. I could see the rise and fall of his chest, and I knew that at least he was alive.

I couldn't enjoy the relief I knew was inside me, though. Not when I couldn't see Braelynn or Luken.

Not when I didn't know how we were going to get out of here.

I had saved us from the knight's magic, from the knight's Wielding by unlocking my Earth element.

But, in the end, it hadn't been enough.

Were we now in the knight's clutches? Or were we with Queen Cameo?

I didn't know, but from the scent of fire in the air and the soot all around us, I knew we were still in the Fire territory. It was logically the only place we could be if the wall of flame had brought us here.

I heard a groan to my right, far deeper into the shadows, and I tried to turn my body so I could see who it was.

I held back a moan myself, as I winced at the movement. I hurt too much to even breathe, but I had to see who was behind me. It could be an enemy, or it could be my friends.

Or, it could mean the death of me.

I didn't say a word, but I was somehow able to turn to see who it was. Luken's light hair glinted in the sliver of light that hit him, and I let out a relieved breath.

This time, I could be slightly more relieved. At least I'd found one of them. Luken met my gaze, and I could just barely see him in the shadows, but I knew he was awake. I knew he was alive. And as another bundle moved next to him and his eyes widened before he clutched whoever it was to his chest, I knew it was Braelynn that I couldn't see. I knew that she was alive and awake.

That meant Rhodes was the only one not awake yet. That worried me.

I used up a lot of my strength to get to a kneeling position and crawl to

Rhodes. I put my hand on his cheek. His face was warm and yet clammy. It was so dark in here, I couldn't see the shade of his skin. Because his eyes were closed, I couldn't see that silver. I needed to see that silver. That would tell me we'd be okay.

But his eyes stayed closed.

"Rhodes," I whispered. "Rhodes, wake up. We need you. Wake up. Please." I pleaded, and finally, he slowly opened his eyes.

This time, the relief running through me was like a hammer to a nail. I blinked back tears, annoyed with myself for letting the emotion get to me. But he had been so still, so quiet. Rhodes was only still when he was sleeping. And even then, he rolled from side to side with his dreams. Not the nightmares I had, but I knew he dreamt. I knew he sometimes talked in his sleep, but the words never made any sense.

I wanted to know so much more about him, but I needed him to be fully awake. I needed him to help us get out of here.

I just needed him.

"Lyric?" His voice was a rough rasp, and he coughed before slowly moving himself to a sitting position. I helped him, and then we leaned into each other as we both fought to catch our breaths. Something had knocked us out and had done it so hard that we all looked as if we'd been hit by a battering ram. Soon, Luken and Braelynn made their way over to us, and somehow, we all got to our feet, our legs shaky, our faith even shakier.

"Where are we?" I asked. "Do you know?"

In the sliver of light, I saw Rhodes nod. "We're at the Fire Estate. The Lord and Lady of Fire live here, as does their son. As do a lot of people for that matter."

I reached out and gripped Rhodes' hand, giving it a squeeze. "We got out of the Earth Estate. We can get out of this."

Rhodes' jaw tightened, and he gave me a nod again. "We got out of that because the Lord of Dirt wants something. We're going to get out of this, too. But, that wall of fire? That magic pushed us from one side of the Fire territory to the other. We're on the exact opposite side of the territory from the court. We're opposite of where we need to be to find my sister. And it's going to take us a hell of a long time to get back there. That is, if they even let us out."

"We'll fight." I paused. "Right?"

"We will. You have two elements now, and that has to count for something."

The way he'd said it made me worry because he was always so confident. But something had shaken him, and I needed to know what. I needed all the information if I was going to get out of this. Because things kept changing, and I had no idea what was going on. I hated it, and I loathed being in the dark.

"Then what do we do."

"You come with us." A new voice entered the room, and we all whirled to the person behind us. Fire surged in all of the lanterns around us, illuminating the room in harsh yet warm tones.

A man stood in front of us, his black battle leathers worn as if he had seen the battlefield, but there were red stones—rubies maybe?—on his chest plate. He looked like a regal warrior, and from the way he held himself, I knew this had to be someone high on the hierarchy, if not the Lord of Fire himself.

"Griffin. Why did you bring us here?" Rhodes asked, his voice so rough and angry I almost took a step back.

I knew Rhodes would never hurt me, but I didn't know everything about him. Even though we had spent weeks together at this point, there were so many facets to him that I still needed to know. And he was a warrior—so strong, so deadly. Maybe there were things that I didn't need to know.

"I wondered why you were in my territory. Going after the queen, are you, Rhodes?" the man asked, a grin on his face.

This had to be the Lord of Fire.

"Let us go, I don't have any quarrel with you."

"Of course, you do," the Lord of Fire snapped. "You are Lumière. This is Obscurité. You are our enemy. It's just the way things are. The way things need to be done." There was an undercurrent in this conversation that I didn't understand. Once again, I was two steps back, and I hated it. No matter how many things I learned, no matter how many elements I unlocked, I never seemed to know what I needed to in any situation.

That was going to change. I didn't know how, but as soon as we found Rosamond, I was going to get my answers.

Either that or die trying.

"Come with us." The Lord of Fire turned on his heel, and that was when I noticed a stunning woman with long, dark hair, creamy, brown skin, and dark eyes staring at us. In her black and red robes, I knew this had to be the Lady of Fire. She mesmerized me.

She stared at me as if she had seen a ghost, and I almost took a step back, but I held myself still. I didn't know why she was staring at me, but maybe it was because she knew what I could be. Or perhaps it was because I reminded her of someone. I didn't know, but I really didn't like the way she looked at me.

Then she turned on her heel. Suddenly, the guards were around us, their black leathers similar to the Lord of Fire's—minus the rubies—and we were being led out of the room we had been placed in and into the throne room.

The Lord of Fire took his seat next to his lady. There was an empty seat next to them, and I remembered Rhodes had said there was a child, a lord or prince of Fire.

"So, what are you doing here?" the Lord of Fire asked.

"Griffin, you're the one that sent the magic to us. I didn't know you had learned new tricks."

Griffin smiled and looked pleased with himself. He was a warrior, that much was evident from the scars I could see on his hands and even on his face. He didn't look like a bad man, didn't look like the enemy. But there was something about him that made me not trust him. Then again, I'd just been torn through a wall of fire and shoved into a place I didn't know. There wasn't much trust when it came to any of that.

"Did you like it? Yes, I've been learning new things. Ones that don't require the sacrifices I know most Fire Wielders use. We aren't all barbarians. But, no, it's a new trick, a new Wielding. I didn't realize it would hurt you that much, though. Banged you up a bit, didn't it?" He looked at Rhodes this time, and I almost reached out to grip Rhodes' hand. But I didn't want to put the attention back on me. Of course, the Lady of Fire was still staring at me.

"Shimmer, what's wrong?" Griffin asked his wife, and I looked over at the woman named Shimmer, the Lady of Fire.

"It's her. I know who she is." Then, Shimmer smiled, and I almost went to my knees. She had to be the most beautiful woman I had ever seen in my life. And there was just something about her that drew me in.

And that meant she had to be dangerous.

"Yes, she's with Rhodes. Though the mix of Air and Earth is quite peculiar."

When Griffin looked at me again, I raised my chin. I didn't say anything, but it wasn't like I needed to.

"Spirit Priestess," Shimmer whispered.

"Truly?" Griffin's eyes went wide, and he almost took a step towards us before Rhodes put his body between us and the thrones.

"Let us go. We need to get my sister, and then we'll leave your territory. I know it's not your fault that your queen took Rosamond. But as soon as we get her, we'll leave. And then it won't be an act of war between the two kingdoms."

Griffin narrowed his eyes and waved Rhodes off. "We've been at war for centuries, boy. There can't be a declaration of what's already begun. But, now that I see you have a Dane with you as well as the possible Spirit Priestess, I guess it makes sense that you should see this." He snapped his fingers, and the guards brought in a chained and shackled person covered in a tunic and a long robe. Whoever it was, was small and didn't say anything. Instead, they allowed themselves to be dragged into the space between the three thrones and the four of us.

But when the person in the robe threw back their hood, I almost fell, my mouth dropped open in shock.

"Emory?"

No. It couldn't be. Emory had to be home. We would have heard something by now if she weren't. This couldn't be happening. I shouldn't have let her leave. I shouldn't have made her come at all. I should have made her stay.

I should have done something other than let her get under my skin like she always did.

Now she was shackled here in the Fire territory. Yet there was something… different about her.

Emory met my gaze, and her eyes narrowed. There was evil in those depths that made my skin crawl.

There was darkness, something putrid, something stark.

"We found your friend it seems. Emory, is it? She wouldn't tell us her name. Of course, she's an adnomination. The Earth Wielders forced *something* into her system, and now she's different. But she used to be a Dane, that much is clear. Or maybe human?"

The Lord of Fire looked over at Braelynn and gave us a nod.

"Maybe she was human. But that human girl you have next to you, I think she might be more of a Dane than you think. Not that it matters."

"What?" Braelynn asked.

"You, you aren't fully human. Are you? But that doesn't matter now. Your friend? Emory? She isn't human anymore, either. Whatever took her, as you say, forced an Earth Wielder's power into her. And then she was sent here to take some of our power from our stores."

I just stared at my friend as she thrashed against her shackles. But she didn't fight against those who chained her. Instead, she kept lunging at me as if she wanted to come at me.

"I hope you die," Emory screamed. "You're the one who did this. It's all your fault. If you had just been good and stayed… But, no, you had to save the world. Perfect Lyric and her perfect life. Nothing is ever good enough for you. You thought you could love a woman? No. Now, you just have to love the cutest boy in town. Now, you think you're something special? You're nothing. I'm the one who's special. I'm the one with this Earth power. Maybe I'm the Spirit Priestess. Maybe you're nothing. It doesn't matter, though, because you left me."

I just blinked at her, trying to catch up with her words. This didn't make any sense. I knew she'd changed, I knew she'd started down this path long before she was forced into this new version of herself, but I still couldn't quite believe what I saw and heard. "You left *us*. What happened? Why did you go?"

"You didn't give me a choice. You never do. You're nothing, just like your little friend Braelynn here. But that's fine, I'm doing just fine."

She said this while chained and looking as if she had truly gone insane. I didn't understand it. I didn't understand anything.

"The Fire and Earth territories are fighting now?" Rhodes asked, his voice susceptibly calm. "I thought you were allies and under the queen's rule."

"A lot's changed since you've been gone, boy. You spent so long looking for the Spirit Priestess that you seem to have forgotten that our people needed the warriors. Instead, we have pirates and people dying all around us. People who think they can take the Wielding and the magic. People who try to add Wielding that they stole from others as they killed them. People who try to take that Wielding and force it into humans. There's so much you're missing, boy. But it's fine. You can go back home to your little Lumière and pretend that we're the only bad guys around."

"Griffin, take a breath, please." Shimmer looked over at her husband and then reached out and patted his hand.

Then she looked over at me, and I forced my gaze away from Emory and her hatred.

Shimmer gave me a small smile, and I held back a frown at the action. "My son, Teagan, would have liked to meet you. He's a warrior, just like your Rhodes, just like Luken here. I know there are things you don't understand, but it is a blessing that you are here. You're the one who will save us, that much I know."

I did not understand this woman or her motivations. The Fire Estate had my friend chained up, my ex who had been irrevocably changed, and I didn't understand why.

"If you want us to stop fighting, why do you have Emory chained?" My voice sounded steady, but I was anything but.

"Because your friend here is a siphon. Whatever they did to her, she can now leach powers from others. The chains that she's in keep her at bay. I don't know what the Earth Wielders who changed her were planning, and I don't even know if it was actually Earth Wielders that did it. She's keeping quite mum on the subject. But don't worry, we have ways of getting answers."

"She's our friend," I whispered. I cleared my throat and forced my voice to be stronger. "We didn't know she was here. Let us take her with us, we'll figure out what to do. But let us keep our friend."

Emory spat at me, her eyes filled with a fire that wasn't an element but pure hatred.

"Screw you. I want nothing to do with you. You left me to be taken."

"No, you're the one that left." I shook my head. "We never wanted you hurt."

Emory narrowed her eyes and then shrugged her shoulders. "Whatever. I found who actually cares about me. And when they come for me. You'll all be sorry."

The Lord of Fire rolled his eyes and let out a large sigh before snapping his fingers.

Emory vanished in a puff of smoke, and I fell to my knees, screaming. "No!" Blood rushed to my face, and my ears pounded to the beat of my pulse.

"What have you done?" Braelynn asked. "What did you do to Emory?"

Tears streamed down my face, and I reached out my hand toward the ash where my friend had just been. Emory. Emory was gone. Again.

What was going on?

"It's fine," Griffin said softly. "I don't actually burn people to ash just because they annoy me. She's just in the dungeon."

"Nice display of power there," another voice said as the body behind it strolled into the room. I leapt up to my feet, wiping my tears as I stood by Rhodes' side.

Easton came in, a sneer on his face. I hated that look. "Hey, fam. Thanks for letting me know that you found the one my mother is looking for. Mom's really looking forward to seeing you all."

"You've got to be kidding me, Easton," Rhodes snapped. "You're working for your mother now? I thought you were out there looking for the Spirit Priestess. I thought that something mattered to you beyond just these petty differences."

Easton met Rhodes' gaze for a moment before moving to face me. "I told you, you should have left, girl. You know it's not safe here."

Unbelievable. "You're taking us to the enemy. I guess you're the one who's making it not safe."

I raised my chin and met his gaze. His eyes were so dark, so black that I felt as if he could see into my soul. There was something about him that unnerved me, something that made me want to take a step back, yet move forward at the same time.

"You don't know what you're talking about. I'm here to protect you all. My mother is not who you think she is. And the man beside you? He's not who you think he is either. Nothing is. You've only been told one side of the story. Maybe if you open your eyes, you would see the other side. Or maybe you're just too young and foolish to truly understand anything."

"Shut up," Rhodes snapped. "Shut up. You don't know what you're talking about. Your mother took my sister. She kidnapped her. She sent the Negs after us. We've been traveling for *weeks* trying to get to her. And everything that comes at us is because of your mother's kingdom."

"And you're the one in the wrong kingdom, right, Rhodes? You're the one in the so-called enemy territory. My mother had nothing to do with this. My mother wants to save this realm. And just because you think you found the Spirit Priestess, doesn't mean you really want to save us."

Easton looked at me then. "Why don't you ask him, Lyric? Why don't you ask him why he wants you."

"I don't have to ask him. I already know."

He wanted me because of our connection.

He wanted me to save the kingdoms.

He wanted me to save the realm.

Because it was mine as much as it was his. Like Brae had said, I didn't belong where I thought I did this entire time. I belonged here.

Easton just glared at me and then shook his head.

"You'll learn. You'll learn because you have to."

And then he held out his hands, smoke billowing between them, and I could see the dark crystal in the shadows. The symbol that had been haunting my dreams. The one that had tried to kill me before.

Had Easton been the shadow before?

Had he been the one to hurt me?

Or had it been the knight? Or the queen?

It didn't matter because as soon as Easton snapped his fingers, we weren't in the Fire Estate any longer.

We had made it to the Obscurité Court.

Now, everything would change.

CHAPTER 30

O nce again, we had been pulled into a new place, but this time, it didn't feel like my bones were broken along the way. Rhodes reached out, gripping my hand, pulling me closer to him. Easton stood in front of us, his gaze narrowing at the contact, and it took everything within me not to just roll my eyes at him or even flip him off.

Why did he care so much that I was here?

Why did he want me to leave?

There had to be a reason. Easton always called me "girl" or "little girl," always told me to leave. I didn't want to know the answer to his motives. I didn't want to hear anything he had to say honestly.

His mother was the reason Rosamond had been taken. His mother and maybe even the knight. Because if the knight were her right-hand man, then she had to know what was going on.

Braelynn and Luken were behind us, not saying a word, but I knew they were there, waiting. Braelynn's hand was on the edge of her dagger, and I knew everyone else, including me, was ready to use our Wielding.

I didn't know where we were, but I had a feeling Easton had taken us to the court.

Because I had never seen anything as glamorous as this.

Everything was clean and sparkling under the lights. There was dark marble tile on the ground and dark stone on the walls.

It made sense that everything was dark here, this was the Obscurité, after all, the dark kingdom. But nothing seemed shadowed or dirty. Instead, the marble glittered as if the stone itself held opulence.

Draperies hung on the windows—black, silver, and even white that made it all stand out against the darkness. Everything was wrought iron and black crystal with just a little bit of white and silver to balance.

I had no idea what the Lumière Kingdom would look like if I ever made it there, but the court of the Obscurité Kingdom was something out of my dreams.

And now that I thought about it, maybe I had dreamt of this once. Perhaps I had seen all of this. I knew this wasn't a dream anymore, not with the pain in my side and the aches of my body for the past few weeks.

This was all too real. And Easton had brought us here.

It had to be the court. There was nowhere else we could go, not if he was taking us to his mother, the queen.

"You can change if you want to, and I'll have some food brought 'round."

"So, you're going to feed us before you torture us?" I asked, no idea where the words had come from.

Easton narrowed his eyes and then snorted. "I'm not going to torture you. I brought you here because my mother asked to see you. I brought the others here because they were trespassing."

Why had I been singled out? Why did the queen want to see me?

Did she truly have Rosamond? And if she did, what had Rosamond Seen and told the queen?

Or, maybe the queen had heard I was a Spirit Priestess. After all, others had already noticed who I was. And it wouldn't take long for word to travel. Word traveled faster than people.

"We don't need anything from you, Easton." Rhodes glared at Easton, and I just looked between the two men, noticing their similarities, yet knowing that there was so much difference between them.

"You can do whatever the heck you want," Easton said, his tone leisurely. "I don't care. All I care about is that you're spreading rumors about my mom. About my queen. You don't have loyalty to your court, I do."

"You're out of line," Luken snapped. "He's the Prince of Lumière. He has more loyalty in his pinky than you will ever have."

Easton glared at Luken and shook his head. "You say that, but when's the last time he's been to his court?"

"Keeping tabs on me now, Easton?" Rhodes asked. There was such anger in his tone that I squeezed his hand. I didn't know how to give comfort, but at least I was here. Of course, I had no idea how I had ended up here.

But that was par for the course these days.

"We always keep tabs on our enemies, isn't that right, Rhodes?" Easton asked. "But, really, he looks like he hasn't showered in weeks, and he looks exhausted. Just change. Eat. I'll even eat in front of you so you know the food's not poisoned. We're not the ones you need to worry about with that. Isn't that right? Isn't that what your dear uncle likes to do?"

"Stop talking about my family, Easton."

"And stop calling my mother the names I know you're thinking. And don't blame her for the loss of your sister."

There was such animosity between the guys that it was all I could do not to step between them and tell them to stop. Luckily though, Luken did that for us.

"I'll take the new leathers. After all, taking anything from you guys so you don't have it is a good thing, I don't mind."

Easton just rolled his eyes and led the way to another set of doors.

Again, we changed, just like we had in the Earth territory. We hadn't been at the Fire Estate long enough to change or even eat. Easton had taken us away in such a blur of movement, I hadn't been able to even get my thoughts in order.

We had left Emory behind, but it hadn't been the Emory I remembered. I had no idea when we were going to get her back, or if we could. She hated me.

But could I blame her?

In a way, we had left her. I had left her.

And now, she wasn't herself anymore.

I knew I had been planning to phase her out of my life before this, but I hadn't meant for it to happen this way. There had been no way I'd thought it *could* happen this way.

"Stop blaming yourself," Braelynn whispered. "I know you're thinking about Emory."

I turned to look at Braelynn, who had changed into soft gray leathers. Almost a dove gray. She had her dagger on her hip—the one Luken had found for her. She had braided her hair back, much like I had done with mine, and she looked far more like a warrior than she had a few weeks ago. Weeks. It seemed like years at this point.

"I still should have tried to help her."

"You say that, but there was no helping her, and no stopping her. There never was. And while I know we're all going to blame ourselves just a little bit for not going after her, we both knew we needed to be where we were at the time. We're finally close to Rosamond. We're finally close to saving her. Maybe we can go and save Emory, as well. But she's the one who left. She's going to have to take some responsibility."

I shook my head, fastening my leather pants. My leathers looked just like Braelynn's, but they were black. In fact, they were the same color and design as Easton's. I had to wonder if the man had done that on purpose just to annoy Rhodes.

The two seem to enjoy irritating each other.

"I can't blame the victim," I said, my voice soft.

"No, but you can make someone responsible for their actions, and then we can hit the people who did that to her. We can save her. But first, I think we have to save ourselves."

I nodded and then held my best friend, wondering once again what we were going to do.

Rhodes came into the room, Luken right behind him. Luken and Rhodes both wore dark brown leathers and looked like a matching pair, Braelynn and I seemed separate.

I had to wonder what the reason behind that was. Or maybe I was just looking into things too deeply.

I tended to do that when I was out of my depth.

"Are you ready to eat with the Prince of Obscurité?" Rhodes asked before leaning down and brushing my lips with his.

I held myself back from leaning into him, knowing we didn't have time for anything more. Not that we had done anything more. I wasn't anywhere near ready for that, and I wasn't sure I ever would be, considering we hadn't stopped moving for weeks.

"Why are we here?"

"Because the queen wants to see you. I think she knows you're the Spirit

Priestess."

I nodded in agreement. "I guess that's a good answer for why we're here."

"It'll be okay. We'll meet with the queen. We'll get Rosamond. And then we'll go back to the Lumière Kingdom."

"I've never been there before. I guess I won't be going back to the human realm."

"Are you okay with that, Lyric? That we're going to the Lumière Court after this? Unless Rosamond has us going somewhere else, I think it's the best place to go. I don't know when we're going back to the human realm. Your parents are surely missing you at this point."

I nodded, knowing that he was right. I was afraid that my parents might be launching a full-scale search for me by now. Braelynn, as well. And what were we going to tell Emory's parents if we ever got back?

If.

"I suppose we'll figure all of that out when we get there. First, I guess it's dinner with royalty."

"You've been having dinner with royalty every night since you came here," Luken mumbled.

I knew that was true, but this felt different. Everything felt different.

We sat at a large, opulent table of dark stone and diamond. Crystals lined the walls and practically shone under the lights. This was the Royal Court of Earth and Fire. That meant the guards around me could rumble the earth, could play with the flame and could dance within both.

And while I had one of those elements, this didn't feel like home.

I didn't know if the Lumière Kingdom would either.

If my role here was connected to both, how was either supposed to feel like home when they were jagged pieces of themselves?

"You know, you can take a bite, it's not going to kill you." Easton glared at me from the other end of the table, and I took a bite then, my gaze never breaking from his. It was roast beef covered in gravy, with a side of potatoes.

And it had to be the most decadent thing I'd had in years.

It took everything within me not to just shove my face into my plate and eat it all in one bite.

But I had to look like a lady. Or a Spirit Priestess. Or at least appear like I didn't want to just shove everything into my mouth.

"Nice. Our cook knows what he's doing."

"Is your mother going to grace us with her presence?" Rhodes asked. He had nibbled a few bites, so I'd known that nothing would poison us. Plus, I didn't really think that was Easton's plan. At least not yet.

Maybe I would poison *him*—if he annoyed me enough.

"She'll be here soon. She had matters to discuss with her knight."

I met Rhodes' gaze, and he gave me a tight nod.

Easton didn't miss the look between us, but I ignored him. I ignored most things when it came to Easton. There was just something about him that set my teeth on edge. I didn't trust him, that much I knew, but still…

"Your court doesn't look any worse for wear, considering that your people are dying."

Easton glared at Rhodes at that statement. "I know my people are dying. Why do you think I'm out there? I gave up hope while looking for the Spirit Priestess. The more I left, the more I abandoned my own people. And, unlike you, I needed to focus on those that I could actually help rather than looking for a fairy tale."

"And yet, I found her, didn't I?"

I whipped around to Rhodes at that statement. So, we were just going to come out with it then? Just let everyone know who I was?

"You say she is, and maybe that's true. Good for you. Because the Spirit

Priestess isn't on one side or the other, isn't that right, Rhodes?"

Easton glanced at me, his dark eyes vibrant. "If you are the Spirit Priestess, you are supposed to unite us. I can already feel the Earth element within you. You can wield that and Air? Because you didn't have Earth before. That means you're almost halfway through your Unlocking. If you are a Spirit Priestess, you aren't on the Lumière's side. You aren't on the Obscurité's side. You're on the side of the Maisons. Remember that. Remember that you're neutral. You are peace. And don't listen to the vitriol that Rhodes puts out."

"That's enough," Rhodes snapped.

I shook my head. "Maybe it's not," I said, my voice calm though I was anything but. Rhodes glanced at me, and I shook my head. "I don't know my purpose. And I'm tired of feeling like I'm falling behind."

"We just need Rosamond," Rhodes said.

"You haven't told her anything?" Easton asked. "You're waiting for your precious sister, the one you think my mother kidnapped?"

"She did. The Negs she sent scented of Earth and Fire. We tracked the trail to the border, and others said they saw your mother's guards with the knight's guards, and that's who took her. That's why we're here. It's not just rumors."

Easton sat still for a moment, and I wondered what he was thinking.

I reached out and put my hand on Rhodes' thigh, giving it a squeeze. He reached down and did the same to my hand before we both let go.

Once again, Easton didn't miss the movement. Once again, I didn't care.

"This court isn't what you think it is," Easton whispered. "It never was. I just don't understand why you don't see that, Rhodes."

Before I could ask why Easton sounded so different just then, the doors opened, and a woman who looked much like the Lady of Earth walked into the dining room.

Easton stood, and the guards went straight to attention. And though she wasn't my queen, I rose, as well. My friends did as I did, but I knew it wasn't for the respect that Easton and the guards were giving the queen. I didn't even know if I was giving her respect. I just knew that this was a queen, she was the queen of one of my elements.

She might not be my queen, but right then, I had to see who she was. Her long, dark hair fell in waves. Her skin was visibly soft, her cheekbones straight and edged. She had Easton's eyes, a black that seemed to see into a person's spirit. She wore robes of night—dark purples and midnight blues with blacks and silvers. Silver moons were etched and sewn into her cape, and her crown was made of deeply colored crystals.

They looked so much like the dark crystal I had seen in my dreams, the same one that had brought us here to the court. I almost gasped.

But it wasn't the same crystal.

The crown itself had diamonds and other gems, but everything was dark, everything was midnight-hued.

This was the Queen of Obscurité.

Rhodes' enemy.

And yet, this could be my future.

I didn't know why I thought that. I wasn't a queen, I wasn't ever going to *be* a queen. But this person had something to do with my future, the whispers in my head, those of the Spirit Wielders in my dreams, told me so.

Maybe I was losing my mind, but there was a reason I was here.

There was a reason for everything.

"Where's my sister?" Rhodes asked, his voice sharp.

Easton opened his mouth to speak, most likely to yell at Rhodes for daring to talk to his mother in that way, but Cameo held up her hand to silence her son.

Confusion slid over the queen's face, and she shook her head.

"I do not have your sister, Rhodes. Why these lies?"

"The others say you took her. The Negs who took her smelled of your land. You know my sister's a Seer, the strongest there is. Why else would you have taken her?"

The queen shook her head again. "We do not have her."

We.

She and the knight? Or her and Easton? Were these lies? Or maybe the knight had taken Rosamond, and Cameo didn't know. Or maybe the queen was a skilled liar.

And then Cameo looked directly at me and stared.

I stood up straight and was thankful that Rhodes hadn't stepped between us. I needed to stand on my own, had to fight my own battles. But I knew from the way that Rhodes held himself, it was taking every fiber of his being not to protect me.

"You are the Priestess. I should've known you'd come."

"You say that, and yet Easton says you wanted to see me. That doesn't make any sense."

"No, I meant you came to the Maison realm. What's left of it, that is. You're the one who's going to save us all. I was afraid that you were forever lost to us. I was frightened the others had found you and took you away. I'm glad that isn't the case."

"Are you saying that the King of Lumière wants Lyric dead?" Rhodes asked. "Because from the way your kingdom's been acting, I have to say it's more likely the opposite."

Queen Cameo shook her head. "My kingdom is dying because the crystal is fading. The crystal is dimming because my father and your grandfather decided it was better to fight in a battle that had no winners. Our world is disappearing because men decided to toss away their histories in order to subjugate those who were weaker than them. Or at least those they thought were weaker than them. I want my kingdom to flourish. I want the Maison realm back. And I will do anything to make that happen."

"Anything? Including kidnapping a Seer?"

"I didn't kidnap Rosamond. I would never touch a Seer. I cannot touch that magic, and know never to trust my own with it. To hold a Seer against her will is to ask for death."

"So you say," Rhodes snapped.

Easton was quiet, his gaze on me the entire time. It was unnerving, and I wanted him to stop. But before I could say anything, another man walked in.

This man, I knew. I had seen him in my nightmares. I'd seen him strip the powers from others when I had thought it was only a dream.

His skin was pale, so white it almost looked translucent. He had a dark widow's peak of long, black hair that fell past his shoulders. His eyes were a green so vivid it looked like the Earth powers themselves.

This was the knight.

The queen's knight.

"You brought her," the knight, Lore, said to Easton.

I looked at Easton then, wondering why I felt betrayed. I shouldn't feel that way. Easton wasn't on my side.

Rhodes was.

"What?" Easton asked, confusion in his tone.

"The Spirit Priestess is here. Let the prophecy unite us."

The knight threw his head back and laughed.

And then the screams began.

CHAPTER 31

Rhodes pushed me to the ground, knocking the breath out of my lungs. Then he rolled on top of me, coming to his feet above me.

I glared at him, wanting to know why he pushed me out of the way when I could fight for myself, and then I looked up at the knight.

The man looked the same as he had when he first walked into the dining room, but his eyes were different.

There was an evil in them, something that spoke of danger.

And I knew this was the man I had seen in my dreams, the one who had burned Rhodes and me.

This was the enemy.

I didn't know if anyone else in this room was, but this was the foe that I knew I needed to fight right then.

"What's the meaning of this?" Cameo asked, wiping the blood from the corner of her mouth. The screams had come from Braelynn and the queen when the knight had flung out his arms, tossing Fire and Earth towards us. Chunks of granite from the walls and other stones came at all of us in the explosion.

Luken had used his sword to knock the fire out of the way, his Air Wielding strong.

But Braelynn had been burned again. It didn't matter how good of a fighter Braelynn was, she was still human—or maybe she was a Dane. I didn't know, none of us did for sure, but this wasn't a fight that Braelynn should be a part of. I wasn't even sure this was a fight *I* should be a part of.

"Like you don't know what I've been doing all this time. You may play the innocent queen, Cameo, the one who fights to protect her people, but you're just as ruthless as anyone." The knight glared at his queen and then tossed another bout of Fire Wielding towards us.

Easton moved in quicker than the rest of us could, throwing up his hands and blocking the Fire with his own Fire Wielding.

The queen had also put up her hands, but Easton was faster.

He was protecting his mother, his queen, and yet there was just something in the way the knight held himself. I wasn't sure it was all going to be okay in the end. We might not be strong enough to defeat this guy, even as a united front.

I might not know much about what was going on, but I knew that look in his eyes.

I knew the danger that was to come.

The queen raised her chin. "I know nothing. Nothing of what you speak. You took that girl, didn't you? You took the Seer."

Rhodes growled, taking a step forward. I was already on my feet when I put my hand on his arm, knowing that he needed to see what the knight was up to. We couldn't hurt him or kill him just then. Not until he told us where Rosamond was. Or what else he had planned. Because if I knew anything, he had far more planned than just tossing around a few pieces of furniture and Wielding flames with his fingertips.

There was something far darker going on beneath the surface. There always had been. Ever since I had my first dream, ever since I stepped into the Spirit territory.

"Seer? Whatever do you mean, my queen?" The knight threw up his hands, and a wall of dirt slid between us. But the particles were so fine, we could see through it. It was as if he had made each molecule tiny so it would protect him from the other elements, but we could still see what he was doing.

I didn't even know that type of Wielding existed, and from the look on Luken's face, he hadn't either. Yet the queen, Easton, and Rhodes didn't look surprised. Maybe they had seen this type of Wielding before. Maybe the two Obscurité royals could do it themselves.

"You're lying," Rhodes shouted. "Where is my sister?"

Lore glared at us, pink and blue Fire coming to life at his fingertips again. "You've sure journeyed a long way for just a rumor."

"It wasn't a rumor," I put in. "Rhodes said the Negs smelled of this territory. Of this kingdom. And from the way you're acting, it was you."

"You've got a lot to learn, girl," Lore spat. I resisted looking at Easton.

When Easton called me "girl," it annoyed me. When Lore did it just then, it made my skin crawl. There was a difference between being arrogant and being pure evil.

I really wish I didn't know the difference between the two.

"Tell us where she is," Easton said, his voice low and a little dangerous.

"I don't have to tell you anything. I've been working for the queen for longer than you've been alive, *my prince*." He sneered the last two words, and I wanted to turn my Air Wielding at him. I didn't know how to use the Earth Wielding. I'd only used it in a time of terror and pressure.

I had no idea who was even going to train me. It wasn't like I could ask for help.

I only knew my Air Wielding, and I knew I had to rely on the others around me to get it done.

"I've been working for the queen as her dear knight for so long, sometimes, I almost forget exactly why I took the position."

Cameo scoffed. "You took the position because you had nothing else. You took it because you wanted to be my king and I had already found my soulmate. Zeke was mine. He was my king. And even though he wasn't as strong as you when it comes to Wielding, he was stronger of the heart, and you never liked that."

Cameo was tapping into a history far older than the war, something beyond the Fall. I really didn't want to be part of a lovers' quarrel. All I wanted to do was find Rhodes and go home. Then I would come back and try to save this realm. Save my ex. But really, I just wanted my own bed, I wanted my mesh jacket. I just wanted to be home.

But I didn't think there was any getting out of this kind of bad.

"Zeke was just too weak." Lore laughed. "Huh, I wonder why it took me so long to come up with that rhyme. Probably should have come up with it a couple hundred years before this. It doesn't matter because he's dead. And I'm the one who killed him."

He threw his head back and laughed, and Easton lunged at him, the need for retribution clear on his face. Cameo held her son back, throwing up a wall of Earth touching Fire to protect her son.

And from what I saw, it wasn't that she didn't want Easton to attack, it was that Lore had been ready. Fire streams pierced the thin layer of Earth and wrapped its tendrils around the blockade that Cameo had put up. If Easton had been there, if she hadn't been quick enough, Cameo's son might have died.

Because I knew putting your emotions into your Wielding could sometimes lead to disaster. And if Eason was focused on the fact that the knight had killed his father? He probably wouldn't have been thinking clearly enough to protect himself from the knight's Wielding.

I looked at the terror on Easton's face, the pain on Cameo's, and I knew that Lore would not survive this day.

But, hopefully, we would find out what his plans were, and where he put Rosamond before his life ended.

From the way he glared at me, I knew that if I had a chance, I would probably kill Lore, as well. I'd never killed anyone before, not that I knew. Because I didn't know if using my power when I first gained Air had hurt anyone. I didn't know if I had hurt anyone or worse when I tried to save my friends. And yet, I knew I wouldn't feel guilty about this. I couldn't. Not with what I could see in the knight's eyes.

"Zeke was in my way, and now he's dead. You wouldn't take me as your king, you kept me as your knight. And now you're going to get what you deserve. I should have been King of Obscurité. I was the one with the plans. You were the one who was too weak to fight the Lumieré."

Cameo shook her head, a single tear falling down her cheek. But the rest of her face was pure hatred, utter anger. She was going to kill him and make it slow.

"I should have let you go when I had the chance. But it is always good to keep your enemies close. I just didn't know what kind of enemy you were, I didn't know the depth of your vile lies."

Lore tilted his head to the side and laughed, looking like the villain he was. "Oh, shut up, *Your Highness*. You've always been too weak to make the decisions that matter. It's just like a woman, waiting for a man to do what's needed."

"Shut up." Once again, there was an edge to Easton's voice.

"Where is my sister, you bastard?" Rhodes asked again, bringing the knight's attention to us. "I'm sure the queen and her prince are going to kill you. Before they do, I want to know where you took my sister. And why."

"Fine, I guess you have me. I guess you all do. Of course, I took Rosamond. She's the best Seer in the entire realm. She's the best Seer of all time. And she wouldn't tell me a damn thing, if that makes you happy. But I still have time, and I'll make her talk. I'll make her tell me what she's Seen."

My blood grew cold, and I barely resisted the urge to grab Rhodes' hand. We needed our hands free to protect ourselves and use our Wielding.

At least we knew Rosamond was alive.

But I didn't know what might have been done to her in the time we were apart.

I didn't know Rosamond as well as I did Rhodes and the others. But she had been nice to me. She had tried to be my friend. I know it might have been because she thought I was the Spirit Priestess, but I knew there was something else beneath all of that, too.

Lore would pay for what he had done.

"So, what is your endgame here?" Easton asked, his voice sounding bored. "You were just going to become King of Obscurité and rule us all? I don't think so. You have something more planned. Why don't you just tell us what it is and lord it over us? You know you want to. After all, you say you're the strongest Wielder in the world. You're going to want to prove that. But, really, I know you'll feel better if you just tell us."

I looked over at Easton, wondering what the hell he was thinking, goading the knight like that. But then again, we needed to know what the rest of Lore's plans were. And I didn't think he was going to get out of here alive for us to ask him later.

"The crystal is dying, dimming because of the poor decision-making of your mother and that bastard's uncle." Lore gestured towards Rhodes, and Rhodes raised his chin.

"You're saying that you could have taken down my uncle before this?"

"I'm saying that *she* should have done that long before this. We would have had one kingdom, one court. Instead, we have two thrones, and it's destroying us all. We're too weak to do anything. That's why I used the crystal like I did."

I saw the others stiffen as I tried to figure out what Lore was saying. "What do you mean?" I knew I wasn't going to like his answer, but I needed to hear it.

The Spirit Wielders whispered in my ear again, and I closed my eyes as I listened.

Make sure he pays for what he's done.

Make sure he pays.

Protect yourself.

You're the voice of reason.

Know that there are answers.

"The crystal needed help. And because the crystal doesn't discriminate, I had to be the one who did."

"What have you done?" Easton asked, his voice a growl.

"I did what had to be done. Those weak didn't deserve the powers they held. So, I took them away. I stripped them and gave them to the crystal."

And to himself.

He didn't have to say it, but I knew that was what had happened.

There was no way he could be this strong without it. Because even I could feel the depth of his depravity and the strength of the power within him.

And if I could sense it, the others in this room with far more experience could definitely tell.

"How could you?" Queen Cameo asked, her voice razor sharp. "Those are our people. And you stripped them of their Wielding? That's part of their soul."

"I did what had to be done," Lore repeated. "I did it because you were too weak to do it. If you were any type of leader, you'd have used the crystal when you should have. Those who were too weak to actually hold onto their Wielding deserved what they got. If I didn't kill them, they'd just end up killing themselves. And that is evolution, isn't it? They die, and we lose the weak. And our kingdom is stronger for it. The crystal is stronger for it. And then, in the end, we'll be stronger than all the Lumière. And we will fight them. And we will kill them. And we will be the only court that matters."

This man had truly lost his mind.

All those people I had seen in the Earth territory, even in the Fire lands that looked downtrodden, sad, and sick. Who looked as if part of their lives had been stripped away from them...it had been because of this knight.

This knight who thought he was better than everyone else and had been trusted enough by the queen to be part of the court.

I knew I had to blame the queen for some of this, but with the look of pain on her face for her people and her king, I couldn't quite do it yet.

This was either an elaborate façade on the queen's part, or the knight was truly evil and was doing all of this on his own.

And we had to stop him.

We couldn't lose any more people. We couldn't lose any more Wielders.

"You will pay for what you've done." The queen glared at Lore, rolling her shoulders back. I did the same, trying to show any strength I had. It was hard, though, when I was so shaken.

"You say that as if that's my endgame. When, after all, I brought you here because I needed her. But I also brought you all here because I knew he would bring *her.*"

And that's when I looked up into the knight's eyes and knew he was talking about me.

"Why?"

"Why? You know why. You are the fabled and prophesized Spirit Priestess. You're the one who's supposed to bring us together. But maybe that's not exactly what the scrolls said."

I froze once again. "What do you mean?"

"In order for the courts to be together, there must be one king and one queen. I am going to be that king. And if you're lucky, girl, you'll be my queen."

I swallowed down the bile rising in my throat and tried not to think about exactly what he wanted. I was going to kill him—if Rhodes and Easton didn't get to him first.

"I just need all of your elements unlocked. And the only way to do that is to put you into high-pressure situations. If I put you and those you love near death, you'll unlock the rest of your magics, and you'll do exactly what I need you to do. Because I need you to be the Spirit Priestess. I need you to help me bring about the end of this, the end of this world. Once you do so, you'll be perfection. And you'll be mine."

It was too much. So much. I was already weakened from unlocking two elements, that much I knew. Because while I was still learning how to be an Air Wielder, and I knew I could reach my Earth Wielding—even if it wasn't easy—each time a new element unlocked, my body grew weaker, if only for the moment. And I had just unlocked two elements in rapid succession. Yes, there had been a couple of weeks between, but my body still knew that it had been too quick.

I wasn't supposed to unlock my elements so quickly. That much I knew. And that meant I wasn't strong enough to unlock the others yet. Yet this man wanted to do it. He wanted to put me in life-or-death situations. Wanted to do the same to my friends.

I knew if Braelynn or Rhodes or Luken, or maybe even the queen and Easton at this point, were in danger, my elements might just unlock to save them.

And I might not make it out of that situation alive.

But there was nothing I could do, not when it looked like Lore had a plan far greater than the rest of us believed.

"You're a monster," Braelynn suddenly said, her voice far stronger than I'd heard it before. "And you're going to pay for what you've done."

The knight snorted. "Sure, honey. Whatever you say. You're just a little human, after all. I'm sure you know exactly what you're talking about."

And then he held out his hands, and the earth shook.

The castle trembled around us, the walls vibrating, the chandeliers shaking. Easton and his mother held out their hands, using their Earth Wielding as well, and it calmed some of the shaking.

But then the knight threw out his hand towards the wall near me, and it crumbled.

Rhodes pulled me back, Luken doing the same with Braelynn.

Suddenly, we could see into the throne room, to the dark crystal that was at the center of everything, of us all.

It looked black and purple in some lights. It had multiple facets that shone in the light, even if some of the inner light had dimmed and swirled with a rot that I knew had come from the knight's abuse of power and from the Fall itself.

It sat in the center of the room, though it faced an open area that looked out over the rest of the kingdom.

While some royalty might have wanted to hide it from enemies, safeguard it from others, the queen had left it where anyone who looked up could see parts of it. She had put it where it could watch over its people, as well.

Maybe I had been wrong about the queen. Maybe she wasn't evil.

Maybe these were just two kingdoms that kept fighting because that was all they knew.

"You're going to open up your new elements, and I know how to do it."

Lore threw out his hands again, this time towards the crystal itself. And then he pulled, that dark rot mixing with the purple and blacks of the crystal's magic. He pulled it out in a long stream and sent it directly towards Braelynn.

I screamed, trying to get closer. Luken blocked Braelynn's body, but it wasn't enough. The knight used his other hand and tossed Luken into a wall, knocking my friend unconscious.

Rhodes and I ran towards Braelynn, but I was too late.

The bolt of magic pierced her heart, and her eyes went wide. She screamed, her hands shaking.

Tears ran down my face, and I knew that whatever was happening to her would be too much.

I didn't know how Emory had been turned into a Wielder, but I knew it hadn't been like this.

The knight was forcing too much into Braelynn all at once. She wasn't strong enough to hold that magic. I didn't think anybody was.

And she was going to die if we didn't stop this.

I reached into myself and tried to locate the Spirit or the Fire or the Water. Any element that I could unlock to try and stop this. Because maybe if I unlocked an element, even as weak as I was, the knight would stop.

But then Braelynn turned to us, her eyes wide but with a knowledge deep in them that I knew meant something.

Acceptance.

She gave me a sad smile, and then she was gone.

Nothing but ash where she had been, the magic from the crystal slamming into the wall behind where she had slumped. And then it was gone, as well.

There was nothing left.

My friend was gone.

My best friend was dead.

I fell to my knees.

CHAPTER 32

No. I had to be wrong.

I wasn't seeing this.

It wasn't over.

She wasn't gone.

She hadn't smiled.

She hadn't breathed her last.

There wasn't ash.

But as Luken's bellowing scream echoed off the walls, I knew that maybe, just maybe, I wasn't wrong.

I had to be wrong, though. This had to be wrong.

But the ash in front of me shifted in the wind, the barest top layer of it blowing around as if it would fade away to nothing. As if it would be gone forever.

As if Braelynn would be forever gone.

No. This wasn't real. This had to be another dream.

All of this had to be another nightmare.

Maybe I had never met Rhodes. Maybe Rosamond was just going to be a friend that would help me figure out the next part of my life. The bit that didn't have anything to do with the Maison realm or Wielders. Maybe this was all fake. It had to be. Because if it was real, then my best friend was dead. My best friend had turned to ash.

Ashes to ashes. Dust to dust.

She was gone.

My best friend was gone.

I didn't realize I was screaming until my voice mixed with Luken's. It was a haunting melody, one that shouldn't have been melodic at all. Luken ran to the pile, the place where Braelynn had been. The spot where part of her still had to be.

But she was gone.

Blood poured from a wound on the side of Luken's head, but still, he fell to his knees. Still, he screamed her name. Still, the anger in his eyes met mine for a brief moment.

And then he turned towards the knight, the Wielder that had killed my friend, who had murdered the person I'd thought Luken could love.

He had killed Braelynn.

Rhodes had his hand on my arm and pulled me back. I hadn't even realized I had even taken a step forward until he did it.

This couldn't be happening.

If I kept saying that, maybe it would stop happening.

But there was no stopping this. There never would be any stopping this.

"What have you done?" the queen asked, her voice sharp. There wasn't any grief in her words, she hadn't known Braelynn. Hadn't known the way Brae did anything to make someone happy. Hadn't known the smiles my friend had when she shared a secret that no one else could know. She hadn't seen the way Braelynn had been so sure of herself even when others weren't sure of her. She hadn't known the Braelynn that I knew and loved.

Instead, she had just seen my best friend die in front of us.

So, there was anger there, but there wasn't grief.

That grief was in me. Was in Luken. Was in Rhodes.

That grief ate at me.

And Lore was going to pay.

"I did what I had to. She'll open up. She wasn't fast enough before, but maybe if I aim the power at the prince here, she'll actually do what she needs to do and fight. She's weak now. But she'll be strong. And she'll be my weapon. The Spirit Priestess is the one who's supposed to unite us all. And she will be mine."

"I hate you," I said, my voice a whisper.

"You're young. Naive. You're just a girl. I don't really care if you hate me because I'll use that hate and I'll hone it and make it into what is needed. We will rule this kingdom, just like it should have been before. There will be no fighting, no more war. Because those weaker than us, those who stand against us? They'll be dead. Just like they should be now."

Lore shot out with his hands again, this time the Fire breaking through the Earth barrier he had made. Easton pushed out his hands, and another wall of Earth—this one much darker, almost obsidian—slammed up between me and the Fire stream.

"You'll answer for your crimes. An easy death won't be what you get this time." Easton moved to step forward, and the knight pulled on the magic of the crystal once more, forcing the elemental powers of Wielding throughout the entire room.

My back slammed into the wall, and I hadn't known that my feet were off the ground until I could hear the ringing in my head.

Rhodes was on his feet before me, but he didn't even stop to help me up. For that, I was grateful. I got to my feet quickly and followed him as we ran toward the knight.

Luken had his sword out, Air Wielding wrapped around the blade. He swung, forcing the Air toward the knight. But the Wielding bounced off the Earth barrier. The knight was far too strong for us.

Now it all made sense as to why he was so strong. He was using magic that wasn't his, Wielding that wasn't his. And in the process, he was sacrificing people's lives and their ways of life.

If Rhodes was right, and I thought he was, Lore had killed, *sacrificed* the Spirit Wielders in the past to get where he was today.

Maybe that's why the Spirit Wielders had talked to me, why they had told me to focus.

I knew I wasn't going to be strong enough to take Lore down alone, but maybe I could help.

Because Braelynn would be avenged. Emery would be avenged.

And I would be avenged. This wasn't fair. But nothing in this life was. I didn't know why I thought it ever could be.

The others started to fight back, using Wielding in ways I had never seen before. Or at least in ways I had only dreamt of. Easton threw out his hands, his fingers spread wide, and then he brought his palms together as if cupping them in front of his chest before pushing them out again. A thin layer of the stone beneath our feet slid as if he had scraped it away in order to form a weapon. It created a wave, slamming through the Earth barrier that the knight had made.

Lore screamed and then sent out another wave of flame. This time, the Wielding made firedrakes dance along the edge.

I knew it wasn't the sweet mystical animals I had seen out in the desert, but for a moment, I paused, wondering how on earth the knight could do things like this. What depravity and sacrifices had he committed in order to be this powerful?

"You'll die tonight," Easton said. "By my hand."

"You would think so, wouldn't you, Easton? You know nothing. You've always been a petulant child who thought he could do what he wants. You thought you were saving your people, but instead, you just led me to the ones who needed the Wielding the least. They were the weakest, so you helped them the most. And in doing so, I knew exactly who to target. So, thank yourself for all of this, Easton. Without you, it would have been much harder for me to take them all out. You really do know how to target the right people."

Easton screamed, his arms going out wide before he slammed his palms together in front of his body with his arms straight. A new wave of flame, this one almost purple with its heat, swirled around us before slamming into Lore.

The knight hit the wall behind him, but he wasn't burned. At the last moment, he had slammed up another wall of Earth to protect himself.

I had no idea how they could use their elements like they did, but, damn it, I was going to learn. I wasn't going to stand back and not be able to fight. Not anymore.

Rhodes moved to Easton's side, putting his body in front of mine, and then used his Air and Water Wielding to try and take out the knight. The two worked side by side, Easton and Rhodes each using their two elements to figure out exactly how to take down the knight who had crossed lines so many times that he had become the strongest elemental there was.

Unless there was something far darker that I didn't know about.

I looked down at the ash that had been my friend and watched the way Luken was still guarding it as if he hoped to bring her back to life.

Something broke inside of me.

My friend would not be coming back.

There would be no saving her.

My best friend was gone.

And I wasn't going to let this stand.

The ground rumbled beneath my feet, but I knew it had nothing to do with the other Earth Wielders in the room. This was me. It was unpracticed, my power raw, but I had enough of it. Papers swirled around me, and I knew the Air Wielding could be seen moving from my fingertips as it grew in strength.

I was going to beat this man. The others could distract him, but he wouldn't expect me, nobody ever did.

Cracks formed in the walls around me, and the Earth Wielding almost overtook me it was so powerful, so strong.

A wave of Air slammed into me from behind, and I knew it was my own, so I pointed my fingers at the knight in front of me and told the power where to go.

A wave of Earth mixed with the Air, and a tornado of both elements rocketed toward the knight. The others watched me wide-eyed, apparently as surprised as I was. But then the knight looked up and smiled.

I took a step back, my body weak. I had used way too much Wielding just then.

I was so angry. So upset.

Braelynn was supposed to be here. She was always supposed to be here. We were supposed to figure out why she had been drawn to this place and why someone thought she was a Dane. I was supposed to hear whispers of why she was falling for Luken and what they did once we had time to breathe. I wanted to tell her about what I felt for Rhodes as soon as I figured it out myself. I wanted her to be by my side once we figured out this Wielding stuff.

I wanted to take her back home so we could figure out the next step in *her* journey.

I needed her.

She had so much left to give.

And now she was gone.

My tunnel of Earth and Air slammed into the knight, but he remained standing as if it hadn't hit him at all. That's when I realized that he had put up another shield, this one even thinner than the first. He was drawing on the crystal itself, and there was nothing we could do but pray we could eventually kill him. And then I took a breath, hoping I could find something else within me that I could use to stop him. Hoping that one of us could stop him.

The knight looked at me, tilted his head, and then pulled out a long sword from beneath his cloak.

A blade much like Luken's but far different. The hilt had dark crystals on it, almost as if they had been torn from the core crystal of Obscurité itself.

The queen rushed towards Lore, her arms outstretched as she sent all of her elements into him. But he blocked them, his eyes still on me. The others fought him, trying to stop him, but the knight only had eyes for me.

And then he threw the sword, flame dancing along the blade as it came right for me.

I almost didn't feel it puncturing my skin. It was warm as if I had stood too close to a fire.

But it didn't hurt.

The sword slid into my body just like cutting into butter before you put it on a roll. The force of it knocked me back into the wall, and the tip of the blade buried itself in the stone behind me. Lore must have used extra Earth Wielding because the blade kept going into that stone, pulling the sword deeper into me as it did.

He was using metal Wielding, something only some Earth Wielders could use. Or so I'd been told.

And he was using it on me.

I tried to let out a breath but I couldn't find the energy, couldn't find the space in my lungs.

Blood pooled from the wound and ran down my side, and I looked at it, wondering how this could be part of me when it didn't hurt. Wasn't this supposed to hurt?

He'd impaled me with a sword and stuck me to a wall. It should have hurt.

I put one hand on the blade, wincing as I cut myself. I was thoroughly confused now. That hurt. My hand hurt from that cut.

But my side didn't. It should have hurt.

I wiped the blood from the corner of my mouth, I knew I was dying. This would be it. Because if I were already bleeding from my mouth, I had to have internal injuries. After all, a sword slicing through my abdomen had probably cut a few important things.

I was going to die, not by Wielding, but by a sword in my gut.

This wasn't how I thought it would end.

This wasn't how I thought anything would end.

Rhodes ran towards me, Easton right on his heels.

Easton also had a cut on his body, and he was bleeding profusely from the wound. I wondered where and when he had gotten hurt. Maybe it was from all the debris and the stones flying around the room. With all the Earth and Air Wielding going on, it was a wonder we weren't all covered in more cuts and bruises. Yes, there were little nicks in everyone's flesh, but not the way Easton looked.

I hoped he would be okay. I thought maybe he was strong enough to help the Obscurité.

Rhodes and Luken would be strong enough to help the Lumière.

But as it turned out, I wasn't strong enough to be the Spirit Priestess.

Maybe I was never strong enough to be one. Perhaps I was just one of the lucky Wielders who happened to have two different elements. I didn't understand it, but then again, I didn't understand much of anything anymore.

Rhodes pulled at the sword, trying to free me from the wall, while Easton held up my arms, holding my body so my weight wasn't on the sword.

And then it started to hurt, and the pain was overwhelming. The heat began where the blade had embedded itself into my flesh before spreading out and then arcing back with a wave of agony and defeat.

Everything started to fade around me, and I knew this was it. I knew I wouldn't give up, but fighting was a little harder than I had planned.

I met Easton's gaze and then looked over at Rhodes. I saw the fear there.

I didn't want to die today.

But it didn't look like I had much choice.

CHAPTER 33

I barely kept my eyes open, but I knew if I weren't careful, I wouldn't be able to resist the darkness.

While Easton and Rhodes were working on me, Luken and the queen were fighting the knight. I tried to speak, attempted to tell them something, but all that came out was a groan.

"You fight, Lyric. You fight. We'll get you out of this."

I looked down at Rhodes as he spoke and tried to nod at him. Although I think my head just lolled to the side. I thought I was stronger than this, but apparently, being impaled by a sword didn't make me very robust.

Easton cursed under his breath and lifted me higher. Without him, I knew the sword would hurt even more inside my stomach, but I didn't really know how to say thank you.

I didn't know what to say to him at all.

"You wake up, little girl. I told you to go away but now that you're here you're going to fight. Look at me. You look at me, Lyric."

So I did. I looked into those dark eyes of his and tried to stay awake.

I slid down on the sword by an inch, and I screamed, blood pouring from my side.

"Get her off the sword," the queen screamed. "Make sure she's okay, and then we will get out of here." The queen threw another Fire Wielding spell towards the knight, but he blocked it, using a wall of Earth.

Luken used his sword, throwing more Air at the knight, but again, the knight was able to shield himself from it all.

He was using the crystal's power, siphoning it from the people of his land, and the knight was far too strong for us to win.

I was going to die, but I didn't want anyone else to.

Braelynn was already gone.

And I didn't want to lose anyone else.

"Lyric!" Rhodes shouted over the din of the battle behind us. "I can't get the sword out of the wall. He used Earth Wielding."

Easton cursed again under his breath.

"Switch with me. I'll try to get her off the sword." I tried to look at both of them, but I was having trouble focusing.

"Hold her up, and I'll use my Earth Wielding."

"Okay, but don't you dare hurt her."

"Shove off."

I wondered why they were fighting, why they were always fighting. I needed to ask Rhodes that. I needed to ask him so much. But I didn't think I would have a chance.

I didn't want to die.

But I couldn't quite find the breath to make that not happen.

As soon as Easton let go of me, a wave of nausea slammed into my body, and I tried not to throw up.

Instead, I just coughed up blood right into Rhodes' face. It was disgusting, but he didn't even blink. Instead, he looked at me, keeping me up against the wall so I wouldn't slide down on the sword any more than I already was.

"You're going to be fine."

I didn't believe him.

Then again, it was hard to believe much of anything.

Easton cursed again, and I wondered why he kept swearing. There was nothing that could do but get you into trouble at school. Of course, he wasn't at school. None of us were. I didn't know how old he was, but he was probably a century or four older than me.

And...I was getting loopy.

Maybe if I just went to sleep...

"Wake up, little girl. I told you to go home, but you didn't. So now you're going to have to deal with this."

"Stuff it, Easton."

"No, you stuff it, Lyric. Keep your eyes open. This is going to hurt."

"Don't you dare hurt her."

"I'm pulling a bloody, a literal bloody sword out of her and the wall. Lore used his Earth Wielding to embed it all the way in. The only reason that it's not fully up to the hilt is that her body's blocking it. So, yeah, it's going to hurt. You're probably going to scream, and then you'll want to kick me. Use all the Wielding you want later, but right now, just focus on not dying. You get me, Lyric? You can hurt me later, but right now, you need to stay alive."

I agreed, at least I thought I did. No sound came out, but my mouth at least moved in the right way. Maybe.

Rhodes met my gaze, and I looked at the blood on his face, some of it mine, some of it his. We'd all been hurt, and now as Lore, the queen, and

Luken fought behind us, I knew we might get hurt even more.

So far, there was a tunnel of Fire and Earth growing around us, looking as if it were a vortex. Even if I got off the sword, I might not make it out of here.

The guys were so focused on me, they weren't looking at the dangers around them. The queen was fighting, and so was Luken.

But I didn't think they would be strong enough.

Not against the Wielding that the knight had stolen and the power of the crystal.

And then I screamed again, sheer agony ripping through me. Rhodes looked like he was ready to rip Easton's head off his shoulders, but he kept his hands on me, keeping me from falling down onto the sword.

Easton used his Earth Wielding, let out a breath, and then he screamed with me.

The sword burst into flames, its metal hot and red. Easton used both his Earth and Fire Wielding to slide the sword out of the stone and out of me. And then the weapon was free, in his hands, still aflame. And I had fallen into Rhodes' arms, trying to catch my breath.

I wasn't sure if I would be able to.

Blood poured out of me, and I knew the sword had been keeping the bleeding at bay a bit. But now it wasn't there anymore, and I was going to die.

I didn't know how to heal this. I didn't know if there was any way to heal this.

Easton was on his knees by us, and I hadn't even realized until then that I was on the ground and lying in Rhodes' lap. I looked up at him, my eyes taking a bit too long to track and focus. There was fear on Rhodes' face, his brown skin pale as he looked down at me.

I swallowed hard as I stared into those silver eyes, wondering if this would be the last time I saw them.

"Heal her," Easton barked. "You know that soulmates can heal one another. Mortal wounds like this, if you don't have the mortal wound yourself yet, you can heal her. There's a way."

"That's only myth," Rhodes answered.

"It's been done. I've seen it. Cover her wound with your hand and try to focus on the bond between you."

"We're not bonded," Rhodes said softly, and I winced, the pain in my heart and my side intensifying.

"It doesn't matter. You have a connection, I've seen the two of you. You already act like you're bonded soulmates. So, cover the wound and focus on what could be. Heal her."

Easton sounded so sure, and I desperately wanted him to be right. He had to be right. I didn't want to die, and if Rhodes were truly mine, then he could save me. I needed him to save me.

Rhodes put his hand over my wound and met Easton's eyes before he looked down at me again. There was such intensity in that silver gaze that I sucked in a breath.

I was his. He was mine.

This was going to work.

It had to work

I waited.

And waited.

Nothing happened.

Something was supposed to happen, right? Because there was supposed to be healing.

"What?" I gasped.

Rhodes shook his head and pressed down on my wound even harder. I sucked in a breath, blood all around us, the viscous liquid coming out of my mouth and now trickling out of my nose. Easton was screaming at Rhodes, telling him to heal me, but I didn't think it was working.

Wasn't it supposed to work?

"I can't do it," Rhodes snapped. And then he looked over at Easton. "How am I supposed to do it? They don't tell you how soulmates work. But I feel a connection to her. She's my soulmate. She has to be. Why can't I heal her? Why can't I heal her, Easton?"

And then I wasn't so warm anymore. I was cold.

Because Easton was looking right at me, and I suddenly knew the answer. *Rhodes isn't my soulmate.*

That connection? That wasn't what he thought it was. Wasn't what *I* thought it was.

It might not matter that I still had feelings for him, and I knew he had feelings for me. He wouldn't be able to heal me through the magical Wielding of soulmates.

Because he wasn't my destiny, wasn't my fate.

I wasn't his.

As the look of horror dawned on him, and he looked down at me, I knew he realized it, too.

I was bleeding out on the floor all around him, my blood pumping through his fingers as he tried to stop the deluge.

But he couldn't.

"It's okay," I whispered. Somehow, my voice had come back, maybe it was because I knew that Rhodes needed to hear this.

He hadn't told me that I was his soulmate, not in so many words. But I knew that's what he thought.

But it wasn't true.

He couldn't heal me. Therefore, I wasn't his. He wasn't mine.

I didn't know why I felt like I was breaking inside. I was dying, I wasn't supposed to shatter at the same time.

My fingertips buzzed, and it became hard for me to breathe, my heart shattering into a million pieces as I realized that what I thought was true wasn't.

"Find a way to save her anyway," Easton said, his voice dark. "My mother and Luken can't save us all. Try to help her, figure something out. I'll get the knight, but we need her, Rhodes. Not just because you thought she was your soulmate, but because she's the Spirit Priestess. She's going to be the one who saves us all. And she can't do that if she's dead."

And then Easton was on his feet, staggering away and practically slipping in my blood before he went to fight the knight again. The sword was still in his hand, the blade covered in my blood. Maybe that would kill the knight. After all, it had already killed me.

"I'm so sorry, Lyric." Rhodes leaned down and put his head on mine. "I know some healers in Air and Water can heal using Wielding, but I don't know how. That's not my specialty. Soulmates…soulmates, that's what we were supposed to be. I'm so sorry, Lyric. I thought you were mine."

Why couldn't I still be his? If I lived through this, why couldn't we be together? Why did it have to be soulmates that could save each other? Why did he look like he was going to walk away? As if now that I wasn't *his* as the Wielding decreed, I wouldn't ever be his?

"It's fine," I whispered—or tried to, but no words came out.

The queen and Luken and Easton were fighting, and screams reverberated throughout the room. I didn't want to die, I wanted to help. If Rhodes couldn't save me, and if I didn't want to give up, I needed to save myself.

So, I closed my eyes and thought of the elements that I had within me. Air and Earth. They weren't opposites, but they weren't the same. They were just two of four elements, two of five of the realm. One I could feel on my skin if I closed my eyes, the other held me against the ground, the warm marble, the heat of my blood cradling me like I was a child.

I could feel the wound pulsating as my life's blood spilled out of me. But maybe, just maybe I could do this.

"You can do this," I whispered to myself.

Only it wasn't a whisper.

We will help.

We can help.

Focus on the wound, focus on your energy.

Imagine the Air around you coming to life, spiraling and holding you in its arms.

Imagine the Earth, warm and full of life.

Imagine it as a cocoon as it holds you close.

Imagine all of it and see yourself healed.

We cannot do this again.

But you are the Spirit Priestess.

You are one of us.

You are stronger than you know.

And then my back arched off the ground, and Rhodes pulled away, his eyes wide. I hadn't known my eyes were open until I looked at him and saw the stark fear and wonder on his face.

I hadn't known those two emotions could mix like that, but it was Rhodes. That was the boy I was supposed to love. The one who was supposed to be my soulmate.

But he wasn't.

I didn't want to die today.

No boy was going to save me.

I would have to save myself.

So I did what the Spirit Wielders told me to do, knowing that it was taking a lot of energy for them to reach me.

I don't know why I knew that, I just did. I had so many questions, and I needed so many answers. I didn't want to see Braelynn again, not like this. I didn't want to see my best friend when we were both dead. I would have to wait.

Because I was going to live.

Luken fell to his knees near us, screaming. As I looked out of the corner of my eye, I saw Braelynn's ashes blowing away in the wind. And then Rhodes left me, getting up to fight for his friend because there was a gash on Luken's shoulder that was bleeding profusely, and the knight was coming after him.

Rhodes had to save Luken, his best friend for ages because he couldn't save me.

I didn't feel anything about that.

I didn't feel anything at all.

I didn't want to face my mortality. I didn't want to face the world. But the universe had put its faith in me, and I wasn't going to give up. I did as the Spirit Wielders instructed, and when the warmth and the heat turned to coolness, I looked down and saw only blood and newly pink skin.

I stood up on shaky legs, wondering how on earth I did that.

It didn't make any sense. I wasn't supposed to be able to heal myself. I wasn't supposed to do anything like this.

But I had.

I was a Spirit Priestess.

And I didn't want to be.

I'd lost my best friend. And I might lose the only other friends I had left if I didn't do something. I'd almost lost my life, and I still could lose it.

This may be all a dream. But I wasn't going to let it end as a nightmare.

Easton and Rhodes were fighting the knight, and a group of men that had come in that seemed to be working for the knight. I hadn't known that they had walked into the room, but the wolf on each of their chest plates showed me that they were the knight's guard. So much had happened when I had had my eyes closed, as I tried to knit myself back together using magic I didn't understand.

Rhodes fought next to Easton as if they were two warriors of old, as if they had been fighting alongside each other for ages rather than fighting against one another. The queen looked as if she were walking through a wind tunnel, her hair blowing around her as she wielded Fire and Earth with such fierceness that it surprised me.

I looked at Rhodes again. He was so strong, he was everything, and I did not want to die today.

"Stop," I said, my voice strong.

Everyone and everything seemed to freeze around me, and then the knight turned my direction.

Lore sneered. "I see you've learned to use your powers. That's just the tip of the iceberg, Lyric. Come closer, and you can be mine. I can show you the world."

I raised my chin and met his gaze. "You're nothing. You're going to die today. And you'll know exactly what you've done. You killed my best friend. And you almost killed me."

He *had* killed me.

I had died, if only for a moment.

And I didn't want to die again.

"If that's the choice you've made. You must know the consequences. Another Priestess will come if I make it so. If I can't have you, then no one will."

And then the knight shot out power from the crystal again, using all of his strength. It came towards me, and I put out my hands, my Air Wielding spiraling around us and knocking down the Fire and Earth walls. The ground rumbled beneath me, and my Earth Wielding shot out in a wave, knocking the knight's men out of the way. With one strike, I had taken out his men.

With another strike, I took out the flames that threatened us all.

I could do this again. I could fight, and I could win against the crystal's magic that came at me.

But then I didn't need to.

Because someone else stepped in the way.

But it wasn't the boy I was supposed to love.

It wasn't the one who had fallen for my best friend.

It wasn't the man that had tried to save me.

It was the queen I had thought was my enemy.

She put her back to the knight, her hands outstretched as a wall of flame covered her, trying to protect herself, but it wasn't going to be enough. She met my gaze, and I wondered why she would do this. Why would she sacrifice herself for me?

And then she opened her mouth, and I couldn't hear the words other than in my head.

Be brave, Lyric. Save us all. My Spirit Priestess.

And then she was on the ground, though not dust as Braelynn had been. The queen had been strong enough to not turn to ash from the amount of power coursing through her, but she hadn't been strong enough to withstand it all.

Easton yelled, screamed, used his Earth and Fire Wielding to send out all his magic. Luken and Rhodes did the same. But the knight stood in a circle of protection thanks to the crystal as Fire, Earth, Air, and Water flew at him. The only thing missing was Spirit. But there were no Spirit Wielders left in this realm.

And because of that, it looked like Lore would survive.

Live because he thought he was stronger than us all.

Everything was moving so fast, and there was still just enough of the crystal coming at me. I bent down and picked up the sword that Easton had dropped moments earlier and put it in front of myself, closing my eyes for a moment as the power of the crystal slammed into the sword once more.

I could feel it reverberate through my bones, rattling my teeth and clenching my muscles.

This was the power of a people, the power of Wieldings through generations, and the souls of those lost in infamy.

I opened my eyes and let the sword fall forward, pointing the tip at my enemy. And because I knew that this was what was supposed to happen, the magic flew back at the knight, and he screamed. Between the crystal's magic and the elements of the three warriors in the room, the knight's protection fell, and he turned to ash—just like Braelynn had. He wasn't as strong as the queen without his stolen power, and he hadn't been able to keep his physical body.

The knight was dead.

The queen was dead.

And as I looked down at the blood around me, at the fallen soldiers and the fallen leader, I wasn't sure if I was alive. I couldn't feel anything. No pain. No loss. No triumph. There were no winners here, just loss.

And I was numb.

I looked at everything. Looked at Easton, who, if I was right, was now the High King of Obscurité. The boy who had just lost his mother.

I looked at Rhodes, who wasn't my soulmate, wasn't my future.

And I couldn't feel anything.

Instead, I swayed on my feet and hit the ground as the others reached out for me.

And this time, I let the darkness come. This time, I let it come and soothe me and hold me in its warm embrace.

Because the darkness was what I needed.

I didn't want to run anymore.

CHAPTER 34

Something was pawing at my hair. Was it…chewing on it?

I really didn't want to open my eyes to find out. My head hurt, the pounding intense.

In fact, now that I thought about it, every single part of me hurt. That was the only reason I knew I was awake and not still dreaming.

Though I hadn't really dreamed the night before. Everything was clouded in darkness.

Maybe I'd only slept for the first time in what felt like months.

That chewing sensation on my hair came back, and I frowned, trying to wiggle away. Whatever had been chewing on me made a little mewing sound and then batted at my face.

Batted at me?

Since when did I have something in my room that could bat at me?

That's when it all came back to me.

The fall. The mountain. The journey. The realm. The fight.

Emory.

Braelynn.

Luken.

Rhodes.

Easton.

The queen.

The knight.

It all came back, and my eyes shot open. I wasn't in my room. Instead, I was somewhere I didn't recognize. The room smelled of flowers and a dark perfume that wasn't something I knew. There were dark purple drapes over the window, though I could see light peeking out, telling me it was daylight.

I didn't know how much time had passed or, honestly, what time it had been when the fight began. So much had happened all at once that it was hard for me to truly follow anything at this point.

I had fallen near the throne room and had closed my eyes, not knowing if I would ever wake up again.

But where was I?

Suddenly, something moved near my head and I almost sat up, but my body felt too heavy to do so. Instead, I frowned as a small cat walked around my head, licked my forehead, and then continued walking down the bed towards my feet.

A cat?

Wherever I was, apparently, there was a cat.

I looked down, trying to focus.

A cat. With black wings.

Maybe I *had* died, and this was a version of the afterlife.

Because that was definitely a cat. A feline, now that I looked closer, that had extra toes like a polydactyl cat. A polydactyl cat with black bat wings.

Yep, I had officially lost my mind.

"You're not losing your mind, Lyric."

I froze, having been unaware that someone else was in my room. Or at least this room with me in it.

And from the sound of it, whoever this person was, was at the foot of my bed.

But I knew that voice, I just hadn't heard it in a while.

I rolled over onto my back and then put my hand down on the bed so I could force myself into a seated position.

Someone had changed me into a tee shirt and jeans, human clothes. I hadn't really expected to be wearing anything like this again, maybe ever, so I was a little distracted by the fact that someone had dressed me. Then I realized exactly who was sitting at the foot of my bed with a cat in her lap—a cat with wings.

"Rosamond."

She smiled at me, and I tried to see if everything was okay with her. There were shadows under her eyes, and scrapes and bruises on her face and her hands.

She was wearing human clothes, as well—a turtleneck with long sleeves—so I didn't know if there was anything else wrong with her.

But Rosamond was alive. And she was sitting on my bed. Petting a cat. A cat with wings. Maybe I really was dead.

"You're not dead," Rosamond said.

"So you're a Seer, *and* you can read my mind?"

Rosamond shook her head, scratching the cat under the chin. "No, you're saying the words aloud. Although your voice is a bit scratchy. Would you like me to get you some water?"

I shook my head, ignoring the way that it made my brain pulse. Maybe shaking my head wasn't such a good idea. "I'm fine. I just didn't realize that I had spoken aloud."

"Most don't when they first wake up. You don't talk in your sleep, so that's good to know."

"Are you okay?" The last time I had seen Rosamond, she was being pulled into a portal by the Negs. I'd thought she could be dead, even though I planned to do everything I could to find her.

And even though we had journeyed through the entire Obscurité Kingdom and its associated elemental territories to find her, we'd only found the knight who had kidnapped her for her powers. I hadn't truly known if we would ever see Rose again.

But here she was, petting a cat with wings.

"I'm fine. And that's not a lie. Lore didn't really hurt me. Not the way my brother seems to think."

I stiffened at the mention of her brother. I didn't really want to think about Rhodes and what it meant that he hadn't been able to heal me. Maybe if I hadn't been thrust into this new world of Wielders and fate, I wouldn't feel like I had lost something. But I couldn't help it just then.

"I'm glad. But can I ask you a question?"

"You're always welcome to ask, Lyric."

"Why are you petting a cat with wings?"

Rosamond looked down at the cat as if just noticing it. She smiled.

"This is a Familiar. And I think you know who she is."

I shook my head, looking at the cat. "It's a cat with wings. How am I supposed to know who that is?"

"Because like I said, Braelynn is a Familiar."

I stiffened. "Braelynn?"

"When someone you love dies as a sacrifice, sometimes, the magic in their soul is just right so they can come back. Maybe not like you knew them, but in a way that they're needed. So, yes, this is Braelynn, the same Braelynn you always knew. When she concedes to this new body, you'll get to know her better. But she is yours. Your Familiar."

Tears stung my eyes, and I looked down at the cat who just blinked at me with wide eyes.

With Braelynn's eyes.

"This can't be my best friend."

"She is. She's just a little different. She's getting used to this new part of herself. Soon, she'll discover exactly what it means to be a Familiar, the same as you will. But she is yours, and she'll take care of you. Just like you will take care of her."

At that moment, Braelynn padded off Rosamond's lap and ended up on mine. I stuck out my hand so she could scent it, wondering how my life had taken this turn.

Braelynn sniffed my hand and then licked it before nuzzling my thigh and then circling around on my lap to take a nap.

I let my fingers trail along her back, feeling the bat wings that were slightly leathery yet soft.

It didn't make any sense, but then again, nothing did anymore.

"Once she figures out who she is, she'll come into her own. Some Familiars can speak to their humans. Or rather, their Wielders. Some have much more than what you see. But that will come later. If it does."

"Oh." I didn't really know what else to say. What was there to say when I just found out that my best friend was now a cat with bat wings?

"I want to apologize, Lyric."

I looked up at Rosamond, still petting Braelynn as she purred in my lap. Well...*that was a weird sentence.*

"For what?"

"For everything. I'm sorry I couldn't tell you everything right away. I just couldn't. Because it wouldn't have worked out the way it needed to if I had told you everything."

I looked into her eyes and knew she was talking about Seeing something. I didn't know the cost of Seeing the future, to See so many roads ahead of you, yet not know which one is the truth. But I knew there was something there that cost way too much. She had Seen a future where, if she had told me, things wouldn't have worked out the way they should.

And I knew it was too much for me to think about right then.

The weight on Rosamond's shoulders was heavy, but then again, so was the weight on mine.

"Where is Rhodes?" I asked, not realizing that I was going to ask that until I did.

"He's...he's here." Rosamond let out a breath and leaned against the wall. "But he needs to go home soon because this court isn't the only one that is failing. All of our territories need to rally together. I just don't think that's going to happen without force."

I tried to understand what she was saying. Rhodes was here, but he hadn't waited for me to wake up? He wasn't here waiting for me.

Did that mean he didn't want to be? Or was it because he was planning on going home, to the Lumière Kingdom?

And did he want me to go with him? Because I didn't know if I could.

I wanted to go home.

I wanted to remember who I was, or at least who I had been.

I had almost died. My best friend had been killed and was now a cat in my lap.

It was all too much. I really just wanted to go home.

And I didn't think the Maison realm was that for me.

"Lyric, you are that force. The force that will bring us together."

At her words, I looked up at Rosamond and shook my head. "No, I'm not. I need to go home." I wasn't that force. I hadn't been strong enough to save someone that I loved. I had somehow been able to heal myself, but only with the other Spirit Wielders. Without them, I would have died. The Queen of Obscurité had died for me. So many people had been hurt because of me. I wasn't worth this. I might be stronger than I had been when I first stepped foot into this realm, but I knew I needed to go home. I needed to go home and figure out exactly what I needed to be before I figured out what would happen next.

"I can't do this. I don't think I'm your Priestess." I sucked in a breath, trying to get my thoughts in order. I couldn't be the person they needed me to be. I wasn't strong enough. There had to be someone out there that wouldn't get her friends killed along the way. I had done so many things wrong because I'd thought they were right. I needed to get better, *be* better. There had to be someone else out there that could help the Maisons.

Because if I were truly who they thought I was, if I was the Spirit Priestess, I wouldn't have been so weak, I wouldn't have almost died as I did.

I thought of the whispers in my head from the Spirit Wielders and the fact that I had to focus on what they had told me and not what the others could do for me. On what Rhodes hadn't been able to do for me.

I had succumbed to the darkness.

I had died.

But now, I lived.

I shook my head, trying to put my thoughts into words. "Everything's changed here. The queen is dead. Easton lost his mother. We almost lost you. All I did was come here and make it worse."

"The knight is dead. The crystal cannot stop its purpose since the knight's magic is seemingly irreversible. But now that the Obscurité know about it, they can perhaps save their people."

"And yet...yet he could have found that out on his own. Easton could have. I didn't do anything except get in the way."

Rosamond looked up at me, but she didn't shake her head, didn't look disappointed. In fact, it looked like she had been expecting this.

Well, she was a Seer. I guess that is exactly what it meant to know the future.

Maybe she had Seen that I would need time to myself, or at least time away from the world that pulled at me. I didn't want to run away, I knew that, but I really needed to regroup. And I didn't know where else to do that but home.

I couldn't stay here, not in the kingdom where I had been complicit in the queen's death, where I had lost Braelynn and even some of myself.

I didn't know if I could go with Rhodes to another kingdom either. Where I would have to meet more people and find out more about a world I didn't know if I could save. I didn't know if I could go hand-in-hand with Rhodes when I wasn't sure he wanted me anymore.

Where I didn't know if I was good enough for him.

And because those thoughts kept coming at me, I knew I just needed time to breathe.

I just didn't know how much time I had.

"Okay." Rosamond got up, and I ignored the sense of disappointment I felt that she wasn't going to try and make me stay. I didn't want to. Not really. I was scared, and I just wanted to go home, even if only for a moment.

People relied on me, and I didn't know if I would be good enough to measure up.

"But take this," Rosamond said, thrusting a large book at me.

I took it in my hands, the weight far heavier than a book of that size should be. It smelled of old parchment and leather and felt of something greater than the volume itself.

The History of the Maison.

I let my fingers run along the raised letters. It was a leather tome with scrolls and runes on the front and sides of the cover. The history of my people. But who *were* my people? I had been born in the human realm. Raised there. And though I could dance air along my fingers and feel the earth quake beneath my feet, I didn't know if I was a true Wielder. How could I be when I didn't know who I was?

"Learn your history. You cannot look toward the future without knowing the past that's behind you." Rosamond looked at my face, her eyes dark and distant. And then I knew she was Seeing a future, one that was important.

I just didn't know if I was part of that.

"Rosamond?"

She shook her head, turning towards the door. She paused before she left, then looked over her shoulder and smiled.

"Don't forget your cat."

CHAPTER 35

I found out that I had been staying in a room next to Easton's at the Obscurité Court. It had been the cleanest and emptiest room that hadn't been damaged in the fight. They'd put me there to sleep, and Rosamond had changed me into human clothes, putting a spell on them so they wouldn't disintegrate. The others hadn't questioned her. Maybe that was because she had Seen that I wanted to go back to the human realm before I had even known I wanted to.

I didn't understand what any of it meant, but I knew that I needed to go home, at least for a little bit. I was shaky, scared, and even though I was holding my best friend, I didn't really feel like that was true. I was holding a cat named Braelynn, one that Rosamond told me was my best friend, just in Familiar form.

Was that true?

Or was I just seeing things?

I had been imagining things too often.

First were the shadows that I later learned were Negs once I almost died on the mountain.

Because when I almost died, Rosamond had used her Wielding, and it had unlocked something inside of me. Because that part of myself had been unlocked, I had been able to see the truth in the shadows. I had been able to see the Negs and what they truly were. I'd been able to see it all.

And then I had walked through these Obscurité territories and had seen people who needed help. People who the knight had been hurting simply because he could.

I didn't know how I was supposed to help them, or how I was supposed to help the other two territories that I didn't even know. And then there was the Spirit territory, barren and vacant. I hadn't traveled to the northern Spirit territory yet, but I had a feeling it would look just like the southern one. I hadn't met the Spirit Wielders outside of my dreams. I hadn't done anything of import but watch the queen die and try to unravel the mess that was the Maison realm.

I just needed to go home. I needed to make sure my parents knew I was okay. I needed to figure out a story for what to tell Braelynn's moms. What to tell Emory's parents. Maybe if I regrouped, maybe if I figured out what I needed to do, I could go back and help. Or maybe they could find someone who could do it better.

"So, you're leaving." It wasn't a question, but I turned to Rhodes anyway.

There was a dark mark on his jaw as if he'd been bruised, and a few cuts on his face. But other than that, he looked just the same.

His soft brown skin, his dark hair falling over his forehead, and those silver, silver eyes.

But he didn't look at me.

It didn't seem like he could look at me.

He was distant.

And I couldn't help but think that he was disappointed. Disappointed in me. Disappointed in the fact that things didn't turn out like he thought they would.

"I'm sorry."

"Don't be sorry. I understand that you need to go. I just don't like it."

"I know I told you I would go with you to the Lumière Kingdom, but now…" My voice trailed off, and he shook his head.

"That was before."

Before I almost died. Before I did die if I really thought about it. Before Rhodes hadn't been enough to save me because we weren't soulmates.

That was all before.

And now, this was the after.

"I don't know what the next step is, Lyric." He took a step forward but didn't reach out to touch me. He didn't touch me.

Why wouldn't he touch me?

Were soulmates the only true way to fall for someone in this realm? Because if that was the case, I didn't want one.

I wanted Rhodes.

But I didn't think that was going to happen. Because he looked so hurt. I knew I had to push him away. I had to be stronger than this.

"I need to go home," Rhodes said. "We're in the enemy's territory, but Easton sure isn't acting like the enemy." He looked off into the distance, and I wondered what that comment meant. Because, yes, Rhodes and Easton had fought side by side, and Easton was letting us stay in his place, even with all the turmoil around us.

The princes hadn't been acting like enemies, but I was afraid that would change as soon as we left this place.

"I need to go to court. There's a war brewing. The Queen of Obscurité is dead, and who knows what her knight and his people did. I need to go. I thought you needed to go with me."

He thought.

I needed to push him away. He needed to find his soulmate. And that wasn't me.

"I'm not yours, Rhodes. I never was."

My voice broke, but I held back the tears. Hid the hurt.

Everything hurt.

But Rhodes didn't fight for me.

He didn't say a word.

"I need to go home to the human realm. I need to see my parents. And I need to remember who I am. Because I don't think I know who Lyric is anymore."

"Lyric," Rhodes said, but he didn't say anything else.

Easton walked in at that point, his head high and his eyes on fire as he looked between Rhodes and me. "Let her go home. You can't keep her here."

"Just remember, High King, you can't either."

There was hurt in Easton's eyes at that. At the words *High King*. He had lost his mother, and now he was a king. So much would happen next, and yet I really just wanted to take a step back and try to focus. Because I couldn't let it all happen all at once. Maybe I was weak, but I didn't care. I would fight for what was right, and I would do all that needed to be done.

But I needed to breathe first.

I just wanted my bed. I needed to wake up from this nightmare.

But because I knew that wasn't going to happen, not really, I knew I just needed space.

If only for a moment.

Rhodes turned away from Easton, took a step, and then brushed his lips along mine.

I stood frozen for a moment before leaning in and savoring his taste, his touch. I let the tears fall this time, and I knew that if I let myself, I could love him in truth.

If it weren't for the fact that the Maisons apparently needed soulmates, he could be mine. Why did there have to be soulmates?

"I wish it was you," he whispered and then turned away.

He didn't see my wince. But Easton did.

Easton, apparently, saw far too much.

Then Rhodes was gone, Luken coming out of the shadows to walk by his side.

My new friends would leave me and go back to the Lumière Kingdom so they could protect their people. I didn't know what would happen with Easton, and I didn't know how this was all going to mesh together. I didn't know anything.

Easton just stood there, looking at me. I didn't look back at him. I just looked at the doorway that Rhodes had left through. I thought about his parting comment and whispered, "And I you."

Because Rhodes wasn't lying.

He never had been.

But it didn't matter that I had wanted him to be mine.

I was alone.

I might always be.

CHAPTER 36

"I'm going to be the one that takes you home," Easton said, pulling me out of my thoughts. My self-pitying ruminations now that I thought about it.

I really hated self-pity.

"What?"

"Rosamond needs to go with her brother because the Lumière need to see that she's okay. I offered to take you home." He winked, and I wanted to throw something at him.

"Why?"

"Because my mother died to protect you, and I don't want her death to be in vain. So, I'm going to make sure you get home, make sure you're all nice and closeted away and protected. And then I'm going to come back here and try to figure out what the hell to do with this kingdom. I hope that's okay

I knew why he was being mean to me, why he was so caustic. And I deserved it.

His mother had died for me.

He had told me to go home, told me to get away from all of this. Maybe if I had listened, the queen would be okay.

Perhaps if I had listened, the cat in my arms would just be my best friend and not a winged feline that I had no idea what to do with.

"How am I supposed to go home with a cat with bat wings?"

Easton sighed. "I'm going to do a spell that will glamour her. Everyone will just see a polydactyl cat. Anyone with the Sight will know that she's a Familiar. A special one."

"What do you mean *special*, besides the wings?"

He winked then, a small smile on his face before he shook his head. "You'll see. She's a bit…feisty."

"Okay." I had no idea what he was saying or what it meant, but I figured he just liked to tease me. Annoy me.

"Your family won't realize that you've been gone for too long. The same with Braelynn's family and Emory's. I never met Emory, though I hear she's a little interesting."

"Let's not talk about her." I didn't know what Emory was doing, or how I could help her, but before I could even think on that, I needed to get my head on straight. And I couldn't do that here.

Easton held up his hands in surrender and shrugged. "No problem. I'll set up the glamour so no one really knows how long you've been gone, and won't question that Braelynn and Emory are still gone."

"You can do that?"

"Yes, I'm the High King of Obscurité. I can do many things."

I looked at him then and wanted to apologize. I wanted to reach out and tell him that I was sorry. But what could I do? He didn't know me, and I didn't know him.

"I can't stay long because, like Rhodes said, there's a war coming and, apparently, I'm the king now. I have a feeling this won't be the last time you walk on these lands, though."

I raised my chin as Braelynn shifted in my arms, rubbing the top of her head against my chin.

"I don't know if I'm coming back. I want to, I think I need to. But I need to figure out exactly what I'm going to do. And I can't do that here. I can't do that with all the responsibility pushing at me."

"I get it. I want to hide away, too, I just don't have the option right now."

"That's not fair."

"Life isn't fair, Lyric. But you've already figured that out, haven't you? And, yeah, you're new to this. You didn't have centuries of knowing that you could be the high queen one day if your mother stepped down. You didn't have centuries of war and strife coming at you. You've had a few weeks. So, yeah, you're allowed to go home and lick your wounds. But you're the Priestess, Lyric. You might not know what that means, but then again, none of us do. You're only a legend."

"Stop saying that. I can't be a legend when I couldn't even decide on a major when I was in the human realm."

Easton just shook his head, laughing. But there was no humor in the sound. "Maybe there was a reason you never could."

"I can't believe in reasons."

I didn't want to believe in them. And now I was just whining. I needed to go home, just for a while. Once I did, I'd be able to figure out what to do. But I couldn't do that here. I couldn't do it in the place where I'd lost my best friend, at least the part of her that I had known. I couldn't do that where I'd had a sword thrown through my body.

I couldn't do that in a place where everyone I knew had been hurt, where Easton's mother had died.

I just needed time and space to breathe.

And then I would be stronger.

"Let's get you home, then." For some reason, Easton reached out and put his hand on my shoulder. Flames erupted all around us, and we were once again in the Spirit territory. It didn't make any sense. But then again, nothing did.

Rhodes hadn't been able to take us this way, but apparently, Easton could. Or maybe there were other reasons Rhodes hadn't. After all, he'd been going in secret to the Obscurité Kingdom and had been alone, at first, with three humans. This was different. It was all different. Everything looked barren again, bright, and harsh.

Without words, we walked through the Spirit territory and through the portal that took us to the human realm.

There were still no words between us when we made our way to Rhodes' car. The fact that Easton knew where it was told me that the two had talked to one another about what to do with me.

We didn't say a word as Easton drove me home.

We didn't say a word as he led me inside, the house empty except for Braelynn and me. My parents weren't home yet.

I didn't feel like I was home either.

I was lost.

So lost.

"Lyric?" I looked over at Easton and frowned. "What?"

"I'm not a Seer, but I've seen enough in my years to know that something's coming. No matter how hard we try, we can't hide from what scares us the most. So, I've taken you home. This way, you can see what you had and determine if you can fit here like you thought you did before. But when the time comes, and you need to come back to the Maison realm, all you gotta do is ask. Because you're not done with our realm yet. Not by far."

"Why are you helping me?"

He looked at me then, his eyes dark, and I knew he was going to lie to me. "Because you saved my land. Because my mother's last action in our realm was to save you. I can't let that go unnoticed."

And while I believed that, I knew that that wasn't the whole truth.

Because, as everything with the Maison realm, I only knew part of what was real and what was a legend.

They thought I was the Spirit Priestess. And when I wasn't failing, I thought maybe that was true, as well.

Change was coming.

And I knew I had to be stronger than I was currently in order to survive it.

I had to be the Lyric that others needed me to be.

But first, I had to figure out who I was now.

A NOTE FROM
CARRIE ANN

Thank you so much for reading *From Breath And Ruin*! I do hope if you liked this story, that you would please leave a review! Reviews help authors and readers.

From Breath and Ruin is only the beginning. I had been wanting to write this series for years with Lyric whispering into my ear for far too long.

Lyric's journey is only at its start and there is much more to come, with the second book in the series coming soon. I do love that you came on this journey with me and I cannot wait for you to see what awaits Lyric, her friends, and those she's yet to meet.

Because as I said, From Breath and Ruin was only the first chapter… there is so much more to come.

If you want to make sure you know what's coming next from me, you can sign up for my newsletter at www.CarrieAnnRyan.com; follow me on twitter at @CarrieAnnRyan, or like my Facebook page (www.facebook.com/CarrieAnnRyanAuthor). I also have a Facebook Fan Club (www.facebook.com/groups/CarrieAnnRyanFanClub/) where we have trivia, chats, and other goodies. You guys are the reason I get to do what I do and I thank you.

Make sure you're signed up for my mailing list! (www.carrieannryan.com/faq/how-do-i-sign-up-for-your-newsletter). You will be alerted when the next releases are available as well as find giveaways and FREE READS.

Happy Reading!

THE ELEMENTS OF FIVE SERIES
Book 1: *From Breath and Ruin*
Book 2: *From Flame and Ash*
MORE TO COME!

ABOUT
CARRIE ANN

Carrie Ann Ryan is the *New York Times* and *USA Today* bestselling author of contemporary and paranormal romance. Her works include the Montgomery Ink, Redwood Pack, Talon Pack, and Gallagher Brothers series, which have sold over 2.0 million books worldwide. She started writing while in graduate school for her advanced degree in chemistry and hasn't stopped since. Carrie Ann has written over fifty novels and novellas with more in the works. When she's not writing about bearded tattooed men or alpha wolves that need to find their mates, she's reading as much as she can and exploring the world of baking and gourmet cooking.

FOR MORE INFORMATION, VISIT:
WWW.CARRIEANNRYAN.COM

MORE BOOKS FROM
CARRIE ANN

MONTGOMERY INK: COLORADO SPRINGS

Book 1: Fallen Ink

Book 2: Restless Ink

Book 2.5: Ashes to Ink

Book 3: Jagged Ink

Book 3.5: Ink by Numbers

THE FRACTURED CONNECTIONS SERIES:

A Montgomery Ink Spin Off Series

Book 1: Breaking Without You

Book 2: Shouldn't Have You

Book 3: Falling With You

THE MONTGOMERY INK: BOULDER SERIES:

Book 1: Wrapped in Ink

THE LESS THAN SERIES:

A Montgomery Ink Spin Off Series

Book 1: Breathless With Her

Book 2: Reckless With You

THE ELEMENTS OF FIVE SERIES:

A YA Fantasty Series

Book 1: From Breath and Ruin

Book 2: From Flame and Ash

MONTGOMERY INK:

Book 0.5: Ink Inspired

Book 0.6: Ink Reunited

Book 1: Delicate Ink

Book 1.5: Forever Ink

Book 2: Tempting Boundaries

Book 3: Harder than Words

Book 4: Written in Ink

Book 4.5: Hidden Ink

Book 5: Ink Enduring

Book 6: Ink Exposed

Book 6.5: Adoring Ink

Book 6.6: Love, Honor, & Ink

Book 7: Inked Expressions

Book 7.3: Dropout

Book 7.5: Executive Ink

Book 8: Inked Memories

Book 8.5: Inked Nights

Book 8.7: Second Chance Ink

THE GALLAGHER BROTHERS SERIES:

A Montgomery Ink Spin Off Series

Book 1: Love Restored

Book 2: Passion Restored

Book 3: Hope Restored

THE WHISKEY AND LIES SERIES:

A Montgomery Ink Spin Off Series

Book 1: Whiskey Secrets

Book 2: Whiskey Reveals

Book 3: Whiskey Undone

THE TALON PACK:

Book 1: Tattered Loyalties

Book 2: An Alpha's Choice

Book 3: Mated in Mist

Book 4: Wolf Betrayed

Book 5: Fractured Silence

Book 6: Destiny Disgraced

Book 7: Eternal Mourning

Book 8: Strength Enduring

Book 9: Forever Broken

REDWOOD PACK SERIES:

Book 1: An Alpha's Path

Book 2: A Taste for a Mate

Book 3: Trinity Bound

Redwood Pack Box Set (Contains Books 1-3)

Book 3.5: A Night Away

Book 4: Enforcer's Redemption

Book 4.5: Blurred Expectations

Book 4.7: Forgiveness

Book 5: Shattered Emotions

Book 6: Hidden Destiny

Book 6.5: A Beta's Haven

Book 7: Fighting Fate

Book 7.5: Loving the Omega

Book 7.7: The Hunted Heart

Book 8: Wicked Wolf

The Complete Redwood Pack Box Set (Contains Books 1-7.7)

THE BRANDED PACK SERIES:
(Written with Alexandra Ivy)

Book 1: Stolen and Forgiven

Book 2: Abandoned and Unseen

Book 3: Buried and Shadowed

DANTE'S CIRCLE SERIES:

Book 1: Dust of My Wings

Book 2: Her Warriors' Three Wishes

Book 3: An Unlucky Moon

The Dante's Circle Box Set (Contains Books 1-3)

Book 3.5: His Choice

Book 4: Tangled Innocence

Book 5: Fierce Enchantment

Book 6: An Immortal's Song

Book 7: Prowled Darkness

The Complete Dante's Circle Series (Contains Books 1-7)

HOLIDAY, MONTANA SERIES:

Book 1: Charmed Spirits

Book 2: Santa's Executive

Book 3: Finding Abigail

The Holiday, Montana Box Set (Contains Books 1-3)

Book 4: Her Lucky Love

Book 5: Dreams of Ivory

The Complete Holiday, Montana Box Set (Contains Books 1-5)

THE HAPPY EVER AFTER SERIES:

Flame and Ink

Ink Ever After

SINGLE TITLE:

Finally Found You

CPSIA information can be obtained
at www.ICGtesting.com
Printed in the USA
LVHW08012240519
619025LV00015B/530/P